Praise for the Novels of the Dresden Files

"One of the most enjoyable marriages of the fantasy and mystery genres on the shelves."   —*Cinescape*

"What's not to like about this series? . . . It takes the best elements of urban fantasy, mixes it with some good old-fashioned noir mystery, tosses in a dash of romance and a lot of high-octane action, shakes, stirs, and serves."
     —*SF Site*

"An invariably entertaining series."   —*Locus*

"Harry is as fine and upstanding and dangerous and wounded as any old-time noir detective. . . . Jim Butcher has done nicely in this series, developing and coloring snapshots of Harry Dresden's character."
     —*The San Diego Union-Tribune*

"The body count from the magical melees would do any hard-boiled gumshoe proud. Butcher's believable, likable set of characters goes for the jocular."
     —*Publishers Weekly*

"Entertaining. . . . Butcher keeps the writing jocular and lively with generous sprinklings of pop-culture references."   —*The Kansas City Star*

"Think *Buffy the Vampire Slayer* starring Philip Marlowe . . . a fast and furious adventure with winking nods to Bugs Bunny and John Carpenter."
     —*Entertainment Weekly*

continued . . .

ALSO BY JIM BUTCHER

THE DRESDEN FILES

THE CINDER SPIRES

THE CODEX ALERA

JIM BUTCHER

PROVEN GUILTY

A NOVEL OF THE DRESDEN FILES

ROC
New York

ROC
Published by Berkley
An imprint of Penguin Random House LLC
penguinrandomhouse.com

ISBN: 9780451461032

Roc hardcover edition / May 2006
Roc premium mass-market edition / February 2007

Printed in the United States of America
23   25   27   29   31   32   30   28   26   24

Chapter

One

Blood leaves no stain on a Warden's grey cloak.

I didn't know that until the day I watched Morgan, second in command of the White Council's Wardens, lift his sword over the kneeling form of a young man guilty of the practice of black magic. The boy, sixteen years old at the most, screamed and ranted in Korean underneath his black hood, his mouth spilling hatred and rage, convinced by his youth and power of his own immortality. He never knew it when the blade came down.

Which I guess was a small mercy. Microscopic, really.

His blood flew in a scarlet arc. I wasn't ten feet away. I felt hot droplets strike one cheek, and more blood covered the left side of the cloak in blotches of angry red. The head fell to the ground, and I saw the cloth over it moving, as if the boy's mouth were still screaming imprecations.

The body fell onto its side. One calf muscle twitched spasmodically and then stopped. After maybe five seconds, the head did too.

Morgan stood over the still form for a moment, the bright silver sword of the White Council of Wizards' justice in his hands. Besides him and me, there were a dozen Wardens present, and two members of the Senior

Council—the Merlin and my one-time mentor, Ebenezar McCoy.

The covered head stopped its feeble movements. Morgan glanced up at the Merlin and nodded once. The Merlin returned the nod. "May he find peace."

"Peace," the Wardens all replied together.

Except me. I turned my back on them, and made it two steps away before I threw up on the warehouse floor.

I stood there shaking for a moment, until I was sure I was finished, then straightened slowly. I felt a presence draw near me and looked up to see Ebenezar standing there.

He was an old man, bald but for wisps of white hair, short, stocky, his face half covered in a ferocious-looking grey beard. His nose and cheeks and bald scalp were all ruddy, except for a recent, purplish scar on his pate. Though he was centuries old he carried himself with vibrant energy, and his eyes were alert and pensive behind gold-rimmed spectacles. He wore the formal black robes of a meeting of the Council, along with the deep purple stole of a member of the Senior Council.

"Harry," he said quietly. "You all right?"

"After that?" I snarled, loudly enough to make sure everyone there heard me. "No one in this damned building should be all right."

I felt a sudden tension in the air behind me.

"No, they shouldn't," Ebenezar said. I saw him look back at the other wizards there, his jaw setting stubbornly.

The Merlin came over to us, also in his formal robes and stole. He looked like a wizard should look—tall, long white hair, long white beard, piercing blue eyes, his face seamed with age and wisdom.

Well. With age, anyway.

"Warden Dresden," he said. He had the sonorous voice of a trained speaker, and spoke English with a high-class British accent. "If you had some evidence that you felt would prove the boy's innocence, you should have presented it during the trial."

"I didn't have anything like that, and you know it," I replied.

"He was proven guilty," the Merlin said. "I soulgazed him myself. I examined more than two dozen mortals whose minds he had altered. Three of them might eventually recover their sanity. He forced four others to commit suicide, and had hidden nine corpses from the local authorities, as well. And every one of them was a blood relation." The Merlin stepped toward me, and the air in the room suddenly felt hot. His eyes flashed with azure anger and his voice rumbled with deep, unyielding power. "The powers he had used had already broken his mind. We did what was necessary."

I turned and faced the Merlin. I didn't push out my jaw and try to stare him down. I didn't put anything belligerent or challenging into my posture. I didn't show any anger on my face, or slur any disrespect into my tone when I spoke. The past several months had taught me that the Merlin hadn't gotten his job through an ad on a matchbook. He was, quite simply, the strongest wizard on the planet. And he had talent, skill, and experience to go along with that strength. If I ever came to magical blows with him, there wouldn't be enough left of me to fill a lunch sack. I did *not* want a fight.

But I didn't back down, either.

"He was a kid," I said. "We all have been. He made a mistake. We've all done that too."

The Merlin regarded me with an expression somewhere between irritation and contempt. "You know what the use of black magic can do to a person," he said.

Marvelously subtle shading and emphasis over his words added in a perfectly clear, unspoken thought: *You know it because you've done it. Sooner or later, you'll slip up, and then it will be your turn.* "One use leads to another. And another."

"That's what I keep hearing, Merlin," I answered. "Just say no to black magic. But that boy had no one to tell him the rules, to teach him. If someone had known about his gift and *done* something in time—"

He lifted a hand, and the simple gesture had such absolute authority to it that I stopped to let him speak. "The point you are missing, Warden Dresden," he said, "is that the boy who made that foolish mistake died long before we discovered the damage he'd done. What was left of him was nothing more nor less than a monster who would have spent his life inflicting horror and death on anyone near him."

"I *know* that," I said, and I couldn't keep the anger and frustration out of my voice. "And I *know* what had to be done. I *know* it was the only measure that could stop him." I thought I was going to throw up again, and I closed my eyes and leaned on the solid oak length of my carved staff. I got my stomach under control and opened my eyes to face the Merlin. "But it doesn't change the fact that we've just *murdered* a boy who probably never knew enough to understand what was happening to him."

"Accusing someone else of murder is hardly a stone you are in a position to cast, Warden Dresden." The Merlin arched a silver brow at me. "Did you not discharge a firearm into the back of the head of a woman you merely *believed* to be the Corpsetaker from a distance of a few feet away, fatally wounding her?"

I swallowed. I sure as hell had, last year. It had been one of the bigger coin tosses of my life. Had I incorrectly judged that a body-transferring wizard known as the Corpsetaker had jumped into the original body of Warden Luccio, I would have murdered an innocent woman and a law-enforcing member of the White Council.

I hadn't been wrong—but I'd never . . . never just *killed* anyone before. I've killed things in the heat of battle, yes. I've killed people by less direct means. But Corpsetaker's death had been intimate and coldly calculated and not at all indirect. Just me, the gun, and the limp corpse. I could still vividly remember the decision to shoot, the feel of the cold metal in my hands, the stiff pull of my revolver's trigger, the thunder of the gun's report, and the way the body had settled into a limp bundle of limbs on the ground, the motion somehow too simple for the horrible significance of the event.

I'd killed. Deliberately, rationally ended another's life.

And it still haunted my dreams at night.

I'd had little choice. Given the smallest amount of time, the Corpsetaker could have called up lethal magic, and the best I could have hoped for was a death curse that killed me as I struck down the necromancer. It had been a bad day or two, and I was pretty strung out. Even if I hadn't been, I had a feeling that Corpsetaker could have taken me in a fair fight. So I hadn't given Corpsetaker anything like a fair fight. I shot the necromancer in the back of the head because the Corpsetaker had to be stopped, and I'd had no other option.

I had executed her on suspicion.

No trial. No soulgaze. No judgment from a dispassionate arbiter. Hell, I hadn't even taken the chance to get in a good insult. *Bang. Thump.* One live wizard, one dead bad guy.

I'd done it to prevent future harm to myself and others. It hadn't been the best solution—but it had been the *only* solution. I hadn't hesitated for a heartbeat. I'd done it, no questions, and gone on to face the further perils of that night.

Just like a Warden is supposed to do. Sorta took the wind out of my holier-than-thou sails.

Bottomless blue eyes watched my face and he nodded slowly. "You executed her," the Merlin said quietly. "Because it was necessary."

"That was different," I said.

"Indeed. Your action required far deeper commitment. It was dark, cold, and you were alone. The suspect was a great deal stronger than you. Had you struck and missed, you would have died. Yet you did what had to be done."

"Necessary isn't the same as *right*," I said.

"Perhaps not," he said. "But the Laws of Magic are all that prevent wizards from abusing their power over mortals. There is no room for compromise. You are a Warden now, Dresden. You must focus on your duty to both mortals and the Council."

"Which sometimes means killing children?" This time I didn't hide the contempt, but there wasn't much life to it.

"Which means always enforcing the Laws," the Merlin said, and his eyes bored into mine, flickering with sparks of rigid anger. "It is your duty. Now more than ever."

I broke the stare first, looking away before anything bad could happen. Ebenezar stood a couple of steps from me, studying my expression.

"Granted that you've seen much for a man your age," the Merlin said, and there was a slight softening in his tone. "But you haven't seen how horrible such things can become. Not nearly. The Laws exist for a reason. They *must* stand as written."

I turned my head and stared at the small pool of scarlet on the warehouse floor beside the kid's corpse. I hadn't been told his name before they'd ended his life.

"Right," I said tiredly, and wiped a clean corner of the grey cloak over my blood-sprinkled face. "I can see what they're written in."

Chapter
Two

I turned my back on them and walked out of the warehouse into Chicago's best impression of Miami. July in the Midwest is rarely less than sultry, but this year had been especially intense when it came to summer heat, and it had rained frequently. The warehouse was a part of the wharves down at the lakeside, and even the chill waters of Lake Michigan were warmer than usual. They filled the air with more than the average water-scent of mud and mildew and eau de dead fishy.

I passed the two grey-cloaked Wardens standing watch outside and exchanged nods with them. Both of them were younger than me, some of the most recent additions to the White Council's military-slash-police organization. As I passed them, I felt the tingling presence of a veil, a spell they were maintaining to conceal the warehouse from any prying eyes. It wasn't much of a veil, by Warden standards, but it was probably better than I could do, and there weren't a whole hell of a lot of Wardens to choose from since the Red Court's successful offensive the previous autumn. Beggars can't be choosers.

I tugged off my robe and my cloak. I was wearing sneakers, khaki shorts, and a red tank top underneath. It didn't make me any cooler to remove the heavy clothes— just marginally less miserable. I walked hurriedly back to my car, a battered old Volkswagen Beetle, its windows rolled down to keep the sun from turning the interior into an oven. It's a jumble of different colors, as my mechanic has replaced damaged portions of the body with parts from junked Bugs, but it started off as a shade of powder blue, and that had earned it the sobriquet of the Blue Beetle.

I heard quick, solid footsteps behind me. "Harry," Ebenezar called.

I threw the robe and cloak into the Beetle's backseat without a word. The car's interior had been stripped to its metal bones a couple of years back, and I had made hurried repairs with cheap lumber and a lot of duct tape. Since then, I'd had a friend redo the inside of the car. It wasn't standard, and it still didn't look pretty, but the comfortable bucket seats were a lot nicer than the wooden crates I'd been using. And I had decent seat belts again.

"Harry," Ebenezar said again. "Damnation, boy, stop."

I thought about getting into the car and leaving, but instead stopped until the old wizard approached and shucked off his own formal robes and stole. He wore a white T-shirt beneath denim Levi's overalls, and heavy leather hiking boots. "There's something I need to speak to you about."

I paused and took a second to get some of my emotions under control. Those and my stomach. I didn't want the embarrassment of a repeat performance. "What is it?"

He stopped a few feet behind me. "The war isn't going well."

By which he meant the war of the White Council against the Red Court of vampires. The war had been a whole lot of pussyfooting and fights in back alleys for several years, but last year the vampires had upped the ante. Their assault had been timed to coincide with vicious activity from a traitor within the Council and with the attack of a number of necromancers, outlaw wizards who raised the dead into angry specters and zombies—among a number of other, less savory things.

The vampires had hit the Council. Hard. Before the battle was over, they'd killed nearly two hundred wizards, most of them Wardens. That's why the Wardens had given me a grey cloak. They needed the help.

Before they'd finished, the vampires killed nearly forty-five thousand men, women, and children who happened to be nearby.

That's why I'd taken the cloak. That wasn't the sort of thing I could ignore.

"I've read the reports," I said. "They say that the Venatori Umbrorum and the Fellowship of St. Giles have really pitched in."

"It's more than that. If they hadn't started up an offensive to slow the vamps down, the Red Court would have destroyed the Council months ago."

I blinked. "They're doing that much?"

The Venatori Umbrorum and the Fellowship of St. Giles were the White Council's primary allies in the war with the Red Court. The Venatori were an ancient, secret brotherhood, joined together to fight supernatural darkness wherever they could. Sort of like the Masons, only with more flamethrowers. By and large, they were academic sorts, and though several of the Venatori had various forms of military experience, their true strength lay in utilizing human legal systems and analyzing information brought together from widely dispersed sources.

The Fellowship, though, was a somewhat different story. Not as many of them as there were of the Venatori, but not many of them were merely human. Most of them, so I took it, were those who had been half turned by the vampires. They'd been infested with the dark powers that made the Red Court such a threat, but until they willingly drank another's lifeblood, they never quite stopped being human. It could make them stronger and faster and better able to withstand injury than regular folks, and it granted them a drastically increased life span. Assuming they didn't fall prey to their constant, base desire for blood, or weren't slain in operations against their enemies in the Red Court.

A woman I'd once cared for very much had been taken by a Red Court vampire. In point of fact, I'd kicked off the war when I went and took her back by the most violent means at my disposal. I brought her back, but I didn't save her. She'd been touched by that darkness, and now her life was a battle—partly against the vampires who had done it to her, and partly against the blood-thirst they'd imposed upon her. Now she was a part of the Fellowship, whose members included those like her and, I'd heard, many other people and part-people with no home anywhere else. St. Giles, patron of lepers and outcasts. His Fellowship, while not a full-blown powerhouse like the Council or one of the Vampire Courts, was nonetheless proving to be a surprisingly formidable ally.

"Our allies can't challenge the vampires in face-to-face confrontations," Ebenezar said, nodding. "But they're wreaking havoc on the Red Court's supply chains, intelligence, and support, attacking from the mortal end of things. Red Court infiltrators within human society are unmasked. Humans controlled by the Red Court have been arrested, framed, or killed—or else abducted to be forcibly freed of their addiction. The Fellowship and the Venatori continue to do all in their power to provide information to the Council, which has enabled us to make a number of successful raids against the vampires. The Venatori and the Fellowship haven't appreciably weakened the vampires, but the Red Court has been slowed down. Perhaps enough to give us a fighting chance to recover."

"How's the boot camp coming?" I asked.

"Luccio is confident of her eventual success in replacing our losses," Ebenezar replied.

"Don't see what else I can do to help," I said. "Unless you're wanting someone to go start fathering new wizards."

He stepped closer to me and glanced around. His expression was casual, but he was checking to see if anyone was close enough to overhear. "There's something you don't know. The Merlin decided it was not for general knowledge."

I turned to face him and tilted my head.

"You remember the Red Court's attack last year," he said. "That they called up Outsiders and assaulted us within the realm of Faerie itself."

"Bad move, so I've heard. The Faeries are going to take it out of their hides."

"So we all thought," the old man said. "In fact, Summer declared war upon the Red Court and began preliminary assaults on them. But Winter hasn't responded— and Summer hasn't done much more than secure its borders."

"Queen Mab didn't declare war?"

"No."

I frowned. "Never thought she'd pass up the chance. She's all about carnage and bloodshed."

"It surprised us as well," he said. "So I want to ask a favor of you."

I eyed him without speaking.

"Find out why," he said. "You have contacts within the Courts. Find out what's happening. Find out why the Sidhe haven't gone to war."

"What?" I asked. "The Senior Council doesn't know? Don't you have an embassy and high-level connections and official channels? Maybe a bright red telephone?"

Ebenezar smiled without much mirth. "The general turbulence of the war has stretched everyone's intelligence-gathering abilities," he replied. "Even those in the spiritual realms. There's another level entirely to the war in the conflict between spiritual spies and emissaries of everyone involved. And our embassy to the Sidhe has been . . ." He rolled a weathered, strong shoulder in a shrug. "Well. You know them as well as anyone."

"They've been polite, open, spoken with complete honesty, and left you with no idea what is going on," I guessed.

"Precisely."

"So the Senior Council is asking me to find out?"

He glanced around again. "Not the Senior Council. Myself. A few others."

"What others?" I asked.

"People I trust," he said, and looked at me directly over the rims of his spectacles.

I stared at him for a second and then said in a whisper, "The traitor."

The vampires of the Red Court had been a little too on top of the game to be merely lucky. Somehow, they had been obtaining vital secrets about the dispositions of the White Council's forces and their plans. Someone on the inside had been feeding the vampires information, and a lot of wizards had died because of it—particularly during their heaviest attack, last year, in which they'd violated Sidhe territory in pursuit of the fleeing Council.

"You think the traitor is someone on the Senior Council."

"I think we can't take any chances," he said quietly. "This isn't official business. I can't order you to do it, Harry. I'll understand if you don't want to. But there's no one better for the job—and our allies cannot maintain the current pace of operations for long. Their best weapon has always been secrecy, and their actions have forced them to pay a terrible cost of lives to give us what aid they have."

I folded my arms over my stomach and said, "We need to help them, sure. But every time I look sideways at Faerie, I get into deeper trouble with them. It's the last thing I need. If I do this, how—"

Ebenezar's weight shifted, gravel crunching loudly. I glanced up to see the Merlin and Morgan emerge from the building, speaking quietly and intently.

"I wanted to talk to you," Ebenezar said, evidently for the benefit of anyone listening. "Make sure Morgan and the other Wardens are treating you square."

I went along with him. "When they talk to me at all," I said. "About the only other Warden I ever see is Ramirez. Decent guy. I like him."

"That says a lot for him."

"That the Council's ticking time bomb has a good opinion of him?" I waited for Morgan and the Merlin to leave, but they paused a little way off, still talking. I stared at the gravel for a long time, and then said, much more quietly, "That could have been me in there today. I could have been that kid."

"It was a long time ago," Ebenezar said. "You were barely more than a child."

"So was he."

Ebenezar's expression became guarded. "I'm sorry you had to see that business."

"Is that why it happened here?" I asked him. "Why come to Chicago for an execution?"

He exhaled slowly. "It's one of the great crossroads of the world, Harry. More air traffic comes through here than anywhere else. It's an enormous port city for shipping of any kind—trucks, trains, ships. That means a lot of ways in and out, a lot of travelers passing through. It makes it difficult for any observers from the Red Court to spot us or report our movements." He gave me a bleak smile. "And then there's the way Chicago seems to be inimical to the health of any vampire who comes here."

"That's a pretty good cover story," I said. "What's the truth?"

Ebenezar sighed and held up his hand in a conciliatory gesture. "It wasn't my idea."

I looked at him for a minute and then said, "The Merlin called the meeting here."

Ebenezar nodded and arched a shaggy grey brow. "Which means . . . ?"

I chewed on my lower lip and scrunched up my eyes. It never helped me think any better, but that was no reason not to keep trying it. "He wanted to send me a message. Kill two birds with one stone."

Ebenezar nodded. "He wanted you stripped of your position as a Warden, but Luccio is still the technical commander of the Wardens, though Morgan commands in the field. She supported you and the rest of the Senior Council overruled him."

"Bet he loved that," I said.

Ebenezar chuckled. "I thought he was having a stroke."

"Joy," I said. "I didn't want the job to begin with."

"I know," he said. "You got rocks and hard places, boy. Not much else."

"So the Merlin figures he'll show me an execution and scare me into toeing the line." I frowned, thinking. "I take it there's no word on the attack last year? No one found with mysterious sums of money dumped into their bank accounts that would incriminate a traitor?"

"Not yet," Ebenezar said.

"Then with the traitor running around loose, all the Merlin has to do is wait for me to screw something up. Then he can call it treason and squish me."

Ebenezar nodded, and I saw the warning in his eyes— another reason to take the job he was offering. "He genuinely believes that you are a threat to the Council. If your behavior confirms his belief, he'll do whatever is necessary to stop you."

I snorted. "There was another guy like that once. Name of McCarthy. If the Merlin wants to find a traitor, he'll find one whether or not one actually exists."

Ebenezar scowled, a hint of a Scots burr creeping into his voice, as it did anytime he was angry, and he glanced at the Merlin. "Aye. I thought you should know."

I nodded, still without looking up at him. I hated being bullied into anything, but I didn't get the vibe that Ebenezar was making an effort to maneuver me into a corner. He was asking a favor. I might well help myself by doing him the favor, but he wasn't going to bring anything onto my head if I turned him down. It wasn't his style.

I met his eyes and nodded. "Okay."

He exhaled slowly and nodded back, silent thanks in his expression. "Oh. One other thing," he said, and passed me an envelope.

"What's this?"

"I don't know," he answered. "The Gatekeeper asked me to give it to you."

The Gatekeeper. He was the quietest of the wizards

on the Senior Council, and even the Merlin showed him plenty of respect. He was taller than me, which is saying something, and he stayed out of most of the partisan politics of the Senior Council, which says even more. He knew things he shouldn't be able to know— more so than most wizards, I mean—and as far as I could tell, he'd never been anything but straight with me.

I opened the envelope. A single piece of paper was inside. Letters in a precise, flowing hand read:

> *Dresden,*
> *In the past ten days there have been repeated acts of black magic in Chicago. As the senior Warden in the region, it falls to you to investigate and find those responsible. In my opinion, it is vital that you do so immediately. To my knowledge, no one else is aware of the situation.*
> *Rashid*

I rubbed at my eyes. Great. More black magic in Chicago. If it wasn't some raving, psychotic, black-hatted bad guy, it was probably another kid like the one who'd died a few minutes ago. There wasn't a whole lot of in-between.

I was hoping for the murderous madman—sorry, political correctioners; mad*person*. I could deal with those. I'd had practice.

I didn't think I could handle the other.

I put the letter back in the envelope, thinking. This was between the Gatekeeper and me, presumably. He hadn't asked me publicly, or told Ebenezar what was going on, which meant that I was free to decide how to handle this one. If the Merlin knew about this and officially gave me the assignment, he'd make damned sure I didn't have much of a choice in how to handle it—and I'd have to do the whole thing under a microscope.

The Gatekeeper had trusted me to handle whatever was wrong. That was almost worse.

Man.

Sometimes I get tired of being the guy who is supposed to deal with un-deal-withable situations.

I looked up to find Ebenezar squinting at me. The expression made his face a mass of wrinkles.

"What?" I asked.

"You get a haircut or something, Hoss?"

"Uh, nothing new. Why?"

"You look . . ." The old wizard's voice trailed off thoughtfully. "Different."

My heartbeat sped up a little. As far as I knew, Ebenezar was unaware of the entity who was leasing out the unused portions of my brain, and I wanted to keep it that way. But though he had a reputation for being something of a magical brawler, his specialty the summoning up of primal, destructive forces, he had a lot more on the ball than most of the Council gave him credit for. It was entirely possible that he had sensed something of the fallen angel's presence within me.

"Yeah, well. I've been wearing the cloak of the people I spent most of my adult life resenting," I said. "Between that and being a cripple, I've been off my sleep for almost a year."

"That can do it," Ebenezar said, nodding. "How's the hand?"

I bit back my first harsh response, that it was still maimed and scarred, and that the burns made it look like a badly melted piece of wax sculpture. I'd gone up against a bad guy with a brain a couple of years back, and she'd worked out that my defensive magic was designed to stop kinetic energy—not heat. I found that out the hard way when a couple of her psychotic goons sprayed improvised napalm at me. My shield had stopped the flaming jelly, but the heat had gone right through and dry roasted the hand I'd held out to focus my shield.

I held up my gloved left hand and waggled my thumb and the first two fingers in jerky little motions. The other two fingers didn't move much unless their neighbors pulled them. "Not much feeling in them yet, but I can hold a beer. Or the steering wheel. Doctor's had me playing guitar, trying to move them and use them more."

"Good," Ebenezar said. "Exercise is good for the body, but music is good for the soul."

"Not the way I play it," I said.

Ebenezar grinned wryly, and drew a pocket watch from the front pocket of the overalls. He squinted at it. "Lunchtime," he said. "You hungry?"

There wasn't anything in his tone to indicate it, but I could read the subtext.

Ebenezar had been a mentor to me at a time I'd badly needed it. He'd taught me just about everything I thought was important enough to be worth knowing. He had been unfailingly generous, patient, loyal, and kind to me.

But he had been lying to me the whole time, ignoring the principles he had been teaching me. On the one hand, he taught me about what it meant to be a wizard, about how a wizard's magic comes from his deepest beliefs, about how doing evil with magic was more than simply a crime—it was a mockery of what magic meant, a kind of sacrilege. On the other hand, he'd been the White Council's Blackstaff the whole while—a wizard with a license to kill, to violate the Laws of Magic, to make a mockery of everything noble and good about the power he wielded in the name of political necessity. And he'd done it. Many times.

I had once held the kind of trust and faith in Ebenezar that I had given no one else. I'd built a foundation for my life on what he'd taught me about the use of magic, about right and wrong. But he'd let me down. He'd been living a lie, and it had been brutally painful to learn about it. Two years later, it still twisted around in my belly, a vague and nauseating unease.

My old teacher was offering me an olive branch, trying to set aside the things that had come between us. I knew that I should go along with him. I knew that he was as human, as fallible, as anyone else. I knew that I should set it aside, mend our fences, and get on with life. It was the smart thing to do. It was the compassionate, responsible thing to do. It was the *right* thing to do.

But I couldn't.

It still hurt too much for me to think straight about it.

I looked up at him. "Death threats in the guise of formal decapitations sort of ruin my appetite."

He nodded at me, accepting the excuse with a patient and steady expression, though I thought I saw regret in his eyes. He lifted a hand in a silent wave and turned away to walk toward a beat-up old Ford truck that had been built during the Great Depression. Second thoughts pressed in. Maybe I should say something. Maybe I should go for a bite to eat with the old man.

My excuse hadn't been untrue, though. There was no way I could eat. I could still feel the droplets of hot blood hitting my face, still see the body lying unnaturally in a pool of blood. My hands started shaking and I closed my eyes, forcing the vivid, bloody memories out of the forefront of my thoughts. Then I got in the car and tried to leave the memories behind me.

The Blue Beetle is no muscle car, but it flung up a respectable amount of gravel as I left.

The streets weren't as bad as they usually were, but it was still hotter than hell, so I rolled down the windows at the first stoplight and tried to think clearly.

Investigate the faeries. Great. That was absolutely guaranteed to get complicated before I got any useful answers. If there was one thing faeries hated doing, it was giving you a straight answer, about anything. Getting plain speech out of one is like pulling out teeth. Your *own* teeth. Through your *nose*.

But Ebenezar was right. I was probably the only one on the Council with acquaintances in both the Summer and Winter Courts of the Sidhe. If anyone on the Council could find out, it was me. Yippee.

And just to keep things interesting, I needed to hunt down some kind of unspecified black magic and put a stop to it. That was what Wardens spent all their time doing, when they weren't fighting a war, and what I'd done two or three times myself, but it wasn't ever pretty. Black magic means a black practitioner of some kind, and they tended to be the sorts of people who were both happy to kill an interfering wizard and able to manage it.

Faeries.

Black magic.

It never rains but it pours.

Chapter

Three

Between one heartbeat and the next, the passenger seat of the Blue Beetle was suddenly occupied. I let out a yelp and nearly bounced my car off of a delivery truck. The tires squealed in protest and I started to slide. I turned into it and recovered, but if I'd had another coat of paint on my car I'd have collided with the one next to me. My heart in my throat, I got the car moving smoothly again, and turned to glare at the sudden passenger.

Lasciel, aka the Temptress, aka the Webweaver, apparently some kind of photocopy of the personality of a fallen angel, sat in the passenger seat. She could look like anything she chose, but her most common form was that of a tall, athletic blonde wearing a white Greek-style tunic that fell almost to her knee. She sat with her hands in her lap, staring out the front of the car, smiling very slightly.

"What the hell do you think you're doing?" I snarled at her. "Are you trying to get me killed?"

"Don't be such a baby," she replied, her tone amused. "No one was harmed."

"No thanks to you," I growled. "Put the seat belt on."

She gave me a level look. "Mortal, I have no physical form. I exist nowhere except within your mind. I am a mental image. An illusion. A hologram only you can see. There is no reason for me to wear my seat belt."

"It's the principle of the thing," I said. "My car, my brain, my rules. Put on the damned seat belt or get lost."

She heaved a sigh. "Very well." She twisted around like anyone would, drawing the seat belt forward around her waist and clicking it. I knew she couldn't have picked up the physical seat belt and done that, so what I was seeing was only an illusion—but it was a convincing one. I would have had to make a serious effort to see that the actual seat belt hadn't moved.

Lasciel looked at me. "Acceptable?"

"Barely," I said, thinking furiously. Lasciel, as she appeared to me now, was a portion of a genuine fallen angel. The real deal was trapped inside an ancient silver denarius, a Roman coin, which was buried under a couple of feet of concrete in my basement. But in touching the coin, I'd created a kind of outlet for the demon's personality—embodied as an entirely discrete mental entity living right in my own head, presumably in the ninety percent of the brain that humans never use. Or in my case, maybe ninety-five. Lasciel could appear to me, could see what I saw and sense what I sensed, could look through my memories to some degree and, most disturbing, could create illusions that I had to work hard to see through—just as she was now creating the illusion of her physical presence in my car. Her extremely attractive and wholesome-looking and entirely desirable presence. The bitch.

"I thought we had an understanding," I growled. "I don't want you coming to see me unless I call you."

"And I have respected our agreement," she said. "I simply came to remind you that my services and resources are at your disposal, should you need them, and that the whole of my self, currently residing beneath the floor of your laboratory, is likewise prepared to assist you."

"You act like I wanted you there in the first place. If I knew how to erase you from my head without getting killed, I'd do it in a heartbeat," I replied.

"The portion of me that shares your mind is nothing but the shadow of my true self," Lasciel said. "But have a care, mortal. I am. I exist. And I desire to continue to do so."

"Like I said. If I could do it without getting killed," I growled. "In the meanwhile, unless you want me to chain you into a little black closet in my head, get out of my sight."

Her mouth twitched, maybe in irritation, but nothing more than that showed on her face. "As you wish," she said, inclining her head. "But if black magic truly is once more rising within Chicago, you may well have need of every tool at hand. And as you must survive for *me* to survive, I have every reason to aid you."

"A tiny black box," I said. "Without holes in the lid. Smelling like my high school locker room."

Her mouth curled again, an expression of wary amusement. "As you wish, my host."

And she was gone, vanishing back into the undeveloped vaults of my mind or wherever she went. I shivered, making sure my thoughts were contained, shielded from her perceptions. There was nothing I could do to prevent Lasciel from seeing and hearing everything I did, or from rummaging randomly in my memories, but I had learned that I could at least veil my active thoughts from her. I did so constantly, in order to prevent her from learning too much, too quickly.

That would only help her reach her goal—that of convincing me to unearth the ancient silver coin buried under my lab and sealed within spells and concrete. Within the coin, the old Roman denarius—one of a collection of thirty—dwelt the whole of the fallen angel Lasciel.

If I chose to ally myself with her, it would get me all kinds of strength. The power and knowledge of a fallen angel could turn anyone into a deadly and virtually immortal threat—at the low, low cost of one's soul. Once you signed on with one of the literal Hell's Angels, you weren't the only one in the captain's chair anymore. The more you let them help you, the more you surrendered your will to them, and sooner or later it's the fallen angel that's calling the shots.

I'd grabbed the coin a heartbeat before a friend's toddler could reach down for it, and touching its surface had transferred a portion of the personality, the intellect of Lasciel into my head. She helped me survive several nasty days the previous autumn, and her assistance had been invaluable. Which was the problem. I couldn't allow myself to continue relying on her help, because sooner or later, I'd get used to it. And then I'd enjoy it. And at some point, digging up that coin in my basement wouldn't seem like such a bad idea.

All of which meant that I had to stay on my guard against the fallen angel's suggestions. The price may have been hidden, but it was still there. Lasciel wasn't wrong, though, about how dangerous situations involving true black magic could become. I might well find myself in need of help.

I thought about those who had fought beside me before. I thought about my friend Michael, whose kid had been the one about to pick up the coin.

I hadn't seen Michael since then. I hadn't called. He'd called me a couple of times, invited me to Thanksgiving dinner a couple of times, asked if I was all right a couple of times. I had turned down his invitations and cut every phone conversation short. Michael didn't know that I'd picked up one of the Blackened Denarii, taken possession of a token that could arguably make me a member of the Knights of the Blackened Denarius. I'd fought some of the Denarians. I'd killed one of them.

They were monsters of the worst sort, and Michael was a Knight of the Cross. He was one of three people on the face of the earth who had been chosen to wield a holy sword, an honest-to-Goodness holy sword, each of them with what was supposed to be a nail from the Cross, capital C, worked into the blade. Michael fought dark and evil things. He beat them. He saved children and innocents in danger, and he would stand up to the darkest creatures imaginable without blinking, so strong was his faith that the Almighty would give him strength enough to defeat the darkness before him.

He had no love for his opposites, the Denarians, power-hungry psychopaths as determined to cause and spread pain and suffering as Michael was to contain them.

I never told him about the coin. I didn't want him to know that I was sharing brain space with a demon. I didn't want him to think less of me. Michael had integrity. Most of my adult life, the White Council at large had been sure that I was some kind of monster just waiting for the right time to morph into its true form and start laying waste to everything around me. But Michael had been firmly on my side since the first time we'd met. His unwavering support had made me feel a whole hell of a lot better about my life.

I didn't want him to look at me the way he'd looked at the Denarians we'd fought. So until I got rid of Lasciel's stupid mental sock puppet, I wasn't going to ask him for help.

I would handle this on my own.

I was fairly sure that my day couldn't get much worse.

No sooner had I thought it than there was a horrible crunching sound, and my head snapped back hard against the headrest on the back of the driver's seat. The Beetle shuddered and jounced wildly, and I fought to keep it under control.

You'd *think* I would know better by now.

Chapter

Four

I managed to get one wild look around, and it showed me someone in a real battleship of an old Chrysler, dark grey, windows tinted, and then the car slammed into the Beetle again and nearly sent me into a deadly spin. My head snapped to one side and hit the window, and I could almost smell the smoldering of my tires as they all slid forward and sideways simultaneously. I felt the car hit the curb, and then bounce up. I wrenched at the steering wheel and the brakes, my body responding to things my stunned brain hadn't caught up to yet. I think I kept it from becoming a total disaster, because instead of spinning off into oncoming traffic or hitting the wall at a sharp angle, I managed to slam the Beetle's passenger-side broadside into the building beside the street. Brick grated on steel, until I came to a halt fifty feet later.

Stars swarmed over my vision and I tried to swat them away so that I could get a look at the Chrysler's plates—but it was gone in a heartbeat. Or at least I think it was. Truth be told, my head was spinning so much that the car could have been doing interpretive dance in a lilac tutu and I might not have noticed.

Sitting there seemed like a really good idea, so I sat. After a while I got the vague notion that I should make sure everyone was all right. I looked at me. No blood, which was positive. I looked blearily around the car. No screaming. No corpses in my rearview mirror. Nothing was on fire. There was broken safety glass everywhere from the passenger-side window, but the rear window had been replaced with a sheet of translucent plastic a while back.

The Beetle, stalwart crusader against the forces of evil and alternative fuels, was still running, though its engine had acquired an odd, moaning wheeze as opposed to the usual surly wheeze. I tried my door. It didn't open. I rolled down my window and hauled myself slowly out of the car. If I could get up the energy to slide across the hood before I got back in, I could audition for *The Dukes of Hazzard*.

"Here in Hazzard County," I drawled to myself, "we don't much cotton to hit-and-run automotive assaults."

It took an unknown number of minutes for the first cop to arrive, a patrolman I recognized named Grayson. Grayson was an older cop, a big man with a big red nose and a comfortable gut, who looked like he could bounce angry drunks or drink them under the table, take your pick. He got out of his car and started asking me questions in a concerned tone of voice. I answered him as best I could, but something between my brain and my mouth had shorted out, and I found him eyeing me and then looking around the inside of the Beetle for open containers before he sat me down on the ground and started routing traffic around. I got to sit down on the curb, which suited me fine. I watched the sidewalk spin around until someone touched my shoulder.

Karrin Murphy, head of Chicago PD's Special Investigations department, looked like someone's cute kid sister. She was maybe a rose petal over five feet tall, had blond hair, blue eyes, a pug nose, and nearly invisible freckles. She was made all of springy muscle; a gymnast's build that did not preclude feminine curves. She was in a white cotton shirt and blue jeans that day, a Cubs ball cap on her head, reflective sunglasses over her eyes.

"Harry?" she asked. "You okay?"

"Uncle Jesse is gonna be awful disappointed that one of Boss Hogg's flunkies banged up the General Lee," I told her, waving at my car.

She stared at me for a moment and then said, "Did you know you have a bruise on the side of your head?"

"Nah," I said. I poked a finger at it. "Do I?"

Murphy sighed and gently pushed my finger down. "Harry, seriously. If you're so loopy you can't talk to me, I need to get you to a hospital."

"Sorry, Murph," I told her. "Been a long day already. I got my bells rung pretty good. I'll be fine in a minute."

She exhaled, and then nodded and sat down on the curb with me. "Mind if I have one of the EMTs look at you? Just to be careful?"

"They'd want to take me to a hospital," I said. "Too dangerous. I could short out someone's life support. And the Reds are watching the hospitals, putting hits on our wounded. I could draw fire onto the patients."

"I know that," she said quietly. "I won't let them take you."

"Oh. Okay, then," I said. An EMT checked me out. He shined a light into my eyes, for which I kicked him lightly in the shins. He muttered at me for a minute, poked me here and there, examined and measured and counted and so on. Then he shook his head and stood up. "Maybe a mild concussion. He should see a doctor to be safe, Lieutenant."

Murphy nodded, thanked the EMT, and looked pointedly at the ambulance. He sidled away, his expression disapproving.

Murphy sat down with me again. "All right, spill. What happened?"

"Someone in a dark grey Chrysler tried to park in my backseat." I waved a hand, annoyed, as she opened her mouth. "And no. I didn't get the plates. I was too busy considering a career as a crash test dummy."

"You've got the dummy part down," she said. "You into something lately?"

"Not yet," I complained. "I mean, Hell's bells, Murphy. I got told half a freaking hour ago that there's bad juju going down somewhere in Chicago. I haven't even had time to start checking into it, and someone is already trying to make me into a commercial for seat belts and air bags."

"You sure it was deliberate?"

"Yeah. But whoever it was, he wasn't a pro."

"Why do you say that?"

"If he had been, he'd have spun me easy. No idea he was there until he'd hit me. Could have bumped me into a spin before I could have straightened out. Flipped my car a few times. Killed me pretty good." I rubbed at the back of my neck. A nice, full-body ache was already spreading out into my muscles. "Isn't exactly the best place for it, either."

"Attack of opportunity," Murphy said.

"Whassat?"

She smiled a little. "When you weren't expecting the shot, but you see it and take it before the opportunity passes you by."

"Oh. Yeah, probably one of those."

Murphy shook her head. "Look, maybe I should get you to a doctor anyway."

"No," I said. "Really. I'm okay. But I want to get off the street soonest."

Murphy inhaled slowly and then nodded. "I'll take you home."

"Thanks."

Grayson came ambling over to us. "Wrecker's on the way," he said. "What do we got here?"

"Hit and run," Murphy said.

Grayson lifted his eyebrows and eyed me. "Yeah? Looked to me like you got hit a couple of times. On purpose-like."

"For all I know it was an honest accident," I said.

Grayson nodded. "There's some clothes in your back-seat. Looks like they have blood on them."

"Leftovers from last Halloween," I said. "It's costume stuff. A cloak and robes and such, had fake blood all over them. It looked cheesy as hell."

Grayson snorted. "You're worse than my kid. He's still got some of his football jerseys in his backseat from last fall."

"He probably has a nicer car." I glanced up at the Beetle. It was a real mess, and I winced. It wasn't like the Beetle was a priceless antique or anything, but it was *my* car. I drove it places. I liked it. "In fact, I'm sure it's a nicer car."

Grayson let out a wry chuckle. "I need to fill out some papers. You okay to help me fill in the blanks?"

"Sure," I told him.

"Thanks for the call, Sergeant," Murphy said.

"De nada," Grayson replied, touching the brim of his cap with a finger. "I'll get those forms, Dresden, soon as the wrecker gets here."

"Cool," I said.

Grayson moved off, and Murphy stared at me steadily for a moment.

"What?" I asked her quietly.

"You lied to him," she said. "About the clothes and the blood."

I twitched one shoulder.

"And you did it well. I mean, if I didn't know you . . ." She shook her head. "It surprises me about you. That's all. You've always been a terrible liar."

"Um," I said. I wasn't sure how to take that one. "Thank you?"

She let out a wry chuckle. "So what's the real story?"

"Not here," I said. "Let's talk in a bit."

Murphy studied my face for a second, and her frown deepened. "Harry? What's wrong?"

The limp, headless body of that nameless young man filled my thoughts. It brought up too many emotions with it, and I felt my throat tighten until I knew I wouldn't be able to speak. So I shook my head a little and shrugged.

She nodded. "You going to be all right?"

There was a peculiar gentleness in her voice. Murphy had been playing in what amounted to a boys-only league in her work with CPD, and she put off a tough-as-nails aura that made her seem almost as formidable as she actually was. That exterior almost never varied, at least out in the open, with other police officers nearby. But as she looked at me, there was a quiet, definite, and unashamed vulnerability in her voice.

We've had our differences in the past, but Murphy was one hell of a good friend. I gave her my best lopsided smile. "I'm always all right. More or less."

She reached out and twitched a stray bit of hair from my forehead. "You're a great big girl, Dresden. One little fender bender and you go all emotional and pathetic."

Her eyes flickered to the Beetle again, and suddenly burned with a cold blue fire. "Do you know who did this to you?"

"Not yet," I growled as the wrecker arrived. "But you can bet your ass I'm going to find out."

Chapter

Five

By the time we got back to my place, my head was starting to run at its normal speed, the better to inform me how much it hurt. I had a nice, deep-down body ache to go along with the bruised skull. The light of the afternoon sun stabbed at my eyes in a cheerfully vicious fashion, and I was glad when I shambled down the steps to my basement apartment, disarmed my magical wards, unlocked the door, and shoved hard at it.

It didn't open. The previous autumn, zombies had torn apart my steel security door and wrecked my apartment. Though I was getting a modest paycheck from the Wardens now, I still didn't have enough money to pay for all the repairs, and I had set out to fix the door on my own. I hadn't framed it very well, but I try to think positive: The new door was arguably even more secure than the old one—now you could barely get the damned thing open even when it wasn't locked.

While I was in home-renovation mode, I put down linoleum in the kitchen, carpet on the living room and bedroom floors, and tile in the bathroom, and let me tell you something.

It isn't as easy as those Time-Life homeowner books make it look.

I had to slam my shoulder against it three or four

times, but the door finally groaned and squealed and came open.

"I thought you were going to have a contractor fix that," Murphy said.

"When I get the money."

"I thought you were getting another paycheck now."

I sighed. "Yeah. But the rate of pay was set in 1959, and the Council hasn't given it a cost-of-living increase since. I think it comes up for review in a few more years."

"Wow. That's even slower than City Hall."

"Always thinking positive." I went inside, stepping onto the large wrinkle that had somehow formed in the carpet before the door.

My apartment isn't huge. There's a fairly roomy living room, with a miniature kitchen set in an alcove opposite the door. The door to my tiny bedroom and bathroom is on the right as you come in, with a red-brick fireplace set in the wall beside it. Bookshelves, tapestries, and movie posters line the cold stone walls. My original *Star Wars* poster had survived the attack, though my library of paperbacks had taken a real beating. Those darned zombies, they always dog-ear the pages and crack the spines the minute they're done oozing foul goop and smashing up furniture.

I have a couple of secondhand sofas, which aren't hard to get cheap, so replacing them wasn't too bad. A pair of comfortable old easy chairs by the fire, a coffee table, and a large mound of grey-and-black fur rounded out the furnishings. There's no electricity, and it's a dim little hole, but it's a dim, *cool* little hole, and it was a relief to get out of the broiling sun.

The small mountain of fur shook itself, and something thudded against the wall beside it as it rose up into the shape of a large, stocky dog covered in a thick shag of grey fur, complete with an almost leonine mane of darker fur around his neck, throat, chest, and upper shoulders. He went to Murphy straightaway, sitting and offering up his right front paw.

Murphy laughed, and grabbed his paw briefly—her fingers couldn't have stretched around the offered limb. "Hiya, Mouse." She scratched him behind the ears. "When did you teach him that, Harry?"

"I didn't," I said, stooping to ruffle Mouse's ears as I went past him to the fridge. "Where's Thomas?" I asked the dog.

Mouse made a chuffing sound and looked at the closed door to my bedroom. I stopped to listen for a moment, and heard the faint gurgle of water in the pipes. Thomas was in the shower. I got a Coke out of the fridge and glanced at Murphy. She nodded. I got her one too, and doddered over to the couch to sit down slowly and carefully, my aches and pains complaining at me the whole while. I opened the Coke, drank, and settled back with my eyes closed. Mouse lumbered over to sit down by the couch and lay his massive head on one knee. He pawed at my leg.

"I'm fine," I told him.

He exhaled through his nose, doggie expression somehow skeptical, and I scratched his ears, to prove it. "Thanks for the ride, Murph."

"Sure," she said. She brought out a plastic sack she'd carried in and tossed it on the floor. It held my robe, stole, and cloak, all of them spattered with blood. She walked over to the kitchen sink and started filling it with cold water. "So let's talk."

I nodded and told her about the Korean kid. While I did that, she put my stole in the sink, then started washing it briskly in the cold water.

"That kid is what wizards mean when they talk about warlocks," I said. "Someone who has betrayed the purpose of magic. Gone bad, right from the start."

She waited a moment and then said, in a quiet, dangerous voice, "They killed him here? In Chicago?"

"Yes," I said. I felt even more tired. "This is one of our safer meeting places, apparently."

"You saw it?"

"Yes."

"You didn't stop it?"

"I couldn't have," I said. "There were heavyweights there, Murphy. And . . ." I took a deep breath. "I'm not sure they were completely in the wrong."

"Like hell they weren't," she snarled. "I don't give a good God damn what the White Council does over in England or South America or wherever they want to hang around flapping their beards. But they came here."

"Had nothing to do with you," I said. "Nothing to do with the law, that is. It was internal stuff. They would have done the same to that kid, no matter where they were."

Her movements became jerky for a moment, and water splashed over the rim of the sink. Then she visibly forced herself to relax, put the stole aside, and went to work on the robe. "Why do you think that?" she asked.

"The kid had gone in for black magic in a big way," I said. "Mind-control stuff. Robbing people of their free will."

She regarded me with cool eyes. "I'm not sure I understand."

"It's the Fourth Law of Magic," I said. "You aren't allowed to control the mind of another human. But . . . hell, it's one of the first things a lot of these stupid kids try—the old Jedi mind trick. Sometimes they start with maybe getting homework overlooked by a teacher or convincing their parents to buy them a car. They come into their magic when they're maybe fifteen or so, and by the time they're seventeen or eighteen they've got a full-grown talent."

"And that's bad?"

"A lot of times," I said. "Think about how men that age are. Can't go ten seconds without thinking about sex. Sooner or later, if someone doesn't teach them otherwise, they'll put the psychic armlock on the head cheerleader to get a date. And more than a date. And then more girls, or I guess other guys if I'm going to be PC about it. Someone else gets upset about losing a girlfriend or a daughter getting pregnant and the kid tries to fix his mistakes with *more* magic."

"But why does that mandate execution?" Murphy asked.

"It . . ." I frowned. "Getting into someone's mind like that is difficult and dangerous. And sooner or later, while you're changing them, you start changing yourself, too. You remember Micky Malone?"

Murphy didn't exactly shudder, but her hands stopped moving for a minute. Micky Malone was a retired police officer. A few months after he'd gotten out of the game, an angry and vicious spiritual entity had unleashed a psychic assault on him, and bound him in spells of torment to boot. The attack had transformed a grandfatherly old retired cop into a screaming maniac, totally out of control. I'd done what I could for the poor guy, but it had been really bad.

"I remember," Murphy said quietly.

"When a person gets into someone's head, it inflicts all kinds of damage—sort of like what happened to Micky Malone. But it damages the one doing it, too. It gets easier to bend others as you get more bent. Vicious cycle. And it's dangerous for the victim. Not just because of what might happen as a direct result of suddenly being forced to believe that the warlock is the god-king of the universe. It strains their psyche, and the more uncharacteristically they're made to feel and act, the more it hurts them. Most of the time, it devolves into a total breakdown."

Murphy shivered. "Like those office workers Mavra did it to? And the Renfields?"

A flash of phantom pain went through my maimed hand at the memory. "Exactly like that," I said.

"What can that kind of magic do?" she asked, her voice more subdued.

"Too much. This kid had forced a bunch of people to commit suicide. A bunch more to commit murder. He'd turned a whole gang of people, most of them his family, into his personal slaves."

"My God," Murphy said quietly. "That's hideous."

I nodded. "That's black magic. You get enough of it in you and it changes you. Stains you."

"Isn't there anything else the Council can do?"

"Not when the kid is that far gone. They've tried it all," I said. "Sometimes the warlock seemed to get better, but they all turned back in the end. And more people died. So unless someone on the Council takes personal responsibility for the warlock, they just kill them."

She thought about that for a moment. Then she asked, "Could you have done that? Taken responsibility for him?"

I shifted uncomfortably. "Theoretically, I guess. If I really believed he could be salvaged."

She pressed her lips together and stared at the sink.

"Murph," I said, as gently as I knew how. "The law couldn't handle someone like that. You couldn't arrest them, contain them, without some serious magic to neutralize their powers. If you tried to bring an angry war-lock into holding down at SI, it would get ugly. Worse than the loup-garou."

"There's got to be another way," Murphy said.

"Once a dog goes rabid, you can't bring him back," I said. "All you can do is keep him from hurting others. The best solution is prevention. Find the kids displaying serious talent and teach them better from the get-go. But the world population has grown so much in the past century that the White Council can't possibly identify and reach them all. Especially with this war on. There just aren't enough of us."

She tilted her head, staring at me. "Us? That's the first time I've heard you reference the White Council with yourself included in it."

I wasn't sure what to say to that, so I drank the rest of my Coke. Murphy went on washing for a minute, set the robe aside, and reached for the grey cloak. She dropped it into the sink, frowned, and then held it up. "Look at this," she said. "The blood came out when it hit the water. All by itself."

"It's like that kid never died. Cool," I said quietly.

Murphy watched me for a moment. "Maybe this is what it feels like for civilians when they see cops doing some of the dirty work. A lot of times they don't under-stand what's happening. They see something they don't like and it upsets them—because they don't have the full story, aren't personally facing the problem, and don't know how much worse the alternative could be."

"Maybe," I agreed.

"It sucks."

"Sorry."

She cast me a fleeting smile, but her expression grew serious again when she crossed the room to sit down near me. "Do you really think what they did was necessary?"

God help me, I nodded.

"Is this why the Council was so hard on you for so long? Because they thought you were a warlock about to relapse?"

"Yeah. Except for the part where you're using the past tense." I leaned forward, chewing on my lip for a second. "Murph, this is one of those things the cops can't get involved in. I told you there would be things like this. I don't like what happened any more than you do. But please, don't push this. It won't help anyone."

"I can't ignore a dead body."

"There won't be one."

She shook her head and stared at the Coke for a while more. "All right," she said. "But if the body shows up or someone reports it, I won't have any choice."

"I understand." I looked around for a change of subject. "So. There's black magic afoot in Chicago, according to an annoyingly vague letter from the Gatekeeper."

"Who is he?"

"Wizard. Way mysterious."

"You believe him?"

"Yeah," I said. "So we should be on the lookout for killings and strange incidents and so on. The usual."

"Right," Murphy said. "I'll keep an eye out for corpses, weirdos, and monsters."

The door to the bedroom opened and my half brother, Thomas, emerged, freshly showered and smelling faintly of cologne. He was right around six feet in height, and was built like the high priest of Bowflex—all lean muscle, sculpted and well formed, not too much of a good thing. He wore a pair of black trousers and black shoes, and was pulling a pale blue T-shirt down over his rippling abs as he came into the room.

Murphy watched him, blue eyes gleaming. Thomas is

awfully pretty to look at. He's also a vampire of the White Court. They didn't go in for fangs and blood so much as pale skin and supernaturally hot sex, but just because they fed on raw life force rather than blood didn't make them any less dangerous.

Thomas had worked hard to make sure that he kept his hunger under control, so that when he fed he wouldn't hurt anyone too badly—but I knew it had been a difficult struggle for him, and he carried that strain around with him. It was visible in his expression, and it made all of his movements those of a lean, hungry predator.

"Monsters?" he asked. He smiled pleasantly and said, "Karrin, good afternoon."

"That's Lieutenant Murphy to you, Prettyboy," she shot back, but her face was set in an appreciative smile.

He grinned back at her from under his hair, which even when wet and uncombed was carelessly curling and attractive. "Why, thank you for the compliment," he said. He reached down to scratch Mouse's ears, nodded to me, and seized up his big black gym bag. "You have some more business come to town, Harry?"

"That's the scuttlebutt," I said. "I haven't had time to look into it yet."

He tilted his head to one side and frowned at me. "What the hell happened to you?"

"Car trouble."

"Uh-huh," he said. He slung the bag's strap over his shoulder. "Look, you need some help, just let me know." He glanced at the clock and said, "Gotta run."

"Sure," I said to his back. He shut the door behind him.

Murphy arched an eyebrow. "That was abrupt. Are you still getting along?"

I grimaced and nodded. "He's . . I don't know,

Murph. He's been very distant lately. And gone almost all of the time. Day and night. He sleeps and eats here, but mostly when I'm at work. And when I do see him, it's always like that—in passing. He's in a hurry to get somewhere."

"Where?" she asked.

I shrugged.

"You're worried about him," she said.

"Yeah. He's usually a lot more tense than this. You know, the whole incubus hunger thing. I'm worried that maybe he's decided appetite control was for the birds."

"Do you think he's hurting anyone?"

"No," I said at once, a little too quickly. I forced myself to calm down and then said, "No, not as such. I don't know. I wish he'd talk to me, but ever since last fall, he's kept me at arm's length."

"Have you asked him?" Murphy said.

I eyed her. "No."

"Why not?"

"It isn't done that way," I said.

"Why not?"

"Because guys don't do it like that."

"Let me get this straight," Murphy said. "You want him to talk to you, but you won't actually tell him that or ask him any questions. You sit around with the silence and tension and no one says anything."

"That's right," I said.

She stared at me.

"You need a prostate to understand," I said.

She shook her head. "I understand enough." She rose and said, "You're idiots. You should talk to him."

"Maybe," I said.

"Meanwhile, I'll keep my eyes open. If I find anything odd, I'll get in touch."

"Thank you."

"What are you going to do?"

"Wait for sundown," I said.

"Then what?" she asked.

I rubbed at my aching head, feeling a sudden surge of defiance for whoever had run me off the road and whatever black-magicky jerk had decided to mess around with my hometown. "Then I put on my wizard hat and start finding out what's going on."

Chapter

Six

Murphy stayed until she was sure I wasn't going to suddenly drop unconscious, but made me promise to call her in a couple of hours to be sure. Mouse escorted her to the door when she left, and Murphy swung it shut with two hands and a grunt of effort in order to make it close snugly into the frame. Her car started, departed.

I prodded my brain with a sharp stick until it figured out my next move. My brain pointed out that I knew the current Summer Knight of the Summer Court, and that the guy owed me some fairly big favors. I'd saved his life when he'd just been a terrified changeling trying not to get swallowed up by an incipient war between Winter and Summer. When everything settled, he was the new Summer Knight, the mortal champion of the Summer Court. It gave him a lot of influence with fully half of the Sidhe realm, and he'd probably know more about what was going on there than any other native of the real world. My brain thought it would be really wonderful if maybe I could make one little phone call to Fix and get all the information I needed about the Sidhe Courts handed to me on a silver platter.

My brain is sometimes overly optimistic, but I indulged it on the off chance that I came up a winner in the investigative lottery.

I reached for the phone. It rang eleven times before someone answered. "Yes?"

"Fix?" I asked.

"Mmmph," answered a rumpled-sounding male voice. "Who is this?"

"Harry Dresden."

"Harry!" His voice brightened with immediate, if somewhat sleepy, cheer, which seemed far more appropriate to the Summer Knight of the Sidhe Courts. "Hey, how are you? What's up?"

"That's the question of the day," I said. "I need to talk to you about Summer business."

The sleepiness vanished from his voice. So did the friendliness. "Oh."

"Look, it's nothing big," I started. "I just need to—"

"Harry," he said, his voice sharp. Fix had never cut me off before. In fact, if you'd asked my professional opinion a year before, I'd have told you he never interrupted anyone in his life. "We can't talk about this. The line might not be secure."

"Come on, man," I said. "No one can monitor the phone line with a spell. It'd burn out in a second."

"Someone isn't playing by the old rules anymore, Harry," he said. "And a phone tap is not a difficult thing to engineer."

I frowned. "Good point," I allowed. "Then we need to talk."

"When?"

"Soonest."

"Accorded neutral territory," he responded.

He meant McAnally's pub. Mac's place has always been a hangout for the supernatural crowd in Chicago. When the war broke out, someone managed to get it placed on a list of neutral territories where, by the agreements known as the Unseelie Accords, everyone respected the neutrality of the property and was expected to behave in a civil fashion when present. It might not have been a private rendezvous, but it was probably the safest place in town to discuss this kind of thing. "Fine," I said. "When?"

"I've got business tonight. The soonest I can do it is tomorrow. Lunch?"

"Noon," I replied.

There was a sleepy murmur on the other end of the phone—a woman's voice.

"Shhhhh," Fix said. "Sure, Harry. I'll see you there."

We hung up, and I regarded the phone with pursed lips. Fix sleeping this late in the day? And with a girl in bed with him, no less. And interrupting wizards without a second thought. He'd come a ways.

Of course, he'd had a lot of exposure to the faeries since the last time I'd seen him. And if he had anything like the power that I'd seen the champions of the Sidhe display before, he'd have had time to get used to his new strength. You can never tell how someone is going to handle power—not until you hand it to them and see what they do with it. Fix had certainly changed.

I got a little twist in my gut that told me I should employ a great deal more than average caution when I spoke to him. I didn't like the feeling. Before I could think about it for too long, I made myself pick up the phone and move on with what my brain told me was a reasonable step two—checking around to see if anyone had heard anything about bad juju running around town.

I called several people. Billy the Werewolf, recently married. Mortimer Lindquist, ectomancer. Waldo Butters, medical examiner and composer of the "Quasimodo

Polka," a dozen magical small-timers I knew, plus my ex's editor at the *Midwestern Arcane*. None of them had heard of anything, and I warned them all to keep an ear to the ground. I even put in a call to the Archive, but all I got was an answering service, and no one returned my call.

I sat and stared at the phone's base for a moment, the receiver buzzing a dial tone in my gloved left hand.

I hadn't called Michael, or Father Forthill. I probably should have, working on the basic notion that more help was better help. Then again, if the Home Office wanted Michael on the case, he'd be there regardless of whether or not anyone called him and how many immovable objects stood in the way. I've seen it happen often enough to trust that it was true.

It was a good rationalization, but it wasn't fooling anyone. Not even me. The truth was that I didn't want to talk to either one of them unless I really, really, really had to.

The dial tone turned into that annoying *buzz-buzz-buzz* of a no-connection signal.

I hung the phone back up, my hand unsteady. Then I got up, reached down to the clumsily trimmed area of carpet that covered the trapdoor set in the apartment's floor, and pulled it open onto a wooden stepladder that folded out and led down into my laboratory.

The lab is in the subbasement, which is a much better name for it than the basement-basement. It's little more than a big concrete box with a ladder leading up and out of it. The walls are lined with overflowing white wire shelves, the cheap kind you can get at Wal-Mart. In my lab, they store containers of every kind, from plastic bags to microwave-safe plastic dinnerware to heavy wooden boxes—and even one lead-lined, lead-sealed box where I store a tiny amount of depleted uranium dust. Other books, notebooks, envelopes, paper bags, pencils, and apparently random objects of many kinds crowd each other for space on the shelves—all except for one plain, homemade wooden shelf, which held only candles at either end, four romance novels, a Victoria's Secret catalog, and a bleached human skull.

A long table ran down the middle of the room, leaving a blank section of floor at the far end kept perfectly clear of any clutter whatsoever. A ring of plain silver was set into the floor—my summoning circle. Underneath it lay a foot and a half or so of concrete, and then another heavy metal box, wrapped with its own little circle of wards and spells. Inside the box was a blackened silver coin.

My left palm, which had been so badly burned except for an outline of skin in the shape of Lasciel's angelic symbol, suddenly itched.

I rubbed it against my leg and ignored it.

My worktable had been crowded with material for most of the time it had been down in my lab. But that no longer was the case.

At that point I felt I owed someone an apology. When Murphy had asked me about the money from the Council, the answer I'd given her was true enough. They'd set the pay rate for Wardens in the fifties—but even the Council wasn't quite hidebound enough to ignore things like standard inflation, and the Warden's paychecks had kept pace through discretionary funding in— my God, I'm starting to sound like part of the establishment.

Long story short. The Wardens have sneaky ways of getting paid more, and the money I was getting from them, while not stellar, was nothing to sneeze at, either. But I hadn't been spending it on things like fixing up my apartment.

I'd been spending it on what was on my worktable.

"Bob," I said, "wake up."

Orangish flames kindled wearily to life inside the open eye sockets of the skull. "Oh for crying out loud," a voice from within complained. "Can't you take a night off? It'll be finished when it's finished, Harry."

"No rest for the wicked, Bob," I said cheerfully. "And that means we can't slack off either, or they'll outwork us."

The skull's voice took on a whiny tone. "But we've been tinkering with that stupid thing every night for six months. You're growing a cowlick and buck teeth, by the way. You keep this up and you'll have to retire to a home for magical geeks and nerds."

"Pish tosh," I said.

"You can't say pish tosh to that," Bob grumped. "You don't even know what it means."

"Sure I do. It means spirits of air should shut up and assist their wizard before he sends them out to patrol for fungus demons again."

"I get no respect," Bob sighed. "Okay, okay. What do you want to do now?"

I gestured at the table. "Is it ready?"

"Ready?" Bob said. "It isn't ever going to be *ready*, Harry. Your subject is fluid, always changing. Your model must change too. If you want it to be as accurate as possible, it's going to be a headache keeping it up-to-date."

"I do, and I know," I told him. "So talk. Where are we? Is it ready for a test run?"

"Put me in the lake," Bob said.

I reached up to the shelf obligingly, picked up the skull, and set it down on the eastern edge of the table.

The skull settled down beside the model city of Chicago. I'd built it onto my table, in as much detail as I'd been able to afford with my new paycheck. The skyline rose up more than a foot from the tabletop, models of each building made from cast pewter—also expensive, given I'd had to get each one made individually. Streets made of real asphalt ran between the buildings, lined with streetlights and mailboxes in exacting detail—and all in all, I had the city mapped out to almost two miles from Burnham Harbor in every direction. Detail began to fail toward the outskirts of the model, but as far as I'd been able to, I modeled every building, every road, every waterway, every bridge, and every tree with as much accuracy as I knew how.

I'd also spent months out on the town, collecting bits and pieces from every feature on my map. Bark from trees, usually. Chips of asphalt from the streets. I'd taken a hammer and knocked a chip or two off every building modeled there, and those pieces of the originals had been worked into the structure of their modeled counterparts.

If I'd done it correctly, the model would be of enormous value to my work. I'd be able to use various techniques to do all kinds of things in town—track down lost objects, listen in on conversations happening within the area depicted by the model, follow people through town from the relative safety of my lab—lots of cool stuff. The model would let me send my magic throughout Chicago with a great deal more facility and with a far broader range of applications than I could currently manage.

Of course, if I *hadn't* done it correctly . . .

"This map," Bob said, "is pretty cool. I'd have thought you would have shown it off to someone by now."

"Nah," I said. "Tiny model of the city down here in my basement laboratory. Sort of projects more of that evil, psychotic, Lex Luthor vibe than I'd like."

"Bah," Bob said. "None of the evil geniuses I ever worked for could have handled something like this." He paused. "Though some of the psychotics could have, I guess."

"If that's meant to be flattering, you need some practice."

"What am I if not good for your ego, boss?" The skull turned slowly, left to right, candleflame eyes studying the model city—not its physical makeup, I knew, but the miniature ley lines that I'd built into the surface of the table, the courses of magical energy that flowed through the city like blood through the human body.

"It looks . . ." He made a sound like someone idly sucking a breath through his teeth. "Hey, it looks not bad, Harry. You've got a gift for this kind of work. That model of the museum really altered the flow around the stadium into something mostly accurate, speaking thaumaturgically."

"Is that even a real word?" I asked.

"It should be," he said with a superior sniff. "Little Chicago might be able to handle something if you want to give it a test run." The skull spun around to face me. "Tell me that this doesn't have something to do with the bruises on your face."

"I'm not sure it does," I said. "I got word today that the Gatekeeper—"

Bob shivered.

"—thinks that there's black magic afoot in town, and that I need to do something about it."

"And you want to try to use Little Chicago to find it?"

"Maybe," I said. "Do you think it will work?"

"I think that the Wright Brothers tested their new stuff at Kitty Hawk instead of trying it over the Grand Canyon for a reason," Bob said. "Specifically, because if the plane folded due to flawed design, they might *survive* it at Kitty Hawk."

"Or maybe they couldn't afford to travel," I said. "Besides, how dangerous could it be?"

Bob stared at me for a second. Then he said, "You've been pouring energy into this thing every night for six months, Harry, and right now it's holding about three hundred times the amount of energy that kinetic ring you wear will contain."

I blinked. At full power, that ring could almost knock a car onto its side. Three hundred times that kind of energy translated to . . . well, something I'd rather not experience within the cramped confines of the lab. "It's got that much in it?"

"Yes, and you haven't tested it yet. If you've screwed up some of the harmonics, it could blow up in your face, worst-case scenario. Best case, you only blow out the project and set yourself back to ground zero."

"To square one," I corrected him. "Square one is the beginning of a project. Ground zero is the area immediately under a bomb blast."

"One may tend to resemble the other," Bob said sourly.

"I'll just have to live with the risk," I said. "That's the exciting life of a professional wizard and his daring assistant."

"Oh, please. Assistants get paid."

In answer, I reached down to a paper bag out of sight below the table and withdrew two paperback romances.

Bob let out a squeaking sound, and his skull jounced and jittered on the blue-painted surface of the table that represented Lake Michigan. "Is that it, is that it?" he squeaked.

"Yes," I said. "They're rated 'Burning Hot' by some kind of romance society."

"Lots of sex *and* kink!" Bob caroled. "Gimme!"

I dropped them back into the bag and looked from Bob to Little Chicago.

The skull spun back around. "You know what kind of black magic?" he asked.

"No clue. Just black."

"Vague, yet unhelpful," Bob said.

"Annoyingly so."

"Oh, the Gatekeeper didn't do it to annoy you," Bob said. "He did it to prevent any chance of paradox."

"He . . ." I blinked. "He what?"

"He got this from hindsight, he had to," Bob said.

"Hindsight," I murmured. "You mean he went to the future for this?"

"Well," Bob hedged. "That would break one of the Laws, so probably not. But he might have sent himself a message from there, or maybe gotten it from some kind of prognosticating spirit. He might even have developed some ability for that himself. Some wizards do."

"Meaning what?" I asked.

"Meaning that it's possible nothing *has* happened, yet. But that he wanted to put you on your guard against something that's coming in the immediate future."

"Why not just tell me?" I asked.

Bob sighed. "You just don't get this, do you?"

"I guess not."

"Okay. Let's say he finds out that someone is going to steal your car tomorrow."

"Heh," I said bitterly. "Okay, let's say that."

"Right. Well, he can't just call you up and tell you to move your car."

"Why not?"

"Because if he significantly altered what happened with his knowledge of the future it could cause all sorts of temporal instabilities. It could cause new parallel realities to split off from the point of the alteration, ripple out into multiple alterations he couldn't predict, or kind of backlash into his consciousness and drive him insane." Bob glanced at me again. "Which, you know, might not do much to deter you, but other wizards take that kind of thing seriously."

"Thank you, Bob," I said. "But I still don't get why any of those things would happen."

Bob sighed. "Okay. Temporal studies 101. Let's say that he hears about your car being stolen. He comes back to warn you, and as a result, you keep your car."

"Sounds good so far."

"But if your car never got stolen," Bob said, "then how did he know to come back and warn you?"

I frowned.

"That's paradox, and it can have all kinds of nasty backlash. Theory holds that it could even destroy our reality if it happened in a weak enough spot. But that's never been proven, and never happened. You can tell, on account of how everything keeps existing."

"Okay," I said. "So what's the point in sending the message at all, if it can't change anything?"

"Oh, it can," Bob said. "If it's done subtly enough, indirectly enough, you can get all kinds of things changed. Like, for example, he tells you that your car is going to be stolen. So you move it to a parking garage, where instead of getting stolen by the junkie who was going to shoot you and take the car on the street, you get jacked by a professional who takes the car without hurting you—because by slightly altering the fate of the car, he indirectly alters yours."

I frowned. "That's a pretty fine line."

"Yes, which is why not mucking around with time is one of the Laws," Bob said. "It's possible to change the past—but you have to do it indirectly, and if you screw it up you run the risk of Paradox-egeddon."

"So what you're saying is that by sending .me this warning, he's indirectly working some other angle completely?"

"I'm saying that the Gatekeeper is usually a hell of a lot more specific about this kind of thing," Bob said. "All of the Senior Council take black magic seriously. There's got to be a reason he's throwing it at you like this. My gut says he's working from a temporal angle."

"You don't have any guts," I said sourly.

"Your jealousy of my intellect is an ugly, ugly thing, Harry," Bob said.

I scowled. "Get to the point."

"Right, boss," said the skull. "The point is that black magic is very hard to find when you look for it directly. If you try to bring up instances of black magic on your model, like Little Chicago is some kind of evil-juju radar array, it's probably going to blow up in your face."

"The Gatekeeper put me on guard against black magic," I said. "But maybe he's telling me that so that I can watch for something else. Something black-magic related."

"Which might be a lot easier to find with your model," Bob said cheerfully.

"Sure," I said. "If I had the vaguest idea of what to look for." I frowned, scowling. "So instead of looking for black magic, we look for the things that go along with black magic."

"Bingo," Bob said. "And the more normal the better."

I pulled out my stool and sat down, frowning. "So, how about we look for corpses? Blood. Fear. Those are pretty standard black wizardry accessories."

"Pain, too," Bob said. "They're into pain."

"So's the BDSM community," I said. "In a city of eight million there are tens of thousands like that."

"Oh. Good point," Bob said.

"One would almost think you should have thought of that one," I gloated. "But for the BDSM crowd, the pain isn't something they fear. So you just look for the fear instead. Real fear, not movie-theater fear. Terror. And there can't be a lot of spilled human blood in places with no violent activity, unless someone slips at the hospital or something. Ditto the corpses." I drummed the fingers of my good hand thoughtfully on the table beside Bob. "Do you think Little Chicago could handle that?"

He considered for a long moment before he said, in a cautious tone, "Maybe one of them. But this will be a very difficult, very long, and very dangerous spell for you, Harry. You're good for your years, but you still don't have the kind of fine control you'll get as you age. It's going to take all of your focus. And it will take a lot out of you—assuming you can manage it at all."

I took a deep breath and nodded slowly. "Fine. We treat it as a full-blown ritual, then. Cleansing, meditation, incense, the works."

"Even if you do everything right," Bob said, "it might not work. And if Little Chicago turns out to be flawed, it would be very bad for you."

I nodded slowly, staring at the model city.

There were eight million people in my town. And out of all of them, there were maybe two or three who could stand up to black magic, who had the kind of knowledge and power it took to stop a black wizard. Not only that, but odds were good that I was the only one who could actively find and counter someone before he got the murder-ball rolling. I was also, presumably, the only one who was forewarned.

Maybe it would be better to slow this down. Wait for developments my friends would report to me. Then I could get a better read on the threat, and how to deal with it. I mean, was it worth as much as my life to try this spell, when patience would get me information that was almost as good?

It might not be worth my life, but it would probably cost someone else's. Black magic isn't the kind of thing that leaves people whole behind it—and sometimes the victims it kills are the lucky ones. If I didn't employ the model, I'd have to wait for the bad guys to make the first move.

So I had to do it.

I was tired of looking at corpses and victims.

"Pull together everything you know about this kind of spell, Bob," I told him quietly. "I'm going to get some food and then we'll lay out the ritual. I'll start looking for fear come sundown."

"Will do," Bob said, and for once he was serious and didn't sass me.

Yikes.

I started back up my ladder before I thought about it too much and changed my mind.

Chapter

Seven

Ritual magic is not my favorite thing in the whole world. It doesn't matter what I'm trying to accomplish; I still feel sort of silly when it comes time to bathe and then dress myself up in a white robe with a hood, lighting candles and incense, chanting, and mucking around with a small arsenal of candles, wands, rods, liquids, and other props used in ritual magic.

Self-conscious as I might be, though, the props and the process offered an overriding advantage when it came to working with heavy magic—they freed up my attention from the dozens of little details that I would normally be forced to imagine and keep firmly in mind. Most of the time I never gave the proper visualization a second thought. I'd been doing it for so long that it was practically second nature. That was fine for short-term work, where I had to hold my thoughts in perfect balance only for a few seconds, but for a longer spell I would need an exponentially greater amount of focus and concentration. It took someone with a lot more mental discipline than me to cast a spell through a half-hour ritual without help, and while there were probably experienced wizards who could manage it, few bothered to try it when the alternative was usually simpler, safer, and more likely to work.

I rounded up the props I would need for the ritual,

with the elements first. A silver cup, which I would fill with wine, for water. A geode the size of my fist, its internal crystals vibrant shades of purple and green, for earth. Fire would be represented by a faerie-made candle, formed from unused beeswax, its wick braided from the hairs of a unicorn's mane. Air would be anchored by a pair of hawk-wing feathers wrought from gold with impossibly fine detail and precision by a band of svartalves whose mortal contact sold examples of their craftsmanship out of a shop in Norway. And for the fifth element, spirit, I would use my mother's silver pentacle amulet.

Other props followed, to engage the senses. Incense for scent and fresh grapes for taste. Tactile forces would depend upon a double-sided three-inch square I'd made from velvet on one side and sandpaper on the other. A rather large, deeply colored opal set within a silver frame reflected back every color of the rainbow, and would hold down the sight portion of the spell. And when I got rolling I would strike my old tuning fork against the floor for sound.

Mind, body, and heart came last. For mind, I would use an old K-Bar military knife as my ritual *athame,* as I usually did. Fresh droplets of my blood upon a clean white cloth would symbolize my physical body. For heart, I placed several photos of those who were dear to me inside a sack of silver-white silk. My parents, Susan, Murphy, Thomas, Mouse and Mister (my thirty-pound grey tomcat, currently on walkabout), and after a brief hesitation, Michael and his family.

I prepared the ritual circle on my lab floor, carefully sweeping it, mopping it, sweeping it again, then cleansing it with captured rainwater poured from a small, silver ewer. I brought in all the props and laid them out, ready to go.

Then I prepared myself. I lit sandalwood incense and more faerie-candles in the bathroom, started up the shower, then went step by step through a routine of washing, while focusing my mind on the task at hand. The water sluicing over me would drain away any random magical energies, a crucial step in the spell—contaminating the spell's energy with other forces would cause it to fail.

I finished bathing, dried, and slipped into my white robe. Then I knelt on the floor at the head of the stairs down to the lab, closed my eyes, and began meditating. Just as no other energies could be allowed into the ritual, my concentration had to be of similar purity. Random thoughts, worries, fears, and emotions would sabotage the spell. I focused on my breathing, upon stilling my thoughts, and felt my limbs grow a little chill as my heartbeat slowed. Worries of the day, my aches and pains, my thoughts of the future—all had to go. It took a while to get myself in the proper frame of mind, and by the time I was finished it had been dark for two hours and my knees ached somewhere in the background.

I opened my eyes and everything came into a brilliantly sharp focus that discounted the existence of anything except myself, my magic, and the ritual awaiting me. It had been a long, wearying preparation, and I hadn't even started with the magic yet, but if the spell could help me nail the bad guys quicker, the hours of effort would be well worth it.

Silence and focus ruled.

I was ready.

And then the fucking phone rang about a foot from my ear.

It is possible that I made some kind of unmanly noise when I jumped. My posture-numbed legs didn't respond as quickly as I needed them to, and I lurched awkwardly to one side, half falling onto the nearest couch.

"Dammit!" I screamed in sudden frustration. "Dammit, dammit, dammit!"

Mouse looked up from his lazy drowse and tilted his head to one side, ears up and forward.

"What are you looking at?" I snarled.

Mouse's jaw dropped open into a grin, and his tail wagged.

I rubbed my hand at my face while the phone kept on ringing. It had been a while since I'd done any seriously focused magic like that, and granted, I really don't get very many calls, but all the same I should have remembered to unplug the phone. Four hours of preparation gone to waste.

The phone kept ringing, and my head pounded in time with it. I ached. Stupid phone. Stupid car crash. I tried to think positive, because I read somewhere that it's important to do that at times of stress and frustration. Whoever wrote that was probably selling something.

I picked up the phone and growled, "Screw thinking positive," into the handset.

"Um," said a woman's voice. "What did you say?"

"Screw thinking positive!" I half shouted. "What the hell do you want?"

"Well. Maybe I have the wrong number. I was calling to speak to Harry Dresden?"

I frowned, my mind taking in details despite my temper's bid to take over the show. The voice was familiar to me; rich, smooth, adult—but the speaker's speech patterns had an odd hesitancy to them. Her words had an odd, thick edge on them, too. An accent?

"Speaking," I said. "Annoyed as hell, but speaking."

"Oh. Is this a bad time?"

I rubbed at my eyes and choked down a vicious response. "Who is this?"

"Oh," she said, as if the question surprised her. "Harry, it's Molly. Molly Carpenter."

"Ah," I said. I clapped one palm to my face. My friend Michael's oldest daughter. Way to role-model, Harry. You sure do come off like a calm, responsible adult. "Molly, didn't recognize you at first."

"I'm sorry," she said.

The "s" sound was a little bit thick. Had she been drinking? "Not your fault," I said. Which it hadn't been. For that matter, the interruption might have been a stroke of luck. If my head was still too scrambled from that afternoon's automobile hijinks to remember to unplug the phone, I didn't have any business trying to cast that spell. Probably would have blown my own head off. "What do you need, Molly?"

"Um," she said, and there was nervous tension in her voice. "I need . . . I need you to come bail me out."

"Bail," I said. "You're being literal?"

"Yes."

"You're in *jail*?"

"Yes," she said.

"Oh my God," I said. "Molly, I don't know if I can do that. You're sixteen."

"Seventeen," she said, with sparks of indignation and another thick "s."

"Whatever," I said. "You're a juvenile. You should call your parents."

"No!" she said, something near panic in her voice. "Harry, please. I can't call them."

"Why not?"

"Because I only get the one call, and I used it to call you."

"Actually, I don't think that's exactly how it works,

Molly." I sighed. "In fact, I'm surprised that . . ." I frowned, thinking. "You lied about your age."

"If I hadn't, Mom and Dad would be here already," she said. "Harry, please. Look, there's . . . there's a lot of trouble at home right now. I can't explain it here, but if you'll come get me, I swear, I'll tell you all about it."

I sighed again. "I don't know, Molly . . ."

"Please?" she said. "It's just this once, and I'll pay you back, and I'll never ask something like this of you again, I promise."

Molly had long since earned her PhD in wheedling. She managed to sound vulnerable and hopeful and sad and desperate and sweet all at the same time. I'm pretty sure she wouldn't need half that much effort to wrap her father around a finger. Her mother, Charity, was probably a different story, though.

I sighed. "Why me?" I asked.

I hadn't been talking to Molly, but she answered. "I couldn't think who else to call," she said. "I need your help."

"I'll call your dad. I'll come down with him."

"Please, no," she said quietly, and I didn't think she was feigning the quiet desperation in her voice. "Please."

Why fight the inevitable? I've always been a sucker for ye olde damsel in distress. Maybe not as big a sucker now as I had been in the past, but the insanity did not seem much less potent than it had always been.

"All right," I said. "Where?"

She gave me the location of one of the precincts not too far from my apartment.

"I'm coming," I told her. "And this is the deal: I'll listen to what you have to say. If I don't like it, I'm going to your parents."

"But you don't—"

"Molly," I said, and I felt my voice harden. "You're already asking me for a lot more than I feel comfortable with. I'll come down there to get you. You tell me what's up. After that, I make the call, and you abide by it."

"But—"

"This isn't a negotiation," I said. "Do you want my help or not?"

There was a long pause, and she made a frustrated little sound. "All right," she said. After a beat she hurried to add, "And thank you."

"Yeah," I said, and eyed the candles and incense, and thought about all the time I'd thrown away. "I'll be along within the hour."

I would have to call a cab. It wasn't the most heroic way to ride to the rescue, but walkers can't be choosers. I got up to dress and told Mouse, "I'm a sucker for a pretty face."

When I came out of the bedroom in clean clothes, Mouse was sitting hopefully by the door. He batted a paw at his leash, which hung over the doorknob.

I snorted and said, "You ain't pretty, furface." But I clipped the leash to his collar, and called for a cab.

Chapter

Eight

The cabby drove me to the Eighteenth District of the CPD, on Larrabee. The neighborhood around it has seen a couple of better days and thousands of worse ones. The once-infamous Cabrini Green isn't far away, but urban renewal and the efforts of local neighborhood watches, community groups, church congregations from several faiths, and cooperation with the local police department had changed some of Chicago's nastier streets into something resembling actual civilization.

The nasty hadn't left the city, of course—but it had been driven away from what had once been a stronghold of decay and despair. What was left behind wasn't the prettiest section of town, but it bore the quiet, steady signs of a place that had a passing acquaintance with law and order.

Of course, the cynical would point out that Cabrini Green was only a short walk from the Gold Coast, one of the richest areas of the city, and that it was no coincidence that funds had been sent that way by the powers that be through various municipal programs. The cynical would be right, but it didn't change the fact that the people of the area had worked and fought to reclaim their homes from fear, crime, and chaos. On a good day, the neighborhood made you feel like there was hope for us, as a species; that we could drive back the darkness with enough will and faith and help.

That kind of thinking had taken on whole new dimensions for me in the past year or two.

The police station wasn't new, but it was free of graffiti, litter, and shady characters of any kind—at least until I showed up, in jeans and a red T-shirt, bruised and unshaven. I got a weird look from the cabby, who probably didn't get all that many sandalwood-scented fares to drop off there. Mouse presented his head to the cabby while I paid through the driver's window, and got a smile and a polite scratching of the ears in reply.

Mouse has better people skills than me.

I turned to walk up to the station, stubbornly putting my money back in my wallet with my stiff left hand as I walked, and Mouse walked beside me. The hair on the back of my neck suddenly crawled, and I looked up at the reflection in the glass doors as I approached them.

A car had pulled up on the far side of the street behind me, and was stopped directly under a No Parking sign. I saw a vague shadow inside the car, a white sedan I did not recognize and which certainly wasn't the dark grey car that had run me off the road earlier. But my instincts told me I was being tailed by someone. You don't park illegally like that, in front of a police station no less, just because you're bored.

Mouse let out a low rumble of a growl, which made me grow a shade more wary. Mouse rarely made noise at all. When he did, I had begun to think it was because there was some kind of dark presence around—evil magic, hungry vampires, and deadly necromancers had all earned snarls of warning. But he never made a peep when the mailman came by.

So adding it up, someone from the nasty end of my side of the supernatural street was following me around town. Good grief; at least I usually know who I'm pissing off, and why. By the time an investigation gets to the point where I'm being followed, there's usually been at least one crime scene and maybe even a corpse or two.

Mouse growled another warning.

"I see him," I told Mouse quietly. "Easy. Just keep walking."

He fell silent again, and we never broke stride up to the door.

Molly Carpenter appeared and opened the door for us.

The last time I'd seen Molly, she'd been an awkward adolescent, all skinny legs, bright-eyed interest, and hesitation of movement offset by an appealing personal confidence and frequent smiles and laughter. But that had been years ago.

Since then, Molly had gotten all growed up.

She strongly favored her mother, Charity. Both of them were tall for women, only an inch or two under six feet, both of them blond, fair, blue-eyed, and both of them built like the proverbial brick house, somehow managing to combine strength, grace, and beauty that showed as much in their bearing, expression, and movement as it did in their appearance. Charity was a rose wrought of stainless steel. Molly could have been her younger self.

Of course, I doubted Charity had ever worn an outfit like Molly's.

Molly stood facing me in a long, gauzy black skirt, shredded artistically in several places. She wore fishnet tights beneath it, showing more leg and hip than any mother would prefer. The tights, too, were artfully torn in patches to display pale, smooth skin of thigh and calf. She had army-surplus combat boots on her feet, laced up with neon pink and blue laces. She wore a tight tank top, its fabric white, thin, and strained by the curves of her breasts, and a short black bolero jacket bearing a huge, gaudy button printed with the logo "SPLATTER-CON!!!" in dripping red letters. Black leather gloves covered her hands.

But wait, that's not all.

Her blond hair had been dyed, parti-colored, one half of her head bubblegum pink, the other sky blue, and it had been cut at a uniform length that ended just below her chin and left most of her face covered by a close veil of hair. She wore a lot of makeup; way too much eye liner and mascara, and black lipstick colored her mouth. Bright rings of gold gleamed in both nostrils, her lower lip, and her right eyebrow, and there was a bead of gold in that little dent just under her lower lip. There were miniature barbell-shaped bulges at the tips of her breasts, where the thin fabric emphasized rather than concealed them.

I didn't want to know what else had been pierced. I know I didn't, because I told myself that very sternly. I didn't want to know, even if it was, hell, a little intriguing.

But wait, that's *still* not all.

She had a tattoo on the left side of her neck in the shape of a slithering serpent, and I could see the barbs and curves of some kind of tribal design flickering out from the neckline of her tank top. Another design, whirling loops and spirals, covered the back of her right hand and vanished up under the sleeve of the jacket.

She watched me with one eyebrow arched, waiting for me to react. Her posture and expression both made the effort to say that she was way too cool to care what I thought, but I could practically taste the uncertainty she was working to hide, and her anxiety.

"Long time, no see," I said, finally.

"Hello, Harry," she replied. The words came out a little thick, and I saw more gold flash near the tip of her tongue.

Of course.

"It's odd," I said. "From here, it doesn't look like you're in jail at all."

"I know," she said. She managed to keep her voice mostly steady, but her face and throat colored pink in a guilty flush. She shifted her weight restlessly, and an odd clicking sound came from her mouth. Good grief. She'd picked up a tic of rattling her tongue piercing against her teeth when she was nervous. "Um. I should apologize, I guess. Uh . . ."

She floundered. I let her. A long silence made her look more flustered, but I had no intention of politely helping her out of it.

Mouse sat down between me and Molly, watching her intently.

Molly smiled at the dog and reached down to pet him.

Mouse tensed up, and a low rumbling came from his chest. Molly moved her hand toward him again, and my dog's chest suddenly rumbled with a deep and warning growl.

The last time Mouse had growled at anything—for that matter, made much noise at all—it had been a crazed sorcerer who made fair headway toward eviscerating me, and summoned a twenty-foot-long demon cobra to kill my dog. Mouse killed it instead. Then, at my command, Mouse killed the sorcerer, too.

And now he was growling at Molly.

"Be polite," I told him firmly. "She's a friend."

Mouse gave me a look and then fell quiet again. He sat calmly as Molly let him sniff her hand and scratch at his ears, but his wary body language didn't change.

"When did you get a dog?" Molly asked.

Mouse was spooked, though not the way he was when serious bad guys were around. Interesting. I kept my tone neutral. "Couple years ago. His name is Mouse."

"What breed is he?"

"He's a West Highlands Dogasaurus," I said.

"He's huge."

I said nothing, and the girl floundered some more. "I'm sorry," she said, finally. "I lied to you to get you to come down here."

"Really?"

She grimaced. "I'm sorry. I just . . . I really need your help. I just thought that if I could talk to you in person about it, you might be . . . I mean . . ."

I sighed. Regardless of how intriguingly rounded her tight shirt was, she was still a kid. "Call a spade a spade, Molly," I said. "You figured if you could get me to come all the way down here, you'd have a chance to flutter your eyelashes and get me to do whatever it is you really want me to do."

She glanced aside. "It isn't like that."

"It's just like that."

"No," she began. "I didn't want this to be a bad thing . . ."

"You manipulated me. You took advantage of my friendship. How is that *not* a bad thing?" My headache started rising up again. "Give me one reason I shouldn't turn and walk away right now."

"Because my friend is in trouble," she said. "I can't help him, but you can."

"What friend?"

"His name is Nelson."

"In jail?"

"He didn't do it," she assured me.

They never did. "He's your age?" I asked.

"Almost."

I arched an eyebrow.

"Two years older," she amended.

"Then tell legal-adult Nelson he should call a bail bondsman."

"We tried that. They can't get to him before tomorrow."

"Then tell him to bite the bullet and spend a night in the lockup or else to call his parents." I turned to go.

Molly caught my wrist. "He *can't*," she said, desperation in her voice. "There's no one for him to call. He's an orphan, Harry."

I stopped walking.

Well, dammit.

I'd been an orphan, too. It hadn't been fun. I could tell you some stories, but I make it a personal policy not to review them often. They amount to a nightmare that started with my father's death, followed by years and years of feeling acutely, perpetually alone. Sure, there's a system in place to care for orphans, but it's far from perfect and it is, after all, a system. It isn't a *person* looking out for you. It's forms and carbon copies and people with names you quickly forget. The lucky kids more or less randomly get tapped by foster parents who genuinely care. But for all the puppies at the pound who don't get chosen, life turns into one big lesson on how to look out for yourself—because there's no one in this world who cares enough to do it for you.

It's a horrible feeling. I don't care to experience even the faded memory of it—but if I just hear the word "orphan" aloud, that empty fear and quiet pain come rushing back from the darker corners of my mind. For a long time I'd been stupid enough to assume that I could handle everything on my own. That's vanity, though. Nobody can handle everything by themselves. Sometimes, you need someone's help—even if that help is only giving you a little of their time and attention.

Or bailing you out of jail.

"What's your friend Nelson in for?"

"Reckless endangerment and aggravated assault." She took a breath and said, "It's kind of a long story. But he's a sweet guy, Harry. There isn't a violent bone in his body."

Which emphasized to me just how young Molly really was. There are violent bones in everyone's body, if you look deep enough. About two hundred and six of them. "What about your dad? He saves people all the time."

Molly hesitated for a second, and her cheeks turned pink. "Um. My parents don't like Nelson very much. Especially my dad."

"Ah," I said. "Nelson's *that* kind of friend." Things started adding up. I asked the loaded question. "Why is it so important for him to get out tonight?"

Wait for it.

Molly let go of my wrist. "Because he might be in danger. The weird kind of danger. He needs your help."

And there it was.

Sometimes it's almost as though I'm psychic.

Chapter

Nine

Boyfriend Nelson had been arraigned two hours before. His bail had been set at enough money to make me glad that over the past year I had made it a habit to keep a chunk of cash around, just in case I needed it in a hurry. I got the fisheye from a hard-faced office matron as I counted it out in twenties. She counted it, too.

"Thank you," I said. "It's a wonderful feeling to be trusted."

She did not look amused. She pushed some papers at me. "Sign here, please. And here."

I signed, while Molly hovered nervously in the background holding Mouse's leash. Then we sat down and waited. Molly fidgeted until they brought her honey-bunny out to sign the last couple of papers before being released.

Boyfriend Nelson wasn't what I'd expected. He was an inch or two taller than Molly. He had a long, narrow face, and I would have hesitated to touch his cheekbones for fear of slicing my fingers on them. He was thin, but it was that kind of lean, whipcord thinness rather than anything that would denote frailty. He moved well, and I pegged him as a fencer or a martial artist of some other kind. Dark hair fell around his head in an even mop. He wore square-shaped, silver-rimmed spectacles, chinos, and a black T-shirt with another SPLATTERCON!!! logo on it. He looked tired and needed a shave.

The second he was free, he hurried over to Molly and they hugged, speaking quietly to one another. I didn't listen in. It didn't seem right to invade their privacy. Besides, body language told me enough. The hug went on a second or two longer than Molly wanted it to. Then, when Nelson bent his head down to kiss her, she gave him a sweet smile, turning her cheek to meet his lips. After that, he got the point. He bit his lower lip a little and stepped back from her, rubbing his hands on his pants as if unsure what else to do with them.

"Save me from awkward relationship melodrama," I muttered to Mouse under my breath, and got onto a pay phone to call a cab. Being a learned wizardly type I had, of course, discovered the cure for tangling up an otherwise orderly life with relationship issues: Don't have a relationship. It was better that way.

If I repeated it to myself often enough, I almost believed it.

Molly and boyfriend Nelson walked over to me a minute later. Nelson didn't look up at me when he offered me his hand. "Uh. I guess, thank you."

I shook his hand and squeezed hard enough to hurt a little. Me annoyed alpha male, ungh. "How could I refuse such a polite and straightforward request for help?" I took Mouse's leash from Molly, who looked away, turning pink again.

"I don't want to seem ungrateful," Nelson said, "but I have to get moving now."

"No, you don't," I said.

His weight had already shifted to move into his first step, and he blinked at me. "Excuse me?"

"I just got you out of a cage. Now comes the part where you tell me what happened to you. Then you can go."

His eyes narrowed and his weight shifted again, centering his balance. Definitely a student of martial arts. "Are you threatening me?"

"I'm telling you how it's going to be, kid. So talk."

"And if I don't?" he demanded.

I shrugged. "If you don't, maybe I'll knock your block off."

"I'd like to see you try," he said, more anger in his voice.

"Suit yourself," I said. "But we're in sight of the cop at the entry desk. He probably won't see who threw the first punch. You just got out on bail. You'll go back, probably for assault, committed within two minutes of being freed. There isn't a judge in town who would grant you bail again."

I saw him think about it furiously, which impressed me. A lot of men his age, when angry, wouldn't bother with actual thought. Then he shook his head. "You're bluffing. You'd be arrested too."

"Hell's bells, kid," I said. "When did you fall off the turnip truck? They'll interview me. I'll tell them you threw the first punch. Who do you think they're going to believe? I'll be out in an hour."

Nelson's knuckles popped as he clenched his fists. He stared at me, and then at the building behind him.

"Nelson," Molly urged quietly. "He's trying to help you."

"He's got a hell of a way of showing it," Nelson spat.

"Just balancing the scales a bit," I said, glancing at Molly. Then I sighed. Nelson was holding on to his pride. He didn't want to back down in front of Molly.

Insecurity, thy name is teenager.

It wouldn't kill me to help Nelson save face. "Come

on, kid. Give me five minutes to talk to you and I'll pay your fare back to wherever you're heading. I'll throw in some fast food."

Nelson's stomach made a gurgling sound and he licked his lips, glancing aside at Molly. The wary focus slid out of his posture and he nodded, brushing his hand back through his hair. He let out a long exhale and said, "Sorry. Just . . . been a bad day."

"I had one of those once," I said. "So talk. How'd you wind up in jail?"

He shook his head. "I'm not sure what actually happened. I was in the bathroom—"

I held up my hand, interrupting him with the gesture. Eat your heart out, Merlin. "What bathroom? Where?"

"At the convention," he said.

"Convention?" I asked.

"SplatterCon," Molly offered. She waved a hand at her button and at Nelson's shirt. "It's a horror movie convention."

"There's a convention for that?"

"There's a convention for everything," Nelson said. "This one screens horror movies, invites in directors, special-effects guys, actors. Authors, too. There are discussion panels. Costume contests. Vendors. Fans show up to the convention to get together and meet the industry guests, that kind of thing."

"Uh-huh. You're a fan, then?"

"Staff," he said. "I'm supposed to be in charge of security."

"Okay," I said. "Get back to the bathroom."

"Right," he said. "Well. I'd had a lot of coffee and potato chips and pretzels and stuff, so I was just sitting in there with the stall door closed."

"What happened?"

"I heard someone come in," Nelson said. "The door

was really squeaky." He licked his lips nervously. "And then he started screaming."

I arched an eyebrow. "Who?"

"Clark Pell," he said. "He owns the old movie theater next to the hotel. We rented it out for the weekend so we could play our favorites on the big screen. Nice old guy. Always supports the convention."

"Why was he screaming?"

Nelson hesitated for a second, clearly uncomfortable. "He . . . you have to understand that I didn't actually *see* anything."

"Sure," I said.

"It sounded like a fight. Scuffling sounds. I heard him let out a noise, right? Like someone had startled him." He shook his head. "That's when he started screaming."

"What happened?"

"I jumped up to help him, but . . ." His cheeks turned red. "You know. I was kind of in the middle of something. It took me a second to get out of the stall."

"And?"

"And Mr. Pell was there," he said. "He was unconscious and bleeding. Not real bad. But he looked like he'd taken a real pounding. Broken nose. Maybe his jaw, too. They took him to the hospital."

I frowned. "Could someone have slipped in or out?"

"No," Nelson said, and his voice was confident on that point. "That damned door all but screams every time it swings."

"Could someone have come in at the same time as Pell?" I asked.

"Maybe," he said. "On the same opening of the door. But—"

"I know," I said. "But they would have had to open the door to leave." I rubbed at my chin. "Could someone have held the door open?"

"The hall was crowded. You could hear the people when the door was open," Nelson said. "And there was a cop standing right outside. He was the first one in, in fact."

I grunted. "And with no other obvious suspects, they blamed you."

Nelson nodded. "Yes."

I mused for a moment and then said, "What do you think happened?"

He shook his head, several times, and very firmly. "I don't know. Someone must have gotten in and out somehow. Maybe there's an air vent or something."

"Yeah," I said. "Maybe that's it."

Nelson checked his watch, and swallowed. "Oh, God, I've got to get to the airport. I'm supposed to meet Darby in thirty minutes and take him to the hotel."

"Darby?" I asked.

"Darby Crane," Molly supplied. "Producer and director of horror films. Guest of honor at SplatterCon."

"He do any work I might have seen?" I asked.

Molly nodded. "Maybe. Did you ever see *Harvest*? The one with the Scarecrow?"

"Uh," I said, thinking. "Where it smashes through the wall of the convent and eats the nuns? And the librarian sets it on fire and it burns down the library and himself with it?"

"That's the one."

"Heh," I said. "Not bad. But I'll take a Corman flick any day."

"Excuse me," Nelson said, "but I *really* need to get moving."

As he spoke, the cab I'd called pulled up to the curb. I checked, and found my shadowy tail still outside, patient and motionless.

Mouse let out another almost subaudible growl.

My shadow wasn't exactly going out of his way not to be noticed, which meant that he almost certainly wasn't a hit man. A hired gun would do everything he could to stay invisible, preferably until several hours after I was cold and dead. Of course, he could be trying reverse psychology, I supposed. But that kind of circular reasoning could trigger a paranoia-gasm and drive me loopy fast.

Odds were good he was just supposed to keep an eye on me, whoever he was. Better, then, to keep him in sight, rather than trying to shake him. I was happier knowing where he was than worrying about him being out of sight. I'd play it cool—give him a while to see if I could figure out what he was up to. I nodded to myself, and strode out to the curb, Mouse at my side.

"Okay, kids," I called over my shoulder. "Get in the cab."

Mouse and I took the backseat. Molly didn't give Nelson a chance to choose. She got into the passenger seat in front, and boyfriend Nelson settled into the backseat beside me.

"Which?" I asked him.

"O'Hare."

I told the driver, and we took off for the airport. I watched my shadow in vague reflections in the windows. The car's lights came on and followed us all the way out to O'Hare. We got Nelson there in time to meet his B-movie mogul, and he all but leapt from the car. Molly opened her door to follow him.

"Wait," I said. "Not you."

She shot me a glance over her shoulder, frowning. "What?"

"Nelson's out of jail and he's talked to me about what happened, and he's in time to meet Darby Crane. I think I pretty much lived up to what I said I would do."

She frowned prettily. "Yes. So?"

"So now it's your turn. Close the door."

She shook her head. "Harry, don't you see that he's in some kind of trouble? And he doesn't believe in . . ." She glanced at the cabby and back to me. "You know."

"Maybe he is," I said. "Maybe not. I'm going to get over to the convention tonight and see if there's anything supernatural about the assault on Mr. Pell. Right after we get done talking to your parents."

Molly blanched. "What?"

"We had a deal," I said. "And in my judgment, Molly, we need to go see them."

"But . . ." she sputtered. "It isn't as though I need them to bail me out or anything."

"You should have thought about that before you made the deal," I said.

"I'm not going there," she said, and folded her arms. "I don't want to."

I felt cold stone flow into the features of my face, into the timbre of my voice. "Miss Carpenter. Is there any doubt in your mind—any at all—that I could take you there regardless of what you want to do?"

The change in tone hit her hard. She blinked at me in surprise for a second, lips parted but empty of sound.

"I'm taking you to see them," I said. "Because it's the smart thing to do. The legal thing to do. The right thing to do. You agreed to do it, and by the stars and stones, if you try to weasel out on me I will wrap you in duct tape, box you up, and send you UPS."

She stared at me in utter shock.

"I'm not your mom or your dad, Molly. And these days I'm not a very nice person. You've already abused my friendship tonight, and diverted my attention from work that could have saved lives. People who *really* need my help might get hurt or die because of this stupid stunt." I leaned closer, staring coldly, and she leaned away, declining to make eye contact. "Now buckle the fuck up."

She did.

I gave the cabby the address and closed my eyes. I hadn't seen Michael in . . . nearly two years. I regretted that. Of course, not seeing Michael meant not seeing Charity either, which I did *not* regret. And now I was going to drive up in a cab with their daughter. Charity was going to like that almost as much as I like cleaning up after Mouse on our walks. In her eyes, my mere presence near her daughter would make me guilty of uncounted (if imaginary) transgressions.

The angelic sigil on my left palm burned and itched furiously. I poked at it through the leather glove, but it didn't help. I'd have to keep the glove on. If Michael saw the sigil, or if he somehow sensed the shadow of Lasciel running around in my head, he might react in a manner similar to his wife's—and that didn't take into consideration a father's desire to protect his . . . physically matured daughter from any would-be, ah, invaders.

I predicted fireworks of one kind or another. Fun, fun, fun.

Should I survive the conversation, I would then be off to a horror convention, where a supernatural assault might or might not have happened, with a mysterious stranger following me while an unknown would-be assassin ran around loose somewhere, probably practicing his offensive driving skills so that he could polish me off the next time he saw me.

Let the good times roll.

Chapter

Ten

I told the cabby to keep the meter running and headed for the Carpenters' front door. Molly remained cool, distant, and untouchably silent all the way over the small lawn. She walked calmly up the steps to the porch. She faced the door calmly—and then broke out into a sweat the moment I rang the bell.

Nice to know I wasn't the only one. I wasn't looking forward to speaking with Michael. As long as I kept the conversation brief and didn't get too close to him, he might not sense the presence of the demon inside me. Things might work out.

My already sore head twinged a little more.

Beside me, Molly rolled her shoulders in a few jerky motions and pushed at her hair in fitful little gestures. She tugged at her well-tattered skirts, and grimaced at her boots. "Can you see if there's any mud on them?"

I paused to consider her for a second. Then I said, "You have two tattoos showing right now, and you probably used a fake ID to get them. Your piercings would set off any metal detector worth the name, and you're featuring them in parts of your anatomy your parents wish you didn't yet realize you had. You're dressed like Frankenhooker, and your hair has been dyed colors I previously thought existed only in cotton candy." I turned to face the door again. "I wouldn't waste time worrying about a little mud on the boots."

In the corner of my eye, Molly swallowed nervously, staring at me until the door opened.

"Molly!" shrieked a little girl's voice. There was a blur of pink cotton pajamas, a happy squeal, and then Molly caught one of her little sisters in her arms in a mutual hug.

"Hiya, Hobbit," Molly said, catching the girl by an ankle and dangling her in the air. This elicited screams of delight from the girl. Molly swung her upright again. "How have you been?"

"Daniel is the boss kid now, but he isn't as good as you," the girl said. "He yells lots more. Why is your hair blue?"

"Hey," I said. "It's pink, too."

The girl, a golden-haired moppet of six or seven, noticed me for the first time and promptly buried her face against Molly's neck.

"You remember Hope," Molly said. "Say hello to Mister Dresden."

"My name is Hobbit!" the little girl declared boldly—then lowered her face into the curve of Molly's neck and hid from me. Meanwhile, the house erupted with thudding feet and more shouts. Lights started flicking on upstairs, and the stairwell shuddered as brothers and sisters pounded down it and ran for the front door.

Another pair of girls made it there first, both of them older than Hope. They both assaulted Molly with shrieks and flying hugs. "Bill," the smaller of the pair greeted me, afterward. "You came back to visit."

"My name is Harry, actually," I said. "And I remember you. Amanda, right?"

"I'm Amanda," she allowed cautiously. "But we already have a Harry. That's why you're Bill."

"And this is Alicia," Molly said of the other, a child as gawky and skinny as Molly had been when I first met her. Her hair was darker than the others, trimmed short, and she wore black-rimmed glasses over a serious expression. "She's the next oldest girl. You remember Mister Dresden, don't you, Leech?"

"Don't call me Leech," she said in the patient tone of someone who has said something a million times and plans on saying it a million times more. "Hello, sir," she told me.

"Alicia," I said, nodding.

Evidently the use of her actual name constituted a gesture of partisanship. She gave me a somewhat relieved and conspiratorial smile.

A pair of boys showed up. The older might have been almost ready to take a driver's test. The next was balanced precariously between grade school and pimples. Both had Michael's dark hair and solid, sober expression. The younger boy almost threw himself at Molly upon seeing her, but restrained himself to a hello and a hug. The older boy only folded his arms and frowned.

"My brother Matthew," Molly said of the younger. I nodded at him.

"Where have you been?" the older boy said. He stood there frowning at Molly for a moment.

"Nice to see you too, Daniel," she replied. "You know Mister Dresden."

He gave me a nod, said to Molly, "I'm not kidding. You just took off. Do you have any idea of how much it messed things up here?"

Molly's mouth firmed into a line. "You didn't think I was going to just hang around forever, did you?"

"Is it Halloween wherever it is you live?" Daniel demanded. "Look at you. Mom is going to freak out."

Molly stepped forward and half tossed Hope into

Daniel's chest. "When does she do anything else? Shouldn't these two be in bed?"

Daniel grimaced as he caught Hope and said, "That's what I was trying to do before someone interrupted bedtime." He took Amanda's hand, and over halfhearted protests took the two youngest girls back into the house.

There was a creak from the upstairs of the house and Alicia thumped Matthew firmly with her elbow. The two vanished as heavy steps descended from the second floor.

Michael Carpenter was almost as tall as me and packed a lot more muscle. He had the kind of face that told anyone who looked that he was a man of honesty and kindness who nonetheless could probably kick the crap out of you if you offered him violence. I wasn't sure how he managed that. Something about the strength of his jawline, maybe, bespoke the steady power of both body and mind. But as for the kindness, that went all the way down to his soul. You could see it in the warmth of his grey eyes.

He wore khaki pants and a light blue T-shirt. A hard-cased plastic cylinder, doubtless the one he used to transport his sword, hung from a strap over one shoulder. An overnight bag hung over the other, and his hair was damp from the shower. He came down the stairs at the pace of a man with places to be—until he looked up and saw Molly and me standing in the doorway.

He froze in place, a smile of surprised delight illuminating his face as he saw Molly. The overnight bag thumped to the floor as he strode forward and crushed his oldest daughter to his chest in a hug.

"Daddy," she protested.

"Hush," he told her. "Let me hug you."

Her eyes flickered to the case still held against one

shoulder, and her expression became tainted with a sudden worry. "When are you going?"

"You just caught me," he said. "I'm glad."

She hugged her father back, and closed her eyes. "It's just a visit," she said.

He rose from the hug a moment later, studying her face, worry in his eyes. Then he nodded, smiled, and said, "I'm glad anyway." He jerked his head back a moment later, as if the rest of her appearance had only then registered on him, and his eyes widened. "Margaret Katherine Amanda Carpenter," he said, his voice hushed. "God's blood, what have you done to your . . ." He looked her up and down, gentle dismay on his face. ". . . your . . ."

"Self," I suggested. "Yourself."

"Yourself," Michael sighed. He looked Molly up and down again. She was doing that thing where she tried to display how much she didn't care what her daddy thought of her look, and it was almost painfully obvious that she cared a great deal. "Tattoos. The hair wasn't so bad, but . . ." He shook his head and offered me his hand. "Tell me, Harry. Am I just too old?"

I didn't want to shake Michael's hand. Lasciel's presence in me, even if it wasn't the full-blown version, wasn't something he would miss—not if he made actual physical contact with me. For a couple of years I had been avoiding him with every excuse I had, hoping I could take care of my little demon issue without bothering him about it.

More accurately, I supposed, I had been too ashamed to let him see what had happened. Michael was probably the most honest, decent human being I had ever had the privilege to know. He had always thought well of me. It had been something that had given me comfort in a low spot or two, and I hated the thought of losing his trust and friendship. Lasciel's presence, the collaboration of a literal fallen angel, would destroy that.

But friendship isn't a one-way street. I had brought his daughter back because I had thought it was the right thing to do—and because I thought he'd do the same for someone else in a similar circumstance. I respected him enough to do that. And I respected him too much to lie to him. I had avoided the confrontation long enough.

I shook his hand.

And nothing in his manner or expression changed. Not an ounce.

He hadn't sensed Lasciel's presence or mark.

"Well?" he asked, smiling.

"If you think she looks silly, you're too old," I said after a moment. "I'm moderately ancient by the standards of the younger generation, and I think she only looks a little over the top."

Molly rolled her eyes at us both, her cheeks pink.

"I suppose a good Christian should be willing to turn the other cheek when it comes to matters of fashion," Michael said.

"Let he who hath never stonewashed his jeans cast the first stone," I said, nodding.

Michael laughed and gripped my shoulder briefly. "It's good to see you, Harry."

"And you," I said, trying a smile. I glanced at the plastic case on his shoulder. "Business trip?"

"Yes," he said.

"Where to?"

He smiled. "I'll know when I get there."

I shook my head. Michael was entrusted to wield one of the blades of the Knights of the Cross. He was one of only two men in the world who were entrusted with such potent weapons against dark powers. As such, he had a lot of planet to cover. I wasn't clear exactly how his itinerary was established, but he was often called away from his home and family, apparently summoned to where his strength was most needed.

I don't go in big for religion—but I believe in the Almighty. I had seen a vast power at work supporting Michael's actions. Coincidence seemed to go to insane lengths, at times, to make sure he was where he needed to be to help someone in trouble. I had seen that power strike down seriously twisted foes without Michael so much as raising his voice. That power, that faith, had carried him through dangers and battles he had no business surviving, much less winning.

But I hadn't ever thought too much about how hard it must be for him to leave his home when the Archangels or God or Whoever sent up a flare and called him off to a crisis.

I glanced aside at Molly. She was smiling, but I could see the strain and worry beneath the surface.

Hard on his family, too.

"Haven't you left?" called a woman's voice from upstairs. The house creaked again and Michael's wife appeared at the top of the stairway, saying, "You'll be—"

Her voice cut off suddenly. I hadn't ever seen Charity in a red silk kimono before. Like Michael, her hair was damp from the shower. Even wet, it still looked blond. Charity had nice legs, clearly defined muscles in her calves shifting as she stepped to the head of the stairs, and what I could see of the rest of her looked much the same— strong, fit, healthy. She bore a sleeping child on one hip—my namesake, Harry, the youngest of the bunch. His arms and legs splayed in perfect relaxation, and his head was pillowed on her shoulder. His cheeks were pink with that look very young children get while sleeping.

Blue eyes widened in utter surprise and for just a moment she froze, staring at Molly. She opened her mouth for a second, words hesitating on her tongue. Then her eyes shifted to me and surprise fell to recognition, which was followed by a mélange of anger, worry, and fear. She clutched her kimono a little more tightly to her, her mouth working for a second more, then said, "Excuse me for a moment."

She vanished and reappeared a moment later, sans little Harry, this time covered in a long terrycloth bathrobe, her feet inside fuzzy slippers.

"Molly," she said quietly, and came down the stairs.

The girl averted her eyes. "Mother."

"And the wizard," she said, her mouth hardening into a line. "Of course he's here." She tilted her head to one side, her expression hardening further. "Is this who you've been with, Molly?"

The air pressure in the room quadrupled, and Molly's face darkened from pink to scarlet. "So what if it is?" she demanded, defiance making the words ring. "That's no business of yours."

I opened my mouth to assure Charity that I had nothing to do with anything (not that it would actually alter the nature of the conversation), but Michael glanced at me and shook his head. I zipped my lips and awaited developments.

"Wrong," Charity said, her stance belligerent and unyielding. "You are a child and I am your mother. It is precisely my business."

"But it's my *life*," Molly replied.

"Which you clearly lack the discipline and intelligence to manage."

"Here we go again," Molly said. "Go go gadget control freak."

"Do *not* take that tone of voice with me, young lady."

"Young lady," Molly singsonged back in a nasal impersonation of her mother's voice, her fists now on her hips. "What's the point? Stupid of me to think that you might actually be willing to talk with me instead of telling me how to live every second of my life."

"I fail to see the error in that when you clearly have no idea what you're doing, young lady. *Look* at you. You look like . . . like a savage."

My mouth went off on reflex. "Ah, yes, a savage. Of the famous Chromotonsorial Cahokian Goth tribe."

Michael winced.

The look Charity turned on me could have withered the life from small animals and turned potted flowers black. "Excuse me, Mister Dresden," she said, words clipped. "I do not recall speaking to you."

"Beg pardon," I said, and gave her my sweetest smile. "Don't mind me. Just thinking out loud."

Molly turned to glare at me, too, but hers was a pale imitation of her mother's. "I do not need you to defend me."

Charity's attention shifted back to her daughter. "You will *not* speak to an adult in that tone of voice so long as you are in this house, young lady."

"Not a problem," Molly shot back, and then she whirled on her heel and opened the door.

Michael put his hand out, not with any particular effort, and the door slammed shut again with a sharp, booming impact.

Sudden silence fell over the Carpenter household. Both Molly and Charity stared at Michael with expressions of utter shock.

Michael took a deep breath and then said, "Ladies. I try not to involve myself in these discussions. But obviously your conversation this evening is unlikely to resolve the differences you've had." He looked at them in turn, and his voice, while still gentle, became something more immovable than a mountain's bones. "I don't have any feeling that my trip will be an extended one," he said, "but we never know what He has planned for us. Or how much time is left to any of us. This house has been upset long enough. The strife is hurting everyone. Find a way to resolve your troubles before I return."

"But . . ." Molly began.

"Molly," Michael said, his tone of voice inexorable. "She is your mother. She deserves your respect and courtesy. You will give them to her for the length of a conversation."

Molly set her jaw, but looked away from her father. He stared at her for a moment, until she gave him a brief nod.

"Thank you," he said. "I want you both to make an effort to set the anger aside, and talk. By God, ladies, I will not go forth to answer the call only to come home to more conflict and strife. I get enough of that while I'm gone."

Charity stared at him for a second longer, and then said, "But Michael . . . surely you aren't going to leave now. Not when . . ." She gestured vaguely at me. "There will be trouble."

Michael stepped over to his wife and kissed her gently. Then he said, "Faith, my love."

She closed her eyes and looked away from him after the kiss. "Are you sure?"

"I'm needed," he said with quiet certainty. He touched her face with one hand and said, "Harry, would you walk me to the car?"

I did. "Thank you," I said, once we were outside. "I'm glad to get out of there. Tension, knife."

Michael nodded. "It's been a long year."

"What happened to them?" I asked.

Michael tossed his case and his bag into the back of his white pickup truck. "Molly was arrested. Possession."

I blinked at him. "She was possessed?"

He sighed and looked at me. "Possession. Marijuana and Ecstasy. She was at a party and the police raided it. She was caught holding them."

"Wow," I said, my voice subdued. "What happened?"

"Community service," he said. "We talked about it. She was clearly repentant. I thought that the humiliation and the sentence of the law were enough to settle matters, but Charity thought we were being too gentle. She tried to restrict which people Molly was allowed to spend time with."

I winced. "Ah. I think I can see how this played out."

Michael nodded, got into his truck, and leaned on the open window, looking up at me. "Yes. Both of them are proud and stubborn. Friction rose until it exploded this spring. Molly left home, dropped out of school. It's been . . . difficult."

"I can see that," I said, and sighed. "Maybe you should pitch in with Charity. Maybe the two of you could sit on her until she gets back on the straight and narrow."

Michael smiled a little. "She's Charity's daughter. A hundred parents sitting on her couldn't make her surrender." He shook his head. "A parent's authority can only go so far. Molly has to start thinking and choosing for herself. At this point, twisting her arm until she cries uncle isn't going to help her do that."

"Doesn't seem like Charity agrees with you," I said.

Michael nodded. "She loves Molly very much. She's terrified of the kinds of things that could happen to her little girl." He glanced at the house. "Which brings me to a question for you."

"Yeah?"

"Is there some kind of dangerous situation developing?"

I chewed on my lip and then nodded. "It seems probable, but I don't have anything specific yet."

"Is my daughter involved in it?"

"Not to my knowledge," I told him. "Her boyfriend got arrested tonight. She talked me into bailing him out."

Michael's eyes narrowed a little, but then he caught himself, and I saw him force the angry expression from his face. "I see. How in the world did you get her to come here?"

"It was what I charged for my help," I said. "She tried to back out, but I convinced her not to."

Michael grunted. "You threatened her?"

"Politely," I said. "I'd never hurt her."

"I know that," Michael said, his tone gently reproving. Behind us, the front door opened. Molly stepped out onto the porch, hugging herself with her arms. She stood that way for a moment, ignoring us. A few seconds later, a light on the second floor came on. Charity, presumably, had gone back upstairs.

Michael watched his daughter for a moment, pain in his eyes. Then he took a deep breath and said, "May I ask a favor of you?"

"Yes."

"Talk to her," Michael said. "She likes you. Respects you. A few words from you might do more than anything I could tell her right now."

"Whoa," I said. "I don't know."

"You don't have to negotiate a treaty," Michael said, smiling. "Just ask her to talk to her mother. To be willing to give a little."

"Compromise has to work both ways," I said. "What about Charity?"

"She'll come around."

"Am I the only one who has noticed that Charity really doesn't regard me with what most of the world thinks of as fairness? Or fondness? I am the last person in the world likely to get her to sit down for a reconciliation talk."

He smiled. "Have a little faith."

"Oh, please." I sighed, but there wasn't any real feeling behind it.

"Will you try to help?" Michael asked.

I scowled at him. "Yes."

He smiled at me, mostly in his eyes. "Thank you. I'm sorry you walked into the cross fire tonight."

"Molly told me there had been trouble at home. Bringing her here seemed like the right thing to do."

"I appreciate it." Michael frowned, his eyes distant for a moment, then said, "I've got to get moving."

"Sure," I said.

He met my eyes and said, "If something arises, will you keep an eye on them for me? It would make me feel a lot better to know you were watching over them until I return."

I glanced back at his house. "What happened to having faith?"

He smiled. "Seems a bit lazy to expect the Lord to do all the work, doesn't it?" His expression grew serious again. "Besides. I do have faith, Harry. In Him—and in you."

Demon-infested me writhed in uncomfortable guilt on the inside. "I'll keep an eye on them, of course."

"Thank you," Michael said, and put the truck in gear. "When I get back, I need to talk business with you, if you have the time."

I nodded. "Sure. Good hunting."

"God be with you," he replied with a deep nod, and

then he pulled out and left. Have sword, will travel. Hi-yo, Silver, away.

Get Molly and Charity to sit down and talk things out. Right. I had about as much chance to do that as I did of backpacking my car to the top of Mount Rushmore. I was gloomily certain that even if I did manage to get them together, it would only make things go more spectacularly wrong once they were there. The whole house would probably go up in an explosion when mother met antimother.

No good could come of this one. Why in the world had I agreed to it?

Because Michael was my friend, and because I was in general too stupid to turn down people in need. And maybe because of something more. Michael's house had always been full of hectic life, but it had been a place, in general, of talk and warmth and laughter and good food. The ugly shouts and snarls of Molly and Charity's quarrel had stained the place. They didn't belong there.

I had never had a home like that, growing up. Even now that Thomas and I had found one another, when I thought of a family, I thought of the Carpenter household. I had never had that kind of intimacy, closeness. Those who have such a family seldom realize how rare and precious it is. It was something worth preserving. I wanted to help.

And Michael had a point. I might have a chance to get through to Molly. That was only half the battle, so to speak, but it was probably more than he could manage from his own position.

But whatever higher power arranged these things had a demented sense of timing, given how much I had on my plate already. Hell's bells.

Molly came over to me after Michael's truck had vanished. She stood beside me in the quiet summer evening, silent.

"I guess you need a ride back to your place," I said.

"I don't have any money," she replied quietly.

"Okay," I said. "Where do you need to go?"

"The convention," she replied. "I have friends there. A room for the weekend." She glanced over her shoulder at the house.

"The rug rats seemed glad to see you," I observed.

She smiled fleetingly and her voice warmed. "I didn't realize how much I missed them. Dumb little Jawas."

I thought about nudging her toward her mother for a second, and decided against it. She might decide to do it if she wasn't pressured, but the second she thought I was trying to force her into something, she'd dig in her heels. So all I said was, "They're cute kids."

"Yes," she replied quietly.

"I'm heading for the convention anyway," I told her. "Get in the cab."

"Thank you," she said.

"You're welcome," I said.

Eleven

When people say the word "convention," they are usually referring to large gatherings of the employees of companies and corporations who attend a mass assembly, usually in a big hotel somewhere, for the purpose of pretending to learn stuff when they are in fact enjoying a free trip somewhere, time off work, and the opportunity to flirt with strangers, drink, and otherwise indulge themselves.

The first major difference between a business convention and a fandom convention is that fandom doesn't bother with the pretenses. They're just there to have a good time. The second difference is the dress code—the ensembles at a fan convention tend to be considerably more novel.

SplatterCon!!! (apparently the name of the con was misspelled if the three exclamation points were left out) had populated the hotel with all kinds of costumed fans, unless maybe the costumes were actually clothing trends. Once in a while, it gets hard to tell make-believe and avant-garde fashion apart. The hotel had an entry atrium, which in turn branched off into a pair of long, wide hallways leading to combination ball- and dining rooms, the ones with those long, folding partitions that can be used to break the larger rooms up into smaller halls for seminars and talk panels and so on. There were a couple hundred people in sight, and I could see more entering and leaving various panel rooms.

"I kind of expected a few more people to be here," I said to Molly. I had stopped at my apartment to grab my stuff and drop off Mouse.

"It's Thursday night," she said, as if that should be significant. "And it's getting late, at least for a weeknight. We have more than three thousand people already registered."

"Is that a lot?"

"For a first-year convention? It's a Mongol horde." There was pride in her voice as she spoke. "And we have a really young staff, to boot. But old hands at putting conventions together." She went on like that for a few moments, naming names and citing their experience as though she expected me to whip out a licensing manual or something to make sure the convention was up to code.

Two girls, both too young for me to think adult thoughts about, sidled by in black-and-purple clothing and makeup that left a lot of skin bare, their faces painted pale, trickles of fake blood at the corners of their mouths. One of them smiled at me, and she had fangs.

I had my hand on my staff and the harsh, clear scent of wood smoke filled my nose before I stopped myself from unleashing an instant, violent, and noisily pyrotechnic assault upon the vampire five feet from me. A second's study showed irregular lumps and finger marks on the teeth—the girls had probably made them with their own fingers from craft plastic. I let out my breath in a steady exhalation and relaxed again, releasing the power I'd begun to channel through my staff.

Relax, Harry. Hell's bells, that would be a great story for the papers. Professional Wizard Incinerates Amateur Vampire. News at ten.

The two girls went on by, none the wiser, and even Molly only frowned at them and then back at me for a second, her face tilted into an expression of silent inquiry.

I shook my head. "Sorry, sorry. Been a long day already. Look, I need to get a look at the bathroom where this theater owner was attacked."

"All right," Molly said. "But first we'll get you a name tag at registration."

"We will?" I asked. "Why?"

"Because you're not supposed to have access to the convention if you haven't registered for it," she said. "Con security and hotel security might get confused. It would be inconvenient for you."

"Right," I said. "Good thinking. I'm not sure how I'd react to inconvenience."

I followed her over to a set of tables set up to receive dozens or hundreds of people at once, each designated with white paper signs marked with "A–D," "E–J," and so on down the alphabet. A tired-looking, brown-haired woman of early middle age sat behind the first table, doing some kind of paperwork.

"Molly," she said, and her voice warmed with tired but genuine pleasure. "Who is your friend?"

"Harry Dresden," Molly said. "This is Sandra Marling. She's the convention chair."

"You're a horror fan?" Sandra Marling asked me.

"My life is all about horror, these days."

"You should find plenty here to entertain you," she assured me. "We're showing movies in several rooms as well as in the theater, and there's the vendors' room, and some autograph signings tomorrow, and of course there are several parties active already, and the costume contests are always fun to watch."

"Isn't that something," I said, and tried not to drown in my enthusiasm.

"Sandy," Molly said, stepping in, "I want to use my freebie for Harry, here."

Sandra nodded. "Oh, Rosanna was looking for you a few minutes ago. Have you spoken to her yet?"

"Not since this afternoon," Molly said, and fretted at her lower lip. "Did she remember to take her vitamins?"

"Rest easy, girl. I reminded her for you."

Molly looked visibly relieved. "Thank you."

Sandra, meanwhile, had me filling out a registration form, which I scribbled through fairly quickly. At the end, she passed me a plastic badge folded around a card that said, SPLATTERCON!!! HI, I'M . . . She gave me a black ink marker to go with it and said, "Sorry, the printer's been off-line all day. Just write your name in."

I promptly wrote the words *An Innocent Bystander* onto the name tag before folding it up in the plastic badge and pinning it to my shirt.

"I hope you enjoy SplatterCon, Harry," Sandra said.

I picked up a schedule and glanced at it. "Make Your Own Blood and Custom Fangs," to be followed by "How to Scream Like a Pro." "I don't see how I can avoid being entertained."

Molly gave me a level look as we walked away. "You don't have to make fun of it."

"Actually I do," I said. "I make fun of almost everything."

"It's mean," she said. "Sandra has poured her whole life into this convention for a year, and I don't want to see her feelings hurt."

"Where do you know her from?" I asked. "Not church, I guess."

Molly looked at me obliquely for a second and then said, "She's a part-time volunteer at one of the shelters where I'm doing community service. She helped Nelson out when he was younger. Rosie too, and her boyfriend."

I lifted a hand in acquiescence. "Fine, fine. I'll play nice."

"Thank you," she said, her voice still prim. "It's very adult of you."

I started to get annoyed, but was struck by the disturbing thought that if I did, I would be coming down on the same side of the situation as Charity, which might be one of the signs of the apocalypse.

Molly led me down to the end of one of the long conference room hallways, where there were the usual restroom doors. One of them had been marked over with three bars of police tape, shutting it, and a uniformed cop sat in a chair beside the door.

The cop was a large black man, grey in his hair at the temples, and he sat with the chair leaned on its rear two legs so that his head rested back against the wall. He had on his uniform, but had added on a SplatterCon!!! name tag. He had filled in the name on the card with a marker, too, though his blocky script under the HI, I'M read *An Authority Figure.* The uniform name stripe on his shirt read RAWLINS.

"Well now," the cop said as I walked over to him. He opened his mostly closed eyes and gave me a wary smile. He read my name tag and snorted. "It's the consultant guy. Thinks he's a wizard."

"Rawlins," I said, smiling, and offered him my hand. He took it, his grip lazily strong.

"So you're one of those horror movie fans, huh?" he rumbled.

"Um, yes," I said.

He snorted again.

"I was sort of hoping I could get into the bathroom there."

Rawlins pursed his lips. "There's two more on this floor. One's back near the front desk, and there's another at the end of the other conference hall."

"I like this one," I said.

Rawlins squinted at me and said, "Maybe you can't read so good. You see that tape there, says crime scene and such?"

"The bright yellow and black stuff?" I asked.

"That's it exactly."

"Yep."

"Well, that's what we police use when we have a crime scene and we don't want nosy private investigators stomping all over it in their big boots and contaminating everything," he drawled.

"What if I promise to walk on tippy toe?"

"Then I promise I will stop bouncing you off walls just as soon as I think you're not resisting arrest," he said in a cheerful tone. The smile faded a little and his eyes hardened. "It's a crime scene. No."

"Molly," I said quietly. "Would you mind if I talked to the officer alone?"

"Sure," she said. "There are things I need to handle anyway. Excuse me." She walked away without looking back.

"Do you mind talking about it?" I asked Rawlins.

"Naw," he said. "Look, you seem okay, Dresden. I'll talk. But I'm not letting you in there."

"Why not?" I asked.

"Because it might make things harder on the kid we took in for it."

I frowned and tilted my head. "Yeah?"

Rawlins nodded. "Kid didn't do it," he said. "But hotel security cameras show him going in there, then the victim, and no one else. And I was sitting right here in this spot the whole time. I'm sure no one else went in or out."

"So how do you know the kid didn't attack the old man?" I asked.

Rawlins gave an easy shrug. "Didn't fit him. He wasn't breathing hard, and giving a beating runs you out of breath quick. No damage to his hands or knuckles. No blood on him."

"So why'd you arrest him?" I asked.

"Because the record shows that there's no one else who could have done it," Rawlins said. "And because the old man was too out of it to talk and clear him. Kid didn't beat on the old man, but that doesn't mean that he wasn't in with whoever did. I figured maybe he knows how the attacker got in and out unseen, so I took him down and booked him. I figured if he was an accomplice, he'd spill rather than take the whole fall himself." Rawlins grimaced. "But he didn't spill. Didn't know a damn thing."

"Then why'd he get put away?" I asked.

"Didn't know he had a record until the paperwork was already going. Repeat offender got a real steep hill to climb as a suspect. Makes it look bad for him. He might take the fall on this even if he's innocent."

I shook my head. "You're sure no one could have gone in or out?"

"I was right here," he said. "Anyone went past me without me noticing, they were a Jedi Knight or something."

"Or something," I muttered, glancing at the door.

"The girlfriend," Rawlins said, nodding after the departed Molly. "She get you involved in this?"

"Daughter of a friend," I said, nodding. "Bailed him out."

Rawlins grunted. "Damn shame for that kid. I played it by the book, but . . ." He shook his head. "Sometimes the book don't do enough."

"The girl thinks he's innocent," I said.

"The girl always thinks they're innocent, Dresden," Rawlins said, without malice. "Problem is that there's pretty good evidence that says he ain't. Good enough to send a repeat offender upstate, unless the lab guys find something in there or on the old man to clear him. Which brings us back to why you ain't going in."

I nodded, frowning. "What if I told you it might be something weird?"

He shrugged. "What if you did?"

"Might be something that I could recognize, if I could just get a look at the room. I might be able to help the kid."

He squinted at me. "You think there's spooky afoot?"

"I told the girl I'd look into it."

Rawlins frowned, but then shook his head. "Can't let you in there."

"Could I just look?" I asked. "You open the door, and I don't even go in. I just look. That couldn't hurt anything, could it? And you've already been in there, the EMTs, maybe a detective. Am I right? I couldn't contaminate it all *that* much just from looking in the door."

Rawlins gave me a long, level stare and then sighed. He grunted, and the front legs of his chair thunked down to the floor. He rose and said, "All right. Not one step inside."

"You're an officer and a gentleman," I told him. I used my elbow to nudge the restroom door open. It squealed ferociously. I leaned my head in, my chin just over the level of the top strip of tape, and looked around the bathroom.

Standard stuff. A bathroom. White tile. Stalls, urinals, sinks, a long mirror.

The blood wasn't standard, of course.

There was a large splotch of it on the floor, and it had been smeared around when it had been making the tile all slippery. There were a couple of different footmarks on the floor, outlined in blood, and more smears of it on one of the sinks, where the victim had apparently tried to pull himself up off the floor. It looked fairly gruesome, which wasn't really a surprise. There wasn't as much blood as there would have been at, say, a murder, but there was plenty all the same. Someone had laid into Clark Pell, the victim, with a will. I picked out small blood splatter on the mirror, high on the wall, and in a spot on the ceiling.

"Jesus," I muttered. "It was an unarmed assault? No knives or anything?"

Rawlins grunted. "Old man had broken ribs, bruises, gashes from being slammed around. No cuts or stabs, though."

"No kid did this," I said.

"Wasn't a professional, either. Crowded spot like this. Witness in the bathroom. Cop twenty feet away. Dumbest thug in Chicago wouldn't open up that big a can of whoopass where he'd be seen and caught."

"Someone strong," I muttered. "And really, really vicious. He had to have hit the old guy a few times after he went down."

Rawlins grunted again. "Sound like anyone you know?"

I shook my head. I stared at the room for a second and then chewed on my lower lip for a second, coming to a decision. I closed my eyes, clearing my thoughts.

"That's enough," Rawlins said. "Shut the door before people start to stare."

"One second," I murmured. Then with an effort of focus and will, and a faint sense of illusory pressure on my forehead, I opened my wizard's Sight.

The Sight is something anyone born with enough talent has. It's an extra sense, though when using it almost everyone experiences it as a kind of augmented vision. It shows you the primal nature of things, the true and emotional core of what they are. It also shows you the presence of magical energies that course through pretty much everything on the planet, showing you how that energy flowed and pulsed and swirled through the world. The Sight was especially useful for looking for any active magical constructs—that's spells, for the newbie—and for cutting through illusions and spells meant to obfuscate what was true.

I opened my Sight and it showed me what my physical eyes could not see about the room. It showed me something that, with as many bad things as I had seen in my life, still made me clench my fists and fight to keep from losing control of my stomach.

The site of the attack, the blood, the brutality and pain inflicted upon the victim, had not been a simple matter of desire, conflict, and violence.

It had been a deliberate, gleeful work of art.

I could see patterns in the bloodstain, patterns that showed me the terrified face of an old man, pounded into a lumpy, unrecognizable mass by sledgehammer fists, each one a miniature portrait painted in the medium of terror and pain. When I looked at the smears on the sink, I could hear a short series of grunts meant to be desperate cries for help. And then the old man was hurled back down for another round of splatter portraits of pain.

And just for a second, I saw a shadow on the wall—a brief glimpse, a form, a shape, something that left an outline of itself on the wall where it had absorbed the agonized energy of the old man's suffering.

I fought to push the Sight away from my perceptions

again, and staggered. That was the drawback to using the Sight. The Sight could show you a lot of things, but everything you saw with it was there to stay. It wrote everything you perceived with it upon your memory in indelible ink, and those memories were always there, fresh and harsh when you went back to them, never blurring with the passage of time, never growing easier to endure. The little demonic diorama of bad vibes painted over the white tiles of that bathroom was going to make some appearances in my darker dreams.

It looked like I'd found the black magic the Gatekeeper warned me about. Just as well that I hadn't tried the dangerous spell with Little Chicago.

I took a couple of steps away, shaking away the flickers of color and sparkles of light on my vision that remained for a time when the Sight was gone once more. Rawlins had a hand under one of my elbows.

"You all right, man?" he rumbled a moment later, his voice very quiet.

"Yeah," I said. "Yeah. Thanks."

He looked from me to the closed door and back. "What did you see in there?"

"I'm not sure yet," I said. My voice sounded shaky. "Something bad."

Almost too quietly to be heard, he said, "This wasn't just some thug, was it."

My stomach twisted again. In my mind's eye, I could see a malicious smile reflected in the eyes of the old man, the memory absolutely crystalline. "Maybe not," I mumbled. "It could have been a person, I think. Someone really sick. Or . . . maybe not. I don't know." More words struggled to bubble out of my mouth and I clamped my lips resolutely shut until I'd gotten my thoughts back under control.

I looked around me and realized that the hairs on the

back of my neck were not crawling around at the memory of the energy I'd just brushed.

They were reacting to more of it drifting through the air. Now. Nearby.

"Rawlins," I said. "How many other cops are here?"

"Just me now," he said quietly. He took a look at my face and then peered around, his heavy-lidded eyes deceptively alert, his hand on his gun. "We got trouble?"

"We got trouble," I said quietly, shifting my staff into my right hand.

The lights went out, all of them at once, plunging the hotel into pure blackness.

And the screaming started.

Chapter

Twelve

No more than two or three seconds went by before Rawlins had his flashlight out and he flicked it on. The light flashed white and clean for maybe half a second, and then it dimmed down, as though some kind of greasy soot had coated it, until the light, though still bright, was so vague and veiled that it accomplished little more than to cast a faint glow to maybe an arm's length from Rawlins.

"What the hell," he said, and shook the light a few times. He had his hand on his gun, the restraining strap off, but he hadn't drawn it yet. Good man. He knew as well as I did that the hotel was going to have far more panicked attendees than potential threats.

"We'll try mine," I said, and got the silver pentacle on its chain from around my neck. A gentle whisper and an effort of will and the amulet began to emit a pure, silver-blue light that reached into the darkness around us, burning it away as swiftly as it pressed in, until we could see for maybe fifteen feet around us. Beyond that was just a murky vagueness—not so much a cloud or a mist as a simple lack of light.

I gripped my staff in my right hand, and more of my will thrummed through it, setting the winding spirals of runes and sigils along its length to burning with a gentle, ember orange light.

Rawlins stared at me for a second and then said, "What the hell is going on?"

There were running footsteps and shouts and cries in the gloom. All of them sounded choked, muffled somehow. One of the two teenaged "vampires" stumbled into the circle of my azure wizard's light, sobbing. Several young men blundered along a moment later, blindly, and all but trampled her. Rawlins grabbed the girl with a grunt of, "Excuse me, miss," and hauled her from their path. He lifted her more or less by main strength and pushed her gently against the wall. He forced her to look at him and said, "Follow the wall that way to the door. Stay close to the wall until you get out."

She nodded, tears making her makeup run in a mascara mudslide, and stumbled off, following Rawlins's directions.

"Fire?" Rawlins blurted, turning back to me. "Is this smoke?"

"No," I said. "Believe me. I know burning buildings."

He gave me an odd look, grabbed an older woman who was passing blindly, and sent her off to follow the wall to the door out. He shivered then, and when he exhaled his breath came out in a long, frosty plume. The temperature had dropped maybe forty degrees in the space of a minute.

I struggled to ignore the sounds of frightened people in the dark and focused on my magical senses. I reached out to the cold and the gloom, and found it a vaguely familiar kind of spellworking, though I couldn't remember precisely where I'd encountered it before.

I spun in a slow circle with my eyes closed, and felt the murk grow deeper, darker as I faced back down the hall to the hotel's front desk. I took a step that way, and the murk thickened marginally. The spell's source had to be that way. I gritted my teeth and started forward.

"Hey," Rawlins said. "Where are you going?"

"Our bad guy is this way," I said. "Or something is. Maybe you'd better stay here, help get these people outside safely."

"Maybe you ought to shut your fool mouth," Rawlins replied, his tone one of forced cheer. He looked scared, but he drew his gun and kept the barrel down, close to his side, and held his mostly useless flashlight in his other hand. "I'll cover you."

I nodded once at him, turned, and plunged into the darkness, Rawlins at my back. Screams erupted around us, sometimes accompanied by the sight of stumbling, terrified people. Rawlins nudged them toward the walls, barked at them in a tone of pure paternal authority to stay near them, to move carefully for the exits. The gloom began to press in closer to me, and it became an effort of will to hold up the light in my amulet against it. A few steps more and the air grew even colder. Walking forward became an effort, like wading through waist-deep water. I had to lean against it, and I heard a grunt of effort come out of my mouth.

"What's wrong?" Rawlins asked, his voice tight.

We passed under one of the hotel's emergency light fixtures, its floodlights only dim orange rings in the murk until my amulet's light burned the shadows away. "Dark magic," I growled through clenched teeth. "A kind of ward. Trying to keep me from moving ahead."

He huffed out a breath and muttered, "Christ. Magic. That isn't real."

I stopped and gave him a steady look over my shoulder. "Are you with me or not?"

He swallowed, staring up at the dim circles of light

that were all he could see of another set of emergency lights. "Crap," he muttered, wiping a sudden beading of sweat from his brow despite the cold air. "You need me to push you or something?"

I let out a bark of tense laughter, and forced my power harder against the gloomy ward, hacking at it with the machete of my will until I began to chop a path through the dark working, picking up speed. As I did, the sense of the spell became more clear to me. "It's coming from up ahead of us," I said. "The first conference room in this hall."

"They got it set up for movies," Rawlins said. He seized a sobbing and terrified man in his middle years and deflected him bodily to the wall, snapping the same orders to him. "God, it was packed in there. If the crowd panicked—"

He didn't finish the sentence, and he didn't need to. Chicago has seen more than a few deaths due to a sudden panic in a movie theater. I redoubled my efforts and broke into a heavy, labored jog that led us to a pair of doors leading into the first conference room. One of the doors was shut, and the other had been slammed open so hard that it had wrenched its way clear of one of the hinges.

From inside the room came a sudden burst of terrified screams—not the canned screams you get in horror movies. Real screams. Screams of such base, feral intensity that you could hardly tell they had come from a human throat. Screams you only really hear when there are terrible things happening.

Rawlins knew what they meant. He spat out a low curse, lifting his gun to a ready position, and we rushed forward to the room side by side.

The murk began to do more than simply drag at me when I hit the doorway. The air almost seemed to congeal into a kind of gelatin, and it suddenly became a fight to keep my legs moving forward. I snarled in sudden frustration, and transformed it into more will that I sent coursing down through my silver pentacle amulet. The soft radiance emanating from the symbol became a white-and-cobalt floodlight, driving back the gloom, burning it from my path. It left the large room still coated in shadow, but it was no longer the total occlusion of the magical murk.

It was a long room, about sixty feet, maybe half that wide. At the far end of the room was a very large projection screen. Chairs faced it in two columns. At one point in the aisle between them, a projector sat, running at such a frantic speed that smoke was rising from the reels of celluloid. The projected movie still appeared clearly on the screen, in a frantic fast-motion blur of faces and images from a classic horror film from the early eighties. The soundtrack could only be heard as a single, long, piercing howl.

There were still about twenty people in the room. Immediately beside the door was an old woman, curled on her side on the ground, sobbing in pain. Nearby a wheelchair lay overturned, and a man with braces of some kind on his legs and hips had fallen into an awkward, painful-looking sprawl from which he could not arise. One of his arms was visibly broken, bone pushing at skin. Other people cringed against the walls and beneath chairs. When my wizard light flooded the place, they got up and started staggering away, still screaming in horror.

Straight ahead of me were bodies and blood.

I couldn't see much of them. Three people were down. There was a lot of blood around. A fourth person, a young woman, crawled toward the door making frantic mewling sounds.

A man stood over her. He was nearly seven feet tall and so thick with slabs of muscle that he almost seemed deformed—not pretty bodybuilder muscle, either, but the thick, dull slabs that come from endless physical labor. He wore overalls, a blue shirt, and a hockey mask, and there was a long, curved sickle in his right hand. As I watched, he took a pair of long steps forward, seized the whimpering girl by her hair, and jerked her body into a backward bow. He raised the sickle in his right hand.

Rawlins didn't bother to offer him a chance to surrender. He took a stance not ten feet away, aimed, and put three shots into the masked maniac's head.

The man jerked, twisting a bit, and released the girl's hair abruptly, tossing her aside with a terrible, casual strength. She hit a row of chairs and let out a cry of pain.

Then the maniac turned toward Rawlins and, even though the mask hid his features, the tilt of his head and the tension of his posture showed that he was furious. He went toward Rawlins. The cop shot him four more times, flashes of bright white burning the image of the maniac and the room onto my eyes.

He brought the sickle down on Rawlins. The cop managed to catch the force of it upon his long flashlight. Sparks flew from the steel case, but the light held. The maniac twisted the sickle, so that the tip plowed a furrow across Rawlins's forearm. The cop snarled. The flashlight spun to the ground. The maniac raised the sickle again.

I braced myself, raised my staff and my will, and cried, *"Forzare!"*

Unseen power lashed from my staff, pure kinetic energy that ripped through the air and hit the maniac like a wrecking ball. The blow drove him back down the aisle, through the air. He hit the projector on its stand.

It shattered. He went through it without slowing down. He kept going, the flight of his passage tearing through the large projection screen, and hit the back wall with a thunderous impact.

I sagged in sudden exhaustion, the effort of the spell an enormous drain on me, and had to plant my staff on the ground to keep from falling over. My headache flared up with a vengeance, and the light of my amulet and staff both faded.

There were a few more screams, the quick, light sound of frightened feet, and I whirled. I saw someone flee the room from the corner of my eye, but I didn't get much of a look at them. A second later, the room returned to normal, the lights back, the broken projector still spinning one reel at reduced speed, a loose tongue of film slap-slap-slapping the broken casing.

Rawlins advanced, gun still out, his eyes very wide, down to the far end of the room. He went past the screen and looked behind it, gun in firing position. He looked around for a second, then back at me, his expression baffled.

"He's not here," Rawlins said. "Did you see him go that way?"

I just didn't have enough left in me to speak right at that moment. I shook my head.

"There's a dent in the wall," he reported. "Covered in . . . I dunno what. Some kind of slime."

"He's gone," I grunted. Then I started forward, toward the downed people. Two of them were young men, the third a young woman. "Help me."

Rawlins holstered his weapon and did. One of the young men was dead. There was a crescent-shaped cut in his thigh that had opened an artery. Another lay mercifully unconscious, a bruise on his head, several hideous inches of bloody innards protruding from a slash across his belly. I was afraid that if we moved him, his guts might come popping out. The girl was alive, but the sickle's tip had drawn a pair of long lines down her back along the spine, and the cuts had been vicious and deep. Bits of bone showed and she lay on her belly, her eyes open and blinking but utterly unfocused, either unwilling or unable to move.

We did what we could for them, which wasn't much more than jerking the tablecloths off the water tables in the corner and improvising soft pads out of them to apply to open wounds. The second girl lay on her side nearby, sobbing hysterically. I checked on the old woman, who had just had the wind knocked out of her. I hauled the guy who'd fallen from his wheelchair into a slightly more comfortable position and he nodded thanks at me.

"See to the other victim," Rawlins said. He held the pad against the boy's opened abdomen, putting gentle pressure on it as he jerked out his radio. It squealed with feedback and static when he used it, but he managed to get emergency help headed our way.

I went to the sobbing girl, a tiny little brunette wearing much the same clothes as Molly had been. She'd been bruised up pretty well, and from the way she lay on the floor she could evidently not move without feeling agony. I went to her and felt over her left shoulder gently. "Be still," I told her quietly. "It's your collarbone, I think. I know it hurts like hell, but you're going to be all right."

"It hurts, it hurts, hurts, hurts, hurts," she panted.

I found her hand with mine and squeezed tight. She returned it with a desperate pressure. "You'll be all right," I told her.

"Don't leave me," she whimpered. Her hand was all but crushing mine. "Don't leave."

"It's all right," I said. "I'm right here."

"What the hell is this?" Rawlins said, panting. He looked around him, at the corpse, at the movie screen, at the dent in the wall beyond. "That was the Reaper, the freaking Reaper. From the *Suburban Slasher* films. What kind of psycho dresses up as the Reaper and starts . . ." His face twisted in sudden nausea. "What the hell is this?"

"Rawlins," I said, in a sharp voice, to get his attention.

His frightened eyes darted to me.

"Call Murphy," I told him.

He stared at me blankly for a second, then said, "My captain is the one who has to make the call on that one. He'll decide."

"Up to you," I said. "But Murphy and her boys might actually be able to do something with this. Your captain can't." I nodded at the corpse. "And we aren't playing for pennies here."

Rawlins looked at me. Then at the dead boy. Then he nodded once and picked up his radio again.

"Hurts," the girl whimpered, breathless with pain. "Hurts, hurts, hurts."

I held her hand. I patted it awkwardly with my gloved left hand while we heard sirens approach.

"My God," Rawlins said again. He shook his head. "My God, Dresden. What happened here?"

I stared at the enormous rip in the movie screen and at the Reaper-shaped dent in the wooden panels of the wall behind it. Clear gelatin, the physical form of ectoplasm, the matter of the spirit world, gleamed there against the broken wood. In minutes it would evaporate, and there would be nothing left behind.

"My God," Rawlins whispered again, his voice still stunned. "What happened here?"

Chapter

Thirteen

The authorities arrived and replaced crisis with aftermath.

The EMTs rushed the more badly injured girl and the eviscerated young man to an emergency room, while police officers who arrived on the scene did what they could to take care of the other injured attendees until more medical teams could show up. I stayed with the injured girl, holding her hand. One of the EMTs had examined her briefly, saw that though in considerable pain she was not in immediate danger, and ordered me to stay with her and keep anyone from moving her until the next team could arrive.

That suited me fine. The thought of standing up again was daunting.

I sat with the girl as more police arrived. She had become quiet and listless as her fear faded and her body produced endorphins to dull the pain. I heard a gasp and the sudden sound of pounding feet. I looked up to see Molly slip by a patrolman and fling herself down beside the girl.

"Rosie!" she cried, her face very pale. "Oh my God!"

"Easy, easy," I told her, putting a hand against Molly's shoulder to prevent her from embracing the wounded girl. "Don't jostle her."

"She's hurt," Molly protested. "Why haven't they put her in an ambulance?"

"She's not in immediate danger," I said. "Two other people were. The ambulance took them first. She goes on the next one."

"What happened?" Molly asked.

I shook my head. "I'm not sure yet. I didn't see much of it. They were attacked."

The girl on the floor suddenly stirred and opened her eyes. "Molly?" she said.

"I'm here, Rosie," Molly said. She touched the injured girl's cheek. "I'm right here."

"My God," the girl said. Tears welled from her eyes. "He killed them. He killed them." Her breathing began to come faster, building toward panic.

"Shhhhhhh," Molly said, and stroked Rosie's hair back from her forehead as one might a frightened child. "You're safe now. It's all right."

"The baby," Rosie said. She slid her hand from mine and laid it over her belly. "Is the baby all right?"

Molly bit her lip and looked at me.

"She's pregnant?" I asked.

"Three months," Molly confirmed. "She just found out."

"The baby," Rosie said. "Will the baby be all right?"

"They're going to do everything possible to make sure that you're both all right," I said immediately. "Try not to worry about it too much."

Rosie closed her eyes, tears still streaming. "All right."

"Rosie," Molly asked. "Can you tell me what happened?"

"I'm not sure," she whispered. "I was sitting with Ken and Drea. We'd already seen our favorite scene in the movie and we decided to go. I was bending over to get my purse and Drea was checking her makeup and then the lights went out and she started screaming . . . And then when I could see again, he was there." She shuddered. "He was there."

"Who?" Molly pressed.

Rosie's eyes opened too wide, showing white all around. Her voice dropped to a whisper. "The Reaper."

Molly frowned. "Like in the movie? Someone in a costume."

"It couldn't be," Rosie said, her trembling growing more pronounced. "It was him. It was really him."

The next medical team arrived and headed right for us. Rosie seemed to be on the verge of another panic attack when she saw them, and started thrashing around. Molly leaned in close, whispering to her and continually touching her head, until the EMTs could get to work.

I stepped back. They got Rosie loaded onto a stretcher. When they laid her arm down by her side, I could see several small, round marks, irregular bruises, and damaged capillaries just under the surface of the skin at the bend of her arm.

Molly stared at me for a second, her eyes wide. Then she helped the EMTs throw a blanket over Rosie and her track marks. The EMTs counted to three and lifted the stretcher, flicked out the wheels underneath, and rolled her toward the doors. The girl stirred and thrashed weakly as they did this, letting out whimpering little cries.

"She's frightened," Molly told the EMTs. "Let me ride with her, help keep her calm."

The men traded a look and then one of them nodded. Molly let out a breath of relief, nodded to them, and went to walk by the head of the stretcher, where Rosie could see her.

"Don't worry," said the other EMT. "We'll be right back for you, sir."

"What, this?" I asked, and waved vaguely at my head. "Nah, I didn't get hurt here. This is from earlier. I'm good."

The man's expression was dubious. "You sure?"

"Yep."

They took the girl out. I dragged myself to the wall and propped my back up against it. A minute later, a man in a tweed suit came in and walked directly to Rawlins. He spoke to the officer for a moment, glancing over at me once as they talked, then turned and walked over to me. Of only average height, the man was in his late forties, thirty pounds overweight, balding, and had watery blue eyes. He nodded at me, grabbed a chair, and settled down into it, looking down at me. "You're Dresden?"

"Most days," I said.

"My name is Detective Sergeant Greene. I'm with homicide."

"Tough job," I said.

"Most days," he agreed. "Now, Rawlins back there tells me you were an eyewitness to what happened. Is that correct."

"Mostly," I said. "I only saw what happened at the very end in here."

"Uh-huh," he said. He blinked his watery eyes and absently removed a pen and a small notebook from his pocket. Behind him, cops were surrounding the area where the victims had lain with a circle of chairs and stringing crime scene tape between them. "Can you tell me what happened?"

"The lights went out," I said. "People panicked. We heard screams. Rawlins went to help and I went with him."

"Why?" he asked.

"What?"

"Why," Greene said, his tone mild. "You're a civilian,

Mr. Dresden. It's Rawlins's job to help people in emergencies. Why didn't you just head for the door?"

"It was an emergency," I said. "I helped."

"You're a hero," Greene said. "Is that it?"

I shrugged. "I was there. People needed help. I tried to."

"Sure, sure," Greene said, blinking his eyes. "So what were you doing to help?"

"Holding the light," I said.

"Didn't Rawlins have his own flashlight?"

"Can't have too many flashlights," I replied.

"Sure," Greene said, writing things. "So you held the light for Rawlins. What then?"

"We heard screams in here. We came in. I saw the attacker over that girl they just took out."

"Can you describe him?" Greene asked.

"Almost seven feet tall," I said. "Built like a battleship, maybe three hundred, three twenty-five. Hockey mask. Sickle."

Greene nodded. "What happened?"

"He attacked the girl. There were other people behind him, already down. He was about to cut her throat with the sickle. Rawlins shot him."

"Shot at him?" Greene asked. "Since we don't have a dead bad guy on the floor?"

"Shot at him," I amended. "I don't know if he hit him. The bad guy dropped the girl and swung that sickle at Rawlins. Rawlins blocked it with his flashlight."

"Then what?"

"Then I hit the guy," I said.

"Hit him how?" Greene asked.

"I used magic. Blew him thirty feet down the aisle and through the projector and the movie screen."

Greene slapped his pen down onto the notebook and gave me a flat look.

"Hey," I said. "You asked."

"Or maybe he turned to run," Greene said. "Knocked the projector over and jumped through the screen to get to the back of the room."

"If that makes you feel better," I said.

He gave me another hard look and said, "And then what?"

"And then he was gone," I said.

"He ran out the door?"

"No," I said. "We were pretty much right next to the door. He went through the screen, hit the wall behind it, and poof. Gone. I don't know how."

Greene wrote that down. "Do you know where Nelson Lenhardt is?"

I blinked. "No. Why would I?"

"He apparently attacked someone else at this convention today and beat him savagely. You bailed him out of jail. Maybe you're friends with him."

"Not really," I said.

"Seems a little odd, then, that you dropped two thousand dollars to bail out this guy you're not friends with."

"Yeah."

"Why did you do it?"

I got annoyed. "I had personal reasons."

"Which are?"

"Personal," I said.

Greene regarded me with his watery blue eyes, silent for a long minute. Then he said, patiently and politely, "I'm not sure I understand all of this. I'd appreciate it if you could help me out. Could you tell me again what happened? Starting with when the lights went out?"

I sighed.

We started over.

Four more times.

Greene was never so much as impolite to me, and his mild voice and watery eyes made him seem more like an apologetic clerk than a detective, but I had a gut instinct that there was a steely and dangerous man underneath the tweed camouflage, and that he had me pegged as an accomplice, or at least as someone who knew more than he was saying.

Which, I suppose, was true. But going on about black magic and ectoplasm and boogeymen that disappeared at will wasn't going to make him like me any better. That was par for the course, when it came to cops. Some of them, guys like Rawlins, had run into something nasty at some point in their careers. They never talked much about it with anyone—other cops tend to worry about it when one of their partners starts talking about seeing monsters, and all kinds of well-intentioned counseling and psychological evaluations were sure to follow.

So if a cop found himself face-to-face with a vampire or a ghoul (and survived it), its only existence tended to be in the landscape of memory. Time has a way of wearing the sharpest edges away from that kind of thing, and it's easy to avoid thinking about terrifying monsters, and even more terrifying implications, and get back to the daily routine. If enough time went by, a lot of cops could even convince themselves that what happened had been exaggerated in their heads, bad memories amplified by darkness and fear, and that since everyone around them knew monsters didn't exist, they must therefore have seen something normal, something explainable.

But when the heat was on, those same cops changed. Somewhere deep down, they know that it's for real, and when something supernatural went down again, they were willing, at least for the duration, to forget about anything but doing whatever they could to survive it and protect lives, even if in retrospect it seemed insane. Rawlins would poke fun at me for "pretending" to be a wizard when there was a fan convention in progress. But when everything had hit the proverbial fan, he'd been willing to work with me.

Then there was the other kind of cop—guys like Greene, who hadn't ever seen anything remotely supernatural, who went home to their house and 2.3 kids and dog and mowed their lawn on Saturdays, who watch *Nova* and the Science Channel and subscribe to *National Geographic,* and keep every issue stored neatly and in order in the basement.

Guys like that were dead certain that everything was logical, everything was explainable, and that nothing existed outside the purview of reason and logic. Guys like that also tend to make pretty good detectives. Greene was a guy like that.

"All right, Mr. Dresden," Greene said. "I'm still kind of unclear on a few points. Now, when the lights went out, what did you do?"

I rubbed at my eyes. My head ached. I wanted to sleep. "I've already told you this. Five times."

"I know, I know," Greene said, and offered me a small smile. "But sometimes repeating things can jiggle forgotten little details loose. So, if you don't mind, can you tell me about when it went dark?"

I closed my eyes and fought a sudden and overwhelming temptation to levitate Greene to the ceiling and leave him there for a while.

Someone touched my shoulder, and I opened my eyes to find Murphy standing over me, offering me a white Styrofoam cup. "Evening, Harry."

"Oh, thank God," I muttered, and took the cup. Coffee. I sipped some. Hot and sweet. I groaned in pleasure. "Angel of mercy, Murph."

"That's me," she agreed. She was wearing jeans, a T-shirt, and a very light cotton blazer. She had circles under her eyes and her blond hair was messy. Someone must have gotten her out of bed for this one. "Detective Greene," she said.

"Lieutenant," Greene replied, all courtesy on the surface. "I didn't realize I'd called Special Investigations for help. Maybe someone bumped the speed dial on my phone." He reached into a pocket and took out a cell. He regarded it gravely for a moment and then said, "Oh, wait. My mistake. You aren't on my speed dial. I must have slipped into some kind of fugue state when I wasn't looking."

"Don't worry, Sergeant," Murphy said, smiling sweetly. "If I find out whodunit, I'll tell you so you can get the collar."

Greene shook his head. "This is messy enough already," he said. "Some clown in a horror movie costume cuts a bunch of horror fans to ribbons. The press is going to make piranhas look like goldfish."

"Yep," Murphy said. "Seems to me you should take all the help you can get. Don't want to screw it up in front of all those cameras."

He gave her another flat look and then shook his head. "You aren't exactly famous for your friendly spirit of cooperation with your fellow officers, Lieutenant."

"I get the job done," Murphy said easily. "I can help you. Or I can see to it that the press knows that you're refusing assistance in finding a murderer because of departmental rivalry. Your call."

Greene stared at her for another long minute, then said, "Does calling someone an overbearing, egotistical bitch constitute sexual harassment?"

Murphy's smile grew sunnier. "Come to the gym sometime and we'll discuss it."

Greene grunted and rose, stuffing his pad and pen into his pocket. "Dresden, don't leave town. I might need to speak to you again."

"Won't that be nice," I mumbled, and sipped more coffee.

Greene handed Murphy a card. "My cell number is on it. In case you actually do want to cooperate."

Murphy traded him for one of hers. "Ditto."

Greene shook his head, gave her a barely polite nod, and walked off to speak to the officers near the taped-off section of floor.

"I think he likes you," I told Murphy.

Murphy snorted. "He's had you running in a circle, huh?"

"For an hour." I tried not to sound too disgusted.

"It's annoying," she said. "But it really does work. Greene's probably the best homicide detective in the state. If he had a personality he'd have made captain by now."

"I don't think he's going to be much help on this one."

Murphy nodded, and sat down in the chair Greene had vacated. "So. You want to give me the rundown here?"

"I haven't even finished my coffee," I complained. But I told her, starting with bailing Nelson out of jail and skipping over the details of the visit to Michael's house. I told her about the attack, and how Rawlins and I had presumably cut it short.

She exhaled slowly. "So this thing must have been from the spirit world, right? If it got shot full of bullets, didn't die, then dissolved into goo?"

"That's a reasonable conclusion," I said, "but I didn't exactly have time to make a thorough analysis. It could have been anything."

"Any chance you killed it?"

"I didn't hit it all that hard. Must have had some kind of self-destruct."

"Dammit," Murphy said, missing the reference. No one loves the classics anymore. "Will it come back?"

"Your guess is as good as mine," I said.

"That's not good enough."

I sighed and nodded. "I'll see what I can figure out. How's Rawlins?"

"Hospital," she reported. "He'll need a bunch of stitches for that cut he took."

I grunted and rose. It was an effort, and I wobbled a little, but as soon as I got my balance I walked over to the remains of the projector on its stand. I bent down and picked up a large round tin, the one the movie reel had come in. I flipped it over and read the label.

"Hunh," I said.

Murphy came over and frowned at the tin. *"Suburban Slasher II?"*

I nodded. "This means something."

"Other than the death of classic cinema?"

"Movie fascist," I said. "The guy that jumped them looked like the Reaper."

Murphy gave me a blank look.

"The Reaper," I told her. "Come on, don't tell me you haven't ever seen the Reaper. The killer from the *Suburban Slasher* films. He can't be slain, brings death to the wicked—which includes anyone who is having sex or drinking, apparently. If that's not classic cinema, I don't know what is."

"I guess I missed that one," Murphy said.

"There have been eleven films featuring the Reaper so far," I replied.

"I guess I missed those eleven," Murphy amended.

"You think this was someone trying to look like the Reaper character?"

"Someone," I murmured with exaggerated menace. "Or some *thing*."

She gave me a level look. "How long have you been waiting to use that one?"

"Years," I said. "The opportunity doesn't come up as often as you'd think."

Murphy smiled, but it was forced, and we both knew it. The jokes didn't change the facts. Something had killed one young man only a few feet from where we sat, and the lives of at least two of the wounded hung on the skills of the doctors attending them.

"Murph," I said. "There's a theater right down the street. Run by a guy named Clark Pell. Could you find out what movie was showing there this afternoon?"

Murphy flipped to an earlier page of her notebook and said, "I already did. Something called *Hammerhands*."

"Oldie but a goodie," I said. "Ruffians push this farmer out onto train tracks and the train cuts his hands off at the wrist. They leave him for dead. But he survives, insane, straps sledgehammer heads to the stumps, and hunts them down one at a time."

"And Clark Pell was the victim beaten here earlier today," Murphy said. "Badly beaten with some kind of blunt instrument."

"Maybe it's a coincidence," I said.

She frowned. "Can someone do that? Bring movie monsters to life?"

"Sorta looks that way," I said.

"How do we stop them?" she asked.

I dragged the con schedule out of my pocket and paged through it. "The real question is, how do we stop them before tomorrow night?"

"What's tomorrow night?"

"Movie fest," I said, and held up the film schedule. "Half a dozen films showing here. Another half a dozen in Pell's theater. And most of their monsters aren't nearly as friendly as Hammerhand and the Reaper."

"God almighty," Murphy breathed. "Any chance this could be regular folks playing dress up?"

"I doubt it. But it's possible."

She nodded. "We'll let Greene cover that angle, then. Consider yourself to be on the clock for the department, Harry. What's our next move?"

"We talk to the surviving victims," I said. "And I try to figure out how many ways there are for someone to do something this crazy."

She nodded, and then frowned at me. "First, you get some sleep. You look like hell."

"Thanks," I said. "Feel like I'm about to fall down."

She nodded. "I'll see if I can talk to Pell, if he's even awake. I doubt we'll get to the others before morning. Assuming they survive."

"Right," I said. "I'll need to get back here and do some snooping tomorrow. With any luck, we can track down our bad guy before something else jumps off the movie screen."

Murphy nodded and rose. She offered me a hand. I took it and she hauled me up. Murphy is a lot stronger than she looks.

"Give me a ride home?" I asked.

She already had her keys in her hand. "Do I look like your driver?"

"Thanks, Murph."

We headed for the door. Usually I have to shorten my steps to match Murphy's, but tonight I was so tired that she was waiting for me.

"Harry," she said. "What if we can't find out who is doing it in time?"

"We'll find them," I said.

"But if we don't?"

"Then we fight monsters."

Murphy took a deep breath and nodded as we stepped out into the summer night. "Damn right we do."

Chapter

Fourteen

Murphy drove me home and parked in the gravel lot next to the century-old converted boardinghouse. She killed the engine in the car, and it made those clicking noises they do. We sat there with the windows rolled down for a second. A cool breeze coming off the lake whispered through the car, soothing after the unrelenting heat of the day.

Murphy checked her rearview mirror and then scanned the street. "Who were you watching for?"

"What?" I said. "What do you mean?"

"You rubbernecked so much on the way here, I'm surprised your shoulders aren't bruising your ears."

I grimaced. "Oh, that. Someone was tailing me tonight."

"And you're just now telling me about it?"

I shrugged. "No sense worrying you over nothing. Whoever he is, he's not there now." I described the shadowy man and his car.

"Same one who ran you off the road, do you think?" she asked.

"Something tells me no," I said. "He wasn't making any effort to avoid being spotted. For all I know, he could just be a PI gathering information on me for the lawsuit."

"Christ," Murphy said. "Isn't that thing over with?"

I grimaced. "For a talk show host, Larry Fowler can really hold a grudge. He keeps doing one thing after another."

"Maybe you shouldn't have burned down his studio and shot up his car, then."

"That wasn't my fault!"

"That's for a court to decide," Murphy said in a pious tone. "You got an attorney?"

"I helped a guy find his daughter's lost dog five or six years ago. He's an attorney. He's giving me a hand with the legal process, enough so it hasn't actually bankrupted me. But it just keeps going and going."

Neither of us got out of the car.

I closed my eyes and listened to the summer night. Music played somewhere. I could hear the occasional racing engine.

"Harry?" Murph asked after a while. "Are you all right?"

"Hungry. Little tired."

"You look like you're hurting," she said.

"Maybe a little achy," I said.

"Not that kind of hurt."

I opened my eyes and looked at her, and then away. "Oh. That."

"That," she agreed. "You look like you're bleeding, somehow."

"I'll get over it," I told her.

"Is this about last Halloween?"

I shrugged a shoulder.

She was quiet for a moment. Then she said, "There was a lot of confusion in the blackout and right after. But they found a corpse in the Field Museum that had been savaged by an animal. Lab guessed it was a large dog. They found three different blood types on the floor, too."

"Did they?" I asked.

"And at Kent College. They found eight dead bodies there. Six of them had no discernible means of death. One had its head half severed by a surgically sharp blade. The other had taken a .44 round to the back of the head."

I nodded.

She stared at me for a while, frowning and waiting for me to continue. Then she said, in a quiet, certain voice, "You killed them."

My memory played some bad clips in my head. My stomach twisted. "I didn't do the headless guy."

Her cool, blue eyes stayed steady and she nodded. "You killed them. It's eating at you."

"It shouldn't. I've killed a lot of things."

"True," Murphy said. "But they weren't faeries or vampires or monsters this time. They were people. And you weren't in the heat of battle when they died. You made the choice cold."

I couldn't lift my eyes for some reason. But I nodded and whispered, "More or less."

She waited for me to say more, but I didn't. "Harry," she said. "You're tearing yourself up over it. You've got to talk to someone. It doesn't have to be me or here, but you've got to do it. There's no shame in feeling bad about killing someone, not for any reason."

I let out a short little laugh. It tasted bitter. "You're the last person I'd expect to tell me not to feel bad about committing murder."

She shifted uncomfortably. "Sort of surprised myself," she said. "But dammit, Harry. You remember when I shot Agent Denton?"

"Yeah."

"Took me some time to deal with it, too. I mean, I know he'd lost it. And he was going to kill you if I didn't do it. But it made me feel . . ." She squinted out at the Chicago night. "Stained. To take a life." She swallowed. "And those poor people the vampires had controlled at the shelter. That was even worse."

"All of those people were trying to kill you, Murph. You had to do it. You didn't have an option. You thought about it. You knew that when you pulled the trigger."

"Do you think you had an option?" she asked.

I shrugged and said, "Maybe. Maybe not." I swallowed. "The point is that I never bothered to consider it. Never hesitated. I just wanted them dead."

She was quiet for a long time.

"What if the Council is right about me?" I asked Murphy quietly. "What if I grow into some kind of monster? One who takes life without consideration for anything but his own will. Who cares more about end than means. More about might than right. What if this is the first step?"

"Do you think it is?" Murphy asked.

"I don't—"

"Because if you think so, Harry, then it probably is. And if you decide that it isn't, it probably isn't."

"The power of positive thinking?" I asked.

"No. Free will," she said. "You can't change what has already happened. But you choose what to do next. Which means that you only cross over to the dark side if you choose to do it."

"What makes you think that I won't?" I asked.

Murphy snorted, and reached over to touch my chin lightly with the fingers of one hand. "Because I'm not an idiot. Unlike some other people in this car."

I reached up and gripped her fingers with my right hand, squeezing gently. Her hand was steady and warm. "Careful. That was almost a compliment."

"You're a decent man," Murphy said, lowering her hand without removing it from my fingers. "Painfully oblivious, sometimes. But you've got a good heart. It's why you're so hard on yourself. You're tired, hungry, and hurting, and you saw the bad guys do something you couldn't stop. Your morale is low. That's all."

Her words were simple, frank, and direct. There was no sense of false comfort to her tone, not a trace of indulgent pity. I've known Murphy for a while. I knew that she meant every single word. Knowing that I had her support, even in the face of violation of the laws she worked to preserve, was a sudden and vast comfort.

I've said it before, and I'll say it again.

Murphy is good people.

"Maybe you're right," I said. "Hell's bells, I've got to stop feeling sorry for myself and get to work."

"Start with food and rest," she said. "If you don't hear from me, assume I'll pick you up in the morning."

"Right," I said.

We sat there holding hands for a minute. "Karrin?" I asked.

She looked up at me. Her eyes looked very large, very blue. I couldn't stare at them too long. "Have you ever thought about . . . you know. Us?"

"Sometimes," she said.

"Me too," I said. "But . . . the timing always seems to be off, somehow."

She smiled a little. "I noticed."

"Do you think it'll ever be right?"

She squeezed my hand gently, and then withdrew hers from mine. "I don't know. Maybe sometime." She frowned at her hand, and then said, "It would change a lot of things."

"It would," I said.

"You're my friend, Harry," Murphy said. "No matter

what happens. Sometimes in the past . . . I haven't really done right by you."

"Like when you handcuffed me in my office," I said.

"Right."

"And when you chipped one of my teeth arresting me."

Murphy blinked. "I chipped a tooth?"

"And when—"

"Yes, all right," she said. She gave me a mild glare, her cheeks pink. "The point is that I should have seen that you were one of the good guys a lot sooner than I did. And . . ."

I blinked at her ingenuously, and waited for her to say it.

"And I'm sorry," she growled. "Jerk."

That had cost her something. Murphy has more pride than is good for her. And yes, I am aware of the proverb about glass houses and stones. So I didn't give her any more of a hard time than I already had. "Don't go all romantic on me now, Murph."

She smiled a little and rolled her eyes. "If we ever did get together, I'd kill you inside a week. Now, go get some rest. You're useless to me like this."

I nodded and swung out of the car. "In the morning, then."

"Around eight," she said, and pulled out and back onto the street. She called to me, "Be careful!"

I looked after the car and sighed. My feelings about Murphy were still in a hopelessly complicated tangle. Maybe I should have said something to her sooner. Shared my feelings with her sooner. Acted more swiftly, taken the initiative.

Be careful, she said.

Why did I feel like I'd been too careful already?

Fifteen

My Mickey Mouse alarm clock went off at seven, and buzzed stubbornly at me until I kicked off the covers, sat up, and shut it off. I ached all over, felt stiff all over, but that sense of overwhelming exhaustion had faded, and since I was already vertical, I got moving.

I got into the shower, and tried not to jump too much when the first shock of freezing water hit me. I've had some practice at it. I've never had a water heater last me more than a week without some kind of technical problem coming up—and that was the kind of thing you just did not want to take chances on when you have a gas heater. So my showers were always either cold or colder. Given my dating life, and the inhuman charms available to some of the beings who occasionally faced off with me, it was probably just as well.

But, especially when I had bumps and bruises and sore muscles, I wished I could have a skin-blistering hot shower like everyone else in the country.

And suddenly the water shifted from ice-cold to piping hot. It was a shock, and I actually let out a little yelp and danced around in the shower until I could redirect the shower head so that it wasn't scalding my bits and pieces. After the initial shock of the temperature change, I leaned my aching head and neck into the spray for a second, and let out a long groan. Then I said, "Dammit, I told you to stop that."

Lasciel's voice murmured in a quiet laugh under the sound of the water. The sensation of phantom fingertips dug into the wire-tight muscles at the base of my neck, easing soreness away. "You should use the technique I taught you last autumn to block out the discomfort."

"I don't need to," I said, and tried for grouchy. But the heated water and massaging fingers, illusory though they were, were simply delicious. "I'll be fine."

"Your discomfort is my discomfort, my host," she said, and sighed. "Literally, as all my perceptions can come only through your own."

"This isn't real," I said quietly. "The water isn't really hot. No one is actually massaging my neck. It's an illusion you're laying over my senses."

"Does it not feel soothing?" her disembodied voice asked. "Does it not ease the tension?"

"Yes," I sighed.

"What matter, then? It is real enough."

I waved a hand as though trying to brush off an annoying fly from my neck, and the sensation of those strong, steady fingers retreated. "Go on," I said. "Hands off. I don't want to start my day with a psychic cage match, but if you push me to it, I will."

"As you wish," her voice said, and the sense of presence retreated. Then paused. "My host, I note that you made no mention of the hot water."

I grunted and mumbled something under my breath, ducked my head under the seemingly scalding water for a few seconds, and then said, "Did you pick up on what happened last night?"

"Indeed," the fallen angel replied.

"What was your read, then?"

There was a moment of thoughtful silence, and then

Lasciel responded, "That Karrin feels a certain distance between the pair of you is a professional necessity, but that she is considering that time and circumstance might someday render it irrelevant."

I sighed. "No," I said. "Not *that*. Stars and stones, I don't want dating advice from a freaking helltart. I meant the things that attacked people at the convention."

"Ah," Lasciel said, with no trace of offense in her tone. "It was obviously the attack of a spiritual predator."

Takes one to know one, I thought. I rolled a stiff shoulder under the hot water. "If that's true, then the attacks weren't about violence," I said thoughtfully. "Which explains what I saw in that bathroom, where the old man had been attacked. Whatever did it was intent on causing fear. Causing pain. Then devouring the . . . what? The psychic energy it generated in the victims?"

"That is a somewhat simplistic description," she said, "but one that is as close as I expect a mortal can come to understanding."

"What, you're a mortality bigot now?"

"Now and always," she replied. "I mean no insult by it, but you should know that your ability to comprehend your environment is very strongly defined by your belief in a number of illusions. Time. Truth. Love. That kind of thing. It isn't your fault, of course—but it does impose limits upon your ability to perceive and understand some matters."

"I'm only human," I said. "So enlighten me."

"To do so, you would have to release your hold on mortality."

I blinked and said, "I'd have to die?"

She sighed. "Again, you have only a partial understanding. But in the interest of expediency, yes. You would have to cease living."

"Then don't bother enlightening me," I said. "I have plenty of would-be teachers already." I rinsed and repeated my shampoo and made myself smell like Irish Spring. "The survivors of the attacks, then. They're going to have taken a spiritual mauling."

"If the theory is correct," Lasciel's voice responded. "If they are indeed wounded in spirit, it would seem conclusive."

I shuddered. That kind of damage showed itself in a number of ways, and none of them were pretty. I'd seen men driven to agonies of madness by spiritual attacks. Murphy had been subjected to such an assault and spent years learning to cope with the night terrors it had spawned, until the spiritual and psychological wounds had finally healed. I'd seen some who had been subjected to a psychic sandblasting by vampires of the Black Court who had become nearly mindless bodies, obeying orders, and others of the same ilk who had turned into psychotic killing machines in service to their masters.

The worst part of it all was that almost the only way for me to see something like that was to open my Sight. Which meant that every horribly mangled psyche I'd come across remained fresh and bright in my memory. Always.

The top shelf of my mental trophy case was getting crowded with hideous keepsakes.

The not-truly-hot water coursed over me, a small but suddenly significant comfort. "Go away," I told Lasciel. Then I added, "Leave me the hot water. Just this once."

"As you wish," the fallen angel's voice replied, polite satisfaction in her tone. The sense of her presence vanished entirely.

I stayed in the shower until my fingers shriveled up. Or, more accurately, I stayed there until the fingers of my right hand shriveled up. The skin of my burned left hand always looked withered and shriveled, these days. The second I turned the water off, the full sensation of icy cold returned, and I shivered violently as I toweled off and got dressed.

I took care of Mouse and Mister's various needs, ate several leftover biscuits from the fridge for breakfast, and opened a can of Coke. After a moment's thought, I headed down to my lab and grabbed Bob's skull from the shelf.

Faint orange lights flickered in the sockets. "Hey," Bob mumbled in a sleep-slurred voice. "Where are we going?"

"Investigating," I said. I went back upstairs with the skull and dropped it into my nylon backpack. "I might need you today. But there are going to be straights around, so keep your mouth shut unless I open the pack."

" 'Kay," Bob said with a yawn, and the lights in the skull's eye sockets winked out again.

I strapped on the magical arsenal—my shield bracelet, the energy ring, and my silver pentacle amulet. I slipped my newly carved blasting rod into a side pocket of the pack, leaving the handle out where I could reach up behind my right ear and whip it out in a hurry. I picked up my staff and eyed my leather duster, hanging on its hook by the door. I had layered spells over the duster in an effort to provide myself with a measure of protection against various fangs and claws and bullets and such, and as a result the coat had effectively become a suit of armor.

But, like most suits of armor, it lacked its own air-conditioning system—and if I wore it around in the blazing summer heat, I'd probably die of heat prostration before anyone had the chance to bite, slice, or shoot me. Hell, even the blue jeans I was wearing would feel too heavy long before noon. The duster stayed on its hook.

That rattled me a little. I'm used to the duster, and the spells on its leather had saved my life before. It made me feel a little vulnerable to think of getting into some kind of supernatural conflict without it. So I grabbed Mouse's lead, much to the dog's tail-wagging approval, and clipped it onto his collar. "You're with me today," I told him. "I need someone to watch my back. Maybe to help me eat a hot dog later."

Mouse's tail wagged even more at the mention of hot dogs. He chuffed out a breath, nudged my hip with the side of his head in a fond gesture, and we went outside to wait for Murphy.

She pulled up and eyed Mouse warily as I opened the back door and he jumped up onto the backseat. The car rocked back and forth with his weight and sank a little.

"He's car-broken, right?"

Mouse wagged his tail and gave Murphy an enthusiastic, vacant doggie grin, tilting his head back and forth quizzically. It was easy for my imagination to subtitle the look: *Car-broken? What is that?*

"Wiseass," I muttered at the dog, and got in the passenger side. "Don't worry, Murph. We did an insane amount of work on the whole bodily function issue as soon as I realized how big he was going to get. He'll be good." I glared at the backseat. "Won't you?"

Mouse gave me that same grin and puzzled tilting of his head. I frowned at him more deeply. He leaned forward to nuzzle my shoulder with his heavy muzzle, and settled down in the backseat.

Murphy sighed. "If it was any other dog, I'd make him ride in the trunk."

"That's right," I said. "You have dog issues."

"Big-dog issues," Murphy corrected me. "Just big dogs."

"Mouse isn't big. He's compactly challenged."

She gave me an arch look as she pulled out and said, "You'd fit in the trunk, too, Harry." Then she frowned at me and said, "Your lips are blue."

"Long shower," I said.

She gave me a sudden, swift grin. "Wanted to keep your mind on business? I think I'll interpret that as a compliment to my sexual appeal."

I snorted and buckled in. "You heard anything from the hospital?"

Murphy's smile faded and she kept her eyes on the road. She nodded without looking at me, her face impossible to read.

"Bad, huh?" I asked.

"The young man the paramedics carried off died. The girl who was already down when you came in is going to make it, but she's in some kind of shock. Catatonic. Doesn't focus her eyes or anything. Just lies there."

"Yeah," I said quietly. "I was sort of expecting that. What about the other girl? Rosie?"

"Her injuries were painful but not life-threatening. They closed the cuts and set the bones, but when they heard she was pregnant they kept her at the hospital for observation. It looks like she'll come through without losing the child. She's awake and talking."

"That's something," I said. "And Pell?"

"Still in ICU. He's an old man, and his injuries were severe. They think he'll be all right as long as there aren't any complications. He's groggy, but he's conscious."

"ICU," I said. "Any chance we could talk to him somewhere else?"

"Those doctors can be real funny about not wanting

people in critical condition to nip out for a walk to the vending machines," she said.

I grunted. "You might have to solo him, then. I don't dare go walking in there with all the medical equipment around."

"Even if it was just for a few minutes?" she asked.

I shrugged. "I don't have any control over when things break down." I paused and said, "Well, not exactly. I could blow out the whole floor in a few seconds, if I was trying to do it, but there's not much I can do to keep things from breaking down. Odds are good that if I was only in there for a few minutes, nothing bad would happen. But sometimes things go haywire the second I walk by them. I can't take any chances when there are people on life support."

Murphy arched a brow at me, and then nodded in understanding. "Maybe we can get you on a speaker phone or something."

"Or something." I rubbed at my eyes. "I think this is gonna be a long day."

Chapter

Sixteen

When you get right down to it, all hospitals tend to look pretty much the same, but Mercy Hospital, where the victims in the attack had been taken, somehow managed to avoid the worst of the sterile, disinfected, quietly desperate quality of many others. It was the oldest hospital in Chicago. The Sisters of Mercy had founded the place, and it remained a Catholic institution. The hospital was thought ridiculously large when it was first built, but the famous Chicago fires of the late nineteenth century filled Mercy to capacity. Doctors were able to handle six or seven times as many patients as any other hospital during the emergency, and everyone stopped complaining about how uselessly big the place was.

There was a cop on guard in the hallway outside the victims' rooms, in case the whacko costumed killer came after them again. He might also be there to discourage the press, whenever they inevitably smelled the blood in the water and showed up for the frenzy. It did not surprise me much at all to see that the cop on guard was Rawlins. He was unshaven and still had his Splatter-Con!!! name tag on. One of his forearms was bound up in neatly taped white bandages, but other than that he looked surprisingly alert for someone who had been injured and then worked all through the night. Or maybe his weathered features just took such things in stride.

"Dresden," Rawlins said from his seat. He'd dragged a chair to the hall's intersection. He was dedicated, not insane. "You look better. 'Cept for those bruises."

"The best ones always show up the day after," I said.

"God's truth," he agreed.

Murphy looked back and forth between us. "I guess you'll work with anybody, Harry."

"Shoot," Rawlins drawled, smiling. "Is that little Karrie Murphy I hear down there? I didn't bring my opera glasses to work today."

She grinned back. "What are you doing down here? Couldn't they find a real cop to watch the hall?"

He snorted, stuck his legs out, and crossed his ankles. I noted that for all of his indolent posture, his holstered weapon was clear and near his right hand. He regarded Mouse with pursed lips and said, "Don't think dogs are allowed in here."

"He's a police dog," I told him.

Rawlins casually offered Mouse the back of one hand. Mouse sniffed it politely and his tail thumped against my legs. "Hmmm," Rawlins drawled. "Don't think I've seen him around the station."

"The dog's with me," I said.

"The wizard's with me," Murphy said.

"Makes him a police dog, all right," Rawlins agreed. He jerked his head down the hall. "Miss Marcella is down that way. They got Pell and Miss Becton in ICU. The boy they brought in didn't make it."

Murphy grimaced. "Thanks, Rawlins."

"You're welcome, little girl," Rawlins said, his deep voice grandfatherly.

Murphy gave him a brief glare, and we went down the hall to visit the first of the victims.

It was a single-bed room. Molly was there, in a chair beside the bed, where she had evidently been asleep while mostly sitting up. By the time I got in the room and shut the door, she was looking around blearily and mopping at the corner of her mouth with her sleeve. In the bed beside her was Rosie, small and pale.

Molly touched the girl's arm and gently roused her. Rosie looked up at us and blinked a few times.

"Good morning," Murphy said. "I hope you were able to get some rest."

"A l-little," the girl said, her voice raspy. She looked around, but Molly was already passing her a glass of water with a straw in it. Rosie sipped and then laid her head tiredly back, then murmured a thank you to Molly. "A little," she said again, her voice stronger. "Who are you?"

"My name is Karrin Murphy. I'm a detective for the Chicago Police Department." She gestured at me, and took a pen and a small notebook from her hip pocket. "This is Harry Dresden. He's working with us on the case. Do you mind if he's here?"

Rosie licked her lips and shook her head. Her unin-jured hand moved fitfully, stroking over the bandages on the opposite forearm in nervous motions. Murphy en-gaged the girl in quiet conversation.

"What are you doing here?" Molly asked me in a half whisper.

"Looking into things," I replied as quietly. "There's something spooky going on."

Molly chewed on her lip. "You're sure?"

"Definitely," I said. "Don't worry. I'll find whatever hurt your friend."

"Friends," Molly said, emphasizing the plural. "Have you heard anything about Ken? Rosie's boyfriend? No one will tell us anything."

"He the kid that they took from the scene?"

Molly nodded anxiously. "Yes."

I glanced at Murphy's back and didn't say anything.

Molly got it. Her face went white and she whispered, "Oh, God. She'll be so . . ." She folded her arms and shook her head several times. Then she said, "I've got to . . ." She looked around, and in a louder voice said, "I'm dying for coffee. Anyone else need some?"

Nobody did. Molly picked up her purse and turned around to walk for the door. In doing so, she brushed within a foot or two of Mouse. Instead of growling, though, Mouse leaned his head affectionately against her leg as she went by, and cadged a few ear scratches from the girl before she left.

I frowned at Mouse after Molly had gone. "Are you going bipolar on me?"

He settled down again immediately. Murphy went on asking Rosie fairly predictable questions about the attack.

The clock was running. I pushed the question about Mouse's odd behavior aside for the moment, and let Mouse watch the door while I reached for my Sight.

It was a slight effort of concentration to push away the concerns of the material world, like aches and pains and bruises and why my dog was growling at Molly, and then the mere light and shadow and color of the everyday world dissolved into the riot of flowing energy and currents of light and power that lay beneath the surface.

Murphy looked like Murphy had always looked beneath my Sight. She appeared almost as herself, but clearer, somehow, her eyes flashing, and she was garbed in a quasi angelic tunic of white, stained in places with the blood and mud of battle. A short, straight sword, its blade made of almost viciously bright white light, hung beneath her left arm, where I knew her light cotton blazer hid her gun in its shoulder rig. She looked at me and I could see her physical face as a vague shadow beneath the surface of the aspect I saw now. She smiled at me, a sunny light in it, though her body's face remained a neutral mask. I was seeing the life, the emotion behind her face, now.

I shied away from staring at her lest I make eye contact for too long—but that smile, at least, was something I wouldn't mind remembering.

Rosie was another story.

The physical Rosie was a small, slight, pale young woman with thin, frail features. The Rosie my Sight revealed to me was entirely different. Pale skin became a pallid, dirty, leathery coating. Large dark eyes looked even bigger, and flicked around with darting, avian jerks. They were furtive eyes, giving her the dangerous aspect of a stray dog or maybe some kind of rat—the eyes of a craven, desperate survivor.

Winding veins of some kind of green-black energy pulsed beneath her skin, particularly around the inside bend of her left arm. The writhing strings of energy ended at the surface of her skin, in dozens of tiny, mindlessly opening and closing little mouths—the needle tracks I'd seen the night before. Her right hand kept darting back and forth over the other arm as if trying to scratch a persistent itch. But her fingers couldn't touch. There was a kind of sheath of sparkling motes around her hands, almost like mittens, and she couldn't actually touch those mindlessly hungry mouths. Worse, there were what looked almost like burn marks on her temples—small, black, neat holes, as if someone had bored a hot needle through the skin and skull beneath. There was a kind of phantom blood around the injuries, but her eyes were wide and vague, as if she didn't even notice them.

What the hell? I had seen the victims of spiritual attacks before, and they'd never been pretty. Usually they looked like the victim of a shark attack, or someone who had been mauled by a bear. I hadn't ever seen someone with damage like Rosie's. It looked almost like some kind of demented surgeon had gone after her with a laser scalpel. That pushed the weirdometer a couple of clicks beyond the previous record.

My head started pounding and I pushed the Sight away. I leaned my hip against the wall for a second and rubbed at my temples until the throbbing subsided and I was sure that my normal vision had returned.

"Rosie," I said, cutting into the middle of one of Murphy's questions. "When was your last fix?"

Murphy glanced over her shoulder at me, frowning. Behind her, the girl gave me a guilty look, her eyes shifting to one side. "What do you mean?" Rosie asked.

"I figure it's heroin," I said. I kept my voice pitched to the barest level needed to be audible. "I saw the tracks on you last night."

"I'm diab—" she began.

"Oh please," I said, and let the annoyance show in my voice. "You think I'm that stupid?"

"Harry," Murphy began. There was a warning note in her voice, but my head hurt too much to let it stop me.

"Miss Marcella, I'm trying to help you. Just answer the question."

She was silent for a long moment. Then she said, "Two weeks."

Murphy arched a brow, and her gaze went back to the girl.

"I quit," she said. "Really. I mean, once I heard that I was pregnant . . . I can't do that anymore."

"Really?" I asked.

She looked up and her eyes were direct, though nothing like confident. "Yes. I'm done with it. I don't even miss it. The baby's more important than that."

I pursed my lips and then nodded. "All right."

"Miss Marcella," Murphy said, "thank you for your time."

"Wait," she said, as Murphy turned away. "Please. No one will tell us anything about Ken. Do you know how he's doing? What room he's in?"

"Ken's your boyfriend?" Murphy asked in a careful tone.

"Yes. I saw them load him in the ambulance last night. I know he's here . . ." Rosie stared at Murphy for a second, and then her face grew even more pale. "Oh, no. Oh, no, no, no."

I was glad I'd gotten a gotten a look at her before she found out about her boyfriend. My imagination provided me with a nice image of watching the emotional wounds open up as though an invisible sword had begun slicing into her, but at least I didn't have to see it with my Sight, too.

"I'm very sorry," Murphy said quietly. Her voice was steady, her eyes compassionate.

Molly picked that moment to return with a cup of coffee. She took one look at Rosie, put the coffee down, and then hurried to her. Rosie broke down in choking sobs. Molly immediately sat on the bed beside her, and hugged her while she wept.

"We'll be in touch," Murphy said quietly. "Come on, Harry."

Mouse stared at Rosie with a mournful expression, and I had to tug on his leash a couple of times to get him moving. We departed and headed for the nearest stairwell. Murphy headed for ICU, which was in the neighboring building.

"I didn't see the track marks on her last night," she said after a minute. "You pushed her pretty hard."

"Yes."

"Why?"

"Because it might mean something. I don't know what, yet. But we didn't have time to waste listening to her denial."

"She wasn't straight with you," Murphy said. "No one kicks heroin that fast. Two weeks. She should still be feeling some of the withdrawal."

"Yeah," I said. We went outside to go to the other building. Bright morning sunlight made my head hurt even more, and the sidewalk began revolving. I stopped to wait for my eyes to adjust to the light.

"You all right?" Murphy asked.

"It's hard. Seeing someone like that," I said quietly. "And she's probably the least mangled of the three."

She frowned. "What did you see?"

I tried to tell her what Rosie had looked like. It sounded surreal and garbled, even to me. I didn't think I had conveyed it very well.

"You look terrible," she said when I finished.

"It'll pass. Just got this damned headache." I shook my head and focused on taking steady breaths until I could force the pain to recede. "Okay. I'm good."

"Did you learn what you were hoping for?" Murphy asked.

"Not yet," I said. "I'll need to look at the others, too. See if the injuries on them give me some kind of pattern."

"They're in ICU."

"Yeah. I need to find a way to them without getting too close to someone on life support. I can't stay around to talk. I'll need maybe a minute, ninety seconds to look at them both. Then I'll get out. Let you talk."

Murphy took a deep breath and said, "You sure you should do this?"

"No," I told her. "But I can't help you if I don't get

to look at them. I can't do that any other way. If I can stay calm and relaxed, it shouldn't hurt anything for me to be there for a minute or two."

"But you can't be sure."

"When can I?"

She frowned at me, but nodded. "Let me go ahead of you," she said. "Wait here."

I found a chair, and took it down the hall and sat down with Mouse and Rawlins, who had joined us. We shared a companionable silence. I leaned my head back against the wall and closed my eyes.

My headache finally began to fade away just as Murphy returned. "All right," she said quietly. "We need to go down a floor and then use the back stairs. A nurse is going to let us in. You won't have to walk past any of the other rooms before you get to our witnesses."

"Okay," I said, and stood up. "Let's get this over with."

Chapter

Seventeen

I wasted no time. We went up the stairs, and I was already preparing my Sight. A nurse opened the door to the stairway, and I simply stepped into the first door on my left—the catatonic girl's, Miss Becton's. I stepped into the doorway and raised my Sight.

She was a young girl, still in her late teens, nervously thin, her hair a shocking color of red that for some reason did not strike me as a dye job. She lay on her front, her head turned to the side, muddy brown eyes open and blank. Her back had been covered in bandages.

As my Sight focused on her, I saw more. The girl's psyche had been savagely mauled, and as I watched her, phantom bruises darkened a few patches of skin that remained, and blood and watery fluids oozed from the rest of her torn flesh. Her mouth was set in a continual, silent wail, and beneath the real-world glaze, her eyes were wide with terror. If there'd been enough left of her behind those eyes, Miss Becton would have been screaming.

My stomach rolled and I barely spotted a trash can in time to throw up into it.

Murphy crouched down at my side, her hand on my back. "Harry? Are you okay?"

Anger and empathy and grief warred for first place in my thoughts. Across the room, I was dimly conscious of a clock radio warbling to life and dying in a puff of smoke. The room's fluorescent lights began to flicker as the violent emotions played hell with the aura of magic around me.

"*No,*" I said in a vicious, half-strangled growl. "I'm *not* okay."

Murphy stared at me for a second, and then looked at the girl. "Is she . . ."

"She isn't coming back," I said.

I spat a few times into the trash can and stood up. My headache started to return. The girl's terrified eyes stayed bright and clear in my imagination. She'd been out for a fun time. A favorite movie. Maybe coffee or dinner with friends afterward. She sure as hell hadn't woken up yesterday morning and wondered if today would be the day some kind of nightmarish *thing* would rip away her sanity.

"Harry," Murphy said again, her voice very gentle. "You didn't do this to her."

"Dammit," I said. I sounded bitter. She found my right hand with hers and I closed my fingers around hers with a kind of quiet desperation. "Dammit, Murph. I'm going to find this thing and kill it."

Her hand was steady and strong, like her voice. "I'll help."

I nodded and held tight to her hand for a minute. There wasn't any tension in that contact, no quivering sensation of excitement. Murphy was human and alive. She held my hand to remind me that I was too. I somehow managed to push the sense of visceral horror I'd seen filling the girl from my immediate thoughts, until I felt steadier. I squeezed her hand once and released it.

"Come on," I said, my voice rough. "Pell."

"Are you sure you don't need a minute?"

"It won't help," I said. I gestured at the radio and the lights. "I need to get this over with and leave."

She chewed on her lip but nodded at me, and led me to the door across the hall. I didn't want to do it, but I hauled up my Sight again and braced myself as I followed on Murphy's heels and Looked at Clark Pell.

Pell was a sour-looking old cuss made out of shoe leather and gristle. One arm and both legs were in casts, and he was in traction. One side of his face was swollen with bruising. A plastic tube for oxygen ran beneath his nose. Bandages swathed his head, though bits of coarse grey hair stuck out. One eye was swollen mostly shut. The other was open, dark, and glittering.

Beyond the physical surface, his wounds were very nearly as dire as those the girl had suffered. He had been brutally beaten. Phantom bruises slid around his wrinkled skin, and the shapes of distorted bones poked disquietingly at the surface. And I saw something about the old man, too. Beneath the shoe leather and gristle, there were *more* shoe leather and gristle. And iron. The old man had been badly beaten, but it wasn't the first such he had endured—physically or spiritually. He was a fighter, a survivor. He was afraid, but he was also angry and defiant.

Whatever had done this to him hadn't gotten what it wanted—not like it had with the girl. It had to settle for a physical beating when its attack hadn't elicited the terror and anguish it had expected. The old man had faced it, and he didn't have any power of his own, beyond a lifetime of stubborn will. If he'd done it, as painful and as frightening as it must have been, I could steel myself against Looking at the aftermath.

I released my Sight slowly and took a deep breath. Murphy, poised beside me as if she expected me to abruptly collapse, tilted her head and peered at me.

"I'm all right," I told her quietly.

Pell made a weak but rude sound. "Whiner. Not even a cast."

I faced the old man and said, "Who did this to you."

He shook his head, a feeble motion. "Crazy."

Murphy started to say something but I raised my hand and shook my head at her, and she fell silent, waiting.

"Sir," I said to Pell. "I swear to you. I'm not a cop. I'm not a doctor. I think you saw something strange."

He stared at me, his one eye narrowed.

"Didn't you?" I asked quietly.

"Ha . . . H-h—" he tried to say, but the word broke into a wracking, quiet cough.

I held up my hand and waited for him to recover. Then I said, "Hammerhands."

Pell's lip lifted, a faint little sneer. His good hand moved weakly, and I stepped over closer to him.

"You told Greene it was someone dressed like Hammerhands," I guessed.

Pell closed his eye tiredly. "Pretty much."

I nodded. "But it wasn't just a costume," I said quietly. "This was something more."

Pell gave a slow shudder, before opening his eye again, dull with fatigue. "It was *him*," the old man whispered. "Don't know how. Don't make no sense. But . . . you could feel it."

"I believe you," I told him.

He watched me for a second and then nodded, closing his eye. "Thing is. That was the only damn movie ever scared me. Wasn't even all that good." He gave a weak shake of his head and said, "Buzz off."

"Thank you," I told him quietly. Then I turned and walked toward the door.

Murphy followed at my side, and we headed back down the stairs. "Harry?" she asked. "What was that?"

"Pell," I said. "He gave us what we needed."

"He did?"

"Yeah," I said. "I think he did. This thing has got to be some kind of phobophage."

"A what?"

"It's a spiritual entity that feeds on fear. It attacks in order to scare people, and feeds on the emotion."

"It didn't give Pell those broken bones by shouting 'boo!' " Murphy said.

"Yeah. It's got to manifest a physical body in order to come to the real world. Pretty standard for all those demon types."

"How do we beat it?"

I shook my head. "I don't know yet. First I have to find out what kind of phobophage it is. But I've got a place to pick up a trail now. There are only going to be so many beings who could have crossed over to Chicago from the Nevernever to do what this thing did."

We emerged into the sunshine and I stopped for a minute, lifting my face up to the light.

The horror and misery I'd seen on the victims remained in place, a clear and terrible image, but the sunlight and the equally sharp memory of old Pell's defiance took the edge off.

"You going to be all right?" Murphy asked.

"I think so," I said quietly.

"Can you tell me what you saw?"

I did, in as few words as I could.

She listened, and then nodded slowly. "It hardly seems like what happened to them happened to Rosie."

"Maybe Rawlins and I got there in time," I said. "Maybe it hadn't had time to do more than a little foreplay."

"Or maybe there's another reason," Murphy said.

"Remind me to lecture you about the interest rate on

borrowed trouble," I said. "Simplest explanation is the one to go with until we find out something to the contrary."

Murphy nodded. "If this creature hit the convention twice, it will probably do it again. Seems to me that maybe we should advise them to close it down. No convention, no attacks, right?"

"Too late for that," I said.

She tilted her head. "What do you mean?"

"The creature feeds on fear. It's attracted to it," I said. "If they shut down the convention, it will scare a lot of people."

"News reports will do that, too."

"Not the same way," I said. "A news report might unsettle some folks. But the people at the convention here, the ones who knew the victims, who were in the same buildings—it will hit them harder. It will make what happened here something dangerous. Something real."

"If the attacker is that dangerous, they *should* be afraid," Murphy said.

"Except that intense fear will attract the attacker again," I said. "In fact, enough of it would attract *more* predators of the same nature."

"More?" Murphy said, her voice sharp.

"Like blood in the water draws in sharks," I said. "Only instead of being at the convention, the targets will be scattered all over Chicago. Right now, the only advantage we have is that we know generally where the thing is going to strike again. If the convention closes, we lose that advantage."

"And the next chance we get to pick up its trail will be when the next corpse turns up." Murphy shook her head. "What do you need from me?"

"For now, a ride home," I said. "I'll have some consulting to do, and . . ." I suddenly ground my teeth. "Dammit, I almost forgot."

"What?"

"I've got a lunch meeting I can't miss."

"More important than this?" she asked.

"I can't let it slide," I said. "Council stuff. Maybe important."

She shook her head. "You take too much responsibility on yourself, Harry. You're just one man. A good man, but you're still only human."

"This is what happens when I don't wear the coat," I opined. "People start thinking I'm not a superhero."

She snorted and we started back toward her car. "I'm serious," she said. "You can't be everywhere at once. You can't stop all the bad things that are going to happen."

"Doesn't mean someone shouldn't try," I said.

"Maybe. But you take it personal. You tear yourself up over it. Like with that girl just now." She shook her head. "I hate to see you like that. You've got worries enough without beating yourself up for things you didn't do."

I shrugged and fell quiet until we got back to the car. Then I said, "I just can't stand it. I can't stand seeing people get hurt like that. I hate it."

She regarded me steadily and nodded. "Me too."

Mouse thumped his head against my leg and leaned on me so that I could feel his warmth.

That settled, we all got into Murphy's car, so that I could track down I knew not what, just as soon as I got done opening an entirely new can of worms with the Summer Knight.

Chapter

Eighteen

At my request, Murphy dropped me off a couple of blocks from home so that I could give Mouse at least a little chance to stretch his legs. He seemed appreciative and walked along sniffing busily, his tail fanning the air. I kept a watch out behind me, meanwhile, but my unknown tail did not appear. I kept an eye out for any other people or vehicles that might have been following me, in case he was working with a team, but I didn't spot anyone suspicious. That didn't stop me from keeping a paranoid eye over my shoulder until we made it back to the old boardinghouse, and I went down the stairs to my apartment door.

I muttered my defensive wards down, temporarily neutralizing powerful constructions of magic that I had placed around my apartment shortly after the beginning of the war with the Red Court. I opened the dead bolt on the steel door, twisted the handle, and then slammed my shoulder into the door as hard as I could to open it.

The door flew open to a distance of five or six whole inches. I kicked it a few times to open it the rest of the way, then tromped in with Mouse and looked up to find the barrel of a chopped-down shotgun six inches from my face.

"Those things are illegal, you know," I said.

Thomas scowled at me from the other end of the

shotgun and lowered the weapon. I heard a metallic click as he put the safety back on. "You've got to get that door fixed. Every time you come in it sounds like an assault team."

"Boy," I replied, letting Mouse off his lead. "One little siege and you get all paranoid."

"What can I say." He turned and slipped the shotgun into his bulging sports bag, which sat on the floor by the door. "I never counted on starring in my own personal zombie movie."

"Don't kid yourself," I said. Mister flew across the room and pitched all thirty pounds of himself into a friendly shoulder block against my legs. "It was my movie. You were a spear-carrier. A supporting role, tops."

"It's nice to be appreciated," he said. "Beer?"

"Sure."

Thomas sauntered over to the icebox. He was wearing jeans, sneakers, and a white cotton T-shirt. I frowned at the sports bag. His trunk, an old military-surplus footlocker, sat on the ground beside the bag, padlocked shut. Between the trunk and the bag, I figured pretty much every material possession he owned now sat on the floor by my door. He came back over to me with a couple of cold brown bottles of Mac's ale, and flicked the tops off of both of them at the same time with his thumbs. "Mac would kill you if he knew you were chilling it."

I took my bottle, studying his face, but his expression gave away little. "Mac can come over here and install air-conditioning, then, if he wants me to drink it warm in the middle of summer."

Thomas chuckled. We clinked bottles and drank.

"You're leaving," I said a minute later.

He took another sip, and said nothing.

"You weren't going to tell me," I said.

He rolled a shoulder in a shrug. Then he nodded at an

envelope on the fireplace's mantel. "My new address and phone number. There's some money in there for you."

"Thomas . . ." I said.

He swigged beer and shook his head. "No, take it. You offered to let me stay with you until I got on my feet. I've been here almost two years. I owe you."

"No," I said.

He frowned. "Harry, please."

I stared at him for a minute, and struggled with a bunch of conflicting emotions. Part of me was childishly relieved that I would have my tiny apartment to myself again. A much larger part of me felt suddenly empty and worried. Still another part felt a sense of excitement and happiness for Thomas. Ever since he started crashing on my couch, Thomas had been recovering from wounds of his own. For a while there, I had feared that despair and self-loathing were going to cause him to implode, and I had somehow known that his desire to get out on his own again was a sign of recovery. Part of that recovery, I was sure, was Thomas regaining a measure of pride and self-confidence. That's why he'd left the money on the mantel. Pride. I couldn't turn down the money without taking that pride from him.

Except for scattered memories of my father, Thomas was the only blood family I'd ever had. Thomas had faced danger and death beside me without hesitation, had guarded me in my sleep, tended me when I'd been injured, and once in a while he'd even cooked. We got on each other's nerves sometimes, sure, but that hadn't ever altered the fundamental fact of who we were to one another.

We were brothers.

Everything else was temporary.

I met his eyes and asked quietly, "Are you going to be all right?"

He smiled a little and shrugged. "I think so."

I tilted my head. "Where'd the money come from?"

"My job."

I lifted my eyebrows. "You found a job you could hold?"

He winced a little.

"Sorry," I said. "But . . . I know you'd had so much trouble." Specifically, he'd been subjected to the amorous attentions of various fellow employees who had been drawn to him to such a degree that it had practically been assault. Being an incubus was probably easier at night clubs and celebrity parties than at a drive-through or a cash register. "You found something?"

"Something without people," he said. He smiled easily as he spoke, but I sensed an undercurrent of deception in it. He wasn't telling me the whole truth. "I've been there a while."

"Yeah?" I asked. "Where?"

He evaded me effortlessly. "A place down off Lake View. I've finally earned a little extra. I just wanted to pay you back."

"You must be getting all kinds of overtime," I said. "As near as I can figure it, you've been putting in eighty- and ninety-hour weeks."

He shrugged, his smile a mask. "Working hard."

I took another sip of beer (which was excellent, even cold) and thought it over. If he didn't want to talk about it, he wasn't going to talk about it. Pushing him wouldn't make him any more likely to tell me. I didn't get the sense that he was in trouble, and while he had one hell of a poker face, I'd lived with him long enough to see through it most of the time. Thomas hadn't ever supported himself before. Now that he was sure he could do it, it had become something he valued.

Getting out on his own was something he needed to do. I wouldn't be doing him any favors by interfering.

"You sure you'll be okay?" I asked him.

Something showed through the mask, then—embarrassment. "I'll be all right. It's past time for me to get out on my own."

"Not if you aren't ready," I said.

"Harry, come on. So far we've been lucky. The Council hasn't noticed me here. But with all of your Warden stuff, sooner or later somebody's going to show up and find you rooming with a White Court vampire."

I grimaced. "That would be a mess," I agreed. "But I don't mind chancing it if you need the time."

"And I don't mind getting out on my own to avoid making trouble for you with the Council," he said. "Besides, I'm just covering my own ass. I don't want to cross them, myself."

"I wouldn't let them—"

Thomas burst out in a brief, genuine laugh. "Christ, Harry. You're my brother, not my mother. I'll be fine. Now that I won't be here to make you look bad, maybe you can finally start having girls over again."

"Bite me, prettyboy," I said. "You need any help moving or anything?"

"Nah." He finished the beer. "I just have one box and one bag. Cab's on the way." He paused. "Unless you need my help with a case or something. I've got until Monday to move in."

I shook my head. "I'm working with SI on this one, so I've got plenty of support. I think I can get things locked down by tonight."

Thomas gave me a flat look. "Now you've done it."

"What?" I asked.

"You predicted quick victory. Now it's going to get hopelessly complicated. Jesus, don't you know any better than that by now?"

I grinned at him. "You'd think that I would."

I finished my beer and offered my brother my hand. He gripped it. "If you need anything, call me," he said.

"Ditto."

"Thank you, little brother," he said quietly.

I blinked my eyes a couple of times. "Yeah. My couch is always open. Unless there's a girl over."

Outside, wheels crunched on gravel and a car horn sounded.

"There's my ride," he said. "Oh. Do you mind if I borrow the shotgun? Just until I can replace it."

"Go ahead," I told him. "I've still got my .44."

"Thanks." He bent over and swung the heavy footlocker onto one shoulder without effort. He picked up the sports bag, slung the strap over his other shoulder, and opened the door easily with one hand. He glanced back, winked at me, and shut the door behind him.

I stared at the closed door for a minute. Car doors opened and closed. Wheels crunched as the cab drove away, and my apartment suddenly seemed a couple of sizes too large. Mouse let out a long sigh and came over to me to nudge his head underneath my hand. I scratched his ears for a minute and said, "He'll be all right. Don't worry about him."

Mouse sighed again.

"I'll miss him too," I told the dog. Then I shook myself and told Mouse, "Don't get comfortable. We're going to go visit Mac. You can meet the Summer Knight."

I went around getting everything I needed for a formal meeting with the Summer Knight, called another cab, and sat in my too-quiet apartment wondering what it was my brother was hiding from me.

McAnally's pub is on the bottom floor of a building not too far from my office. Chicago being what it is—essentially a giant swamp with a city sinking into it—the building had settled over the years, and to enter the pub you had to come in the door and take a couple of steps down. It's a low-ceilinged room, or at least it's always felt that way to me, and it offers the added attraction of several whirling ceiling fans at my eye level, just as I come in the door, and after stepping down into the room they're still uncomfortably close to my head.

There's a sign Mac's got hanging up at the door that reads ACCORDED NEUTRAL GROUND. It means that the place was supposed to be a no-combat zone, under the terms laid out in the Unseelie Accords, the most recent and influential set of principles agreed upon by most of the various nations of the supernatural maybe ten or twelve years ago. By the terms of the Accords, there's no fighting allowed between members of opposing nations in the bar, and we're not supposed to attempt to provoke anybody, either. If things do get hostile, the Accords say you have to take it outside or risk censure by the signatory nations.

More importantly, at least to me, Mac was a friend. When I came to his place to eat, I considered myself a guest, and he my host. I'd abide by his declared neutrality out of simple respect, but it was good to know that the Accords were there in the background. Not every member of the supernatural community is as polite and neighborly as me.

Mac's place is one big room. There are a baker's dozen of thick wooden support pillars spread through the room, each of them carved with figures from Old World nursery tales. There's a bar with thirteen stools, thirteen tables spread irregularly throughout the room, and the whole place has an informal, comfortable, asymmetrical sort of feel to it.

I came through the door armed for bear and projecting an attitude to match. I bore my staff in my left hand, and I'd slipped my new blasting rod, a shaft of wood two feet long and as thick as my two thumbs together, through my belt. My shield bracelet hung on my left hand, my force ring was on my right, and Mouse walked on my right side on his lead, looking huge and sober and alert.

A couple of people inside looked at my face and immediately tried to look like they had no interest in me. I wasn't in a bad mood, but I wanted to look that way. Since the war with the Red Court had gotten rolling, I had learned the hard way that predators, human and otherwise, sense fear and look for weakness. So I walked into the place like I was hoping to kick someone in the neck, because it was a hell of a lot easier to discourage potential predators ahead of time than it was to slug it out with them when they followed me out afterward.

I crossed the room to the bar, and Mac nodded at me. Mac was a lean man somewhere between thirty and fifty. He wore his usual dark clothes and spotless white apron while simultaneously managing all the bartending and a big wood-burning grill where he cooked various dishes for the customers. The summer heat was fairly well

blunted by the shade and the fans and the partially sub-
terranean nature of the room, but there were still dark
spots of sweat on his clothes and beading along the bare
skin of his scalp.

Mac knew what the tough-guy face was about, and it
clearly didn't bother him. He nodded to me as I sat
down on a stool.

"Mac. You got any cold beer back there somewhere?"

He gave me an unamused look.

I leaned my staff on the bar, lifted both hands in a
placating gesture, and said, "Kidding. But tell me you've
got cold lemonade. It's a zillion degrees out there."

He answered with a glass of lemonade cooled with his
patented lemonade ice cubes, so that you could drink it
cold and not have it get watered down, all at the same
time. Mac is pretty much a genius when it comes to
drinks. And his steak sandwiches should be considered
some kind of national resource.

"Business?" he asked me.

I nodded. "Meeting with Fix."

Mac grunted and went out to a corner table, one with
a clear view of the door. He nudged it out a bit from the
wall, polished it with a cloth, and straightened the chairs
around it. I nodded my thanks to him and settled down
at the table with my lemonade.

I didn't have long to wait. A couple of minutes before
noon, the Summer Knight opened the door and came
in.

Fix had grown, and I mean that literally. He'd been
about five foot three, maybe an inch or so higher. Now
he had towered up to at least five nine. He'd been a wiry
little guy with white-blond hair, and most of that remained true. The wire had thickened to lean cable, but
the shock of spikes he'd worn as a hairdo had gotten
traded in on a more typical cut for faerie nobles—a

shoulder-length do. Fix hadn't been a good-looking guy, and the extra height and muscle and the hair did absolutely nothing to change that. What had changed was his previous manner, which had been approximately equal parts nervous and cheerful.

The Summer Knight projected confidence and strength. They shone from him like light from a star. When he opened the door, the dim shadows retreated somewhat, and a whispering breeze that smelled of pine and honeysuckle rolled through the room. The air around him did something to the light, throwing it back cleaner, more pure, more fierce than it had been before it touched him.

Fix wasn't putting on a face, like I had. This was what he had become: the Summer Knight, mortal champion of the Seelie Court, a thunderstorm in blue jeans and a green cotton shirt. His gaze went first to Mac, and he gave the barkeep a polite little bow of respect. Then he turned to me, grinned, and nodded. "Harry."

"Fix," I said. "Been a while. You've grown."

He looked down at himself and looked briefly like the flustered young man I had first met. "It sort of snuck up on me."

"Life has a way of doing that," I agreed.

"I hope you don't mind. Someone else wanted to speak to you, too."

He turned his head and said something, and a breath later the Summer Lady entered the tavern.

Lily had never been hard on the eyes. The daughter of one of the Sidhe and a mortal, she'd had the looks usually reserved for magazines and movie stars. But, like Fix, she had grown; not physically, though a somewhat juvenile eye might have made certain comparisons to the past and somehow found them even more appealing. What had changed most was the bashful uncertainty that had filled her every word and movement. The old Lily had hardly been able to take care of herself. This was the Summer Lady, youngest of the Seelie Queens, and when she came in the room, the whole place suddenly seemed more alive. The lingering taste of lemonade on my tongue became more intensely sour and sweet. I could hear every whisper of wind around every lazily spinning fan blade in the room, and all of them murmured gentle music together. She wore a simple sundress of green, starkly contrasting the silken waterfall of purest white tresses that fell to her waist.

More than that, she carried around her a sense of purpose, a kind of quiet, gentle strength, something as steady and warming and powerful as summer sunlight. Her face, too, had gained character, the awkward shyness in her eyes replaced with a kind of gentle perception; a continual, quiet laughter leavened with just a touch of sadness. She stepped forward, between two of the carved wooden columns, and the flowers wrought into the wood upon them twitched and then burst into sudden blooms of living color.

Everyone there, myself included, stopped breathing for a second.

Mac recovered first. "Lily," he said, and bowed his head to her. "Good to see you."

She smiled warmly at his use of her name. "Mac," she replied. "Do you still make those lemonade ice cubes?"

"Two," Fix said, grinning more broadly. He offered his arm to Lily, and she laid her hand upon it, both gestures so familiar to them that they didn't need to think about them anymore. They came over to the table, and I rose politely until Fix had seated Lily. Then we mere menfolk sat down again. Mac came with drinks and departed.

"So," Fix said. "What's up, Harry?"

Lily sipped lemonade through a straw. I tried not to stare and drool. "Um. I've been asked to get in touch with you," I said. "After the Red Court's attack last year, when they encroached on Faerie territory, we were kind of expecting a response. We were wondering why there hadn't been one."

"We meaning the Council?" Lily asked quietly. Her voice was calm, but something just under its surface warned me that the answer might be important.

"We meaning me and some people I know. This isn't exactly, ah, official."

Fix and Lily exchanged a look. She nodded once, and Fix exhaled and said, "Good. Good, I was hoping that would be the case."

"I am not permitted to speak for the Summer Court to the White Council," Lily explained. "But you have a prior claim of friendship to both myself and my Knight. And there is nothing to prevent me from speaking to an old friend regarding troubled times."

I glanced back and forth between them for a moment before I said, "So why haven't the Sidhe laid the smack down on the Red Court?"

Lily sighed. "A complicated matter."

"Just start at the beginning and explain it from there," I suggested.

"Which beginning?" she asked. "And whose?"

I felt my eyebrows arch up. "Hell's bells, Lily. I wasn't expecting the usual Sidhe word games from you."

Calm, remote beauty covered her face like a mask. "I know."

"Seems to me that you're a couple of points in the red when it comes to favors given and received," I said. "Between that mess in Oklahoma and your predecessor."

"I know," she said again, her expression showing me less than nothing.

I leaned back into my chair for a second, glaring at her, feeling that same old frustration rising. Damn, but I hated trying to deal with the Sidhe. Summer or Winter, they were both an enormous pain in the ass.

"Harry," Fix said with gentle emphasis. "She isn't always free to speak."

"Like hell she isn't," I said. "She's the Summer Lady."

"But Titania is the Summer Queen," Fix told me. "And if you'll forgive me for pointing out something so obvious, it wasn't so long ago that you murdered Titania's daughter."

"What does that have to do with anything," I began, but snapped my lips closed over the last word. Of course. When Lily had become the Summer Lady, she got the whole package—and it went way beyond simply turning her hair white. She would have to follow the bizarre set of limits and rules to which all of the Faerie Queens seemed bound. And, more importantly, it meant she would have to obey the more powerful Queens of Summer, Titania and Mother Summer.

"Are you telling me that Titania has ordered you both not to help me?" I asked them.

They stared back at me with faerie poker faces that told me nothing.

I nodded, beginning to understand. "You aren't permitted to speak officially for Summer. And Titania's laid some kind of compulsion on you both to prevent you from helping me on a personal level," I said. "Hasn't she?"

Had there been crickets, I would have heard them clearly. Had my table companions been statues, I'd have gotten more reaction from them.

"You're not supposed to help me. You're not supposed to tell me about the compulsion." I followed the chain of logic a step further. "But you want to help, so here you are. Which means that the only way I could get information out of you is to approach it indirectly. Or else the compulsion would force you to shut up. Am I close?"

Cheep-cheep. If it went on much longer, they'd have to worry about inbound pigeons.

I frowned a little and thought about it for a minute. Then I asked, "Theoretically speaking," I said, "what kinds of things might prevent Winter and Summer from reacting to an incursion by another nation?"

Lily's eyes sparkled, and she nodded to Fix. The little guy turned to me and said, "In theory, only a few things could do it. The simplest would be a lack of respect for the strength of the incurring nation. If the Queens considered them no threat, there would be no need to act."

"Uh-huh," I said. "Go on."

"A much more serious reason would be an issue of the balance of power between the Courts of Summer and Winter. Any reaction to the invasion would alter what resources one would have at hand. If one Court did not act in concert with the other, it would provide an ideal opportunity for a surprise assault while the other had its strategic back turned."

I rubbed my hands along my thighs, squinting one eye shut. "Let me see if I've put this together right. Summer's ready to throw down. But Winter isn't gonna help, because apparently they'd rather take a poke at you guys when you were focused on another threat."

I took Fix's silence as an affirmative.

"That's insane," I said. "If that happens, both Courts are going to suffer. Both of you will be weakened. No matter who came out on top, they'd be easy pickings for the Reds. Theoretically speaking."

"An imbalance between Winter and Summer is nothing new," Lily said. "It has existed since the time when we first met you, Harry. It continues today because of the fate of the current Winter Knight."

I grimaced. "Christ. He's still alive? After . . . what, almost four years?"

Fix shuddered. "I saw him once. The man was a psycho, a drug addict and a murderer—"

"And a rapist," Lily interjected in a quiet, sad voice.

"And that," Fix agreed, his expression grim. "I could break his neck and not lose a minute's sleep. But no one deserves"—he swallowed, his face going pale—"that."

"The moron betrayed Mab," I said quietly. "He knew the risks when he did it."

"No," Fix said, with another shudder. "Believe me, Harry. He didn't know what would happen to him. He couldn't have."

Fix's obvious discomfort made a certain impression on me, especially given that Mab had displayed an unnerving amount of interest in me, and that I still owed her a couple of favors. I shifted uneasily in my chair and tried to blow it off. "Whatever," I said. "There's a Summer Knight. There's a Winter Knight. What's unbalanced about that?"

"He isn't exerting his power," Fix replied. "He's a prisoner, and everyone knows it. He has no freedom, no will. He can't stand on the side of Winter as its champion. So far as the tension between the Courts goes, the Winter Knight might as well not exist."

"All right," I murmured. "Mab's got a man in the penalty box. She wants to take the offensive before Summer pushes a power play, and she's looking for ways to even the odds. If Summer goes running off to take on the Reds, it will give her a chance to strike." I shook my head. "I don't pretend to know Mab very well, but she isn't suicidal. If the imbalance is so dangerous, why is she keeping the Winter Knight alive to begin with? And she must see what the consequences of another Winter-Summer war would be." I looked back and forth between them. "Right?"

"Unfortunately," Lily said quietly, "our intelligence about the internal politics of Winter is very limited—and Mab is not the sort to reveal her mind to another. I do not know if she realizes the potential danger. Her actions of late have been . . ." She closed her eyes for a moment and then said, with some obvious effort, "Erratic."

I propped up my chin on the heel of my hand, thinking. "Mab's a lot of things," I said thoughtfully. "But she sure as hell isn't erratic. She's like some damned big glacier. Not a thing you can do to stop her, but at least you know just how she's going to move. What's the bard say? Constant as the northern star."

Fix frowned, as if struggling with an internal decision for a minute, then let out an exasperated sigh and said, "I think many who know the Sidhe would agree with you."

Which was neither a confirmation nor a denial—technically, at any rate. But then, Sidhe magic and bindings tended to lean heavily toward the technical details.

I sat back slowly again, thoughts flickering over dozens of ideas and bits of information, putting them together into a larger picture. And it wasn't a pretty one. The last time one of the Faerie Queens had come a little bit unbalanced, the situation had become a potential global catastrophe on the same order of magnitude as a middling large meteor impact or a limited nuclear exchange. And *that* had been the youngest Queen of the gentler and more reasonable Summer, Lily's predecessor. Aurora. The late Aurora, I suppose.

If Mab had blown a gasket, matters wouldn't be just as bad.

They would be worse.

A lot worse.

"I've got to know more about this one," I told them quietly.

"I know," Lily said. She lifted her hand to a temple and closed her eyes in a faint frown of pain. "But . . ." She shook her head and fell silent again as Titania's binding sealed her tongue.

I glanced at Fix, who managed to whisper, "Sorry, Harry," before he too closed his eyes and looked vaguely ill.

"I need answers," I murmured, thinking aloud. "But you can't give them to me. And there can't be all that many people who know what's going on."

Silence and faint expressions of pain. After a few seconds, Fix said, "I think we've done all we can here."

I racked my brains for a few seconds more and then said, "No, you haven't."

Lily opened her eyes and looked at me, arching a perfect, silver-white brow.

"I need someone with the right information and who isn't under a compulsion not to help me. And I can only think of one person who fits the bill."

Lily's eyes widened a second after I got done speaking.

"Can you do it?" I asked her. "Right now?"

She chewed her lower lip for a second, then nodded.

"Call her," I said.

Fix looked back and forth between us. "I don't understand. What are you doing?"

"Something stupid, probably," I said. "But this is too big. I need more information."

Lily closed her eyes and folded her hands on her lap,

her expression relaxing into one of deep concentration. I could feel the subtle stir of energy around her.

My stomach rumbled. I asked Mac to whip me up a steak sandwich and settled down to wait.

It didn't take long. My sandwich wasn't halfway done when Mouse let out a sudden, rumbling growl of warning, and the temperature in the bar dropped about ten degrees. The whirling ceiling fans let out mechanical moans of protest and spun faster. Then the door opened and let in sunlight made wan by a patch of dreary grey clouds. The light cast a slender black silhouette.

Fix's eyes narrowed. His hands slid casually out of sight beneath the table, and he said, "Oh. *Her.*"

The young woman who entered the bar could have been Lily's sister. She had the same exotic beauty, the same canted, feline eyes, the same pale, flawless skin. But this one's hair was worn in long, ragged strands of varying lengths, like a Raggedy Ann doll, each one dyed a slightly different color from frozen seas—pale blues and greens, as though each had borrowed its color from a different glacier. Her eyes were a cold, brilliant shade of green, almost entirely darkened by pupils dilated as though with drugs or arousal. A slender silver hoop gleamed at one side of her nose, and a collar of black leather studded with silver snowflakes encircled the graceful line of her slender throat. She wore sandals and cut-off blue jean shorts—very cut-off, and very tight. A tight, white T-shirt strained across her chest, and read, in pale blue letters stretched into intriguing curves, "YOUR BOYFRIEND WANTS ME."

She prowled across the room to us, all hips and lips and fascinating eyes, looking far too young to move with such wanton sensuality. I knew better. She could have been a century old. She chose to look the way she did because of what she was: the Winter Lady, youngest

Queen of the Unseelie Court, Mab's understudy in wickedness and power. When she walked by the flowers that had bloomed in Lily's presence, they froze over, withered, and died. She gave them no more notice than Lily had.

"Harry Dresden," she said, her voice low, lulling, and sweet.

And I said, "Hello, Maeve."

Chapter

Twenty

Maeve stared at me for a long minute and licked her lips. "Look at you," she all but purred. "All pent up like that. You haven't had a woman in ages, have you?"

I hadn't. I really, really hadn't. But that wasn't the kind of thinking that a professional investigator allowed to clog up the gears in his brain. I could have said something back, but I decided that if I ignored the taunt, maybe she'd get bored and leave me alone. So instead of taking up the verbal épée, I rose and drew out a chair for her, politely. "Sit with us, Maeve?"

Her head tilted almost all the way to her shoulder. She stared at me with those intense green eyes. "Just boiling over. Maybe you and I should have a private talk. Just the two of us."

My libido seconded the suggestion, and heartily.

My libido and I generally don't see eye to eye. Dammit.

"I'd rather just sit and have a nice chat," I said to her.

"Liar," Maeve said, smiling.

I sighed. "All right. There are a lot of things I'd love to do. But the only thing that's going to happen is a nice chat. So you might as well sit down and let me get you a drink."

Her head tilted the other way. Her hips shifted in a kind of counterpoint that drew the eye. "How long has it been for you, wizard? How long since you sated yourself."

The answer was depressing. "Last time I saw Susan, I guess."

Maeve made a disgusted sound. "No, not *love*, wizard. Need. Flesh."

"The two aren't mutually exclusive," I said.

She waved that off with an expression of contempt. "I want an answer."

"Looks to me like there's all kinds of things you want that you aren't going to get," I told her. I glanced at Fix and Lily, throwing a mute appeal into it.

Fix gave me an apologetic shrug and Lily sighed. "You might as well indulge her, Harry. She's as stubborn as any of us, the only one who might give you the answers you need, and she knows it."

I looked back at Maeve, who gave me that same eerie, intensely sensual smile. "Tell me, mortal. When was the last time flesh, new and strange to your hand, lay quivering beneath you, hmm?" She leaned down until her eyes were inches from mine. I could smell winter mint and something lush and corrupt, like rotted flowers, on her breath. "When was the last time you could taste and feel some little lovely's cries?"

I regarded her without any expression and said, in a gentle voice, "Technically? When I killed Aurora."

Maeve's expression flickered with an instant of uncertainty.

"You remember Aurora," I told her quietly. "The last Summer Lady. Your peer. Your equal. When she died, she'd been cut several dozen times with cold iron. She was bleeding out. But she was still trying to stick a knife in Lily. So I tackled her and held her down. She kept struggling until she lost too much blood. And then she died in the grass on the hill of the Stone Table."

Dead silence filled the whole place.

"It sort of surprised me," I said, never putting any particular emotion on the words. "How fast it happened. It surprised her, too. She was confused when she died."

Maeve only stared at me.

"I never wanted to kill her. But she didn't leave me any choice." I let the silence fill the room for a moment and stared at Maeve's eyes.

The Winter Lady swallowed and eased her weight a tiny bit away from me.

Then I gestured with one hand at the chair I still held out for her and said, "Let's be polite to one another, Maeve. Please."

She took a slow breath, soulless, inhuman eyes on mine, and then said, "I know now why Mab wants you." She straightened and gave me an odd little bow, which might have looked more courtly had she been wearing a gown. Then she sat and said, "Does the barkeep still have those sweet-lemon chips of ice?"

"Of course," I said. "Mac. Another lemonade for the Lady, please?"

Mac provided it in his usual silence. As he did, the few people who were in the place cleared out. Most of the magical community of Chicago knew the Ladies by reputation, if not on sight, and they wanted nothing to do with any kind of incident between Winter and Summer. They were safer if they were never noticed.

Hell, if I could have snuck out, I would have led the way. When I'd defeated Aurora, there had been a healthy chunk of luck involved. I caught her with a sucker punch. If she'd been focused on taking me out instead of finishing her scheme, I doubt I would have survived the evening. Sure, I might have stared Maeve down, but ultimately I was bluffing—trying to fool the oncoming shark into thinking I might be something that could eat it. If the shark decided to start taking bites anyhow, things would get unpleasant for me.

But this time, at least, the shark didn't know that.

Maeve wrapped her lips idly around the straw, and sipped. Then she settled back into her seat, chewing. Crunching sounds came from her mouth. The lemonade had frozen solid when it passed her lips.

Which made me feel pretty damned smart for avoiding the whole sexual temptation issue.

Maeve looked at Lily steadily as she chewed, and then said, to me, "You know, my last Knight often dragged this one before the Court for performances. All kinds of performances. Some of them hurt. And some of them didn't. Though she still cried out prettily enough." She smiled, her tone polite and conversational. "Do you remember the night he made you dance for me in the red shoes, Lily?"

Lily's green eyes settled on Maeve, calm and placid as a forest pool.

Maeve's smile sharpened. "Do you remember what I did to you after?"

Lily smiled, a tired little expression, and shook her head. "I'm sorry, Maeve. I know how much pleasure you take in gloating, but you can't hurt me with that now. That Lily is no more."

Maeve narrowed her eyes, and then her gaze shifted to Fix. "And this one. I've seen this little man weeping like a child. Begging for mercy."

Fix sipped at his lemonade and said, "For the love of God, Maeve. Would you give the Evil Kinkstress act a rest? It gets tired pretty fast."

The Winter Lady let out an exasperated breath, put down her drink, and folded her arms sullenly across her chest. "Very well," Maeve said, her tone petulant. "What is it you wish to know, wizard?"

"I'd like to know why Mab hasn't been striking back at the Red Court after they trespassed on Sidhe territory during the battle last year."

Maeve arched a brow at me. "That is knowledge, and therefore power. What are you prepared to trade for it?"

"Forgetfulness," I said.

Maeve tilted her head. "I can think of nothing in particular I would like to forget."

"I can think of something you want me to forget, Maeve."

"Can you?"

I smiled, with teeth. "I'd be willing to forget what you did at Billy and Georgia's wedding."

"Pardon?" Maeve said. "I don't seem to recall being present."

She knew the score. She knew that I knew it, too. Her legality pissed me off. "Of course," I replied. "You weren't there. But your handmaiden was. Jenny Greenteeth."

Maeve's lips parted in sudden surprise.

"I saw through her glamour. Didn't you know who shut her down?" I asked her, lifting my own eyebrows in faux innocence. "That was petty cruelty, Maeve, even for you. Trying to ruin their marriage."

"Your wolf children did me a petty wrong," Maeve replied. "They killed a favorite hireling of the Winter Court."

"They owed their loyalty to Dresden when they killed the Tigress," Lily murmured. "Even as did the Little Folk he used against Aurora. They acted with his consent and upon his will, Maeve. You know our laws."

Maeve gave Lily a dirty look that was almost human.

"For what happened that night, they were mine." I put my hands flat on the table and leaned a little toward Maeve, speaking with as much quiet intensity as I could. "I protect what is mine. You should know that by now. I have lawful reason for a quarrel with you."

Maeve's attention moved back to me, and her expression became remote and alien. "What is it you propose?"

"I'm willing to let things go as they are, all accounts settled, in exchange for an honest answer to my question." I settled back in my chair and asked, "Why hasn't Winter moved against the Red Court?"

Maeve regarded me with an odd little twinkle in her eye, then nodded and said, "Mab has not allowed it."

Fix and Lily traded a quick look of surprise.

"Sooth," Maeve said, nodding, evidently enjoying their reaction. "The Queen has readied her forces to strike at Summer, and has furthermore given specific orders preventing her captains from conducting operations against the Red Court."

"That's madness," Lily said quietly.

Maeve folded her hands on the table, frowning at something far away, and said, "It may well be. Dark things stir in Winter's heart. Things even I have never before seen. Dangerous things. I believe they are a portent."

I tilted my head a little, focused on her. "How so?"

"What Aurora attempted was insane. Even among the Sidhe," Maeve replied. "Her actions could have thrown enormous forces out of balance, to the ruin of all."

"Her heart was in the right place," Fix said, his tone mildly defensive.

"Maybe," I told him, as gently as I could. "But good intent doesn't amount to much when the consequences are epically screwed up."

Maeve shook her head. "Hearts. Good. Evil. Mortals are always concerned with such nonsense." She abruptly rose, her mind clearly elsewhere.

Something in her expression or manner gave me a sudden sense that she was worried. Deeply, truly worried. Little Miss Overlord was frightened.

"These mortal notions," Maeve said. "Good, evil, love. All those other things your kind natter on about. Are they perhaps contagious?"

I rose with her, politely. "Some would say so," I told her.

She grimaced. "In the time since her death, I have often thought to myself that Aurora was stricken with some mortal madness. I believe the Queen of Air and Darkness has been taken by a similar contagion." She suddenly shuddered and said, voice curt, "I have answered you with truth, and more than needed be said. Does that satisfy the accounting, mortal?"

"Aye," I told her, nodding. "Good enough for me."

"Then I take my leave." She turned, took half a step, and there was a sudden gust of frozen air that knocked her mostly full glass of lemonade onto the floor. It froze in a lumpy puddle. Somewhere between tabletop and floor, Maeve vanished.

The three of us sat there quietly for a moment.

"She was lying," Fix said.

"She can't lie," Lily and I said at exactly the same moment. Lily yielded the issue to me with a gesture of her hand, and I told Fix, "She can't speak an outright lie, Fix. None of the Sidhe can. You know that."

He frowned and made a frustrated, helpless little gesture with his hand. "But . . . Mab? Insane?"

"It does fit with our concerns," Lily told him quietly.

Fix looked a little green around the edges. "I loved

her like a sister, but Aurora's madness was bad enough. If *Mab* sets out to send the world on a downward spiral . . . I mean, I can't even imagine the kind of things she could do."

"I can," I said quietly. "I would suggest that you relay word of this to Titania, Lady. And take that as official concern from the Council. Please also convey the message that the Council is naturally interested in preserving the balance in Faerie. It would be of value to all of us to cooperate in order to learn more."

Lily nodded once at me. "Indeed. I will do so." She shivered and closed her eyes for a second, her expression distressed. "Harry, I'm very sorry, but the bindings on me . . . I stretch the bounds of my proper place."

Fix nodded decisively and rose. He took Lily's arm. "I wish we could have done more to help you."

"Don't worry about it," I said, rising politely to my feet again. "You did what you could. I appreciate it."

Lily gave me a strained smile. She and Fix departed, quick and quiet. The door never opened, but a breath later they were both gone. Mouse sat there next to the table, cocking his head left and right, his ears attentively forward, as though trying to figure that one out.

I sat at the table and sipped lemonade without much enthusiasm. More trouble in Faerie. Bigger trouble in Faerie. And I'd be willing to bet dollars to navel lint that I knew exactly which stupid son of a bitch the Council would expect to start poking his nose around in it.

I put the lemonade down. It suddenly tasted very sour.

Mac arrived. He took my lemonade. He replaced it with a beer. I flicked the top off with my thumb and put it away in a long pull. It was warm and it tasted too bitter, but the gentle bite of the alcohol in it was pleasant enough to make me want another.

Mac showed up with another.

Mac can sometimes be downright angelic.

"They've changed," I told him. "Fix and Lily. It's like they aren't even the same people anymore."

Mac grunted once. Then he said, "They grew up."

"Maybe that's it." I fell back into a brooding silence, and Mac left me to it. I finished the second beer more slowly, but I didn't have a lot of time to lose. I nodded my thanks to Mac, left money on the table, and took up Mouse's leash. We headed for the door.

I had other business to take care of. Nebulous maybe-threats would have to wait for the monsters I was sure would show up in a few hours. At least I'd gotten out of the whole situation without someone trying to kill me or declaring war on the Council. I'd had a civil conversation with both Lady Winter and Lady Summer and come away from it unscathed.

As I walked toward the door, though, an idle thought gnawed at me.

It had hardly been like pulling out teeth at all.

Chapter

Twenty-one

I headed back for SplatterCon!!! before the afternoon was half gone, this time with my backpack of wizard toys, my staff, my blasting rod, my dog, my gun, and a partridge in a pear tree. I didn't have a concealed-carry permit for the .44, but working on the theory that it was better to have the gun and not need it than to need it and not have it, I put it in the backpack.

When I got to SplatterCon!!!, I decided that it very well might have been better not to have the damned gun on me; there was something of a police presence in evidence.

Two patrol cars were parked in plain sight outside the hotel, and one cop in uniform stood, sweating and miserable-looking, outside the doors. As I paid off the cabby, I picked out at least two loiterers in street clothes who were paying too much attention to who and what approached the building to be casual strollers taking advantage of spots of shade outside the hotel. I clipped on my SplatterCon!!! name tag.

The cop's eyes flicked over me and I could all but see him take stock of me—tall guy, gaunt, mussed hair, dark eyes, big dog, sticks, backpack, one hand in a leather glove . . . and a horror convention name tag. Evidently, in this guy's head, a name tag gave you carte blanche to look weird without being threatening, because when his eyes got to that, he just traded a nod with me and waved me through.

Inside, not only was the convention in full swing, but they had added a press conference to it to boot. The conference wing outside the room where the killer struck was packed with a half circle of reporters and photographers, while industrious satellite personnel held up lights and even a couple of boom microphones. From the door I could see three more uniformed officers. Between the cops, the conference, and the passersby, that whole section of the hotel was packed with a lot of noisy people. The air-conditioning had been pushed well beyond its limits, and it was stuffy and smelled like most crowded buildings.

Mouse sneezed and looked mournful. I agreed with him.

Murphy appeared out of the crowd and made her way to me. She gave me a tight nod, and knelt down to speak to Mouse and scratch behind his ears. "How'd your meeting go?" she asked.

"Survived it. Storm clouds on the horizon." I looked around the place a minute more and said, "For crying out loud, it's a zoo."

"It gets better," Murphy said. "I've been speaking with the convention staff, and they say that since the story hit the news and the radio stations at noon, they've almost doubled the number of attendees."

"Crap," I sighed.

"There's more. Greene called in the Feds," she said.

I frowned. "Last time the Feds showed up was less than fun."

"Tell me about it." She hesitated and then said, "Rick is with them."

I blinked at her for a second, and then remembered. "Oh, right. The ex."

"Ex-husband," Murphy said, her tone sour. Her back was rigidly straight, and her eyes flickered with stormy emotions. "Current brother-in-law."

"Which is icky," I said.

"And I don't like him being here," Murphy said. "But it isn't my call. And it's possible that I have issues."

I snorted.

She gave me a brief smile. "This has been splashy enough that they've got one of the major forensics units from the East Coast on the way."

I scowled. "Maybe he should have blown a few trumpets, too. Or brought in a marching band. I think if he hurries, he can probably rent some of those big swiveling spotlights before dark."

She rolled her eyes. "I get the point, Harry. You don't like all the noise."

"I don't like all the potential victims," I said. "Fifty bucks says the extra attendees are mostly minors."

"No bet," she replied. "Does it matter?"

"Maybe. In general, young people, especially adolescents, feel emotions much more intensely. The whole hormone thing. It can make them easier targets. Richer sources of energy."

"Then why did it hit an old geezer like Pell first?"

I opened my mouth, and then closed it again. "Good point."

"Besides," she continued, "isn't it a good thing if more people are paying attention? From what you've told me, things from the spooky side of the street don't like crowds."

"In general, no," I said. "But the place wasn't exactly a ghost town yesterday when the phobophage showed up."

"You think it will appear right in front of all these people?" she asked.

"I think crowds aren't going to deter it. I think that if something bad happens, the more people there are around, the more fear it's going to generate and the more our killer gets to eat. And a panic with more people means even more people get hurt."

Murphy's pale golden brows knitted into a frown. "So, what options can you give me?"

"There's no guarantee, but I think we'll have until nightfall."

"Why?"

"Because it will be stronger after dark."

Murphy frowned. "You think that's why Pell survived his attack," she murmured. "It was still daylight."

"Got it in one," I said. "Assuming we have until sundown, it gives us a little time to work."

"Doing what?"

"Setting up some wards," I said.

"Like at your place?"

I shook my head. "Nothing that complex. There's no time. I can't build a moat around this place, but I think I can throw together a web that will let us know when and where something comes over from the Nevernever. I'll need to walk around a lot of the building to cover it all."

She nodded. "That doesn't address the crowd issue."

I grimaced. "You know anyone in the fire department?"

"A cousin," she said.

"This place must be over maximum occupancy. Maybe if the fire marshal heard about how crowded it was, they'd clear at least some of these people out. We only need a crowd big enough to tempt the killer in."

She nodded. "I'll see to it."

"And I know it's a long shot, but has CPD turned up anything? Or the ME?"

"Nothing on the autopsy. They didn't give this one to Butters. Brioche handled it, and he didn't find anything out of the ordinary."

"Naturally," I sighed. "Greene?"

"Theories. He had some vague notion that the attack might have been some kind of publicity stunt to attract attention to the convention."

"That's a little cynical," I said.

"Greene isn't a believer," Murphy said. "And he's a trained investigator looking for a solid motive. If he accepts that the killer was just some kind of lunatic, it means he's got almost nothing to work with. So he's grasping at straws and hoping he can find something familiar he can use to nail the killer fast."

I grunted. "Guess I can see that."

"I don't envy him," Murphy said. "I don't like him much, but he's a cop, and he's in a tight spot. Chances are, there's not a damned thing he could do about it. And he doesn't even know it."

There was a little extra weight on the last phrase, something that contained personal pain.

Murphy had faced the same situations as Greene, more or less. Something wild happened, and none of it made any sense. Murphy had her first face-off with the supernatural while she was still a beat cop on patrol. It gave her an advantage as a detective, because at least she knew how much she didn't know. Greene didn't even have that much going for him. I hated to see her like that, feeling helpless to do anything. Hurting. Even if only in memory.

"How about you?" I asked. "You see anything that you think is worth mentioning?"

"Not yet. Someone around here has got to know something useful—even if they don't know that they do." She tilted her head and frowned at me. "Wait. You're asking *me*?"

I shrugged a shoulder. "Murph, you've seen as much weird as most wizards. I think you're more capable than you know."

She studied my face for a long moment. "What do you mean?"

I shrugged again. "I mean that you've been there a time or two. You know what it's like when something is lurking around. There's commonality to it. You'll know it when you feel it."

"What? Am I supposed to be a wizard now?"

I grinned. "Just a savvy cop chick, Murph."

"Cop chick?" she asked, menace in her voice.

"Sorry," I said. "*Police* chick."

She grunted. "That's better."

"Just don't ignore your instincts," I said. "They're there for a reason."

Murphy wasn't listening to that last part, because she'd turned her head sharply to one side, blue eyes narrowing as she focused on a man who had emerged from a conference room doorway and was slipping down the hall.

And Mouse let out a low growl.

"Who's that?" I asked Murphy.

"Darby Crane," Murphy said.

"Ah," I said. "The horror movie director."

Mouse growled again. Murphy and he started after Crane.

Why fight the inevitable? I started walking before Mouse pulled my arms out of their sockets. "Hey, howsabout we go talk to him?"

"You think?" Murphy said.

"Take him. I'll back you up."

She nodded, without turning around. "Excuse me," she told a gang of conventiongoers in front of her. "Coming through, please."

We tried to hurry through the crowd, but it was like trying to run in chest-deep water. The faster you try to move, the more resistance there is. Crane moved through them like an eel, a spare man of medium height in slacks and a dark blazer. Murphy forged ahead, making room for me to follow, while I put my height to good use to keep an eye on Crane.

He beat us to a comparatively empty side hallway that led back to ground-floor guest rooms and elevators. By the time we got into the clear, the elevator doors had opened. Murphy hurried forward and shot a glance over her shoulder at me, then jerked her chin at the elevators.

I grinned. There are times when I hate it that technology has such problems operating around wizards. And then there are the times when it's sort of fun.

I made a mild effort of will, focused my thoughts on the elevators, and murmured, *"Hexus."* Nebulous and unseen energy fluttered down the hallway, and when the hex hit the elevators there was a sudden hiss of sparks at one edge of the panel with the call button, and an oozing smoke dribbled out a moment later. The doors started to close, then a bell went *bing.* The doors sprang open again. That happened a couple of more times before Murphy closed to the elevator and caught up to Darby Crane.

I slowed my pace, holding on to Mouse, and lurked several feet away, trying to blend in by reading a wall full of flyers announcing various parties at the convention.

Crane was a surprisingly good-looking man—slender, stark cheekbones, and his demeanor was more like an actor's than that of someone on the production side. His dark hair was in a short, neat cut, dark eyes deep-set and opaque, and he carried himself in a posture that read nothing but relaxed nonaggression.

Before I'd finished looking him over, I was sure that the whole thing was a calculated lie. There was cruelty lurking below the calm of his features, contempt hiding within the modest posture of his body. As Murphy approached, he stepped out of the elevator, frowning at the smoke. His eyes snapped to her, and around the hallway at once. There were several other people standing not far away, outside of a guest room with an open door.

He judged them, then Murphy for a moment, and then turned to face her, his mouth settling into a polite, bland little perjury of a smile.

"So hard to rely upon technology these days," he said, his glance moving over me as part of the background scenery. I thought. He had a surprisingly deep, resonant voice. "May I help you, Officer?"

"Lieutenant, actually," she told him without rancor. "My name is Karrin Murphy. I'm with . . ."

"Chicago Police Department Special Investigations," Crane said. "I know."

Alarm bells went off in my head. I doubted Crane would recognize it, but Murphy's stance shifted subtly, becoming more wary. "Have we met, Mr. Crane?"

"In a way. I've seen secondhand copies of the film of you gunning down a madman and some sort of animal several years ago. Very impressive, Lieutenant. Have you ever considered work in film?"

She shook her head. "I've been told the camera adds ten pounds. I have problems enough. May I take a few moments of your time, Mister Crane?"

He grinned at her, then, a grin I'm sure he meant to be boyish and flirty. The weasel. "I suppose that depends on what you intend to do with them."

Murphy studied his face for just a moment, as though in wary amusement. "I had a few questions regarding the incident here, and I hope that you can help me out with them."

"I can't imagine what I know that would help you," Crane replied. He glanced at the unmoving elevator doors and sighed. "Bother." He drew a small black cell phone from his jacket pocket, hit a button without looking, and lifted it to his ear. Then he lowered it again and frowned down at it in silence.

Hah. Take that, weasel.

"It won't take much of your time," Murphy said. "I'm sure that you can see how important it is for us to be thorough in this investigation. We would all hate for anyone else to be harmed."

"I'm sure I don't know anything of any importance, Lieutenant," Crane said, his voice turning a little impatient. "I was present during the blackout last night, but I was already in my room. I didn't even come downstairs until this morning."

"I see. Did anyone see you at that time?"

Crane let out a little laugh. "Am I a suspect, that I need an alibi?"

"As a celebrity guest, it's entirely possible that the person or persons responsible for this attack might have an unhealthy interest in you," Murphy replied, matching his fake laugh with her politely professional smile. "I certainly don't mean to imply any sort of accusation— only concern for your safety."

Someone shoved open a door that showed a set of stairs behind it, and a small man in an expensive grey suit emerged from it. He was sort of frog-faced—he had the mouth of someone much larger than he, almost grotesquely thick and wide. He had fine black hair, all limp and stringy, and someone had cut it with the ancient but trusty salad-bowl method. He had bulgy, watery eyes that required extra-large, wide-rimmed glasses to properly encircle.

"Ah, Mr. Crane," the newcomer said. He had a wheezy, nasal voice. "I received your call, but it was apparently cut off just as I answered."

Crane took out his phone again and tossed it underhand to the newcomer. "It seems to have died quite abruptly, Lucius. Like this elevator."

The man caught it and frowned at the phone, then at Murphy with equal amounts of disapproval. "I see."

"Lieutenant Murphy, may I present Lucius Glau, my personal advisor and legal counsel."

Mouse tensed as Glau turned to regard Murphy with his froggy eyes. The little lawyer made a swallowing sound in his throat, and then said, "Is my client under arrest?"

"No," she said. "Naturally n—"

"Then I must insist that this conversation be cut short," Glau said over her. For a pasty little guy, he had a lot of confidence. He squared off in front of Murphy, just to one side of Crane. Murphy's arms relaxed to her sides and I saw her blue eyes flick down to the floor and back up, gauging distances. The tension level went higher.

"We were just talking," Murphy told Glau. I'd seen her wearing that look, right before she went for her gun, more than once. "In an amiable and cooperative fashion."

"As I informed both the FBI and the investigator in charge of the scene with Chicago's police department, my client was in his rooms all night and neither witnessed what happened nor even knew of what had transpired until he came down to breakfast this morning." Glau's voice was clipped, his bulgy eyes impossible to read. I got the feeling it was the expression he used whenever he did anything, be it eating ice cream or drowning puppies. "Continued contact could well be construed as harassment."

"Lucius, Lucius," Crane said, holding out his hand between them, his voice soothing. "Honestly, you react so strongly to the smallest things." He turned that dazzling smile on Murphy and said, "I'm sorry. Lucius has worked for me for a very long time, and he's seen a number of unreasonable people approach me. I certainly don't think of the attentions of so striking a woman as harassment."

Murphy's eyes left Glau for a second as she cocked a golden brow at Crane. "Really?"

"Truly," Crane said, the model of modern gallantry. "Lucius is doubtless concerned about my timetable for today, and I would hate to disappoint any of the fans here to meet me by falling behind my schedule."

He glanced at Froggy as he spoke, and Froggy took a very small step back from Murphy.

Crane nodded at him, continuing to speak. "But if you would permit it, perhaps you would care to let me get you a drink of something later this evening, by way of apology?"

Murphy hesitated, which wasn't much like her. "I don't know . . ." she said.

Crane extended his hand to her to be shaken, still smiling. "If you still had questions, I'd be happy to answer them then. Please, as a token of my intentions, I insist. I would hate you to have the wrong impression of me."

Murphy gave him a look of wary amusement and lifted her hand.

I'm not sure how I got across that much carpet that fast, but I put my hand on Murphy's shoulder and gripped lightly just before she touched him. She froze, sensing the warning in the gesture, and drew her hand back.

Crane's eyes narrowed, studying me, his hand still sticking out. "And who is this?"

"Harry Dresden," I said.

Crane went still. Not still like people go still, where you can see them blinking and swaying slightly and adjusting their balance. He went still like corpses and plastic dressing dummies, and said nothing.

As I am a highly experienced investigator, I drew the conclusion that he recognized the name.

Froggy made a gulping sound in his throat, bulging eyes switching to me. I thought he shrunk in on himself a little, as if suddenly losing an inch or two of height—or tensing to crouch.

He recognized it, too. I felt famous.

Mouse let out a relaxed ripsaw of a growl, so low that it could hardly be heard.

Froggy's eyes went to the dog and widened. He shot a look at Crane.

Everyone froze like that for a moment. Crane and Murphy still smiled their professional smiles. Froggy looked froglike. I went for bored. But I felt my heart speed up as my instincts told me that violence was a hell of a lot closer to the surface than it looked.

"There are witnesses here, Dresden," Crane said. "You can't move on me. It would be seen."

I tilted my head and pursed my lips thoughtfully. "You're right. And you're a public figure. Which means this is a great opportunity for advertising. I haven't been on TV since the last time I was on the *Larry Fowler Show*."

His expression changed then, that cold sneer coming out of the background to twist his lips. "You wouldn't dare reveal yourself to the world."

I snorted at him and said, "Go read the yellow pages in your room. I'm in there. Under 'Wizards.' "

Froggy gulped again.

"You're insane," Crane said.

"Wizards is the kway-zee-est people," I confirmed. "And you don't look very much like a Darby."

Crane's chin lifted, his eyes glittering with some sort of sudden approval. I had no idea why. Dammit, I hate it when someone knows more than me about exactly how deep a hole I'm digging under myself. "No? And what does a Darby look like?"

"I confess, the only one I ever saw was in that leprechaun movie with Sean Connery," I said. "Call it an instinct."

He pursed his lips and fell silent. We all enjoyed another two minutes of wordless, increasingly tense standoff.

Then Murphy said, deadpan, "Say, ten o'clock for that drink, Darby? The hotel's lounge? We'd hate to keep you from your busy schedule."

He glanced from Murphy to me and back, and then lowered his hand. He gave her a little bow of the head, then turned and walked away, back toward the crowd.

Froggy watched us for a three count, then turned and hurried after his boss, checking frequently over his shoulder.

I exhaled slowly, and leaned against the wall. Adrenaline without an outlet is a funny thing. The long muscles in my legs twitched and flexed without me telling them to, and the lights in the hallway suddenly seemed a little too bright. My bruised head twinged some more.

Murphy just stood there, not moving, but I could hear her consciously regulating her breathing, keeping it smooth.

Mouse sat down and looked bored, but his ears kept twitching in the direction the pair had vanished.

"Well," Murphy said a second later, keeping her voice low. "What was *that* all about?"

"We almost started a fight," I said.

"I noticed that," Murphy said, her tone patient. "But why?"

"He's spooky," I murmured.

She frowned, looking over her shoulder and up at me. "What is he?"

"I told you. Spooky." I shook my head. "Other than that I don't know."

She blinked. "What do you mean, you don't know?"

"I don't know," I said. "Something about him hit me wrong. When he offered you his hand, it seemed . . . off. Dangerous."

Murphy shook her head. "I figured he was going to go for the hold-and-caress routine," she said. "It's a little bit insulting, but it isn't all that dangerous."

"Unless maybe it is," I said.

"You're sure he's from your side of things?" she asked.

"Yeah. He recognized me. He started pulling out the standard Old World reasons for avoiding public confrontation. And Mouse didn't like him—or his lawyer, either."

"Vampire?" she asked.

"Could be," I said, chewing on my lip. "Could be a lot of things. Hell, could be human, for that matter. Without knowing more we shouldn't make any assumptions."

"Think he's involved in the attacks?"

"I like him for it," I said. "If I was making the call alone, he'd definitely be our asshole. He's got all the earmarks."

"If he's the guy, he's out of my reach," she said. "He's got a hair-trigger attorney and has already spoken to Greene and Rick. Any police pressure I brought against him would be harassment. Greene won't act on my suspicions."

"Well," I said. "Good thing I'm not Greene."

Chapter

Twenty-two

Murphy and I walked around the hotel, and as we did I popped open a fresh can of blue Play-Doh. At the corners of major intersections and at the exterior exits, I pinched off bits and plunked them down on top of the molding over doorways, inside flowerpots, inside fire extinguisher cabinets, and anywhere else where they wouldn't be easily or immediately noticed. I made sure to leave plenty of them in unnoticed little spots along the hallways chiefly in use for the convention, especially outside the rooms that the schedule designated as showing films as evening approached.

"What are we doing again?" Murphy asked.

"Setting up a spell," I said.

"With Play-Doh."

"Yes."

She gave me a level look.

I shook out the can that still had most of the original material in it, and showed it to her. "The little pieces I've been leaving around are part of this piece. See?"

"Not yet," she said.

"They used to be one piece. Even when they're separated, they still have a thaumaturgical connection to the original," I told her. "It means that I'll be able to use the big piece to reach out and connect to the little pieces."

"That's what you meant by a web?"

"Yes. I'll be able to . . ." I twisted up my face, searching for the words to explain. "I can extend energy out to all the smaller pieces. I'll set it up so that if one of the little pieces picks up on a disturbance of the energies, I'll be able to feel it through the larger piece."

"Like . . . seismographs, sort of," Murphy said.

"Yeah," I said. "And we use blue Play-Doh. Blue for defense."

She arched a brow at me. "Does the color really matter?"

"Yes," I said, then thought about it for a second. "Well, probably no. But yes, for me."

"Huh?"

"A lot of the use of magic is all tied up with your emotions. With what you believe is real. When I was younger, I learned a lot of stuff, like the role of colors in the casting of spells. Green for fertility and prosperity, red for passion and energy, white for purity, black for vengeance, and so on. It could be that the color doesn't matter at all—but if I expect the spell to work because of the color used, then that color is important. If I don't believe in it, the spell won't ever get off the ground."

"Like Dumbo's magic feather?" Murphy asked. "It was his confidence that was really important?"

"Yes," I said. "The feather was just a symbol—but it was an *important* symbol."

I gestured with the can. "So I use blue, because I don't have to do too much introspection, and I don't introduce new doubts in a crisis situation. And because it was cheap at Wal-Mart."

Murphy laughed. "Wal-Mart, huh?"

"Wizarding doesn't pay much," I said. "You'd be surprised how much stuff I get from Wal-Mart." I checked a clock on the wall. "We've got about two hours before the first movie starts showing."

She nodded. "What do you need?"

"A quiet space to work in," I told her. "At least six or seven feet across. The more private and secure, the better. I've got to assume that the bad guy knows I'm around here somewhere. I don't want to get a machete in the back when I'm busy running the spell."

"How long do you need to set it up?"

I shrugged. "Twenty minutes, give or take. What I'm really concerned about is—"

"Mister Dresden!" called a voice from across the crowded convention hallway. I looked up to see Sandra Marling hurrying through the crowd toward me. The convention's chairwoman looked exhausted and too nervous to be awake, much less standing, much less politely pushing her way through a crowd, but she did it anyway. She still wore the same black T-shirt with the red SplatterCon!!! logo on it, presumably the same I'd seen her in the night before.

"Ms. Marling," I said, nodding to her as she approached. "Good afternoon."

She shook her head wearily. "I'm such . . . this is such an enormous amount of . . . but I don't know who else I can turn to about this." Her words failed her, and she started trembling with nerves and weariness.

I traded a frown with Murphy. "Sandra. What's wrong?"

"It's Molly," she said.

I frowned. "What about her?"

"She came here from the hospital a couple of hours ago. The police came to talk to her and I don't think she's come out since then, and none of the officers I've spoken to know where she is. I think—"

"Sandra." I told her, "Take a breath. Slow down. Do you know where Molly is?"

The woman closed her eyes and shook her head,

bringing herself under control, lowering her voice several pitches. "They're still . . . interrogating her, I think? Isn't that what they say? When they try to scare you and ask questions?"

I narrowed my eyes. "Yeah," I said. "Was she arrested?"

Sandra shook her head jerkily. "I don't think so. They didn't handcuff her or read from that little card or anything. Can they *do* that? Just drag her into a room?"

"We'll see," I said. "Which room?"

"Other wing, second door on the right," she said.

I nodded, slung my pack off my back, and took out a small notebook. I scribbled some phone numbers and names on a page, and gave it to Sandra. "Call both of these people."

She blinked at the paper. "What do I tell them?"

"The truth. Tell them what's going on and that Harry Dresden said they need to get down here immediately."

Sandra blinked down at the page. "What are you going to do?"

"Oh, you know. The usual," I said. "Get to that phone."

"I'll catch up in a minute," Murphy said.

I nodded, slung the pack back on, jerked my head at Mouse, and started walking with purposeful strides toward the knot of reporters that had begun to dissolve at the conclusion of the official statements to the press. My dog fell in to pace at my side until I spotted Lydia Stern at the rear of the crowd.

Lydia Stern was a formidable woman, a reporter for the *Midwestern Arcane,* a yellow journal based out of Chicago that did its best to report on the supernatural. Sometimes they managed to get close to the truth, but more often they ran stories that had headlines like Lizard Baby Born in Trailer Park, or maybe Bigfoot and the

Chupacabra, the Unholy Alliance. By and large, the stories were amusing and fairly harmless, but once in a while someone stumbled into something strange and it made it into the paper. Susan Rodriguez had been a lead reporter for the *Arcane,* until she'd run into exactly the wrong story. Now she lived her life somewhere in South America, fighting off the infection in her soul that wanted to turn her into one of the Red Court while she and her half-vampire buddies campaigned against their would-be recruiters.

When Lydia Stern took over Susan's old job a couple of years back, her reporting had taken a different angle. She'd investigated strange events and then demanded to know why the appropriate institutions had been ignoring them. The woman had a scathing intellect and penetrating wit, and she employed both liberally and with considerable panache in her writing. She was unafraid to challenge anyone in her articles, from some small-town animal control unit to the FBI.

It was a shame she was working at a rag like the *Arcane* instead of at a reputable paper in DC or New York. She'd have been a Pulitzer nominee inside of five years. City officials who had to deal with the cases I'd brushed up against had developed a nearly supernatural ability to vanish whenever she was around. None of them wanted to be the next person Lydia Stern eviscerated in print. She had a growing reputation as an investigative terror.

"Ms. Stern," I said in a low, grave voice, extra emphasis on the "z" in "Ms." "I wonder if you might have a few moments."

The terror of the *Midwest Arcane* whirled to face me, and her face broke into a cherubic grin. She was a little over five feet tall, pleasantly plump, and of Asian ancestry. She had a sparkling smile, thick glasses, curly black hair, and was wearing a pair of denim overalls over an old

Queensrÿche T-shirt. Her tennis shoes had bright pink laces on them. "Harry Dresden," she said. She had a sort of breathless, bubbling voice, the kind that seemed like it could barely contain laughter beneath almost every word. "Hah. I knew this one smelled right."

"Could be," I said. I hadn't been real forthcoming with Lydia. It hadn't worked out well with reporters in the past. Whenever I spoke to her, little daggers of guilt stabbed at me, reminders that I could not afford to let careless words get her into too much trouble. Despite that, we'd gotten along, and I'd never lied to her. I hadn't bothered to try. "You busy?"

She gestured at the bag whose strap hung over her shoulder. "I've got recordings, and I'll want to jot down some notes shortly." She tilted her head to one side. "Why do you ask?"

"I need a thug to scare some guys for me," I said.

The dimples in her cheeks deepened. "Oh?"

"Yeah," I said. "Do this for me. I'll give you ten minutes on this." I waved my hand vaguely at the hotel around us. "As soon as I have some time free."

Her eyes brightened. "Done," she said. "What do I do?"

"Hang around outside a doorway and . . ." I grinned. "Just be yourself."

"Good. I can do that." She nodded once, curls bouncing, and followed me to the room where they were grilling my friend's daughter.

I opened the door like I owned the place and walked in.

The room wasn't a big one—maybe the size of a large elementary-school classroom. There was a raised platform about a foot high at one end, with chairs on it behind a long table. More chairs faced it in rows. A sign, now discarded on the floor behind the door, declared that the room was scheduled for something called "filk-ing" between noon and five o'clock today. "Filking" sounded suspiciously like it might be an activity some-how related to spawning salmon, or maybe some kind of bizarre mammalian discussion. I decided that it was probably one of those things I was happier not know-ing.

Greene was in the room, standing on the platform with his arms folded, a sour frown on his face. Molly sat in the first row of chairs, still in the same clothes as the night before. She looked tired. She'd been crying.

Next to her was a man of medium build and unre-markable height, with brown hair just tousled enough to be fashionable. He wore a grey suit, its gravity somewhat offset by a black tie that featured Marvin the Martian. I recognized him. Rick, Murphy's ex. He stood over Molly, passing her a cup of water, the good cop of the usual interrogation equation. He was here in his official capacity, then. Agent Rick.

"Excuse me," Greene said, without looking over at me. "This room isn't open to the public."

"It isn't?" I said, overly ingenuous. "Man. I was really looking forward to a nice afternoon of filking, too."

Molly looked up, and her eyes widened in recognition and what looked like sudden hope. "Harry!"

"Heya, kid," I told her, and ambled in, Mouse in tow. The dog went right over to Molly, wagging his tail and subtly begging for affection by thrusting his broad muzzle underneath her folded hands. Molly let out a little laugh and leaned down, hugging the dog, talking baby talk to him like she did to her youngest siblings.

Greene turned to glower at me. After a moment, Agent Rick did too.

"Dresden," Greene said, his tone peremptory. "You are interfering in an investigation. Get out."

I ignored him to speak to Molly. "How's Rosie?"

She left her cheek on top of Mouse's broad head and said, "Unconscious. She was very upset by the news and the doctors gave her something to help her sleep. They were afraid she would freak out and it would hurt the baby."

"Dresden," Greene snarled.

"Best thing for her right now," I told Molly. "She'll handle it better when she's had some rest."

She nodded and said, "I hope so."

Greene spat a curse and reached for his radio, presumably to summon goons.

Greene was an ass.

Maybe I was going a little hex-happy, but I muttered something under my breath and made a little effort. Sparks shot out of the radio and were followed by curls of smoke. Greene stood there cursing as he tried to get the thing to work. "Dammit, Dresden," he snarled. "Get out before I have you taken downtown."

I kept ignoring him. "Hi there, Rick. How was the wedding?"

"That's it," Greene said.

Rick pursed his lips and then held up a hand toward Greene, a placating gesture. "Everyone survived it," Agent Rick responded, studying me with a steady frown, looking between me and Molly. "Harry, we're working here. You should go."

"Yeah?" I asked. I plopped down into the chair beside Molly and grinned at him. "I'm thinking maybe not. I mean, I'm working, too. I'm a consultant."

"You're obstructing an investigation, Dresden," Greene growled. "You're going to lose your jobs with the city. Your investigative license. Hell, I'll even get you stuck in jail for a month or two."

"No you won't."

"Have it your way, tough guy," Greene said, and started for the door.

Molly, maybe taking it for a cue, rose herself.

"Sit down," Greene said, his voice hard. "You aren't finished yet."

She hesitated for a second and then sat.

"Greene, Greene, Greene," I said. "There's something you're missing here."

He paused. Agent Rick watched me steadily.

"See, Miss Carpenter here can go any time she damned well pleases."

"Not until she's answered a few questions," he said.

I made a game-show buzzing sound. "Wrong. This is a free country. She can walk out and there's not a damned thing you can do about it. Unless you want to arrest her." I grinned at him some more. "You didn't arrest her, did you?"

Molly watched the exchange from the corner of her vision, being very still and keeping her face down.

"We're questioning her in relation to an ongoing investigation," Rick said.

"Yeah? One of you guys got the subpoena, then?"

They hadn't, of course. No one spoke.

"See, you're the one out on a limb here, Greene. You've got nothing on the young lady. No court order. You haven't arrested her. So anything she chooses to tell you is entirely voluntary."

Molly blinked up at me. "It is?"

I put a hand to my chest and mimed an expression of shock. "Greene! I can hardly believe this. Did you lie to this young woman to frighten her? To make her think she was under arrest?"

"I didn't lie," Greene snarled.

"You just led her on," I said, nodding. "Sure, sure. Not your fault if she interpreted you wrong. Say, let's go

back and check the tape and see where the mistake was."
I paused. "You *are* recording this, aren't you? All on the
record and aboveboard?"

Greene looked at me like he wanted to kick my nuts
up into my skull. "You've got nothing but speculation.
Get out. Or, as lead investigator, I will have you barred
from the hotel."

"That a threat?" I asked him.

"Believe it."

I made a show of rubbing at my mouth. "Oh, man.
I'm having quite the moral quandary. Because if you do
that to me, then hell, maybe the press would find out
that you're dismissing professional consultants with a
positive track record with the city." I leaned forward and
added casually, "Oh. And they might find out that you
are illegally interrogating a juvenile."

Greene stared at me, shock on his face. Even Agent
Rick arched an eyebrow. "What?"

"A juvenile," I enunciated, "i.e., one who cannot give
you legal consent on her own. I took the liberty of sending for her parents. I'm sure that they and their attorney
will have a whole lot of questions for you."

"That's blackmail," Greene said.

"No, it's due process," I replied. "You're the one who
tried the end run around the law."

Greene scowled at me and said, "You can talk all you
want, but you've got no proof."

My cheeks ached from smiling so much, and I
chuckled.

The door, which had never fully closed, opened on
cue. Lydia Stern stood there behind it, her press badge
around her neck, a mini-tape recorder in her hand, held
up so that Greene could clearly see it. "So, Detective,"
she asked, "could you please explain why as a part of

your investigation you are interrogating a juvenile without her parents' consent? Is she a suspect in the crime? Or a witness to any of the events? And what about these rumors of interdepartmental noncooperation slowing down the investigation?"

Greene stared at the reporter. He shot a glance at Agent Rick.

Rick shrugged. "He's got you. You took a chance. It didn't pay off."

Greene spat a word that authority figures oughtn't say in front of juveniles, and then stomped out. Lydia Stern winked at me, then followed on his heels, recorder held out toward him, asking a steady stream of questions whose only reasonable answers would make Greene look like an idiot.

Rick watched him go and shook his head. Then he said to me, "What's your stake in this?"

"The girl is my friend's daughter," I said. "Just looking out for her."

He gave me a slight nod. "I see. Greene's under a lot of pressure. I'm sorry you got treated like that."

"Rick," I said in a patient voice, "I'm not a teenage girl. Please don't try to good-cop me."

His polite, interested expression vanished for a second behind a quick, boyish grin. Then he shrugged and said, "It was worth trying."

I snorted.

"You know he can get the subpoena. It's just a question of running through channels."

I rose. "That's not my problem. I'll leave it to the Carpenters' attorney."

"I see," he said. "You actually are interfering with the investigation. He could probably make it stick."

"Come on, Agent. I'm protecting the rights of a juvenile. The ACLU would eat that raw." I shook my head. "Besides. What you're doing is wrong. Bullying girls. Hell's bells, man, that's low."

A flicker of anger touched Agent Rick's expression. "Dresden, I know you don't have a concealed carry permit. You want me to suspect you of carrying a weapon and search you for it?"

Oops. I thought nervously of the revolver in my backpack. If Agent Rick wanted to make an issue of it, I could be in trouble—but I didn't want *him* to know that. I tried to shake it off with a nonchalant shrug. "How is that going to help stop the killer before he strikes again?"

Rick tilted his head to one side and frowned at me. Dammit, I've got to get a better poker face. He oriented on me, eyes searching over me for possible places to hide a gun. "Irrelevant," he replied. "If you're breaking the law, you're breaking the law."

From the doorway there was an impatient sigh, and then Murphy said, "Would it kill you to stop being an asshole for five minutes, Rick?"

I hadn't noticed her arrival, and judging from Agent Rick's expression, neither had he.

"He's a consultant for SI, which is also working the case. We don't have the time to get involved in a pissing contest. People are in danger. We need to work together."

Rick glared at her, then reined in his temper and shrugged a shoulder. "You may be right. But Dresden, I want you to consider leaving of your own will. If you keep interfering, I'll arrest you and toss you in the clink for twenty-four hours."

"No," Murphy said, entering the room. "You won't."

He rounded on her, eyes narrowed. "Dammit, Karrin. You never know when to quit, do you?"

"Of course I do," she said, setting her jaw. "Never."

Agent Rick shook his head. He slammed open the door and departed.

Murphy watched him go. Then she sighed and asked, "Are you all right, miss?"

Molly nodded somewhat numbly. "Yes. Just tired."

A moment later, Sandra Marling hurried in, looked around at all of us, and then went over to give Molly a hug. The girl hugged back, tight.

"Did you reach them?" I asked Sandra.

"Yes. Mrs. Carpenter is on the way."

Molly shuddered.

"Good," I said. "Could you stay with Molly until she arrives?"

"Of course."

I nodded and said to Molly, "Kid, things are getting complicated. I want you to go with your mom. All right?"

She nodded, slowly, without looking up.

I sighed and got up out of my chair. "Good."

I left, Murphy and Mouse flanking me as I headed back into the hotel. "Nice guy, Rick," I commented. "Maybe a little manipulative."

"Just a tad," Murphy said. "What happened?"

I told her.

She let out a wicked chuckle. "Wish I could have seen the look on their faces."

"Next time I'll take a picture."

She nodded. "So what's our next move?"

"Hey, we're in a hotel." I bobbed my eyebrows at her. "Let's get a room."

Under peaceful circumstances, I'm sure that no rooms would have been available. Obviously, though, circumstances were far from peaceful, and there had been a minor avalanche of cancellations and early departures from the hotel—which only goes to show that people occasionally demonstrate evidence of sound judgment. The convention might have doubled the number of folks attending, but that didn't mean that they wanted to *sleep* here.

There was a room available on the fifth floor. I paid an extra fee to allow Mouse to stay, and we got checked in.

There was no one else in the elevator, and we rode in a silence that became increasingly tense. I shifted my weight from side to side and fiddled with one of the two plastic cards the desk clerk had given us. I cleared my throat.

"So here we are," I said. "Heading up to our hotel room."

Murphy's cheeks turned pink. "You are a pig, Dresden."

"Hey, I didn't put any innuendo into that. You did it yourself."

She rolled her eyes, smiling a little.

I watched numbers change on the elevator panel. I coughed. "Yes, sirree. Alone together."

"It's a little weird," she admitted.

"A little weird," I agreed.

"Should it be?" she asked. "I mean, we're just working together. We've done that before."

"We haven't done it in a hotel room."

"Yes, we have," Murphy said.

"But they all had corpses in them."

"Ah. True."

"No corpses this time," I said.

"Heh," Murphy said. "The night is young."

Her reminder of the dangers before us put a bullet through the head of *that* conversation. Her smile vanished, and her face regained its usual color. We went the rest of the way in silence, until the elevator doors opened. Neither one of us moved to get out. It almost felt like there was some kind of invisible line drawn across the floor.

The silence stretched. The doors tried to close. Murphy mashed down on the Door Open button with her thumb.

"Harry," she said finally, her voice very quiet, her blue eyes focused into distance. "I've been thinking about . . . you know. Us."

"Yeah?"

"Yeah."

"How much thinking?"

She smiled a little. "I'm not sure, really. I don't think I wanted to admit that . . . you know."

"Things might change between us?"

"Yes." She frowned at me. "I'm not sure this is something you would want."

"Between the two of us," I said, "I think I probably have more insight into that one."

She frowned. "How do you know it's what you want?"

"Last Halloween," I said, "I wanted to murder Kincaid."

Murphy glanced down as her cheeks turned pink. "Oh."

"Not literally," I said, then paused. "Well. I guess it was literally. But the urge died down a little."

"I see," she said.

"Are you and him . . . ?" I asked, leaving the question open.

"I saw him at New Year's," she said. "But we aren't in anything deep. Neither of us want that. We're friends. We enjoy the company. That's all."

I frowned. "We're friends too," I said. "But I've never taken your pants off."

"We're different," she said, her blush renewing. She gave me an oblique look from beneath pale eyelashes. "Is it something you want?"

My heart sped up a little. "Uh. Pants removal?"

She arched a brow and tilted her head, waiting for an answer.

"Murph, I haven't been with a woman for . . ." I shook my head. "Look, you ask any guy if he wants to have sex and he's going to say yes. Generally speaking. It's in the union manual."

Her eyes sparkled. "Including you?" she pressed.

"I'm a guy," I said. "So yes." I frowned, thinking about it. "And . . . and no."

She smiled at me and nodded. "I know. You couldn't do casual. You commit yourself too deeply. You care too much. We couldn't have something light. You would never settle for that."

She was probably right. I nodded.

"I don't know if I could give you what you want, Harry." Then she took a deep breath and said, "And there are other reasons. We work together."

"I noticed."

She didn't quite smile. "What I mean is . . . I can't let relationships come close to my job. It isn't good for either."

I said nothing.

"I'm a cop, Harry."

My belly twisted a little as I realized the rejection in the words, and the lack of any room for compromise. "I know you are."

"I serve the law."

"You do," I said. "You always have."

"I can't walk away from it. I won't walk away from it."

"I know that too."

"And . . . we're so different. Our worlds."

"Not really," I said. "We sort of hang around in the same one, most of the time."

"That's work," she said quietly. "My work isn't everything about me. Or it shouldn't be. I've tried a relationship built on having that in common."

"Rick," I said.

She nodded. Pain flickered in her eyes. I never would have seen that a few years before. But I'd seen Murphy in good times and bad mostly bad. She'd never say it, never want me to say anything about it, but I knew that her failed marriage had wounded her more deeply than she would ever admit. In a way, I suspected that they explained some of her professional drive and ambition. She was determined to make the career work. Something had to.

And maybe she'd been hurt even more deeply than that. Maybe badly enough that she wouldn't want to leave herself open to it again. Long-term relationships have the potential for long-term pain. Maybe she didn't want to go through it again.

"What if you weren't a cop?"

She smiled faintly. "What if you weren't a wizard?"

"Touché. But indulge me."

She tilted her head and studied me for a minute. Then she said, "What happens when Susan comes back?"

I shook my head. "She isn't."

Her tone turned dry. "Indulge me."

I frowned. "I don't know," I said quietly. "We decided to break it off. And . . . I suspect we'd see a lot of things very differently now."

"But if she wanted to try again?" Murphy asked.

I shrugged. "I don't know."

"Let's say we get together," Murphy said. "How many kids do you want?"

I blinked. "What?"

"You heard me."

"I don't . . ." I blinked a few more times. "I hadn't really thought about it." So I thought about it for a second. I thought about the merry chaos of the Carpenter household. God, I'd have given anything for that when I was little.

But any child of mine would inherit more than my eyes and killer chin. There were a lot of people who didn't think much of me. A lot of not-people thought that way, too. Any child of mine would be bound to inherit some of my enemies, and worse, maybe some of my allies. My own mother had left me a legacy of perpetual suspicion and doubt, and nasty little surprises that occasionally popped out of the hoary past.

Murphy watched me, blue eyes steady and serious. "It's a big question," she said quietly.

I nodded, slowly. "Maybe you're thinking about this too much, Murph," I said. "Logic and reason and planning for the future. What's in your heart doesn't need that."

"I used to think that, too." She shook her head. "I was wrong. Love isn't all you need. And I just don't see us together, Harry. You're dear to me. I couldn't ask for a kinder friend. I'd walk through fire for you."

"You already did," I said.

"But I don't think I could be the kind of lover you want. We wouldn't go together."

"Why not?"

"At the end of the day," she said quietly, "we're too different. You're going to live for a long time, if you don't get killed. Centuries. I'm going to be around another forty, fifty years at the most."

"Yeah," I said. It was one of those things I tried really hard not to dwell on.

She said, even more quietly, "I don't know if I'll get serious with a man again. But if I do . . . I want it to be someone who will build a family with me. Grow old with me." She reached up and touched the side of my face with warm fingers. "You're a good man, Harry. But you couldn't be what I need, either."

Murphy took her thumb from the button and left the elevator.

I didn't follow her right away.

She didn't look back.

Stab.

Twist.

God, I love being a wizard.

Chapter

Twenty-three

The room was typical of my usual hotel experience: clean, plain, and empty. I made sure the blinds were pulled, looked around, and shoved the small round table at one side of the room over against the wall to leave me some open space in the middle of the floor. I slung my backpack down on the bed.

"Need anything?" Murphy asked. She stood in the doorway to the room. She didn't want to come in.

"Think I have it all. Just need some quiet to get it set up." There was no reason not to give Murphy a way out of the awkwardness the conversation had brought on. "There's something I'm curious about. Maybe you could check it out."

"Pell's theater," Murphy guessed. I could hear some relief in her voice.

"Yes. Maybe you could cruise by it and see what's to be seen."

She frowned. "Think there might be something in there?"

"I don't know enough to think anything yet, but it's possible," I said. "You get a bad feeling about anything, don't hang around. Just vamoose."

"Don't worry," she said. "I already planned to do that." She went to the door. "Shouldn't take me long. I'll contact you in half an hour, let's say?"

"Sure," I said. Neither one of us voiced what we both were thinking—that if Murphy missed the check-in, she'd probably be dead, or dying, or worse. "Half an hour."

She nodded and left, shutting the door behind her. Mouse went over to the door, sniffed at it for a moment, then walked in a little circle three times and settled down on the floor to sleep. I frowned down at the carpet and opened my backpack. Chalk wouldn't do for a circle, not on carpet like that. I'd have to go with the old standby of fine, white sand. The maids would doubtless find it annoying to clean up, but life could be hard sometimes. I pulled out a glass bottle of specially prepared sand and put it on the table, along with the main blob of Play-Doh and Bob the skull.

Orange lights kindled in the skull's eye sockets. "Can I talk now?"

"Yeah," I said. "You been listening to things?"

"Yeah," Bob said, depressed. "You are *never* going to get laid."

I glared at the skull.

"I'm just sayin'," he said, voice defensive. "It isn't my fault, Harry. She'd probably bang you if you didn't take it so godawful seriously."

"The subject. Change it," I suggested in a flat voice. "We're working now."

"Right," Bob said. "So you're planning on a standard detection web–ward for the building?"

"Yeah," I said.

"It isn't going to be very helpful," Bob said. "I mean, by the time something manifests enough to set off your web, it's going to be all the way into the real world. While you're running for the stairs, it's already going to be tearing into somebody."

"It isn't perfect," I said. "But it's all I've got. Unless you have a better idea?"

"The thing about having several centuries of experience and knowledge at my disposal is that it doesn't do me any good unless I know what it is you want me to help you fight," Bob said. "So far, all you know is that you've got an inbound phobophage."

"That's not specific enough?"

"No!" Bob said. "I can think of about two hundred different kinds of phobophages off the top of my head, and I could probably come up with two hundred more if I took a minute to think about it."

"That many of them who can do what this thing did? Take a solid form and attack?"

Bob looked at me as though he thought me very thick. "Believe it or not, the old 'take the form of the victim's worst fear' routine is pretty much the most common move in the phobophage handbook."

"Oh. Right." I shook my head. "But this whole place is open territory. There's no threshold to use to anchor anything heavier than a web. At least if I do that much, maybe I can get into position fast enough to directly intervene when the thing shows up again."

"Things," Bob corrected me. "Plural. Phages are like ants. First one shows up, then two, then a hundred."

I exhaled. "Crap," I said. "Maybe we can come at this from a different angle. Is there any way I can redirect them while they're crossing over? Make it harder for them to get here?"

Bob's eyelights brightened. "Maybe. Maybe, yes. You might be able to raise a veil over this whole place—from the other side."

"Urk," I said. "You're saying I could hide this place from the phages, but only from the Nevernever?"

"Pretty much," Bob said. "Even then, it would be a calculated risk."

"How so?"

"It all depends on how they're finding this place," Bob said. "I mean, if these are just naturally arriving phages finding a hunting ground, a veil won't stop them. It might slow them down, but it won't stop them."

"Let's assume that it isn't a coincidence," I said.

"Okay. Assuming that, the next variable is finding out whether they're being summoned or sent."

I frowned. "There are things strong enough to send them through from the other side? I didn't think that ever happened anymore. Hence the popularity of working through mortal summoners."

"Oh, it's doable," Bob assured me. "It just takes a hell of a lot more juice to open the way to the mortal world from the other side."

I frowned. "How much power are we talking?"

"Big," Bob assured me. "Like the Erlking, or an archangel, or one of the old gods."

I got a shivery feeling in my stomach. "A Faerie Queen?"

"Oh, sure. I guess so." He frowned. "You think this is Faerie work?"

"Something is definitely screwy in elfland," I said. "More so than normal, I mean."

Bob made a gulping sound. "Oh. We're not going to go visiting the faeries or anything, are we?"

"Not if I can help it," I said. "I wouldn't take you with me, if it came to that."

"Oh," he sighed. "Good."

"One of these days, you're gonna have to tell me what you did to make Mab want to kill you."

"Yeah, sure," Bob said, in that tone of voice you use while sweeping things under the rug. "But we should also consider the third possibility."

"A summoner," I said. "Given that someone actually

threw a ward in my way the last time the phage showed up, that seems to be the most likely of the three."

"I think so, too," Bob said. "In which case, you're in trouble."

I grunted, and started unpacking candles, matches, and my old army-surplus knife. "Why?"

"Without a threshold to build on, you can't put up any proper defense. And even if you do cross over and set up a veil to try to keep the phages from finding the place . . ."

"Their summoner is going to draw them in," I finished, following the line of reasoning. "It's like . . . I could blanket the surrounding area in fog, but if they have someone on this end, the phages will have a beacon they can use to home in on the hotel."

"Right," Bob said. "And then the summoner just opens the door from his side, and they're in."

I frowned and said, "It's all about finding the summoner, then."

"Which you can't do, until they actually summon something," Bob said.

"Hell's bells," I complained. "There's got to be something we can do to prevent it."

"Not especially," Bob said. "Sorry, boss. Until you know more, you can't do anything but react."

I scowled. "Dammit. Then it's the web or nothing. At least if I use that, I might be able to identify the summoner." At the low, low cost of the phages mauling or killing someone else. Unless . . .

"Bob," I said, frowning over the idea. "What if I didn't try to hide the hotel or keep these things away. What if I, uh . . . just put a little topspin on the phages on the way in?"

Bob's eyelights brightened even more. "Ooooooo, classic White Council doctrine. When the phages come through, you point them straight at the guy who summoned them. Give him a dose of his own medicine."

"Right up the ass," I confirmed.

"There's an image," Bob said. "A summoning suppository."

"It's doable, isn't it?"

"Sure," Bob said. "I mean, you have everything you need for that. You know the phages are after fear, and that they're probably using his power as a beacon. Your web tells you something is stirring. You conjure up a big ball of fear, target the same beacon the phages are using, and let it fly."

"It'll be like hanging a steak around his neck and throwing him to the lions," I said, grinning.

"Hail Caesar," Bob confirmed. "The phages will go right after him."

"And once he's out of the game, I veil the hotel from the phages. No more convention attendees get hurt. Bad guy gets a lethal dose of dramatic irony."

"The good guys win!" Bob cheered. "Or at least you do. You're still a good guy, right? You know how confusing the whole good-evil concept is for me."

"I'm thinking about changing it to 'them' and 'us,' for simplicity's sake," I said. "I like this plan. So there's got to be a catch to it somewhere."

"True," Bob admitted. "It's gonna be a little tricky when it comes to the timing. You won't be able to sense the beacon until the phages actually step through from the Nevernever and take material form. If you haven't redirected them by then, it'll be too late."

I nodded, frowning. "That gives me what? Maybe twenty seconds?"

"Only if they're really lame," Bob said. "Probably ten seconds. Maybe even less."

I frowned. "Dammit, that's a small window." I

thought of another problem. "Not only that, but I'll be shooting blind. There won't be any way to tell who I'm setting the phages after. What if he's standing in a crowd?"

"He's going to be summoning fiends from the netherworld to wreak horror and death on the populace," Bob pointed out in a patient voice. "That won't lend itself to blending into a crowd."

"Good point. He'll probably be somewhere private, quiet." I shook my head. "Even so, I'd be a lot happier if this was a little less dicey. But I don't see any other way to stop these things from hurting anyone else."

"Until we have more information, I don't see what else you could do, boss."

I grunted. "I'd better get this web up and running, then."

Mouse's collar tag clinked against the buckle, and I looked over my shoulder. The dog had lifted his head from the floor, staring intently at the door. A second later, someone knocked.

Mouse hadn't started growling, and his tail thumped the wall a few times as I went to the door, sounding the all-clear. "That was fast," I said, opening the door. "I thought you were going to be half an hour, Murph—"

Molly stood in the hallway, an overnight bag hung over her shoulder. She drooped, the way my house plants always used to when I was still optimistic enough to keep buying new ones. Her pink-and-blue hair hung down listlessly, and her cheeks were marked with the remains of several mascara-laden tear tracks. She looked rumpled, tired, uncertain, and lonely.

"Hi," she said. Her voice wasn't much more than a whisper.

"Hey," I told her. "I thought you were waiting for your mom."

"I was," she said. "I am. But . . . I'm kind of messed up." She waved her hand gingerly at herself. "I wanted to clean up a little, but they won't let me use the bathroom in Nelson's room. I was hoping I could borrow yours. Just for a minute."

It would have been easier to dropkick a puppy than to turn the kid away. "Sure," I said. "Just keep it quiet. Okay?"

I stepped back into the room, and Molly followed me, pausing to scratch Mouse behind the ears. She looked past me, to the open floor space and the things I had set out.

"What are you doing?" she asked me.

"Magic," I said. "What's it look like I'm doing?"

She smiled a little. "Oh. Right."

I waved a hand at my materials. "I'm going to try to prevent another attack from hurting anyone."

"Can you do that?" she asked.

"Maybe," I said. "I hope so."

"I can't believe . . . I mean, I knew there were things out there, but my friends . . . Rosie." Her lower lip quivered and her eyes filled with tears that didn't quite fall.

I didn't have much I could say to comfort her. "I'm going to stop it from happening again," I said quietly. "I'm sorry I didn't move fast enough the first time."

She looked down again, and nodded without speaking. She swallowed several times.

"Listen," I told her quietly. "This is serious stuff. You need to talk about it. Not with me," I added, as she looked up at me. "With your mom."

Molly shook her head. "She isn't—"

"Molly," I sighed. "Life can be short. And cruel. You saw that last night. You got a look at the kind of thing your dad deals with all the time."

She didn't respond.

I said quietly, "Even Knights can die, Molly. Shiro did. It could happen to Michael, too."

She lifted her head abruptly, staring at me as if in shock.

"How does that make you feel?" I asked.

She chewed on her lip. "Scared."

"It scares your mom, too. It scares her a lot. She deals with it by holding on hard to the people around her. Maybe too hard, sometimes. That's why you feel like she's trying to keep you a little kid. She probably is. But it isn't because she's a control freak. It's because she loves you all so much—you, your dad, your family—and she's frightened that something bad could happen. She's desperate to do everything she can to keep you all safe."

Molly didn't look up or respond.

"Life is short," I said. "Too short to waste it on stupid arguments. I'm not saying your mom is perfect, because God knows she isn't. But my God, Molly, you've got the kind of family people like me would kill for. You think they'll always be there later—but they might not be. Life doesn't give you any guarantees."

I let that sink in for a minute, and then said, "I promised your dad that I'd ask you to talk to her. I told him I'd do my best to get the two of you to work things out."

She looked up at me, crying now, silently. More dark makeup trailed down her cheeks.

"Will you sit down with her, Molly? Talk?"

She took a shaking breath and said, "I don't know if it will do any good. We've said so much. . . ."

"I can't force you to do it. No one can do that but you."

She sniffled for a moment. "It won't do any good."

"I don't expect miracles. Just try to talk to her. Please."

She took a breath, and then nodded, once.

"Thank you," I said.

She tried to smile once, and hovered outside the bathroom door for a moment more.

"Molly?" I asked. "Are you okay?"

She nodded, but she didn't move, either.

I frowned. "Something you want to say?"

She looked up at me for just a second. "No," she said then, and shook her head. "No, it's nothing, really. Thank you. I won't be long." She stepped into the bathroom, shut the door, and locked it. The shower started a moment later.

"Wow," Bob said from behind me, somehow inserting a leer into the word. "I didn't realize you liked them quite that . . . fresh, Harry."

I glared at him. "What?"

"Did you see the body on her? Magnificent rack! Blond Nordic babeage, but all pierced and dressed in black, which means she's probably into at least one kind of kink. And all tender and emotional and vulnerable to boot. Taking her clothes off right here in your room."

"Kink? You don't— Look, there's no way to . . ." I sputtered. "No, Bob. Just no. For crying out loud. She's seventeen."

"Better move quick, then," Bob said. "Before anything starts to droop. Taste of perfection while you can, that's what I always say."

"Bob!"

"What?" he said.

"That isn't how things are."

"Not *now*," Bob said. "But you go get in that shower with her and you've got your own personal cable TV erotic movie come true."

I rubbed at the bridge of my nose. "Hell's bells. The whole idea is wrong, Bob. Just . . . wrong."

"Harry, even a nerd should know that it's no coincidence when a girl shows up at a man's hotel room. You know all she really wants is to—"

"Bob," I snapped, cutting him off. "Even if she wanted to, which she doesn't, nothing is happening with the girl. I'm trying to work, here. You aren't helping."

"I'd hate to disrupt your most recent attempt to court death and agony," he said brightly. "You should stick me somewhere else, where I won't distract you. On the counter in the bathroom, for example."

I slapped open one of the empty dresser drawers and tossed the skull in there, instead. Bob sputtered a few muffled curses in ancient Greek, something about sheep and a skin rash.

I looked up from the drawer into the room's mirror, and found myself facing not my reflection, but Lasciel's image instead, angelic and lovely and poised. "The perverted little creep has a point, my host," she said.

I jabbed a finger at the mirror and said, "Bob is *my* little creep, and the only one who gets to call him names is me. Now go away."

"Ah," Lasciel said, and the image faded to translucence, my own reflection appearing to replace it. "Fascinating, though," she added, just before vanishing, "that boyfriend Nelson bears quite the striking physical resemblance to you."

Then she was gone. Dammit. Stupid demons. Always with the last word.

Worse, she had a point. I eyed the bathroom door and reviewed the past day or so, and my interactions with the girl before that. I had always been someone her father respected and her mother disapproved of. I showed up once in a blue moon in a big black coat, usually looking roughed-up and dangerous, and I'd been doing so since she was young enough to be very impressionable. Hell, when you got right down to it, Charity's disapproval alone might have been enough to make me seem interesting to a rebellious teenage girl.

I came to the reluctant conclusion that it was possible Molly might have certain ideas in her head. It might well explain the most recent awkward silences and halting pauses. She'd always liked me, and it wasn't outrageous to think that it might have developed into something more—and that I'd be a right bastard to do anything that might encourage those ideas, even inadvertently. Maybe Bob and Lasciel were wrong, and in fact nothing like that was going on, but the passions of youth, its attractions and desires, were a minefield one took lightly at one's own peril.

Magnificent rack notwithstanding, Molly was still, in every important way, a child—my *friend's* child, to boot. She was hurting. It bothered me, and I wanted to help her, but I had to be aware of the fact that my sympathy could be misinterpreted. The kid had issues and she needed someone to help her work things out. She didn't need someone who would only make her more confused.

Steam curled out from under the bathroom door. An actual hot shower. Not merely the illusion of one.

I shook my head and got back to the detection web.

As spells went, this one was pretty big, but it wasn't complicated. I'd created a long-term version of the same basic working in the neighborhood around my apartment, in order to detect approaching mystical entities. The one I wanted for the hotel was the same thing, but I didn't have to bother with setting it up as a long-term construct. A sunrise, or two at most, would erode the spell, but with any luck I wouldn't need it for any longer.

I took the Play-Doh in hand, grabbed three candles

in their own wooden holders, poured the sand in a circle around me, and began gathering in my power, painstakingly creating mental images of the web of energy I needed to weave between the points of the hotel I'd marked out with Play-Doh. It didn't take me a terribly long time to set it up. Anyone with some basic skills and desire enough could have done something like this—or at least, they could have done it on a smaller scale. Weaving a web throughout the whole building took a lot of heavy lifting, magically speaking, but it wasn't complicated, and fifteen minutes later I solidified the image of the energy patterns in my mind, and whispered, "*Magius, orbius, spiritus oculus.*"

I poured my will and my magic out with the words as I spoke them, and my body briefly lit up with a flood of tingling energy that raced along all of my limbs, down into the lump of Play-Doh, and swirled in tight spirals around the three candles that would serve as my wardflames. The spell's energy flashed, appearing as a tiny stream of faint flickers, like bursts of static electricity, and the candles each flickered to life, steady little flames born of the spell. I broke the circle of sand as I spoke, and the power blossomed out through the hotel, into the shape I'd imagined, invisible strands flickering into instant shape, like ice crystals forming in the space of a heartbeat, spreading unseen strands throughout the hotel.

My balance wobbled a bit as I finished the spell and the energy left me, submerging me in a temporary flood of fatigue. I sat there with my head down, breathing hard for a minute.

"Wow," Murphy said, her tone less than impressed. I looked up to see her shutting the room's door behind her. "What did you do?"

I waved around to indicate the hotel and panted, "If

bad mojo shows up in the hotel, the spell will sense it."
I gestured at the three candles. "Take one with you. If
you see it flare up, it means we've got incoming."

Murphy frowned but nodded. "How much warning
will they give us?"

"Not much," I said. "A couple minutes, maybe less.
Maybe a lot less."

"Three candles," she said. "One for you, one for me,
and . . ."

"I thought we'd see if Rawlins wanted one."

"Is he here?" Murphy said.

"Gut feeling," I said. "He seems like the kind who
sees something through."

"He also seems like the kind who's been injured. No
chance he'd get active duty here."

"He didn't have it at the hospital, either," I pointed
out.

"True," Murphy said.

I caught my breath a little, and asked, "Anything at
Pell's theater?"

Murphy nodded and crossed the room to pick up two
of the candles. "A lot of nothing. Place was locked up
tight. Chains on the front doors, and the back door was
locked. Sign on the door said they were closed until further notice."

I grunted. "You'd think Pell would be wild to have
the place open, if the convention was providing a significant amount of his income—even if he was in a hospital
bed. Hell, *especially* if he was in a hospital bed."

"Unless he doesn't have anyone he trusts to run it for
him."

"But he does have someone he trusts enough to lock
it up?" I said. "That doesn't track. Pell sure as hell didn't
lock up after he was attacked."

Murphy frowned, but she didn't disagree with me. "I

tried to call him to ask him about it, but the nurse said he was sleeping."

I ran my fingers back through my hair, frowning over the situation. "Curiouser and curiouser," I said. "We're missing something here."

"Like what?" Murphy asked.

"Another player," I said. "Someone we haven't seen yet."

Murphy made a thoughtful sound. "Maybe. But imagining invisible perpetrators or hidden conspiracies veers pretty close to paranoia."

"Maybe not another suspect, then," I said thoughtfully. "Maybe another motive."

"Like what?" she asked, though I could see the wheels turning in her head as she followed the logic chain from the notion.

"These phage attacks look fairly simple at first glance. Like . . . I don't know. Shark attacks. Something hungry shows up to eat someone and then leaves. Natural occurrences. Or rather, typical supernatural occurrences."

"But they aren't random," Murphy said. "Someone is sending them to a specific place. Someone who used magic to try to stop you when you interfered with one of the phages."

"Which begs the obvious question . . ." I began.

Murphy nodded and finished the thought. "Why do it in the first place?"

I stuck my left hand out to one side of me and said, "Look over here." Then I mimed a short jab with my right fist.

"It's a rope-a-dope," Murphy said, her eyes narrowing. "A distraction. But from what?"

"Something worse than homicidal, shapeshifting, supernatural predators, apparently," I mused. "Something we'd want to stop a lot more."

"Like what?"

I shook my head and shrugged. "I don't know. Not yet, anyway."

Murphy grimaced. "Leave it to you to make paranoia sound plausible."

"It's only paranoia if I'm wrong," I said.

Murphy glanced over her shoulder and shivered a little. "Yeah." She turned back to me, squared her shoulders, and took a steadying breath. "Okay. What's the play, here? I assume you've got something in mind beyond having a minute or two of warning."

"Yes," I said.

"What?" she asked.

"It gets kind of technical," I said.

"I'll try to keep up," she said.

I nodded. "Anytime something from the spirit world wants to cross into the mortal world, it has to do a number of things to cross the border. It has to have a point of origin, a point of destination, and enough energy to open the way. Then it has to cross over, summon ectoplasm from the Nevernever, and infuse it with more energy to give itself a physical body."

She frowned. "What do you mean by points of origin and destination?"

"Links," I told her. "Sort of like landmarks. Usually, the creature you're calling up can serve as its own point of origin. Whoever is opening the way across is usually the destination."

"Can anyone be the destination?" she asked.

"No," I said. "You can't call up anything that isn't . . ." I frowned, looking for words. "You can't call up anything that doesn't have some kind of reflection inside you, a kind of point of reference for the spirit being. If you want evil, nasty, hungry beings, there's got to be evil, nasty, and hunger inside of you."

She nodded. "Does the way have to be opened from this side?"

"Generally," I said. "It takes a hell of a lot more oomph to get it done from the other side."

She nodded. "Go on."

I told her about my plan to turn the phages back upon their summoner.

"I like that," she said. "Using their own monsters against them. But what does that leave me to do?"

"You buy me time," I said. "There will be a moment just when the phage or phages cross over, where they will be vulnerable. If you're able to see one and distract it, it will give me more time to aim them back at their summoner. And it's possible that my spell might not work. If it goes south, you'll be near enough to help clear people out, maybe do them some good."

Murphy began to speak—then she paused, turned around, and asked, "Harry. Is there someone in the shower?"

"Uh. Yeah," I said, and rubbed at the back of my neck.

She arched a brow and waited, but I didn't offer any explanation. Maybe it was my way of getting petty vengeance for her brutal honesty in the elevator.

"All right then," she said, and took up the candles. "I'll get downstairs and look for Rawlins. Otherwise, I'll grab one of my guys from SI."

"Sounds good," I said.

Murphy left, while I started planning out my redirection spell. It didn't take me long.

Mouse lifted his head suddenly, and a second later someone knocked at the door. I went over and opened it.

Charity stood on the other side, dressed in jeans, a knit tank top, and a blue blouse of light cotton. Her features were drawn with stress, her shoulders clenched in unconscious tension. When she saw me, her features became remote and neutral, very controlled. "Hello, Mister Dresden."

It was probably the friendliest greeting I could expect from her. "Heya," I said.

Standing beside her was an old man, a little under average height. What was left of his hair was grey, trimmed neatly, though hardly a fringe remained. He had eyes the color of robin's eggs, spectacles, a comfortably heavy build, and wore black slacks and a black shirt. The white square of his clerical collar stood out distinctively against the shirt. He smiled when he saw me, and offered me his hand.

I shook it, smiling, and had no need to fake it. "Father Forthill. What are you doing here?"

"Harry," he said amiably. "Lending some moral support, by and large."

"He's my attorney," Charity added.

I blinked. "He is?"

"He is," Forthill said, smiling. "I passed the bar before I entered the orders. I've kept my hand in on behalf of the diocese and my parishioners. I do some pro bono work from time to time, too."

"He's a lawyer," I said. "He's a priest. This does not compute."

Forthill let out a belly laugh. "Oxymoronic."

"Hey, did I start calling *you* names?" I grinned at him. "What can I do for you?"

"Molly was supposed to be waiting for us downstairs," Charity said. "But we haven't found her. Do you know where she is?"

The universe conspired against me. If Charity had asked the question ten seconds sooner, I would have been fine. But instead, the bathroom door opened, and

Molly appeared in a swirl of steam. She had a towel wrapped around her hair, and was holding another around her torso. Hotel towels and Molly's torso being what they were, the towel didn't quite get all the way around her, and barely maintained modesty. "Harry," she said. "I left my bag out he—" She broke off suddenly, staring at Charity.

"This, uh, isn't what it looks like," I stammered, turning back to Charity.

Her eyes blazed with cold, righteous rage. An old Kipling axiom about the female of the species being more deadly than the male flashed through my mind, right about the time Charity introduced my chin to her right hook.

Light flashed behind my eyes and I found myself flat on my back while the ceiling spun around a little.

"Mother," Molly said in a shocked voice.

I looked up in time to see Forthill put a firm hand on Charity's arm, preventing her from following up the first blow. She narrowed her eyes at Forthill, but the old man's fingers dug into her biceps until she gave him a slight nod and took a small step back into the hallway.

"Dress," she told Molly, implacable authority in her tone. "We're leaving."

The kid looked like she might just start falling apart on the spot. She grabbed her bag, ducked into the bathroom, and was dressed in under a minute.

"There was nothing going on," I mumbled. It came out sounding more like, "Mmrphg ggggh oonng."

"I may not be able to keep you away from my husband," Charity said, her tone cold, her diction precise. "But if you come near one of my children again, I will kill you. Thank you for calling me."

She left, the weary Molly following her.

"There was nothing going on," I said again, to Forthill. This time it sounded mostly like English.

He sighed, looking after the pair. "I believe you." He gave me a smile that was one part amusement to four parts apology, and followed them.

Murphy must not have reached the elevators before Charity and Forthill had arrived. She appeared in the doorway, peering inside the room, and then back the way Charity had gone. "Ah," she said. "You all right?"

"I guess," I sighed.

Her mouth twitched, but she didn't quite smile or laugh at me. "Seems to me that you should have seen that one coming."

"Don't laugh at me," I said. "It hurts."

"You've had worse," she said heartlessly. "And it serves you right for letting a little girl into your hotel room. Now get up. I'll be downstairs."

She left, too.

Mouse came over and started patiently nuzzling my chin and putting slobbering dog kisses on the bruise I could feel forming there.

"Women confuse me," I told him.

Mouse sat down, jaws dropping open into a doggie grin. I groaned, pushed myself to my feet, and set about preparing the redirection spell, while outside my room's window the sun raced for its nightly rendezvous with the western horizon.

Chapter

Twenty-four

I shut the door again and rushed to prepare the beacon spell, hurrying, certain that every second counted. I would only get one shot at diverting the phages, and I finished my preparations in feverish haste.

Nothing happened.

The sun set, leaving me mostly in the dark, since I hadn't bothered to turn on any lights.

Nothing continued happening.

I knelt in my circle of sand until my legs cramped and then went numb, and my knees felt like they were resting in molten lead.

And all that nothing just kept on coming.

"Oh come *on*," I snarled. "Bring on the doom, already."

From his spot near the door, Mouse heaved a sigh.

"Oh, shut up," I told him. I didn't dare take a break. If the bad guys moved and I wasn't ready, people would get hurt. So I knelt there, holding the spell ready in my mind, uncomfortable as hell, and swearing sulfurously under my breath. Stupid, lame-ass summoner. What the hell was he waiting for? Any half-competent villain would have had monsters roaming the halls hours ago.

Mouse's tail thumped against the wall, and a moment later the room's lock clicked, and Rawlins opened the door. He was wearing jeans and a long-sleeved shirt that concealed the bandages on his wounded arm, and he carried a wardflame candle in one hand. The blocky, dark-skinned officer leaned down and held his hand out to Mouse, who sniffed Rawlins in typical canine fashion and wagged his tail some more.

Rawlins remained in the doorway and said, "Hello? Dresden?"

"Here," I muttered.

Rawlins thumped at the wall until he found the lights and flicked them on. He stared at me for a minute, eyebrows slowly rising. "Uh-huh. There's something I don't see every day."

I grimaced. "Murphy found you, I see."

"Almost like she's a detective," Rawlins said, grinning.

"Your boss know you're here?" I asked.

"Not so far," he replied. "But I expect someone might notice and tell him about me at some point."

"He won't be happy," I said.

"I just hope I can live with myself later." He waved his little candle. "Murphy sent me up here to make sure you was still alive."

"I'm going to need knee surgery," I sighed. "I never planned on it taking this long."

"Uh-huh," Rawlins said again. "You ain't one of those Satan worshipers are you?"

"No," I said. "More like Pythagoras."

"Pih-who?"

"He invented triangles."

"Ah," Rawlins said, as if that had explained everything. "So, what are you doing here?"

I explained it to him, though it looked like he was having trouble accepting my words. Maybe I lacked credibility. "But I figured he would have moved by now."

"Crooks are funny that way," he agreed. "No respect."

I scrunched up my face in thought. I was hungry, thirsty, tired, hurting, and I had to use the bathroom in the worst way. None of those things were going to become easier to bear as the night went on, and I needed to have all the concentration I could get.

"Okay," I said. "Be smart. Take a break." I leaned down and broke the circle by sweeping the sand aside with my hand, letting the energy of the spell I'd been holding ready drain away. At least I'd already done it once. Getting it back into position wouldn't take nearly as long as the first time.

I tried to rise, but my legs were incommunicado. I grimaced at Rawlins and said, "Give me a hand here?"

He set his candle aside and helped me up. I wobbled precariously for a couple of seconds, but then stumbled to the bathroom and back out.

"You okay?" he asked.

"I'm good. Tell Murphy to hold steady."

Rawlins nodded. "We'll be downstairs." He paused and said, "Hope this happens soon. There's some kind of costume contest going on."

"Is it bad?"

"There are a lot of skimpy getups, and some of those people should *not* be wearing them."

"Call the fashion police," I said.

Rawlins nodded gravely. "They've crossed a line."

"Do me a favor?" I asked him. "Take Mouse out for a walk?" I dug a couple of bills from my back pocket and passed them to Rawlins. "Maybe get him a hot dog or something?"

"Sure," Rawlins agreed. "I like dogs."

The dog's tail thumped rapidly against the wall.

"Whatever you do, don't give him nachos. I didn't bring my gas mask with me."

Rawlins nodded. "Sure."

"Keep your eyes open," I said. "Tell Murph I'll be reset in a couple of minutes."

Rawlins grunted and left.

I had a canteen of fruit punch in my backpack, along with some beef jerky and some chocolate. I went to the bag and started wolfing down all three while pacing back and forth to stretch my legs. Holding myself ready to strike had been more than simply a physical strain. My head felt like someone had packed it in wool, while at the same time my senses seemed slightly distorted; edges made sharper, curves more ambiguous, the whole combining to make the hotel room feel like a toned-down Escher painting. There was no help for that. The use of magic was mostly in the mind, and holding a spell together for a long time often triggered disconcerting side effects.

I polished off the food as fast as I could gulp it down, went easy on the drink, in case I was there for another several hours, and settled back down in my circle, preparing to close it again.

When the room's phone rang.

"Déjà vu," I commented to the empty room. I stood up, my knees creaking, and went to the phone.

"Dresden Taxidermy," I said. "You snuff it, we'll stuff it."

There was a beat of startled silence from the phone, and then a young man's voice said, "Um. Is this Harry Dresden?"

I recognized the voice—Boyfriend Nelson. That made my ears perk up, metaphorically speaking. "Yeah, this is him," I said.

"This is . . ."

"I know who it is," I told him. "How did you know where I was?"

"Sandra," he said. "I called her cell. She told me you'd checked in."

"Uh-huh. *Why* are you calling me?"

"Molly said . . . she said you helped people." He paused to take a breath, and then said, "I think I need your help. Again."

"Why?" I asked. Keep the questions open, I thought. Never give him one with a simple answer. "What's going on?"

"Last night, during the attacks. I think I saw something."

I sighed. "It was going around," I agreed. "But if you saw something, you're a witness to a crime, kid. You need to show up and work with the cops. They get sort of unreasonable with people who go all evasive when they want to ask questions about a murder."

"But I think some . . . thing is following me," he said. An unsteady tremor shook Nelson's voice. "Look, they're just cops, man. They just have guns. I don't think they can help me. I hope you can."

"Why?" I asked him. "What is it that you saw?"

"No," he said. "Not on the phone. I want to meet with you. I want you to promise me your help. I'll tell you then."

Right. Because it wasn't like I had anything better to be doing. "Look, kid . . ."

Nelson's voice suddenly went thready with breathless fear. "Oh, God. I can't stay here. Please. *Please.*"

"Fine, fine," I said, trying to keep my voice strong, steady. The kid was scared—the bone-deep, knee-watering, half-crazy kind of scared that makes rational thinking all but impossible. "Listen to me. Stay around people, as many of them as you can. Go to Saint Mary of the Angels Church. It's holy ground, and you'll be safe there. Ask for Father Forthill. He's a little guy, mostly bald, glasses, bright blue eyes. Tell him everything and tell him I'm coming to collect you as soon as I can."

"Yes, all right, thank you," Nelson said, the words hysterically rushed. There was a brief clatter, and then I heard running footsteps on concrete. He hadn't even gotten the phone back into its cradle before he'd taken off at a dead sprint.

I chewed on my lip. The kid was definitely in trouble, or at least genuinely believed that he was. If so, it meant that maybe he *had* seen something last night, something that made it important for someone to kill him—i.e., some kind of damning evidence that would probably help me figure out what the hell was going on. I felt a stab of anxiety. Holy ground was a powerful deterrent to the things that went bump in the night—or in this case, things that went stab, stab, hack, slash, rip in the night—but it wasn't invulnerable. If something of sufficient supernatural strength really was after the kid, it might be able to force its way into the church.

Dammit, but what choice did I have? If I left my position here, any fresh attack could make last night's look like a friendly round of Candyland. What could he possibly have seen that would make him worth killing? Why the hell was he being followed? I felt like I was floundering around in the dark inside someone else's house, benighted of savoir faire enough to move with assurance. I was spread too thin. If I didn't start finding more pieces of the puzzle and put them together, and soon, more people would die.

I could only be in one place at one time. If the kid was in real trouble, he'd be as safe at the church, with Forthill, as anywhere in town short of the protection of my heavily warded apartment. Meanwhile, there were a bunch of other kids here who looked to be the next meal on the phobophage buffet. I had to act where I could do the most good. It was a cold sort of equation, the calculus of survival, but undeniable. I'd get to Nelson after I had taken care of business at the hotel.

I settled down on my knees again, carefully, closed the circle, and began to pick up the pieces of the redirection spell once more.

The single wardflame candle on the room's dresser suddenly exploded into lurid red light. Simultaneously, I felt a heavy thrumming in the air, where the strands of my web spell had suddenly encountered powerful magic in motion, drawing my thoughts and attention to a back hallway in the hotel, not far from the kitchens, up to the hall outside the hotel's exercise room, and a swift double-thrum from another of the hotel's bathrooms.

Four attackers, this time. Four of them at least.

I had ten seconds to get the spell off.

Nine.

Maybe less.

Eight.

I threw myself into the spell.

Seven.

It had to be fast.

Six.

It had to be perfect on the first attempt.

Five.

If I screwed this one up, someone else would pay for it.

Four.

They'd pay for it in blood.

Three.

Two.

One . . .

Chapter

Twenty-five

I readied my spell, terrified that I was already too late, terrified that I had made a critical mistake, terrified that more innocents were about to face hideous agony and death.

That was how it had to be. If I wanted to lure the phages from their rampage by directing them after a richer source of fear, it had to come from somewhere—specifically, it had to come from me. If I'd tried to use falsified emotion, it would no more have worked on them than an attempt to make a gorilla interested in a plastic banana. The fear had to be genuine.

Of course, I hadn't really planned on being quite *this* afraid. Being taken off my guard and handed a time limit had added an edge of panicked hysteria to the ample anxiety I already had.

The spell coalesced, and time came to an abrupt stop.

In that illusory stasis, my senses were on fire. The presence of the dangerous entities now entering the material world rippled through my detection web; a jittery, fluttering sensation. The energy of the spell burned like an invisible star before my outstretched hands, and my terror rushed into it and fused with the spell. Streamers from the lure whipped out along the lines of power that constituted my detection web, brushing lightly at the entities, attracting their attention, giving them a whiff of rich sustenance.

And somewhere in the middle of all that, I felt a single, quiet, quivering pulse—a living presence that could only be the phages' summoner and beacon.

"Gotcha," I hissed, and with an effort of will broke the circle and sent the spell winging toward him.

Time resumed its course. The energy that powered the spell fled out of me in another rush, and left me lying on my side, struggling to draw in enough breath. I could feel the spell sizzling down the lines of power for the summoner, and a heartbeat later there was a sense of impact as the spell went home. As it happened, the entities my web touched went abruptly still, the web ceasing its trembling—and then they all surged forward into sudden motion, vanishing from the web, and presumably streaking after the lure.

All but one.

A breath or two after the entities had departed, my web trembled again, now growing more agitated, its motion a kind of subliminal pressure against my thoughts.

I had missed one. My spell had gotten out in time to draw away the others, but either my web had failed me at some point or the remaining phage had been quicker on the draw than his buddies from the Nevernever. I could feel it moving from the hotel's kitchens toward the convention halls.

I wanted to curl into a fetal position and go into a coma. Instead, I shoved my wobbly way to my feet, took up my pack, and opened the drawer to get Bob.

"Did it work?" he chirped.

"Almost," I said. "There's one left. Keep your head down."

"Oh, *very* funny . . ." he began.

I zipped the skull into my pack, took up my staff and

blasting rod, and shuffled wheezily out to find the remaining phage before it found someone else.

My legs almost gave out just *thinking* about taking the stairs, so I rode the elevator down to the first floor. I heard nothing until the floor indicator told me we'd just passed the second floor, at which point I began to hear frightened, muffled screams. The elevator hit the first floor, and the doors had just begun to roll open when the power went out.

Blackness fell over the hotel. The screams redoubled. I took out my pentacle amulet and sent enough of my will into it to make it glow with pale blue wizard's light. I jammed my staff into the slightly open elevator doors and levered them apart, then slipped out into the hotel.

Though the sun had set more than an hour before, the crowded convention hall had remained stuffy while its air conditioners labored in vain. I got my bearings and headed for the kitchen. As I did, the air temperature plummeted, sending the hotel's climate from near-sauna to near-freezing in a handful of seconds. The suddenly cooled air could no longer contain the oppressive humidity it had been holding, and this resulted in a sudden, thick fog that coalesced out of nowhere and cut visibility down to maybe three or four long steps.

Dammit. The phages that had appeared so far seemed to be specialists in the up-close-and-personal venue of violence, whereas wheezy wizards like me prefer to do business from across the street, or down the block, or maybe from a neighboring dimension. Farther away, if possible. Wizards have a capacity for recovering from injury that might be more than most humans', but that was a long-term deal. In a bar fight, it wasn't going to do me any good. Hell, I didn't even have my duster with me, and now that the cold had rolled over the hotel, I missed it for multiple reasons.

I put my amulet back on, then shook out my shield bracelet and readied it for use, creating a second source of glowing blue light—though by accident, not design. The silver bracelet I used to focus magic into a tangible plane of force had been damaged in the same fire that took most of my left hand, and sparks of blue light tended to dribble from it whenever I moved my arm around. I had to be ready to use the shield at an instant's notice. It would be the only thing between me and whatever might come rushing from the fog.

I went with my staff in my right hand. When it came to taking apart rampaging monsters, I preferred my blasting rod, but I've had an incident or two involving buildings and fire. If I went blazing away at the thing in a crowded hotel and burned the place down, it would kill more people than the rampage would have. The staff was a subtle tool, not as potent a weapon as the blasting rod, but it was more versatile, magically speaking.

Plus, in a pinch, I could brain someone with it—which isn't subtle, but sure as hell is reassuring.

The emergency lights hadn't snapped on, so either someone had sabotaged them or there was enough raw magical energy flying around to take them out. But as I moved out toward the kitchens, I didn't feel anything like the kind of ambient energy it would take to blow out something as simple as a battery-powered light. That meant that someone had deliberately taken the emergency lights off-line, by magical means or otherwise, and it wasn't hard to guess why.

Gunshots rang out, weirdly muted by the building's acoustics; flat, heavy sounds like someone swinging a baseball bat at a metal trash can. Screams and sounds of confusion, fear, worry, and even pain continued all around me as people fumbled in the dark, tripped, fell, or collided with furniture and one another. The building was already emptying, at least here on the first floor, but the sudden darkness had resulted in a panicked stampede, and people had been injured in the crush. The darkness had created confusion, slowed the intended prey from fleeing, and left wounded behind who could neither defend themselves nor flee the building. Their helplessness would be driving them mad with fear.

It would make them juicier targets for the phage.

A metallic, piercing shriek hit my ears in a sudden, stunning shock wave, and my legs stopped moving. I didn't choose to do it. The sound just hit something primitive in my brain stem, something that made my instincts scream at me to freeze, to not be seen. I dropped to one knee, terror suddenly falling onto my shoulders like a physical weight. In the wake of the shriek, I could hear human throats screaming in fear, nearby to me, and I could see the shapes of people moving around, lumpy shadows in the faint light from my shield bracelet.

A flame suddenly appeared ahead of me, and I got a look at a young woman who crouched down, holding up a cigarette lighter in a hand that shook so badly that it seemed a miracle the lighter stayed aflame.

"No!" I screamed at her. I rose to my feet and lunged toward her. "Put out the light!"

Her face swiveled toward me, ghostly in the light of the tiny flame, her mouth working soundlessly—and then something the size of a mountain lion hit her across the shoulders and flung her to the ground. The lighter flew from her hand, the little lick of flame showing me something black and gleaming and spattered with scarlet gore.

The woman screamed. The dark hallway became a river of terrified people plunging through the darkness. Someone fell against me, and as I stumbled away from them I stepped on someone's fingers in the darkness and tripped when I tried to pull my weight off of them.

I snarled, slammed my back against the wall, held up my staff, and called up Hellfire.

Power flooded down the length of the carved oak, its sigils and runes filling with red-white liquid fire that ran from the base of the staff to its head in a ripple of energy. The crisp, clean scent of wood smoke filled the air, tainted with the barest hint of sulfur, and lurid light washed through the hallway.

I saw people scrambling, screaming, weeping. They were moving away, taking advantage of the light while they had it, and the hall around me cleared rapidly. It left the woman with the lighter. She lay on her side, curled into a fetal position, her arms clasped around her head while . . . the *thing* mauled her.

It was equal parts feline and insect, all lanky arms, powerful legs, and a whipping tail tipped with a serrated point. Its skin was a black, shining carapace, and it had an elongated, eyeless head ending in viscous, slime-covered jaws full of teeth. Though it had no eyes, it somehow sensed the light of my powered staff, and it whipped around toward me with a hiss, body tensing in sinuous grace, jaws gaping, slime dripping from its teeth while a slow, enraged hissing sound emerged from its throat.

I stared at it for all of a second in the shock of recognition. Then I gritted my teeth, got my feet underneath me, pointed the end of my staff at the creature, and snarled, "Get away from her, you *bitch*."

The phage shifted its position, the wounded girl now forgotten, its limbs weirdly jointed, its motion sinuous and eerie. It hissed again, louder. A second pair of jaws emerged from between the first, and they too hissed and parted and drooled in challenge.

"Is this gonna be a standup fight or just another bug hunt?" I taunted.

The phage leapt at me, faster than I would have thought possible—but that's how fast always works. Lots of people and not-people are faster than me, and I'd learned to plan for it a long time ago. A lot of people think that, in a fight, speed is the only thing that matters. It isn't true. Oh, sure, it's enormously advantageous to have greater speed, but a smart opponent can counter it with good footwork, calculating distance to give him the advantage of economy of movement. The phage was fast, but it had to cross eight or nine feet of carpet to get to me. I had to move my hand about ten inches and harden the shield before my left hand with my will. It wasn't that fast.

The phage hit my shield, bringing a ghostly blue quarter dome into shape and sending a cascade of blue sparks flying back around me. At the last second, I turned and angled the shield to deflect the creature's momentum. It caromed off the shield and went tumbling along the hallway beyond me for a good twenty feet.

"You want some of this?" I stepped into the middle of the hall to put myself between the phage and the wounded girl. The phage rose, turning to flee. Before it could move I thrust the end of my staff in its direction and cried, *"Forzare!"*

I hadn't ever used quite that much Hellfire before.

Power rushed out of my staff. Usually, when I employed it like this, the force I unleashed was invisible. This time, it rushed out like a scarlet comet, like a blazing cannonball. The force dipped at the last second, then came up at the phage. The impact threw it against the ceiling with bone-crushing force, and at least twice as much energy as I'd intended. The phage came down, limbs thrashing wildly, bouncing and skittering frantically, like a half-smashed bug.

I hit it again, the runes in my staff blazing, bathing the whole length of the hall in scarlet radiance, slamming the phage into a wall with more crunching sounds. Yellowish liquid splattered, there was an absolutely awful smell, and sudden holes pocked the wall and the floor where the yellow blood fell.

I cried havoc in the hellish light and hit it again. And again. And again. I bounced the murdering phage around that hallway until acid burned a hundred holes in the walls, ceiling, and floor, and my blood sang with the battle, with the power, with triumph.

I lost track of several seconds. The next thing I remember, I stood over the crushed, twitching phage. "It's the only way to be sure," I told it. And then, with cool deliberation, I slammed the end of my staff into the thing's eyeless skull, muscle and magic alike propelling the blow. Its head crunched and fractured like a cheap taco shell, and suddenly there was no phage, no creature. There was only the damaged hallway, the tainted smell of hellish wood smoke, and a mound of clear, swiftly dissolving ectoplasm.

My knees shook and I sat down in the hallway. I closed my eyes. The red light of Hellfire continued to pulse through my staff, lighting the hall, illuminating my eyelids.

The next thing I knew, Mouse pressed up against my side, an enormous, warm, silent presence. Bright lights bobbed toward me. Flashlights. Footsteps. People were shouting a lot.

"Jesus," Rawlins breathed.

Murphy knelt down by me and touched my shoulder. "Harry?"

"I'm okay," I said. "The girl. Behind me. She's hurt."

Rawlins stood shining his flashlight on a bloody section of the hallway. "Jesus Christ."

The phage had killed three people before I got there. I hadn't been able to see much of them during the fight. It was a scene of horror, worse than any slaughterhouse. The phage had taken out a cop. I could see a piece of shirt with a bloodstained CPD badge on it. The second victim might have been a middle-aged man, judging by a bloodied orthopedic shoe that still held a foot. White leg bone showed two or three inches above the shoe.

The third victim had been one of the little vampire girls I'd seen the previous evening. I could only tell because her head had landed facing me. The rest of her was hopelessly intermixed with the other two bodies.

They'd need someone good at jigsaw puzzles to put them back together.

Murphy went to the girl with the lighter, and knelt over her.

"How is she?" I asked.

"Gone," Murphy replied.

I blinked. "What?"

"She's dead."

"No," I said. I was too tired to feel much of the sudden frustration that went through me. "Hell's bells, she was moving just a second ago. I got here in time."

Murphy grimaced. "She bled out."

"Wait," I said, staggering to my feet. "This isn't . . . She shouldn't be . . ."

I felt a sudden sickness in my stomach.

Was she still alive when the phage had turned to run? Could I have stopped or slowed the bleeding, if I had let the thing retreat to the Nevernever?

I thought of the fight again. I thought of the satisfaction of turning the hunter into prey, of extracting vengeance for those it had slain. I thought about the power that raged through me, the sheer, precise *strength* of the Hellfire-assisted assault, and how good it felt to use it on something that had it coming. I'd barely given a thought to the girl's condition.

Had I let her die?

My God. I could have let the phage run.

I could have helped her.

The girl's body lay curled up, still, like a sleeping child. Her dead eyes were open and glassy.

I lunged for a potted plant near me and threw up.

After I did, Rawlins observed, "You don't look so good."

"No," I whispered. The word tasted bitter. "I don't."

Mouse let out one of his not-whine breaths and laid his chin on my shoulder. My eyes couldn't get away from the dead people, not even when they were closed. The hellish light in my staff slowly faded and went dark.

"I've got to organize this clusterfuck," Murphy sighed. "Rawlins, keep an eye on him."

"Yeah."

She nodded once and rose, briskly moving away, snapping orders. "You, you," Murphy said, pointing at two nearby cops. "Get over there and help the wounded. Airway, bleeding, heartbeat. Move." She raised her voice and shouted, "Stallings! Where the hell is my ambulance?"

"Two minutes!" a man shouted down a dimly lit hall leading to the lobby. It looked like someone had pulled a patrol car or three up to the front of the hotel to shine their headlights into the darkened building.

"Clear them a path and call for more EMTs," Murphy barked. She took her radio off her belt and started giving more orders.

Rawlins looked at the remains, and at the acid-scarred walls and the enormous areas of smashed drywall and ceiling that looked like they'd been kissed by a wrecking ball. He shook his head. "What the hell happened here?"

"Bad guy," I said. "I got him. Not fast enough."

Rawlins grunted. "Come on. Best we get up to the lobby. Until they get the lights back on, it might not be safe out here."

"What happened on your end?" I asked.

"Damn candle blew up in my face. Then the lights went out. Thought for a second I'd gone blind."

I grunted. "Sorry."

"Some of the civilians were carrying. That howling thing went by in the dark and everyone panicked. Stampede in the dark. People got trampled and scared. Civilians opened fire, cops opened fire. We got one dead and a couple of dozen wounded by one thing or another."

We reached the lobby and found more police arriving along with the emergency crews. The EMTs set up shop at once in a makeshift triage area, where Murphy had brought most of the wounded. The EMTs started stabilizing, evaluating, resuscitating. They had the worst cases loaded in the ambulance and rushing for the hospital within six or seven minutes.

Murphy's stream of peremptory commands had slowed to a stop, and she stood near the triage area. I sidled over to her and loomed. Mouse pushed his head underneath her hand, but Murphy only patted him absently. I followed her worried blue gaze. The EMTs were working on Rick.

Greene sat in a chair nearby. He had wiped his face with a towel, but it hadn't taken the blood out of the creases. It made a sanguine masque of his features. He held the towel against his head with his left hand.

Murphy said nothing for a while. Then she asked, "Did the spell work?"

"Mostly," I said. "I missed one."

She tensed. "Is it still . . ."

"No. I picked up the spare."

She pressed her lips firmly together and closed her eyes. "When the candle went off, I hit the fire alarm. I wanted to clear the building fast. But someone had broken it. Just like the power and the emergency lights. Something went right by me and hit Greene early on. Now I'm the one in charge of this mess."

"What happened to Rick?"

She spoke dispassionately. "Hit by panic fire. Gut shot. I don't know how bad."

"He'll be all right," I told her. "The EMTs would have taken him out first if he was in real trouble."

She watched a pair of them labor over Rick. "Yeah," she said. "He'll be okay. He'll be all right."

She forced herself to look away from her ex-husband with a visible effort. "I've got to get things under control here, until we get the chain of command straightened out, and I make sure the wounded are cared for. Families notified, God." She shook her head, and watched the EMTs lift Rick onto a stretcher and carry him out. Unspoken apology infused her tone. "After that, there will be questions, and a rain forest worth of paperwork."

"I get it," I told her quietly. "It's your job."

"It's my job." She focused her eyes in the distance. I could feel the trembling tension in her. I've known Murphy for a while now. I'd seen her like that before, when she wanted to fall apart but couldn't take the time to do it. She was better at managing that kind of thing than me. There was nothing in her expression but calm and confidence. "I'll put off everything I can and get back to you as soon as possible. Tomorrow sometime."

"Don't worry about me, Murph," I told her. "And don't be too hard on yourself. If you hadn't gotten in

Greene's face and stayed here, a lot of people would be dead right now."

"A lot of people *are* dead right now," she said. "What about our bad guy?"

I felt my mouth stretch into a sharp-edged, wolfish smile. "He's entertaining unexpected guests."

"Is he going to survive them?"

"I doubt it," I told her cheerfully. "If one of those things had jumped me, instead of vice versa, it would have taken me out. Three of them would filet me."

Murphy's attention was drawn to the door. Several men in wrinkled suits came in and stood around rubbernecking. Murphy straightened her clothing. "What about collateral damage?"

"I don't think it will be an issue. I'll track them and make sure."

Murphy nodded. "Rawlins," she called.

The veteran had been hovering not far away, feigning disinterest.

She hooked a thumb up at me. "Babysit for me?"

"Shoot," Rawlins drawled. "Like I got nothing better to do."

"Suffer," she told him, but she smiled when she said it. She put her hand on my arm and squeezed hard, letting out some of the pressure behind her calm facade through the contact. Then she strode over to the rubbernecking suits.

Rawlins watched her go, his lips pursed. "That is one cast-iron bitch," he said. His tone revealed a quiet respect. "Cast iron."

"Hell of a cop," I said.

Rawlins grunted. "Problem with cast iron. It's brittle. Hit it right and it shatters." He looked around the foyer and shook his head. "This isn't going to go well for her."

"Huh?" I said.

"Department is going to crucify someone for it," Rawlins said. "They have to."

I let out a bitter bark of laughter. "After all, she probably saved a lot of lives tonight."

"No good deed goes unpunished," Rawlins agreed.

Greene blinked blearily at us from his chair and then slurred, "Rawlins? What the hell are you doing down here? I sent you home." Anger gathered on his vague expression. "You son of a bitch. You're defying a direct order. I'll have your ass on a platter."

Rawlins sighed. "See what I mean?"

I lifted my hand with my thumb and first two fingers extended, the others against my palm, and moved it in a vaguely mystical gesture from left to right. "That isn't Rawlins."

Greene blinked at me, and his eyes blurred in and out of focus. The distraction derailed the train of thought he'd been laboriously assembling. It wasn't magic. I've taken head shots before. It takes a while for your brain to start doing its job again, and the vaguest kinds of confusion make things into one big blur.

I repeated the gesture. "That isn't Rawlins. You can go about your business. Move along."

Greene fumbled with a couple of words, then shook his head and closed his eyes and went back to holding the towel against his head.

Rawlins arched an eyebrow. "You ever handle any divorce negotiations?"

I jerked my head at Mouse and said, "Come on. Before his brains unscramble."

Rawlins fell into pace beside me. "Where are we going?"

I gave him the short version of what I'd done with the other three phages. "So now I track them, and make sure the guy who called them up is out of play."

"Demons," Rawlins said. "Wizards." He shook his head.

"Look, man—"

He held up a hand. "No. I think about this too much and I won't be any good to you. Don't explain it. Don't talk about it. Let me get through tonight and you can blow my mind all you want."

"Cool," I told him. "You got a car?"

"Yup."

"Let's go."

We went outside and down the street to the nearest parking garage. Rawlins drove an old blue station wagon. A bumper sticker on the back read MY KID IS TOO PRETTY TO DATE YOUR HONOR STUDENT.

Mouse let out a sudden warning growl. An engine raced. The dog flung his weight at my thigh and sent me slamming up against Rawlins's station wagon. A van rushed at me in my peripheral vision, too fast for me to try to avoid. It missed me by less than six inches.

It didn't miss Mouse. There was a meaty sound. The dog let out a bawl of pain. Brakes screeched.

I turned, furious and terrified, and the runes in my staff seethed with sudden Hellfire.

I had a split second to see Darby Crane swinging a tire iron. Then stars exploded in front of my eyes and the parking garage rotated ninety degrees. I saw Mouse, sprawled motionless on the concrete thirty feet away. Glau, Crane's lawyer, stood beside the open driver's door of the van, holding a gun on Rawlins.

See what I mean about head shots?

Fade to black.

Chapter

Twenty-six

I came to with a headache, and my stomach attempted to slither out of my mouth. Its escape attempt was blocked by some kind of gag. I had the taste of metal in my mouth, and my jaws were forced uncomfortably wide. The blindfold on my face was almost a mercy, given the headache. I was pretty sure any light that got into my eyes would hurt like hell.

My nose was filled with scents. Old motor oil. Gasoline vapors. Dust. Something metallic and elusively familiar. I knew the smell, but I couldn't place it.

I lay prostrate on some cold, hard surface—concrete, at a guess. My arms were held up above my head, my wrists bound in something cold that prickled with many tiny, sharp points. Thorn manacles, then. They were meant, along with the gag and blindfold, to keep me from using my magic. If I tried to start focusing my will, they would bite and freeze. I didn't know where the damned things came from, but Crane wasn't the first bad guy I'd met who kept a pair on hand. Maybe there'd been a sale.

I'd heard one person claim that they'd been invented by a two-thousand-year-old lunatic named Nicodemus, and I'd heard others claim they were of faerie make. Personally, I figured they were more likely a creation of the Red Court, materiel for their war with the Council.

It would certainly be to their advantage to make sure as many people as possible had a set of restraints with no purpose but to render a mortal wizard helpless.

Hell, if I was in the Red Court, I'd be giving the things away like Halloween candy. It was a scary notion, and for more than one reason.

I was in trouble up to my eyebrows, but my nausea was severe enough that it took me several minutes of effort to care. *Come on, Harry. You aren't fighting your way clear of this. Use your head.*

For starters, I was still alive, and that told me something all by itself. If Crane had wanted to kill me, he'd had all the time he would need to do it. He wouldn't even have had to worry about the death curse a wizard could lay down on his enemies on his way into the hereafter. Unconscious wizards can't throw curses. I was still breathing, which meant . . .

I swallowed. Which meant that he had other plans for me. It did not seem like a promising way to begin thinking my way clear.

I tried to say Rawlins's name, but my tongue was being held in place by something, and it sounded like, "Lah-tha?"

"Here," Rawlins replied, his tone very quiet. "How you doing?"

"La tha yahnah."

"They got me cuffed to a wall," he said. "My own damned cuffs, too, and they took my keys. I can't get to you, man. Sorry."

"Ooah ah yee?"

"Where? Where are we?" he asked.

I nodded. "Yah."

"Looks like an old auto workshop," he replied. "Abandoned. Metal walls. Windows are painted over. Doors chained shut. Lots and lots of cobwebs."

"Ooah lah kuh phruh?"

"The light? Big old shop lamp."

"Ah eeoh heh?"

"Anyone here?" Rawlins asked.

"Yah."

"Creepy little guy with fish lips. He won't talk to me, even when I asked pretty please. He's sitting in a chair about three feet from you pretending he's a guard dog."

Anger returned to me in full force, and made my head pound even harder. Glau. Glau'd been driving the van. Glau had killed my dog. Without consciously making the effort, I found myself reaching for my magic, for fire enough to cremate the little toad. The manacles became a frozen agony that wiped anything resembling thought from my head.

I bit down on the mouthpiece and forced myself to relax my will. I could not afford to allow my impulses to control me, or I'd never get out of this. There would come a time when I wouldn't have to bite back on my emotions—but that time was not yet here.

Wait, I promised my anger. *Wait. I need to think for now, to get clear of my captors.*

And as soon as I did, Glau was going to have a real bad day.

I relaxed my will and the pain of the manacles faded. Patience, Harry. Patience.

A door creaked open and footsteps approached. A moment later, Crane's voice murmured, "Awake, I see, Dresden. Your head must be as hard as everyone says. Mr. Glau, if you would be so kind?"

Someone fumbled at the hood over my face, and it withdrew along with the mouthpiece, and I could see that hood and gag were all of a piece. Charming. The mouthpiece had gripped my tongue with two little clamps. I spat the taste of metal out of my mouth, along with a little bit of blood. The hood and muzzle had torn my gums open in a couple of places.

I lay on my back, staring up at a corrugated metal ceiling, then looked around at a dim, ugly, forlorn-looking auto shop. The nagging sense of familiarity increased. The only doors leading out were chained shut and padlocked on the inside, and no keys were in sight.

Crane stood over me, looking down, smiling, as tall and dark and handsome as you please. My eyes went past him to Rawlins. The dark-skinned cop stood leaning against the wall, one wrist cuffed to a metal ring in a steel support beam. A bruise severe enough to show even on his dark skin covered one cheek entirely. Rawlins looked calm, remote, and unafraid. I was fairly sure it was only an act, but if so, it was a good one.

"Crane," I said. "What do you want?"

He smiled a nasty smile. "To build the future," he replied. "Networking is very important in my business."

"Cut the crap and talk," I said in a flat tone.

The smile vanished. "You would be wise not to anger me, wizard. You're hardly in a position to make demands."

"If you were going to kill me, you'd have done it already."

Crane let out a rueful laugh. "I suppose that's true enough. I was going to finish you and drop you in the lake, but imagine my surprise when I made some calls and it turns out that you're . . ."

"Infamous?" I suggested. "Tough? A good dancer?"

Crane showed me his teeth. "Marketable. For an insignificant young man, you've managed to irritate a great many people."

A little chill went through me. I kept it off my face.

Crane's eyes glittered anyway. "Ah. Yes. Fear." He inhaled deeply, his smile turning smug. "You're smart enough to know when you are powerless, at least. In my experience, most wizards are fairly cowardly, when push comes to shove."

I felt a hot reply coming, but again I set my anger aside—temporarily. Crane was trying to push my buttons. He could only get away with it if I allowed him to do so. I met his dark eyes and let one corner of my mouth tilt up into a smile.

"In my experience," I replied, gaze unwavering, "people who have underestimated me regretted it."

I didn't feel like being drawn into a soulgaze with Crane, but I had little to lose. If nothing else, it might provide me with some valuable insight to his character.

Crane's nerve broke first. He turned to walk away from me, pretending that he'd just received a call on his cell phone—he already had a new one. He stood in the shadows on the other side of the room.

I spat more metal taste out of my mouth and wished I had a glass of water. Glau sat in a chair nearby, watching me. The little man had a gun resting in his lap, in hand and ready to go. A briefcase sat on the floor beside his chair.

"You," I said.

Glau looked at me without any readable expression.

"You killed my dog," I said. "Get your affairs in order."

Something ugly flickered through his eyes. "An idle threat. You will not live to see the dawn."

"You'd best hope I do," I said. "Because if I go down, I know where my death curse is going."

Glau's lips peeled back from his teeth, and I swear to God that they were pointed—not like a vampire's fangs or a ghoul's canines, but in solid, serrated triangles, like a shark. He rose, the gun twitching in his hand.

"Glau!" snapped Crane.

Glau froze for a second, and then relaxed and let the gun fall to his side.

Crane shoved the cell phone into his pocket and stalked over to me. "Keep your tongue in your mouth, wizard."

"Or what?" I asked. "You'll kill me? From where I'm standing, that isn't a worst-case scenario."

"True," Crane murmured. He withdrew a small handgun from his pocket and without so much as blinking shot Rawlins in the foot.

The big cop jerked against the cuffs that held him. His face contorted in surprised pain and he fell. The cuffs, fastened to the beam at shoulder level, cut cruelly into his wrists. Rawlins got his legs underneath him and let out a string of sulfurous curse words.

Crane regarded Rawlins for a moment, smiled, and then pointed the gun at the cop's head.

"No!" I shouted.

"It's entirely up to you, wizard, whether or not his children lose their father. Behave." He smiled again. "We'll all be happier."

Again the rage threatened to drown any rational thought in my head. Threatening me is one thing. Threatening someone else to *get* to me is another. I'm sick of seeing decent people suffer. I'm sick of seeing them die.

Patience, Harry. Calm. Rational. I was going to have to discourage Crane from this tactic with extreme prejudice as a deterrent to future weasels. But not yet. Keep him talking.

"Do you understand me?" Crane said.

I jerked my chin in a brief nod.

He smirked. "I want to hear you say it."

I clenched my jaw and said, "I understand."

"I'm so glad we had this talk," he said. There was a low buzzing sound, the almost-silent alert of his cell phone, I suppose, and he walked away again, taking it out of his pocket and lifting it to his ear.

"How long have we been here?" I asked Rawlins.

"Hour," he mumbled. "Hour and a half."

I nodded. "You okay?"

He let out a pained grunt. "Tore open the stitches on my arm," he panted. "Foot, I don't know. Can't feel it. Doesn't look like it's bleeding much."

"Hang in there," I said. "We'll get out of this."

Glau's rubbery lips stretched out into a silent little smile, though he looked at neither of us.

"Bull," Rawlins said. "If you can get out, you should go. Once he gets what he wants, he's going to kill me anyway. Don't stay on my account."

"You're siphoning my noble hero vibe," I told him. "Cease and desist or I'll sue."

Rawlins tried to smile, and leaned against the wall, weight off his injured foot. The lower portion of his left sleeve had soaked through with blood.

Crane returned a moment later, smiling like butter wouldn't melt in his mouth. "Start building more tax shelters, Glau. This is going rather well."

"Yeah?" I asked. "So who's going to pony up for one Harry Dresden, slightly used?"

Crane showed me all his teeth. "I'm holding an auction as we speak. A rather energetic one."

"Yeah?" I asked. "Who's leading?"

His smiled widened. "Why, Paolo Ortega's widow. Duchess Arianna of the Red Court."

I suddenly felt cold, all over.

I was captured by the Red Court once. Held in the dark by a crowd of hissing, monstrous shapes.

They did things.

There was nothing I could do about it.

I still had the nightmares to remind me. Not every night, maybe, but often enough. Often enough.

Crane closed his eyes and inhaled with a satisfied expression. "She'll be quite creative when it comes to dealing with her husband's bane. I don't blame you for feeling terrified. Who wouldn't?"

"Hey," I told him, grasping at straws. "Call the White Council. If nothing else, maybe they'll run the bidding up for you."

Crane laughed. "I already have," he said.

Hope twitched somewhere inside me. If the Council knew I was in trouble, then maybe they would be able to do something. They might be on the way even now. I needed to stall Crane, keep him occupied. "Yeah? What did they say?"

His smile widened. "That the White Council's unyielding policy is one of nonnegotiation with terrorists."

Hope's corpse went through some postmortem twitching.

His phone buzzed again. He stepped away and spoke quietly, his back to us. After a moment he snapped his fingers and said, "Glau, get on the computer. The auction is closing in five minutes and there's always a last-second rush. We'll need to verify an account." He turned back to the phone. "No, unacceptable. A numbered account only. I don't trust those people at PayPal."

"Hey!" I protested. "Are you selling me on *eBay*?"

Crane winked at me. "Ironic, eh? Though I confess a bit of surprise. How do you know what it is?"

"I read," I told him.

"Ahhh," he said. "Glau. Computer."

Glau nodded but said, "They should not be unwatched."

"I can see them," Crane replied, irritation in his voice. "Move."

By his expression, Glau clearly did not agree with Crane, but he went.

I licked my lips, struggling to think through my headache and anxiety and a solid lump of despair. There had to be a way out of this. There was always a way out. I had found ways out of desperate straits before.

Of course, I'd had my magic available then. Damn those manacles. As long as they kept my power constrained, I would never be able to free myself or Rawlins.

So, moron, I thought to myself. *Get rid of the manacles. Get around them. Do something. It's your only chance.*

"How?" I muttered out loud. "I don't know a damned thing about them."

Rawlins blinked at me. I grimaced, shook my head at him, and closed my eyes. I shut away the distractions and turned my focus inward. It was easy to imagine an empty place; flat, dark floor illuminated from above by a single light shining without apparent source. I imagined myself standing beneath it.

"Lasciel," my image-self said quietly. "I seek counsel."

She appeared at once, stepping into the circle of light. She wore her most familiar form, the functional white tunic, the tall, lovely figure, but her golden hair now appeared as a waist-length sheet of deep auburn. She bowed deeply and murmured, "I am here, my host."

"You changed your hair," I said.

Her mouth flirted with a smile. "There are too many blondes in your life, my host. I feared I would be lost in the press."

I sighed. "The manacles," I said. "Do you know of them?"

She bowed again. "Indeed, my host. They are of an ancient make, wrought by the troll-smiths of the Unseelie Court, and employed against those of your talents for a thousand years and more."

I blinked at her. "Faeries made those?"

I was dimly aware that, in my surprise, I had spoken the words aloud. I clenched my physical jaws shut and focused on the image me, briefly wondering just how badly cracked my engine block was going to get by trying to keep track of my own personal internal reality in addition to the actual, threatening reality where Rawlins and I were in deep trouble. Hell, for that matter, I supposed it was entirely possible that I already *had* snapped. It wasn't as though anyone but me had ever seen Lasciel. Perhaps, in addition to existing only in my head, she was all in my imagination, kind of a waking dream.

For a minute, I thought about abandoning the wizarding biz and taking up a career that would let me crawl under rocks and hide, professionally.

"You needn't attempt to keep your inner self separate from your physical self," Lasciel said in a reasonable tone. "I should be happy to advise you from the outside, so to speak."

"Oh, no," I said, keeping all the conversation on the inside. "I've got problems enough without adding a sentient hallucination to the mix."

"As you wish," Lasciel replied. "You are, I take it, seeking a way to overcome the bindings of the thorn manacles?"

"Obviously. Can it be done?"

"All things are possible," Lasciel assured me. "Though some of them are extremely unlikely."

"How?" I demanded of her. "This is not the time to

get coy with me. If I die, you're coming along for the ride."

"I am aware," she replied, arching an eyebrow. "They are a crafting of faerie make, my host. Seek that which is bane to they who made it."

"Iron," I said at once, nodding. "And sunlight. Trolls can't stand either." I opened my actual eyes and glanced around the interior of the garage. "Sunlight's out of town for a few hours yet, but we've got lots and lots of iron. Rawlins has a free hand. If I get a tool to him, maybe he could shatter a link of the manacles' chain. Then I could break his cuffs or something."

"Point of logic," the fallen angel pointed out. "Given that you are not free to retrieve a tool, getting one to Rawlins seems problematic."

"Yeah, but—"

"In addition," she continued, "you are exhausted, and it is reasonable to assume that Crane will finish his negotiations shortly and turn you over to one of your foes. You have insufficient time to recover your strength."

"I guess—"

She continued in the firm tone of a schoolteacher addressing a stubborn child. "You have in the past expressed much frustration and doubt that your control of physical forces was precise enough to break handcuffs without breaking the person held in them."

I sighed. "True, but—"

"The only egress from this place is chained shut and you do not have the key."

"It isn't—"

"And finally," she finished, "lest you forget, you are being guarded by at least one supernatural being who will hardly stand gawking while you attempt escape."

I glowered. "Anyone ever told you that you have a very negative attitude?"

She arched a brow, the expression an invitation to continue the line of thought.

I chewed on my lip and forged another couple of links in the chain of thought. "Which isn't helpful. But your ass is as deep in alligators as mine, and you want to help. So . . ." My stomach sank a little. "You can offer me another option."

She smiled, pleased. "Very good."

"I don't want it," I said.

"Why ever not?"

"Because a freaking fallen angel is offering it, that's why ever not. You're poison, lady. Don't think I don't know it."

She lifted a long-fingered hand to me, palm out. "I ask only that you hear me out. If what I offer is not to your liking, I will of course support your efforts to form an alternate plan."

I upgraded the glower to a glare. She regarded me in perfect calm.

Dammit. The best way to keep yourself from doing something grossly self-destructive and stupid is to avoid the temptation to do it. For example, it is far easier to fend off inappropriate amorous desires if one runs screaming from the room every time a pretty girl comes in. Which sounds silly, I know, but the same principle applies to everything else.

If I let her talk to me, Lasciel would propose something calm and sane and reasonable and effective. It would require a small price of me, if nothing else by making me a tiny bit more dependent upon her advice and assistance. Whatever happened, she'd gain another smidgen of influence over me.

Baby steps on the highway to hell. Lasciel was an immortal. She could afford patience, whereas I could not afford temptation.

It came down to this: If I didn't hear her out and didn't get out of this mess, Rawlins's blood would be on my hands. And whoever was behind the slaughter around the convention might well keep right on escalating. More people could die.

Oh. And I'd wind up enjoying some kind of Torquemadaesque vacation with whichever fiend had the most money and the least lag.

When a concept like that is an afterthought, you know things are bad.

Lasciel watched me with patient blue eyes.

"All right," I told her. "Let's hear it."

Chapter

Twenty-seven

We plotted, the fallen angel and me. It went fast. It turns out that holding an all-mental conversation gets things done at the literal speed of thought, without all those clunky phonemes to get in the way.

Barely a minute had passed when I opened my eyes and said very quietly to Rawlins, "You're right. They'll kill you. We have to get out of here."

The cop gave me a pained grimace and nodded. "How?"

I struggled and sat up. I rolled my shoulders a little, trying to get some blood flowing through my arms, which had been manacled together underneath me. I tested the chain. It had been slipped through an inverted U-bolt in the concrete floor. The links rattled metallically as they slid back and forth.

I checked Crane at the noise. The man kept speaking intently into his cell phone, and took no apparent notice of the movement.

"I'm going to slip one of these manacles off my wrist," I told him. I nodded at a discarded old rolling tool cabinet. "There should be something in there I can use. I'll cut us both out."

Rawlins shook his head. "Those two going to stand there watching while we do all that?"

"I'll do it fast," I said.

"Then what?"

"I kill the lights and we get out."

"Door is chained shut," Rawlins said.

"Let me worry about that."

Rawlins squinted. He looked very tired. "Why not," he said, nodding. "Why not."

I nodded and closed my eyes, slowed my breathing, and began to concentrate.

"Hey," Rawlins said. "How you going to slip your cuffs?"

"Ever heard about yogis, out east?"

"Yogi Berra," he said at once. "And Yogi Bear."

"Not those yogis. As in snake charmers."

"Oh. Right."

"They spend a lifetime learning to control their body. They can do some fairly amazing stuff."

Rawlins nodded. "Like fold themselves up into a gym bag and sit inside it at the bottom of a pool for half an hour."

"Right," I said. I followed Lasciel's instructions, sinking into deeper and deeper focus. "Some of them can collapse the bones in their hands. Use their muscles and tendons to alter tensions. Change the shape." I focused on my left hand, and for a moment was a bit grateful that it was already so badly maimed and mostly numb. What I was about to do, even with Lasciel's instruction, was going to hurt like hell. "Keep an eye out and be ready."

He nodded, holding still and not turning his head toward either Crane or Glau.

I dismissed him, the warehouse, my headache, and everything else that wasn't my hand from my perceptions. I had the general idea of what was supposed to happen, but I didn't have any practical, second-to-second knowledge of it. It was a terribly odd sensation, as though I were a skilled pianist whose fingers had suddenly forgotten their familiarity with the keys.

Not too quickly, murmured Lasciel's voice in my head. *Your muscles and joints have not been conditioned to this.* There was an odd sensation in my thoughts, somehow similar to abruptly remembering how to tie a knot that had once been thoughtlessly familiar. *Like this,* Lasciel's presence whispered, and that same familiarity suddenly thrummed down my arm.

I flexed my thumb, made a rippling motion of my fingers, and tightened every muscle in my hand in a sudden clench. I dislocated my thumb with a sickly little crackle of damaged flesh.

For a second, I thought the pain would drop me unconscious.

No, Lasciel's voice said. *You must control this. You must escape.*

I know, I snarled back at her in my mind. *Apparently nerve damage from burns doesn't stop you from feeling it when someone pulls your fingers out of their sockets.*

Someone? Lasciel said. *You did it to yourself, my host.*

Would you back off and give me room to work?

That's ridiculous, Lasciel replied. But the sense of her presence abruptly retreated.

I took deep, quiet breaths, and twisted my left hand. My flesh screamed protest, but I only embraced the pain and continued to move, slow and steady. I got the fingers of my right hand to lightly grasp the manacle on my left wrist, and began to draw my hand steadily against the cold, binding circle of metal. My hand folded in a way that was utterly alien in sensation, and the screaming pain of it stole my breath.

But it slipped an inch beneath the metal cuff.

I twisted my hand again, in exactly the same motion, never letting up the pressure, working to encompass the pain as something to aid me, rather than distract.

I slipped an inch closer to freeing my hand. The pain became more and more intense despite my efforts to divert it, like an afternoon sun that burns brightly into your eyes even though they're closed. Only a moment more. I only needed to remain silent and focused for a few more seconds.

I bore the pain. I kept up the pressure, and abruptly I felt the cold metal of the cuff flick over the outside of my thumb, one of the few spots on my fingers where much tactile sensation remained. My hand came free, and I clutched tightly to the empty cuff with my right hand, to keep it from rattling.

I opened my eyes and glanced around the garage. Crane paced back and forth in conversation on his phone. I waited until his back was mostly turned to move. Then I rose and slipped the chain through the U-bolt on the floor, until the circle of the cuff pressed against the bolt. I was still tethered by a chain perhaps a foot long, but I moved as silently as I could and reached out with my throbbing left hand for the wheeled tool cabinet.

I had trouble getting my fingers to cooperate, but I slipped the cabinet open. The tools inside it had been there for a long time—several years, at least. They were spotted with rust. I could only see about half the cabinet from where I crouched, and there wasn't anything there that could help me. I hated to do it, but I felt around the unseen portion of the cabinet with my clumsy fingers. I was terrified that I wouldn't be able to feel a tool even if my fingers found it, and even more frightened by the knowledge that I might knock something over and draw attention.

My hand shook, but I felt through the cabinet as quickly and lightly as I could, starting at the top and moving down.

On the floor of the cabinet, I felt an object, the handle of some kind of tool. I drew it out as quietly as I could, and found myself holding a hacksaw. My heart leapt with excitement.

I returned to more or less my original position, with my captors seemingly none the wiser, and took a grip on the saw. My distorted thumb hurt abominably, so I took the hacksaw in my right hand, took a deep breath, and then began slicing at the chain link immediately below the empty manacle.

I could only cut in strokes eight or nine inches long because of the chain still attached to my right wrist, and it made a low, buzzing racket that could not be mistaken for anything *but* a saw. I was sure I would not have time to cut myself free—but the heavy-duty steel of the hacksaw's blade ripped into the silvery metal chain as if it were made of pine. Three, four, five strokes of the hacksaw and the link parted. I jerked hard with my right hand and the chain slid through the U-bolt, the broken link snapping as the cuffs struck the bolt.

I rose, free.

Crane let out a sudden, startled sound, dropped his cell phone, and went for his gun. There was no time to free Rawlins, so I tossed him the hacksaw and then threw myself to one side as Crane let off a shot. Sparks leapt up from the rolling cabinet's surface, and a rush of adrenaline made the pains of my body vanish. I kept my head down as low as I could and scurried to one side, attempting to put the bulk of an old, rusted pickup truck between Crane and me. I reached for my magic, but the cuff still attached to my arm reacted with that same burst of agony, splintering my concentration.

I caught a glimpse of movement. Crane circled to one side, looking for a clear line of fire. I maneuvered like a squirrel, keeping the truck between us and crouching low to deny him a clean shot. I went for the passenger door, hoping to find something, anything I could use to defend myself in the truck.

Locked.

"Glau!" Crane shouted. His second shot shattered the truck's passenger window, the bullet passing within a few inches of my head.

I reached up, unlocked the truck's door, and swung it open. The cab was cluttered with empty cigarette packs, discarded fast-food wrappers, crushed beer cans, a heavy-duty claw hammer, and three or four glass beer bottles.

Perfect.

I clutched the hammer's wrapped steel handle in my teeth, scooped up the bottles, and threw one at the far side of the garage. It shattered loudly. I rose at once, another bottle ready, and hurled it with as much force as I could.

The first bottle had caused Crane to snap his head to one side, looking for the source of the sound. He looked away from me for only a second, but it was distraction enough to allow me to throw.

The bottle tumbled end over end and smashed into the work lamp with a crash of breaking glass. Sparks showered up in a brief cloud of electric outrage, and then heavy darkness slammed down upon us.

Now, I thought to Lasciel.

Darkness vanished, replaced with lines and planes of silver light that outlined the garage, the truck, the tool cabinets and workbenches, as well as the doors and windows and the bolt on the wall where Rawlins was chained.

I was not actually seeing the garage, of course, for

there was no physical light for my eyes to see. Instead, I was looking at an illusion.

The portion of Lasciel in my head was capable of creating illusory sensations of almost any kind, though if I suspected any tampering I could defend myself against it easily enough. This illusion, however, was not meant to deceive. She'd placed it there to help me, gleaning the precise dimensions and arrangements of the garage from my own senses and projecting them to my eyes to enable me to move in the dark.

It wasn't a perfect illusion, of course. It was merely a model. It didn't keep track of animate objects, and if anything moved around I wouldn't know it until I'd knocked myself unconscious on it—but I wouldn't need it for long. I ran for Rawlins.

"Glau!" Crane screamed, no more than ten or twelve feet away. "Cover the door!"

I flung the third bottle to the floor at my feet. It was an exceedingly odd sensation, for the bottle was outlined in silver light until it left my hand. It vanished into the darkness, and shattered on the floor near me.

There was a moment of frozen silence, broken only by the rasp of a hacksaw against Rawlins's cuffs. Crane took a couple of steps toward me, then hesitated, and though I could not see him, I could sense the hesitation. Then he moved again, away from me, probably assuming I was attempting another distraction. My lips stretched into a wolfish smile, and I padded to Rawlins, my steps sure and steady even in the total darkness.

I reached the bolt on the steel beam, and found Rawlins standing beneath it, breathing hard, sawing as fast as he could. He jumped when I touched his shoulder, but I took the hammer in hand and whispered, "It's Harry. Get your head down."

He did. I looked up at the silvery illusion of the bolt,

steadied my breathing, and drew the hammer back very slowly, focusing upon that movement and nothing else. Then I hissed out a breath and struck at the bolt with every ounce of force I could physically muster.

I'm not a weightlifter, but no one's ever accused me of being a sissy, either. More importantly, years and years of my metaphysical studies and practice had given me considerable skill at focus and concentration. The hammer struck the bolt that held the other ring of Rawlins's cuffs. Sparks flew. The bolt, as rusted and ruined as the rest of the building, snapped.

Rawlins dragged me to the ground a heartbeat before Crane's pistol thundered again from the far side of the garage. A bullet caromed off the metal beam with an ugly, high-pitched whine.

"Come on," I hissed. I seized Rawlins's shirt. He grunted and stumbled blindly after me, trying to be quiet, but given his injuries there was only so much he could do. Speed would have to serve where stealth was not available. I hauled him directly across the garage floor, skipping around a mechanic's pit and several stacks of old tires.

"Where are we going?" Rawlins gasped. "Where is the door?"

"We aren't taking the door," I whispered—which was true. I wasn't sure that we'd have a way out of the garage, but we certainly wouldn't leave via the door.

The Full Moon Garage had been abandoned since the disappearance of its previous owners, a gang of lycanthropes with a notable lack of common sense when it came to choosing enemies. It wasn't as big a coincidence as it seemed, that Crane was using the same building. It was old, abandoned, had no windows, was close to the convention center, and easy to get in and out of. More to the point, it had been a place where fairly horrible things happened, and the ugly energy of them still lingered in the air. I wasn't sure what Crane and Glau were, exactly, but a place like this would feel comfortable and familiar to many denizens of the dark side.

I'd been held captive in the building before and my means of egress was still there—a hole beneath the edge of the cheap corrugated metal wall, dug down into the earth and out into the gravel parking lot by a pack of wolves. I got to the wall and knelt down to check Lasciel's mental model against the reality it represented. The hole was still there. If anything, the years had worn it even deeper and wider.

I shoved Rawlins's hands down to let him feel it. "Go," I whispered. "Under the wall and out."

He grunted assent and started hauling himself through it. Rawlins was built a lot heavier than me, but he fit through the time-widened hole. I crouched down to follow him, but heard running footsteps just behind me.

I ducked to one side, my eyes now adjusting enough to let me see faint, ambient city light trickling through the hole. I saw a vague shape in the darkness, and then saw Glau's hands seize Rawlins's wounded foot. Rawlins screamed.

I lunged forward and smashed the claw hammer down onto Glau's forearm. It hit with brutal force and a sound of breaking bone.

Glau let out a wild, falsetto, ululating scream, like that of some kind of primitive warrior. The hammer jerked out of my hands. I heard a *whirr* in the air, and ducked in time to avoid Glau returning the favor. I twisted, swinging the chain still attached to the remaining manacle along at what I estimated to be Glau's eye level. The chain hit. He let out another shrieking cry, falling backward.

I dove for the hole and wriggled through it like a

greased weasel. Crane's gun went off again, punching a hole in the wall ten feet away. Running footsteps retreated, and metal clinked. I heard myself whimpering, and had a flashback to any number of nightmares where I could not move swiftly enough to escape the danger. Any second I expected to take a bullet, or for Glau to lay into me with the hammer or his sharklike teeth.

Rawlins grabbed my wrist and pulled me through. I got to my feet, looking around the little gravel lot wildly for the nearest cover—several stacks of old tires. I didn't have to point at it for Rawlins to get the idea. We ran for it. Rawlins's wounded leg almost gave out, and I slowed to help him, looking back for our pursuers.

Glau wriggled out of the hole just as we had, rose to a crouch, and threw the claw hammer. It tumbled end over end, flying as swiftly as a major-league fastball, and hit me in the ass.

A shock went through me on impact, and my balance wavered as half of my lower body went numb. I tried to clutch at Rawlins for balance, but the hand I'd distorted wasn't strong enough to hold, and the force of the blow threw me down to the gravel. The impact tore open all the defenses I'd rallied against my body's various pains, and for a second I could barely move, much less flee.

Glau drew a long, curved blade from his belt, something vaguely Arabic in origin. He bounded after us. It was hopeless, but Rawlins and I tried to run anyway.

There were a couple of light footsteps, a blurring figure running far too swiftly to be human, and Crane kicked my functional leg out from underneath me. I dropped. He delivered a vicious blow to Rawlins's belly. The cop went down, too.

Crane, his face pale and furious, snarled, "I warned you to behave, wizard." He lifted the gun and pointed it at Rawlins's head. "You've just killed this man."

Chapter

Twenty-eight

A dark figure stepped out of the deep shadows behind the stacks of tires, pointed a sawed-off shotgun at Glau, and said, "Howdy."

Glau whirled to face the newcomer, hand already lifting the knife. The interloper pulled the trigger. Thunder filled the air. The blast threw Glau to the gravel like an enormous, flopping fish.

Thomas stepped out into the wan light of a distant streetlamp, dressed all in loose black clothing, including my leather duster, which fell all the way to his ankles. His hair was ragged and wind-tossed, and his grey eyes were cold as he worked the action on the shotgun, ejecting the spent shell and levering a fresh one into the chamber. The barrel of the shotgun snapped to Crane.

Son of a bitch.

Now I knew who'd been following me around town.

"You," Crane said in a hollow-sounding voice, staring at Thomas.

"Me," Thomas agreed, insouciant cheer thick in his voice. "Lose the gun, Madrigal."

Crane's lip lifted into a sneer, but he did lower the pistol and drop it to the ground.

"Kick it over here," Thomas said.

Crane did it, ignoring me completely. "I thought you'd be dead by now, coz. God knows you made enemies enough within the House, much less the rest of the Court."

"I get by," Thomas drawled. Then he used a toe to flick the gun over to me.

Crane's eyes widened in surprise, then narrowed.

I picked up the revolver and checked the cylinder. My distorted left hand functioned, weakly, but it hurt like hell, and would until I could get enough quiet and focus to get everything back into its proper place. My headache intensified to a fine, distracting agony as I bent over, but I ignored that, too. Though I walk through the valley of the shadow of trauma, I will fear no concussion.

Crane's revolver held freshly loaded rounds, all six of them. I put them back and checked on Rawlins. Between the pain of his recent injuries and the strain of our flight and recapture, the big cop did not look well.

"Isn't bad," he said quietly. "Just hurts. Tired."

"Sit tight," I told him. "We'll get you out of here."

He nodded and lay there, watching developments, his eyes only half aware.

I made sure he wasn't bleeding too badly, then rose, pointed the gun at Crane, and took position between him and Rawlins.

"How's it going, Dresden?" Thomas asked.

"Took you long enough," I said.

Thomas grinned, but it didn't touch his eyes. His gaze never left Crane. "Have you ever met my cousin, Madrigal Raith?"

"I knew he didn't look like a Darby," I said.

Thomas nodded. "Wasn't that a movie with Janet Munro?"

"And Sean Connery."

"Thought so," Thomas said.

Madrigal Raith watched the exchange through narrowed eyes. Maybe it was a trick of the light, but he looked paler now, his features almost eerily fine. Or maybe now that Thomas had identified him as a White Court vampire, I could correctly interpret the warnings my instincts had shrieked at me during our first talk. There was little but contempt in Madrigal's eyes as he stared at my brother. "You have no idea what you're getting yourself involved in, coz. I'll not surrender this prize to you."

"Oh, but you will," Thomas said in his best Snidely Whiplash villain voice.

Crane's eyes flickered with something hot and furious. "Don't push me, little coz. I'll make you regret it."

Thomas's laugh rang out, full of scorn and confidence. "You couldn't make water run downhill. Walk away while you still can."

"Don't be stupid," Madrigal replied. "Do you know what kind of money he's worth?"

"Is it the kind that spends in hell?" Thomas asked. "Because if you keep this up, you'll need it."

Madrigal sneered. "You'd kill family in cold blood, Thomas? You?"

There are statues that don't have a poker face as good as Thomas's. "Maybe you haven't put it together yet, Madrigal. I'm banished, remember? You aren't family."

Madrigal regarded Thomas for a long minute before he said, "You're bluffing."

Thomas looked at me, a quality of inquiry to his expression, and said, "He thinks I'm bluffing."

"Make sure he can talk," I said.

"Cool," Thomas said, and shot Madrigal in the feet.

The light and thunder of the shotgun's blast rolled away, leaving Madrigal on the ground, hissing out a thready shriek of agony. He curled up to clutch at the gory ruins of his ankles and feet. Blood a few shades too pale to be human spattered the gravel.

"Touché," grunted Rawlins, a certain satisfaction in his tone.

It took Madrigal a while to control himself and find his voice. "You're dead," he whispered, pain making the words quiver and shake. "You gutless little swine. You're dead. Uncle will kill you for this."

My half brother smiled and worked the action of the shotgun again. "I doubt my father cares," he replied. "He wouldn't mind losing a nephew. Particularly not one who has been consorting with scum like House Malvora."

"Aha," I said quietly, putting two and two together. "Now I get it. He's like them."

"Like what?" Thomas asked.

"A phobophage," I said quietly. "He feeds on fear the way you feed on lust."

Thomas's expression turned a bit nauseated. "Yes. A lot of the Malvora do."

Madrigal's pale, strained face twisted into a vicious smile. "You should try it some night, coz."

"It's sick, Mad," Thomas said. There was an almost ghostly sense of sadness or pity in his tone, so subtle that I would not have seen it before living with him. Hell, I doubt he realized it was there himself. "It's sick. And it's made you sick."

"You feed on mortal desires for the little death," Madrigal said, his eyes half closing. "I feed on their desire for the real thing. We both feed. In the end, we both kill. There's no difference."

"The difference is that once you've started, you can't let them go running off to report you to the authorities," Thomas said. "You keep them until they're dead."

Madrigal let out a laugh, unsettling for how genuine

it sounded given his situation. I got the sneaking suspicion that the vampire was a couple of Peeps short of an Easter basket.

"Thomas, Thomas," Madrigal murmured. "Always the self-righteous little bleeding heart. So concerned for the bucks and does—as though you never tasted them yourself. Never killed them yourself."

Thomas's expression went opaque again, but his eyes were flat with sudden anger.

Madrigal's smile widened at the response. His teeth shone white in the evening's gloom. "I've been feeding well. Whereas you . . . well. Without your little dark-eyed whore to take—"

Without warning, without a flicker of expression on Thomas's face, the shotgun roared again, and the blast took Madrigal across the knees. More too-pale blood spattered the gravel.

Holy crap.

Madrigal went prone again, body arching in agony, the pain choking his scream down to an anemic little echo of a real shriek.

Thomas planted his boot on Madrigal's neck, his expression cold and calm but for the glittering rage in his eyes. He pumped the next shell in, and held the shotgun in one hand, shoving the barrel against Madrigal's cheekbone.

Madrigal froze, quivering in agony, eyes wide and desperate.

"Never," Thomas murmured, very quietly. "Ever. Speak of Justine."

Madrigal said nothing, but my instincts screamed again. Something in the way he held himself, something in his eyes, told me that he was acting. He'd maneuvered the conversation to Justine deliberately. He was playing on Thomas's feelings for Justine, distracting us.

I spun to see Glau on his feet just as though he hadn't been given a lethal dose of buckshot in the chest from ten feet away. He shot across the parking lot at a full sprint, running for the van parked about fifty feet away. He ran in utter silence, without the crunch of gravel or the creak of shoes, and for a second I thought I saw maybe an inch and a half of space between where he planted his running feet and the ground.

"Thomas," I said. "Glau's running."

"Relax," Thomas said, and his eyes never left Madrigal.

I heard the scrabble of claws on gravel and then Mouse shot out of the shadows that had hidden Thomas. He flashed by me in what was for him a relaxed lope, but as Glau approached the van, Mouse accelerated to a full sprint. In the last couple of steps before Glau reached the van, I thought I saw something forming around the great dog's forequarters, tiny flickers of pale colors, almost like Saint Elmo's fire. Then Mouse threw himself into a leap. I saw Glau's expression reflected in the van's windshield, his too-wide eyes goggling in total surprise. Then Mouse slammed his chest and shoulder into Glau's back like a living battering ram.

The force of the impact took Glau's balance completely, and sent the man into a vicious impact with the van's dented front bumper. Glau hit *hard*, hard enough that I heard bones breaking from fifty feet away, and his head whiplashed down onto the hood and rebounded with neck-breaking force. Glau bounced off the van's front bumper and hood, and landed in a limp, boneless pile on the ground.

Mouse landed, skidded on the gravel, and spun to face Glau. He watched the downed man for a few seconds, legs stiff. His back legs dug twice at the gravel, throwing up dust and rocks in challenge.

Glau never stirred.

Mouse sniffed and then let out a sneeze that might almost have been actual words: *So there*.

Then the dog turned and trotted right over to me, favoring one leg slightly, grinning a proud canine grin. He shoved his broad head under my hand in his customary demand for an ear scratching. I did it, while something released in my chest with a painful little snapping sensation. My dog was all right. Maybe my eyes misted up a little. I dropped to one knee and slid an arm around the mutt's neck. "Good dog," I told him.

Mouse's tail wagged proudly at the praise, and he leaned against me.

I made sure my eyes were clear, then looked up to find Madrigal staring at the dog in shock and fear. "That isn't a dog," the vampire whispered.

"But he'll do anything for a Scooby Snack," I said. "Spill it, Madrigal. What are you doing in town? How are you involved with the attacks?"

He licked his lips and shook his head. "I don't have to talk to you," he said. "And you don't have time to make me. The gunshots. Even in this neighborhood, the police will be here soon."

"True," I said. "So here's how it's going to work. Thomas, when you hear a siren, pull the trigger."

Madrigal made a choking sound.

I smiled. "I want answers. That's all. Give them to me, and we go away. Otherwise . . ." I shrugged, and made a vague gesture at Thomas.

Mouse stared at him and a steady growl bubbled from his throat. Madrigal shot a look over at the fallen Glau, who, by God, was moving his arms and legs in an aimless, stunned fashion. Mouse's growl grew louder, and Madrigal tried to squirm a little farther from my dog. "Even if I did talk, what's to keep you from killing me once I've told you?"

"Madrigal," Thomas said quietly. "You're a vicious little bitch, but you're still family. I'd rather not kill you. We left your jann alive. Play ball and both of you walk."

"You would side with this mortal buck against your own kind, Thomas?"

"My own kind booted me out," Thomas replied. "I take work where I can get it."

"Pariah vampire and pariah wizard," Madrigal murmured. "I suppose I can see the advantages, regardless of how the war turns out." He watched Thomas steadily for a moment and then looked at me. "I want your oath on it."

"You have it," I said. "Answer me honestly and I let you leave Chicago unharmed."

He swallowed, and his eyes flicked to the shotgun still pressed to his cheek. "My oath as well," he said. "I'll speak true."

And that settled that. Pretty much everything on the supernatural side of the street abided by a rigid code of traditional conduct that respected things like one's duties as a host, one's responsibility as a guest, and the integrity of a sworn oath. I could trust Madrigal's oath, once he'd openly made it.

Probably.

Thomas looked at me. I nodded. He eased his boot off of Madrigal's neck and took a step back, holding the shotgun at his side, though his stance became no less wary.

Madrigal sat up, wincing at his legs. There was a low, crackling kind of noise coming from them. The bleeding had already stopped. I could see portions of his calf, where the pants had been ripped away. The skin there actually bubbled and moved, and as I watched a round lump the size of a pea formed in the skin and burst, expelling a round buckshot that fell to the parking lot.

"Let's start simple," I said. "Where's the key to the manacles?"

"Van," he replied, his tone calm.

"My stuff?"

"Van."

"Keys." I held out my hand.

Madrigal drew a rental-car key ring from his pocket and tossed it to me, underhand.

"Thomas," I said, holding them up.

"You sure?" he asked.

"Mouse can watch him. I want this fucking thing off my arm."

Thomas took the keys and paced over to the van. He paused to idly check his hair in the reflection in the windshield before opening the van. Vanity, thy name is vampire.

"Now for the real question," I told Madrigal. "How are you involved with the attacks?"

"I'm not involved," he said quietly. "Not in the planning and not in the execution. I've been scheduled here for more than a year."

"Doesn't scream alibi to me," I said.

"I'm *not*," he insisted. "Of course, I thought them entertaining. And yes, the . . ." His eyelids half lowered and his voice went suddenly husky. "The . . . storm of it. The horror. Empty night, so sweet, all those souls in fear . . ."

"Get off the creepy psychic vampire train," I said. "Answer the question."

He gave me an ugly smile and gestured at his healing legs. "You see. I've fed, and fed *well*. Tonight, particularly. But you have my word, wizard, that whatever these creatures are, they are none of my doing. I was merely a spectator."

"If that's true," I said, "then why the hell did you grab me and bring me here?"

"For gain," he said. "And for enjoyment. I don't let any buck talk to me as you did. Since I'd planned on replying to your arrogance anyway, I thought I might as well turn a profit on it at the same time."

"God bless America," I said. Thomas returned with my magical gear—staff, backpack, a paper sack with my various foci in it, and an old-fashioned key with big teeth. I popped it in the slot on the manacles, fumbling with the stiff, uncooperative fingers of my left hand, and got the thing off my arm. My skin tingled for a moment, and I reached experimentally for my magic. No whiteout of pain. I was a wizard again.

I put on my amulet, bracelet, and ring. I felt the backpack to make sure Bob's skull was still in there. It was, and I breathed a mental sigh of relief. Bob's arcane knowledge was exceeded only by his inability to distinguish between moral right and wrong. His knowledge, in the wrong hands, could be dangerous as hell.

"No," I said quietly. "It isn't a coincidence that you're there, Madrigal."

"I just told you—"

"I believe you," I said. "But I don't think it was a coincidence, either. I think you were there for a reason. Maybe one you didn't know."

Madrigal frowned at that, and looked, for a moment, a little bit worried.

I pursed my lips and thought aloud. "You're high-profile. You're known to feed on fear. You're at war with the White Council." Two and two make four. Four and four make eight. I glanced up at Thomas and said,

"Whoever it is behind the phage attacks, they wanted me to think that Darby, here, was it."

Thomas's eyebrows went up in sudden understanding. "Madrigal's supposed to take the fall."

Madrigal's face turned even whiter. "What do you—"

He didn't get to finish the question.

Glau screamed. He screamed in pure, shrieking terror, his voice pitched as high as a woman's.

Everyone turned in surprise, and we were in time to see something haul the wounded Glau out of sight on the other side of the van. Red sprayed into the air. A piece of him, probably an arm or a leg, flew out from behind the van and tumbled for several paces before falling heavily to earth. Glau's voice abruptly went silent.

Something arched up from behind the van and landed, rolling. It bumped over the gravel and came to a stop.

Glau's head.

It had been physically ripped from his body, the flesh and bone torn and wrenched apart by main strength. His face was stretched into a scream, showing his sharklike teeth, and his eyes were glazed and frozen in death.

Orange light rose up behind the van, and then something, a creature perhaps ten or eleven feet in height, rose up and turned to face us. It was dressed all in rags, like some kind of enormous hobo, and was inhumanly slender. Its head was a bulbous thing, and it took me a second to recognize it as a pumpkin, carved with evil eyes like a jack-o'-lantern's. Those eyes glowed with a sullen red flame, and flashed intensely for a moment as it spied us.

Then it took a long step over the hood of the van and came at us with strides that looked slow but ate up yards with every step.

"Good God," Rawlins breathed.

Mouse snarled.

"Harry?" Thomas said.

"Another phage in a horror movie costume. The Scarecrow, this time," I murmured. "I'll handle it." I took my staff in hand and stepped out to meet the oncoming phage. I called up the Hellfire once more, as I had against the other phage, until my skin felt like it was about to fly apart. I gathered up energy for a strike more deadly than I had used earlier in the night. Then I cried out and unleashed my will against the creature, hitting it as hard as I possibly could.

The resulting cannonball of blazing force struck the Scarecrow head-on while it was twenty feet away, exploding into a column of searing red flame, an inferno of heat and light that went off with enough force to throw the thing halfway across Lake Michigan.

Imagine my surprise when the Scarecrow stepped through my spell as if it had not existed. Its eyes regarded me with far too much awareness, and its arm moved, striking-snake fast.

Fingers as thick and tough as pumpkin vines suddenly closed around my throat, and in a rush of sudden, terrifying understanding, I realized that this phage was stronger than the little one I'd beaten at the hotel. This creature was far older, larger, stronger, more dangerous.

My vision darkened to a star-spangled tunnel as the Scarecrow wrapped its other hand around my left thigh, lifted me to the horizontal over its head, and started to rip me in half.

Chapter

Twenty-nine

"Harry!" Thomas shouted. I heard a rasp of steel, and saw Thomas draw an old U.S. Cavalry saber from inside my duster. He tossed the shotgun to the wounded Rawlins and rushed forward.

Mouse beat him there. The big dog snarled and threw himself at the Scarecrow, obliging the creature to release my leg so that it could swing a spindly arm and fist at my dog. The Scarecrow was strong. It struck Mouse in midleap and batted him into the corrugated steel wall of the Full Moon Garage like he was a tennis ball. There was a crash, and Mouse bounced off the wall and landed heavily on his side, leaving a dent in the steel where he'd hit. He thrashed his legs and managed to rise to a wobbly stand.

Mouse had given Thomas an opening, and my brother leapt to the top of an old metal trash bin, then bounded fifteen feet through the air, whipping the sword down on the wrist of the arm that held me in choke. Thomas was never weak, but he was tapping into his powers as a vampire of the White Court as he attacked, and his skin was a luminous white, his eyes metallic silver. The blow parted the Scarecrow's hand from its arm, and dropped me a good five or six feet to the ground.

Even as I fell, I knew I had to move away from the

creature, and fast. I managed to have my balance more or less in place when I hit, and I fell into a roll, using the momentum to help me rise to a running start. But a problem developed.

That damned Scarecrow's hand had not ceased choking me, and had not lost any of its strength. My head-long retreat turned into a drunken stumble as my air ran out, and I clutched at the tough vine-fingers crushing my windpipe shut. I went to my knees and one hand, and out of the corner of my eye I saw Rawlins lift the shotgun and begin pumping rounds into the oncoming Scarecrow from where he sat on the ground. The rounds slowed the oncoming creature, but they did nothing to harm it.

My throat was on fire, and I knew I had only seconds of consciousness left. In pure desperation, I took my staff and, in a dizzying gesture, dragged it through a complete circle in the gravel at my feet. I touched my hand to the circle, willing power into it, and felt the field of magic that it formed spring up around me in a silent, invisible column.

The circle's power cut the Scarecrow's severed hand off from the main body of the creature, and like the phage in the hallway of the hotel, it abruptly transformed into transparent jelly that splattered down onto the gravel beneath my chin and soaked my shirt in sticky goo.

I sucked in a breath of pure euphoria, and though I was on my knees, I turned to face the Scarecrow and did not retreat. So long as the circle around me maintained its integrity, there was no way for the phage to get to me. It should buy me a little time, to get the air back into my lungs and to work out my next attack.

The Scarecrow let out an angry hissing sound and swung its stump of an arm down at Rawlins. The veteran cop saw it coming and rolled out of the way as though he were an agile young man, barely avoiding the blow. Thomas used an old metal oil drum as a platform for another leap, this time driving his heels into the Scarecrow's back, at what would have been the base of its spine on a human. The impact sent the Scarecrow to the ground, but as it landed it kicked a long leg at Thomas and struck his saber arm, breaking it with a wet snap of bone.

Thomas howled, scrambling back, leaving his fallen sword on the ground. The Scarecrow whirled back to me, eyes blazing with an alien rage, and I could swear that I saw recognition in them. It looked from me to Rawlins, and then with a hissing cackle it went after the cop.

Dammit. I waited until the last second and then broke the circle with a sweep of my foot, snatching up Thomas's sword. I charged forward.

The Scarecrow whirled the moment the circle went down, sweeping out a great fist that could have broken my neck, but it hadn't expected me to charge, and I was inside its reach before it realized what I had done. I let out a shout and struck at one of the Scarecrow's legs, but it was quicker than I thought, and the saber's blade barely clipped the thick, sturdy, viny limb. The Scarecrow let out a hiss loud and sharp enough to hurt my ears and tried to kick me, but I slipped to one side just in time, and the blow intended for me instead scattered several stacks of tires.

Madrigal Raith rose up from among the fallen tires only a couple of feet away from me, shrieking with fear. The Scarecrow's eyes blazed into painfully bright flames when it saw Madrigal, and it started for him.

"Get to the van!" I shouted, hopping back to stand beside Madrigal. "We need wheels if we're going to get away from this—"

Without so much as a second's hesitation, Madrigal stuck out his hand and shoved me between himself and the monster, sending me into a sprawl at the Scarecrow's feet while he turned to flee in the opposite direction.

Before I hit the ground, I was already calling power into my shield bracelet and I twisted to land on my right side, holding my left hand and its shield up. If I'd been half a second slower, the Scarecrow would have stomped its foot down onto my skull. Instead, it hit the half sphere of my sorcerous shield with so much force that the shield sent off a flare of light and heat, so that it looked like an enormous blue-white bowl above me.

Furious, the Scarecrow seized an empty barrel and hurled it down at my shield. I hardened my will as it struck, and turned the force of the throw, sending the barrel bouncing over the gravel, but it had gotten closer to me than the first blow. A second later, its fist hammered down, and then it found a bent aluminum ladder in a pile of junk and slammed it down at me.

I managed to block the attacks, but each one came a little closer to my hide. I didn't dare to let up my concentration for a moment in an effort to move away. The damned thing was so *strong*. I wouldn't survive a mistake. A single blow from one of its limbs or improvised weapons would probably kill me outright. But if I didn't get away, the creature would hammer through the shield anyway.

Mouse charged in again, on three legs this time, bellowing an almost leonine battle roar as he did so. The Scarecrow struck out at Mouse, but the dog's attack had been a feint, and he avoided the blow while remaining just out of the Scarecrow's reach. The Scarecrow turned back to me, but Mouse rushed it again, forcing the Scarecrow to abandon its attack lest Mouse close in from behind.

I rolled clear of the Scarecrow's reach and regained my feet, sword in my right hand, shining blue shield blazing on my left. I'd been throwing an awful lot of magic around tonight, and I was feeling it. My legs trembled, and I wasn't sure how much more I could do.

Mouse and I circled the monster opposite one another, playing wolf pack to the Scarecrow's bear, each of us menacing the creature's flanks when it turned to the other. We held our own for maybe a minute, but it was a losing bet, long-term. Mouse was moving on three legs and tiring swiftly. I wasn't much better off. The second one of us slipped or moved too slowly, the Scarecrow would drive us into the ground like a fence post. A wet, red, squishy fence post.

Light shone abruptly on my back, an engine roared, and a car horn blared. I hopped to one side. Madrigal's rental van shot past me and slammed into the Scarecrow. It knocked the creature sprawling all the way across the parking lot to the edge of the street.

Thomas leaned his head out the window and shouted, "Get in!"

I hurried to oblige him, snatching up my staff on the way, and Mouse was hard on my heels. We piled into the van, where I found Rawlins unconscious in the back. I slammed the side door shut. Thomas threw up a cloud of gravel whirling the van around, banged over the concrete median between the gravel lot and the street, and shot off down the road.

A wailing, whistling shriek of rage and frustration split the air behind us. I checked out the window, and found the Scarecrow pursuing us. When Thomas reached an intersection and turned, the Scarecrow cut across the corner, bounding over a phone booth with ease, and slammed into the back quarter of the van. The noise was horrible and the van wobbled, tires screeching and slithering while Thomas fought to control the slide.

The Scarecrow shrieked and slammed the van again. The wounded Mouse added his battle roar to the din.

"Do something!" Thomas shouted.

"Like what?" I screamed. "It's immune to my fire!"

Another crunch blasted my ears, rocked the van, and sent me sprawling over Rawlins.

"We're going to find traffic in a minute!" Thomas called. "Figure something out!"

I looked frantically around the van's interior, trying to think of something. There was little enough there: Glau's briefcase, an overnight bag containing, presumably, Glau's shower kit and foot powder, and two flats of expensive spring water in plastic bottles.

I could hear the Scarecrow's heavy footsteps outside the van, now, and a motion in the corner of my eye made me look up to see its blazing, terrifying eyes gazing into the van's window.

"Left!" I howled at Thomas. The van rocked, tires protesting. The Scarecrow drove its arm through the van's side window, and its long fingers missed me by an inch.

Do something. I had to do something. Fire couldn't hurt the thing. I could summon wind, but it was large enough to resist anything but my largest gale, and I didn't have the magical muscle to manage that, exhausted as I was. It would have to be something small. Something limited. Something clever.

I stared at the bottled water, then thought of something and shouted, "Get ready for a U-turn!" I shouted.

"What?" Thomas yelled.

I picked up both flats of bottles and shoved them out the broken window. They vanished, and I checked out the rear window to see them tumbling along in our wake, still held together by heavy plastic wrapping. I took up my blasting rod, pointed it at them, and called up the smallest and most intense point of heat I knew how, releasing it with a whispered, *"Fuego."*

The rear window glass flashed; a hole the size of a peanut suddenly appeared, the glass dribbling down, molten. Bottles exploded as their contents heated to boiling in under a second, spattering that whole section of road with a thin and expensive layer of water.

"Now!" I hollered. "U-turn!"

Thomas promptly did something that made the tires howl and almost threw me out the broken window. I got an up-close look at the Scarecrow as the van slewed into a bootlegger reverse. It reached for me, but its claws only raked down the van's quarter panel, squealing as they ripped through the paint. The Scarecrow, though swift and strong, was also very tall and ungainly, and we reversed directions more quickly than it could, giving us a couple of seconds' worth of a lead.

I gripped my blasting rod so hard that my knuckles turned white, and struggled to work out an evocation on the fly. I'm not much of an evocator. That's the whole reason I used tools like my staff and blasting rod to help me control and focus my energy. The very thought of spontaneously trying out a new evocation was enough to make sweat bead on my forehead, and I tried to remind myself that it wasn't a new evocation. It was just a very, very, very skewed application of an old one.

I leaned out the broken window, blasting rod in hand, watching behind us until the Scarecrow's steps carried it into the clump of empty plastic bottles in a shallow puddle.

Then I gritted my teeth, pointed my blasting rod at the sky, and reached out for fire. Instead of drawing the power wholly from within myself, I reached out into the environment around me—into the oppressive summer air, the burning heat of the van's engine, from Mouse, from Rawlins, from the blazing streetlights.

And from the water I'd spread in front of the Scarecrow.

"Fuego!" I howled.

Flame shot up into the Chicago sky like a geyser, and the explosion of sudden heat broke some windows in the nearest buildings. The van's engine stuttered in protest, and the temperature inside the van dropped dramatically. Lights flickered out on the street, the abrupt temperature change destroying their fragile filaments as my spell sucked some of the heat out of everything within a hundred yards.

And the expensive puddle of water instantly froze into a sheet of glittering ice.

The Scarecrow's leading foot hit the ice and slid out from under its body. Its too-long limbs thrashed wildly, and then the Scarecrow went down, awkward limbs flailing. Its speed and size now worked against it, throwing it down the concrete like a tumbleweed until it smacked hard into a municipal bus stop shelter.

"Go, go, go!" I screamed.

Thomas gunned the engine, recovering its power, and shot down the street. He turned at the nearest corner, and when he did the Scarecrow had only begun to extricate its tangle of limbs from the impact. Thomas hardly slowed, took a couple more turns, and then found a ramp onto the freeway.

I watched behind us. Nothing followed.

I sagged down, breathing hard, and closed my eyes.

"Harry?" Thomas demanded, his voice worried. "Are you all right?"

I grunted. Even that much was an effort. It took me

a minute to manage to say, "Just tired." I recovered from that feat and added, "Madrigal pushed me into that thing and bugged out."

Thomas winced. "Sorry I wasn't there sooner," he said. "I grabbed Rawlins. I figured you'd have told me to get him out anyway."

"I would have," I said.

He looked up at me in the rearview mirror, his eyes pale and worried. "You sure you're all right?"

"We're all alive. That's what counts."

Thomas said nothing more until we slid off the highway and he began to slow the van. I busied myself checking Rawlins. The cop had kept going in the face of severe pain and even more severe weirdness. Damned heroic, really. But even heroes are human, and human bodies have limits you can't exceed. Everything had finally caught up to Rawlins. His breathing was steady, and his wounded foot had swollen up so badly that his own shoe held down the bleeding, but I don't think a nuclear war could have woken him.

I ground my teeth at what I had to do next. I set my deformed left hand on the floor of the van at the angle Lasciel had shown me and let my weight fall suddenly onto it. There was an ugly pop, more pain, and then the agony subsided somewhat. It was a giddy feeling, and my hand looked human again, if bruised and swollen.

"So," I said, after I had worked up the energy. "It was you following me around town."

"I didn't want to be seen openly with you," he said. "I figured the Council might take it badly if they found out you had taken a White Court vampire on a Warden ride-along."

"Probably," I said. "I take it you followed them from the parking garage?"

"No, actually," Thomas said. "I tried but I lost them.

Mouse didn't. I followed him. How the hell did they keep him away from you when they grabbed you?"

"They hit him with this van," I said.

Thomas raised his eyebrows and glanced back at Mouse. "Seriously?" He shook his head. "Mouse led me to you. I was trying to figure out how to get into that garage without getting us shot. Then you made your move."

"You stole my coat," I said.

"Borrowed," he corrected.

"They never talk about this kind of crap when they talk about brothers."

"You weren't wearing it," he pointed out. "Hell, you think I'm going to walk into one of your patented Harry Dresden anarchy-gasms without all the protection I can get?"

I grunted. "You looked good tonight."

"I always look good," he said.

"You know what I mean," I told him quietly. "Better. Stronger. Faster."

"Like the Six Million Dollar Man," Thomas said.

"Stop joking, Thomas," I told him in an even tone. "You used a lot of energy tonight. You're feeding again."

He drove, eyes guarded, his face blank.

I chewed on my lip. "You want to talk about it?"

He ignored me, which I took as a "no."

"How long have you been active?"

I was sure he was stonewalling when he said, in a very quiet voice, "Since last Halloween."

I frowned. "When we took on those necromancers."

"Yeah," he said. "There's . . . look, there's something I didn't tell you about that night."

I tilted my head, watching his eyes in the rearview mirror.

"Remember, I said Murphy's bike broke down?"

I did. I nodded.

"It wasn't the bike," Thomas said. He took a deep breath. "It was the Wild Hunt. They came across me while I was trying to catch up with you. Sort of filled up the rest of my evening."

I arched my eyebrows. "You didn't have to lie about something like that, man. I mean, everyone who won't join the Hunt becomes its prey. So it's not your fault the Hunt chased you around." I scratched at my chin. Stubble. I needed a shave. "Hell, man, you should be damned proud. I doubt that more than five or six people in *history* have ever escaped the Hunt."

He was quiet for a minute and then said, "I didn't run from them, Harry."

My shoulders twitched with sudden tension.

"I joined them," he said.

"Thomas . . ." I began.

He looked up at the mirror. "I didn't want to die, man. And when push comes to shove, I'm a predator. A killer. Part of me wanted to go. Part of me had a good time. I don't like that part of me much, but it's still there."

"Hell's bells," I said quietly.

"I don't remember very much of it," he said. He shrugged. "I let you down that night. Let myself down that night. So I figured this time I'd try to help you out, once you told me you were on a job again."

"You've got a car now, too," I said quietly.

"Yeah."

"You're making money. And feeding on people."

"Yeah."

I frowned. I didn't know what to say to that. Thomas had tried to fit in. He tried to get himself an honest job. He tried it for most of two years, but it always ended badly because of who and what he was. I had begun to wonder if there was anyplace in Chicago that *hadn't* fired him.

But he'd had this job, whatever it was, for a while now.

"There anything I need to know?" I asked him.

He shook his head, a tiny gesture. His reticence worried me. Though he'd been repeatedly humiliated, Thomas had never had any trouble talking—complaining, really—about the various jobs he'd tried to hold. Once or twice, he'd opened up to me about the difficulty of going without the kind of intense feeding he'd been used to with Justine. Yet now he was clamming up on me.

An uncharitable sort of person would have gotten suspicious. They would have thought that Thomas must have been engaging in something, probably illegal and certainly immoral, to make his living. They would have dwelt on the idea that, as a kind of incubus, it would be a simple matter for him to seduce and control any wealthy woman he chose, providing sustenance and finances in a single package.

Good thing I'm not one of those uncharitable guys.

I sighed. If he wasn't going to talk, he wasn't going to talk. Time to change the subject.

"Glau," I said quietly. "Madrigal's sidekick, there. You said he was a jann?"

Thomas nodded. "Scion of a djinn and a mortal. He worked for Madrigal's father. Then my father arranged to have Madrigal's father go skydiving naked. Glau stuck with Madrigal after that."

"Was he dangerous?" I asked.

Thomas thought about it for a moment and then said, "He was *thorough*. Details never slipped by. He could play a courtroom like some kind of maestro. He was never finished with something until it was dissected, labeled, documented, and locked away in storage somewhere."

"But he wasn't a threat in a fight."

"Not as such things go. He could kill you dead enough, but not much better than any number of things."

"Funny, then," I said. "The Scarecrow popped him first."

Thomas glanced back at me, arching a brow.

"Think about it," I said. "This thing was supposed to be a phobophage, right? Going after the biggest source of fear."

"Sure."

"Glau was barely conscious when it grabbed him," I said. "It was probably me or Madrigal who was feeling the most tension, but it took out Glau, specifically."

"You think someone sent it for Glau?"

"I think it's a reasonable conclusion."

Thomas frowned. "Why would anyone do that?"

"To shut him up," I said. "I think Madrigal was supposed to go down for these attacks, at least in front of the supernatural communities. Maybe Glau was in on it. Maybe Glau arranged for Madrigal to be here."

"Or maybe the Scarecrow went after Glau because he was wounded and separate from the rest of us. It might have been a coincidence."

"Possible," I allowed. "But my gut says it wasn't. Glau was their cut-out man. They killed him to cover their trail."

"Who do you think 'they' is?"

"Uhhhhhh." I rubbed at my face, hoping the stimulation might move some more blood around in my brain and knock loose some ideas. "Not sure. My head hurts. I'm missing some details somewhere. There should be enough for me to piece this together, but damned if I can see it." I shook my head and fell quiet.

"Where to?" Thomas asked.

"Hospital," I said. "We'll drop Rawlins off."

"Then what?"

"Then I pick up the trail of those phages, and see if I can find out who summoned them." I told him briefly about the events of the afternoon and evening. "If we're lucky, all we'll find is some maniac's corpse with a surprised look on his face."

"What if we aren't lucky?" he asked.

"Then it means the summoner is a hell of a lot better than I am, to fight off three of those things." I rubbed at one eye. "And we'll have to take him down before he hurts anyone else."

"The fun never ends," Thomas said. "Right. Hospital."

"Then circle the block around the hotel. The spell I diverted the phages with had the tracking element worked into it. Sunrise will unravel it, and we don't know how long it will take to follow the trail."

I directed Thomas to the nearest hospital, and he carried the unconscious Rawlins through the emergency room doors. He came back a minute later and told me, "They're on the job."

"Let's go, then. Otherwise someone will want to ask us questions about gunshot wounds."

Thomas was way ahead of me, and the van headed back to the hotel.

I got the spell ready. It wasn't a difficult working, under normal circumstances, but I felt as wrung out as a dirty dishrag. It took me three tries to get the spell up and running, but I managed it. Then I climbed into the passenger seat, where I could see evidence of the phages' passing as a trail of curling, pale green vapor in the air. I gave Thomas directions. We followed the trail, and it led us toward Wrigley.

Not a whole hell of a lot of industry was going on in my aching skull, but after a few minutes something began to gnaw at me. I looked blearily around, and found that the neighborhood looked familiar. We kept on the trail. The neighborhood got more familiar. The vapor grew brighter as we closed in.

We turned a last street corner.

My stomach twisted in a spasm of horrified nausea.

The green vapor trail led to a two-story white house. A charming place, somehow carrying off the look of suburbia despite being inside the third-largest city in America. Green lawn, despite the heat. White picket fence. Children's toys in evidence.

The vapor led up to the picket fence, first. There were three separate large holes in the fence, where some enormous force had burst the fence to splinters. Heavy footprints gouged the lawn. An imitation old-style, wrought-iron gaslight had been bent to parallel with the ground about four feet up. The door had been torn from its hinges and flung into the yard. A minivan parked in the driveway had been crushed, as if by a dropped wrecking ball.

I couldn't be sure, but I thought I saw blood on the doorway.

The decorative mailbox three feet from me read, in cheerfully painted letters: THE CARPENTERS.

Oh, God.

Oh, God.

Oh, *God*.

I'd sent the phages after Molly.

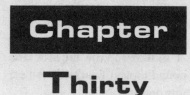

Chapter

Thirty

I got out of the van, too shocked to see anything but the destruction. It made no sense. It made no sense at all. How in the hell could this have happened? How could my spell have turned the phages and sent them here?

I stood on the sidewalk outside the house with my mouth hanging open. The streetlights were all out. Only the lights of the van showed the damage, and Thomas turned them off after only a moment. There was no disturbance on the street, no outcry, no police presence. Whatever had happened, something had taken steps to keep it from disturbing the neighbors.

I don't know how long I stood there. I felt Mouse's presence at my side. Then Thomas's, on the other side of me.

"Harry?" he said, as if he was repeating himself. "What is this place?"

"It's Michael's house," I whispered. "His family's home."

Thomas flinched. He looked back and forth and said, "Those things came here?"

I nodded. I felt unsteady.

I felt so damned tired.

Whatever happened here, it was over. There was nothing I could do at this point, except see who had been hurt. And I did not want to do that. So I stood there staring at the house until Thomas finally said, "I'll keep watch out here. Circle the house, see if there's anything to be seen."

"Okay," I whispered. I swallowed, and my stomach felt like I'd swallowed a pound of thumbtacks. I wanted nothing in the world so much as to run away.

But instead, I dragged my tired ass over the damaged lawn and through the house's broken doorway. Mouse, walking on three legs, followed me.

There were sprinkles of blood, already dried, on the inside of the doorway.

I went on inside the house, through the entry hall, into the living room. Furniture lay strewn all over the place, discarded and broken and tumbled. The television lay on its side, warbling static on its screen. A low sound, all white noise and faint interference, filled the room.

There was utter silence in the house, otherwise.

"Hello?" I called.

No one answered.

I went into the kitchen.

There were school papers on the fridge, most of them written in exaggerated, childish hands. There were crayon drawings up there, too. One, of a smiling stick figure in a dress, had a wavering line of letters underneath that read: I LOVY OU MAMA.

Oh, God.

The thumbtacks in my belly became razor blades. If I'd hurt them . . . I didn't know what I would do.

"Harry!" Thomas called from outside. "Harry, come here!"

His voice was tense, excited. I went out the kitchen door to the backyard, and found Thomas climbing down from a tree house only a little nicer than my apartment, built up in the branches of the old oak tree behind the

Carpenters' house. He had a still form draped over his shoulder.

I drew out my amulet and called wizard light as Thomas laid the oldest son, Daniel, out on the grass in the backyard. He was breathing, but looked pale. He was wearing flannel pajama pants and a white T-shirt soaked with blood. There was a cut on his arm; not too deep, but very messy. He had bruises on his face, on one arm, and the knuckles on both his hands were torn and ragged.

Michael's son had been throwing punches. It hadn't done him any good, but he'd fought.

"Coat," I said, terse. "He's cold."

Thomas immediately took off my duster and draped it over the boy. I propped his feet up on my backpack. "Stay here," I told him. I went in the house, fetched a glass of water, and brought it out. I knelt down and tried to wake the boy up, to get him to drink a little. He coughed a little, then drank, and blinked open his eyes. He couldn't focus them.

"Daniel," I said quietly. "Daniel, it's Harry Dresden."

"D-Dresden?" he said.

"Yeah. Your dad's friend. Harry."

"Harry," he said. Then his eyes flew open wide and he struggled to sit up. "Molly!"

"Easy, easy," I told him. "You're hurt. We don't know how bad yet. Lie still."

"Can't," he mumbled. "They took her. We were . . . Is Mom okay? Are the little ones okay?"

I chewed on my lip. "I don't know. Do you know where they are?"

He blinked several times and then he said, "Panic room."

I frowned. "What?"

"S-second floor. Safe room. Dad built it. Just in case."

I traded a look with Thomas. "Where is it?"

Daniel waved a vague hand. "Mom had the little ones upstairs. Molly and me couldn't get to the stairs. They were there. We tried to lead them away."

"Who, Daniel? They who?"

"The movie monsters. Reaper. Hammerhand." He shuddered. "Scarecrow."

I snarled a furious curse. "Thomas, stay with him. Mouse, keep watch." I stood up and stalked into the house, crossed to the stairs, and went up them. The upstairs hallway had a bunch of bedrooms off it, with the oldest children's rooms being at the opposite end of the hall from the master bedroom, the younger children being progressively closer to mom and dad. I looked inside each room. They were all empty, though the two nearest the head of the stairs had been torn up pretty well. Broken toys and shattered child-sized furniture lay everywhere.

If I hadn't been looking for it, I wouldn't have noticed the extra space between the linen closet and the master bedroom. I checked the closet in the master bedroom and turned up nothing. Then I opened the door to the linen closet, and found the shelves in complete disarray, sheets and towels and blankets strewn on the floor. I hunkered down and held up my mother's amulet, peering closely, and then found a section of the back wall of the closet just slightly misaligned with the corner it met. I reached out and touched that part of the wall, closed my eyes, extending my senses through my fingertips.

I felt power there. It wasn't a ward, or at least it was unlike any ward I had ever encountered. It was more of a quiet hum of constant power, and was similar to the power I'd felt stirring around Michael on several occasions—the power of faith. There was a form of magic protecting that panel.

"Lasciel," I murmured quietly. "You getting this?"

She did not appear, but her voice rolled through my thoughts. *Yes, my host. Angelic work.*

I exhaled. "Real angels?"

Aye. Rafael or one of his lieutenants, from the feel of it.

"Dangerous?"

There was an uncertain pause. *It is possible. You are touched by more darkness than my own. But it is meant to conceal the room beyond, not to strike out at an intruder.*

I took a deep breath and said, "Okay." Then I reached out and rapped hard on the panel, three times.

I thought I heard a motion, weight shifting on a floorboard.

I knocked again. "Charity!" I called. "It's Harry Dresden!"

This time, the motion was definite. The panel clicked, then rolled smoothly to one side, and a double-barreled shotgun slid out, aimed right at my chin. I swallowed and looked down the barrel. Charity's cold blue eyes faced me from the other end of the gun.

"You might not be the real Dresden," she said.

"Sure I am."

"Prove it," she said. Her tone was quiet, balanced, deadly.

"Charity, there's no time for this. You want me to show you my driver's license?"

"Bleed," she said instead.

Which was a good point. Most of the things who could play doppelgänger did not have human plumbing, or human blood. It wasn't an infallible test by any means, but it was as solid as anything a nonwizard could use for verification. So I pulled out my pen knife and cut my already mangled left hand, just a little. I couldn't feel it in any case. I bled red, and showed her.

She stared at me for a long second, and then eased the hammers on the shotgun back down, set the weapon aside, and wriggled out of the space beyond the panel. I saw a candle lit back there. The rest of the Carpenter children, sans Molly, were inside. Alicia was sitting up, awake, her eyes worried. The rest were sacked out.

"Molly," she said, once she'd gained her feet. "Daniel."

"I found him hiding in the tree house," I said. "He's hurt."

She nodded once. "How badly?"

"Bruised up pretty good, groggy, but I don't think he's in immediate danger. Mouse and a friend of mine are with him."

Charity nodded again, features calm and remote, eyes cold and calculating. She had a great cool-headed act going, but it wasn't perfect. Her hands were trembling badly, fingers clenching and unclenching arrhythmically. "And Molly?"

"I haven't found her yet," I said quietly. "Daniel might know what happened to her."

"Were they Denarians?" she asked.

I shook my head. "Definitely not."

"Is it possible that they may return?"

I shrugged. "It isn't likely."

"But possible?"

"Yes."

She nodded once, and her voice had the quality of someone thinking aloud. "Then the next thing to do is to take the children to the church. We'll make sure Daniel is cared for. I'll try to send word to Michael. Then we'll find Molly."

"Charity," I said. "Wait."

Charity thrust the heel of her hand firmly into my chest and pushed my shoulders back against the opposite wall. Her voice was quiet and very precise. "My children are vulnerable. I'm taking them to safety. Help me or stand aside."

Then she turned from me and began bringing her children out. Alicia helped as much as she could, her studious features tired and worried, but the littlest ones were sleepy to the point of hibernation, and remained limp as dishrags. I pitched in, picking up little Harry and Hope, carrying one on each hip. Charity's expression flashed briefly with both worry and thanks, and I saw her control slip. Tears formed in her eyes. She closed them again, jaw clenched, and when she looked up she had regained her composure.

"Thank you," she said.

"Let's move," I replied, and we did.

Tough lady. Very tough. We'd had our differences, but I had to respect the proud core of her. She was the kind of mother you read about in the paper, the kind who lifts a car off of one of her kids.

It was entirely possible that I'd just killed her oldest daughter. If Charity knew that, if she knew that I'd put her children in danger, she'd murder me.

If Molly had been hurt because of me, I'd help.

Saint Mary of the Angels is more than just a church. It's a monument. It's huge, its dome rising to seventeen stories, and covered in every kind of accessory you could name, including angelic statues spread over the roof and ledges. You could get a lot of people arguing over exactly what it's a monument *to*, I suppose, but one cannot see the church without being impressed by its size, by its artistry, by its beauty. In a city of architectural mastery, Saint Mary of the Angels need bow its head to no one.

That said, the back of the place, the delivery doors, looked quite modestly functional. We went there, Charity driving her family's minivan, Thomas, me, and Mouse in Madrigal's battered rental van. Mouse and I got out. Thomas didn't. I frowned at him.

"I'm going to find someplace to park this," he said. "Just in case Madrigal decides to report it as stolen or something."

"Think he'll make trouble for us?" I asked.

"Not face-to-face," Thomas said, his voice confident. "He's more jackal than wolf."

"Look on the bright side," I said. "Maybe the Scarecrow turned around and got him."

Thomas sighed. "Keep dreaming. He's a greasy little rat, but he survives." He looked up at the church and then said, "I'll keep an eye on things from out here. Come on out when you're done."

I got it. Thomas didn't want to enter holy ground. As a vampire of the White Court, he was as close to human as vampires got, and as far as I knew, holy objects had never inconvenienced him. So this wasn't about supernatural allergies. It was about his perceptions.

Thomas didn't want to go into the church because he wasn't optimistic that the Almighty and his institutions would smile on him. Like me, he favored maintaining a low profile with regards to matters temporal. And if he had gone back to older patterns, doing what came naturally to his predator's nature, it might incline him to stay off the theological radar. Worse, entering such a place as the church might force him to face his choices, to question them, to be confronted with the fact that the road he'd chosen kept getting darker and further from the light.

I knew how he felt.

I hadn't been in a church since I'd smacked my hand down on Lasciel's ancient silver coin. Hell, I had a freaking fallen angel in my head—or at least a facsimile of one. If that wasn't a squirt of lemon juice in God's eye, I didn't know what was.

But I had a job to do.

"Be careful," I told him quietly. "Call Murphy. Tell her what's up."

"You'd better get some rest soon, Harry," he replied. "You don't look good."

"I never look good," I said. I offered him my fist. He rapped my knuckles gently with his own.

I nodded and walked over to knock on the delivery doors while he drove off in Madrigal's van. I'd taken my duster back, once Daniel had a blanket on him. Screw the heat. I wanted the protection. Its familiar weight on my shoulders and motion against my legs were reassuring.

Forthill answered my knock, fully dressed, the white of his clerical collar easily seen in the night. His bright blue eyes looked around the parking lot once, and he hurried toward the van without a word being exchanged. I followed him. Forthill moved briskly, and we unloaded the van, Alicia shepherding the mobile kids indoors while he and Charity carried Daniel in between them. I followed with the two little wet dishrags, trying to keep my tired muscles from shaking too obviously.

Forthill led us to the storage room that sometimes doubled as refugee housing. There were half a dozen folded cots against one wall, and another one already opened, set out, and occupied by a lump under a blanket. Forthill and Charity got the wounded Daniel onto a cot first, and then opened the rest of them. We deposited tired children on them.

"What happened?" Forthill asked, his voice quiet and calm.

I didn't want to hear Charity talk about it. "Got a cramp," I told them. "Need to walk it off. Come find me when Daniel gets coherent."

"Very well," Charity said.

Forthill looked back and forth between us, frowning.

Mouse rose with a grunt of effort to limp after me. "No, boy. Stay and keep an eye on the kids."

Mouse settled down again, almost gratefully.

I beat it, and started walking. It didn't matter where. There were too many things flying around in my head. I just walked. Motion wasn't a cure, but I was tired enough that it kept the thoughts, the emotions, from drowning me. I walked down hallways and through empty rooms.

I wound up in the chapel proper. I've been in smaller stadiums. Gleaming hardwood floors shine over the whole of the chapel. Wooden pews stand in ranks, row upon row upon row, and the altar and nave are gorgeously decorated. It seats more than a thousand people, including the balcony at the rear of the chapel, and every Sunday they still have to run eight masses in four different languages to fit everyone in.

More than size and artistry, though, there is something else about the place that makes it more than simply a building. There's a sense of quiet power there, deep and warm and reassuring. There's peace. I stood for a moment in the vast and empty room and closed my eyes. Right then, I needed all the peace I could get. I drifted through the room, idly admiring it, and wound up in the balcony, all the way at the top, in a dark corner.

I leaned my head back against a wall.

Lasciel's voice came to me, very quietly, and sounded odd. Sad. *It is beautiful here.*

I didn't bother to agree. I didn't tell her to get lost. I leaned my head back against the rear wall and closed my eyes.

I woke up when Forthill's steps drew near. I kept my eyes closed, half hoping that if I didn't seem to waken he would go away.

Instead, he settled a couple of feet down the pew from me, and remained patiently quiet.

The act wasn't working. I opened my eyes and looked at him.

"What happened?" he asked quietly.

I pressed my lips together and looked away.

"It's all right," Forthill said quietly. "If you wish to tell me, I'll speak of it to no one."

"Maybe I don't want to talk to you," I said.

"Of course," he said, nodding. "But my offer stands, should you wish to talk. Sometimes the only way to carry a heavy burden is to share it with another. It is your choice to make."

Choices.

Sometimes I thought it might be nice not to make any choices. If I never had one, I could never screw it up.

"There are things I don't care to share with a priest," I told him, but I was mostly thinking out loud.

He nodded. He took off his collar and set it aside. He settled back into the pew, reached into his jacket, and drew out a slender silver flask. He opened it, took a sip, and offered it to me. "Then share it with your bartender."

That drew a faint, snorting laugh from me. I shook my head, took the flask, and sipped. An excellent, smooth Scotch. I sipped again, and I told him what happened at the convention, and how it had spilled over onto the Carpenter household. He listened. We passed the flask back and forth. I finished by saying, "I sent those things right to her door. I never meant it to happen."

"Of course not," he said.

"It doesn't make me feel any better about it."

"Nor should it," he said. "But you must know that you are a man of power."

"How so?"

"Power," he said, waving a hand in an all-encompassing gesture. "All power is the same. Magic. Physical strength. Economic strength. Political strength. It all serves a single purpose—it gives its possessor a broader spectrum of choices. It creates alternative courses of action."

"I guess," I said. "So?"

"So," he said. "You have more choices. Which means that you have much improved odds of making mistakes. You're only human. Once in a while, you're going to screw the pooch."

"I don't mind that," I said. "When I'm the only one who pays for it."

"But that isn't in your control," he said. "You cannot see all outcomes. You couldn't have known that those creatures would go to the Carpenter house."

I ground my teeth. "So? Daniel's still hurt. Molly could be dead."

"But their condition was not yours to ordain," Forthill said. "All power has its limits."

"Then what's the *point*?" I snarled, suddenly furious. My voice bounced around the chapel in rasping echoes. "What good is it to have power enough to kill my friend's family, but not power enough to *protect* them? What the hell do you expect from me? I've got to make these stupid choices. What the hell am I supposed to do with them?"

"Sometimes," he replied, his tone serious, "you just have to have faith."

I laughed, and it came out loud and bitter. Mocking echoes of it drifted through the vast chamber. "Faith," I said. "Faith in what?"

"That things will unfold as they are meant to," Forthill said. "That even in the face of an immediate ugliness, the greater picture will resolve into something all the more beautiful."

"Show me," I spat. "Show me something beautiful about this. Show me the silver fucking lining."

He pursed his lips and mused for a moment. Then he said, "There's a quote from the founder of my order: There is something holy, something divine, hidden in the most ordinary situations, and it is up to each one of you to discover it."

"What's that supposed to mean?" I asked.

"That the good that will come is not always obvious. Nor easy to see. Nor in the place we would expect to find it. Nor what we personally desire. You should consider that the good being created by the events this night may have nothing to do with the defeat of supernatural evils or endangered lives. It may be something very quiet. Very ordinary."

I frowned at him. "Like what?"

He finished off the little flask and then rose. He put it away and put his collar back on. "I'm afraid I'm not the one you should ask." He put a hand on my shoulder and nodded toward the altar. "But I will say this: I've been on this earth a fair while, and one way or another, this too shall pass. I have seen worse things reverse themselves. There is yet hope for Molly, Harry. We must strive to do our utmost, and to act with wisdom and compassion. But we must also have faith that the things beyond our control are not beyond His."

I sat quietly for a minute. Then I said, "You almost make me believe."

He arched an eyebrow. "But?"

"I don't know if I can do that. I don't know if it's possible for me."

The corners of his eyes wrinkled. "Then perhaps you should try to have faith that you might one day have faith." His fingers squeezed and then released my shoulder. He turned to go.

"Padre," I said.

He paused.

"You . . . won't tell Charity?"

He turned his head, and I could see sadness in his profile. "No. You aren't the only one too afraid to believe."

Sudden footsteps clattered into the chapel, and Alicia hurried in, accompanied by Mouse. The big grey dog sat down and stared up at the balcony. Alicia, panting, looked up. "Father?"

"Here," Forthill said.

"Come quick," she said. "Mama said to tell you Daniel's awake."

Thirty-one

We listened to Daniel's recounting of the attack. It was simple enough. He'd heard Molly moving around downstairs and had come down to talk to his sister. There had been a knock at the door. Molly had gone to answer it. There had been an exchange of words, and then Molly had screamed and slammed the door.

"She came running into the living room," Daniel said. "And they broke down the door behind her and came in." He shivered. "They were going upstairs and Molly said we had to distract them, so I grabbed the poker from the fireplace and just sort of jumped them." He shook his head. "I thought they were just costumes. You know. Like . . . really stupid burglars or something. But the Reaper grabbed me. And he was going to . . . you know. Cut me with that curved knife." He gestured vaguely at his wounded arm. "Molly hit him and he dropped me."

"With what?" I asked him.

He shook his head. His thin, awkward, adolescent features were hollow with pain, weariness, and a kind of lingering disbelief. His words were all slightly stiff, wooden, as if reporting events in an unappealing motion picture, rather than actual experiences. "I couldn't see. I think she must have had a bat or something. He dropped me."

"Then what?" I asked him.

He swallowed. "I fell, and bumped my head on the floor. And they grabbed her. The Reaper and the Scarecrow. And they carried her out the door. She was screaming . . ." He bit his lip. "I tried to stop them, but Hammerhand chased me. So I ran out the back and up into the tree house, 'cause I figured, you know. He doesn't have any hands. Just hammers. So how's he going to climb up after me?"

He looked to Charity and said, shame in his voice, "I'm sorry, Mom. I wanted to stop them. They were just . . . too big." Tears welled up in his eyes and his thin chest heaved. Charity caught him in a fierce hug, squeezing him hard and whispering to him. Daniel broke down, sobbing.

I got up and walked to the far side of the room. Forthill joined me there.

"These creatures," I told him quietly, "inflict more than simple physical damage. They rip into the psyches of those they attack."

"This happened to Daniel?" Forthill asked.

"I'd have to take a closer look to be certain, but it's probable. Kid's gonna have it tough for a while," I said. "It's like emotional trauma. Someone dying, that kind of thing. It tears people up the same way. They don't get over it fast."

"I've seen it too," Forthill said. "I haven't brought this up yet, but I thought you should know that Nelson came to me earlier this evening."

I nodded at the cot that had been occupied when we came in. "That him?"

"Yes."

"How'd he strike you?" I asked.

Forthill pursed his lips. "If I didn't know you sent him, I would have thought he was having a bad reaction to drugs. He was almost incoherent. Very agitated. Terrified, in point of fact, though he would not or could not explain why. I managed to get him calmed down and he all but fainted."

I frowned, running the fingers of my right hand back through my hair. "Did you have the sense that anyone was following him?"

"Not at all. Though I might have missed something." He essayed a tired smile. "It's late. And I'm not as spry as I used to be, after ten o'clock or so."

"Thank you for helping him," I said.

"Of course. Who is he?"

"Molly's boyfriend," I said. I glanced across the room, at the mother holding her son. "Maybe Charity doesn't need to know that part, either."

He blinked and then sighed, "Oh, dear."

"Heh. Yeah," I said.

"May I ask you a question?" he asked.

"Sure."

"These creatures, these phages. If they are what you say, beings of the spirit world, then how did they manage to cross the house's threshold?"

"Traditional way," I said. "They got an invitation."

"From whom?"

"Probably Molly," I said.

He frowned. "I have difficulty believing that she would do such a thing."

I felt my mouth tighten. "She probably didn't know they were monsters. They're shapeshifters. They probably appeared to her as someone she knew, and would invite in."

Forthill said, "Ah. I see. Someone such as you, perhaps."

"Perhaps," I said quietly. "Makes it the second time

someone has used my face to get a shot at Michael's family."

Forthill said nothing for a moment. Then he said, "It occurs to me that these creatures killed without compunction in your previous encounters. Why would they carry Molly away instead of simply murdering her?"

"I don't know yet," I said. "I don't know how my spell managed to bring them to Molly. I don't know precisely what these things are, or where they hail from. Which means I can't figure out why they've been showing up, or where they might have taken the girl." I waved a hand in a frustrated gesture. "It's driving me insane. I've got tons of facts and none of them are lining up."

"You're tired," Forthill said. "Perhaps some rest—"

I shook my head. "No, Padre. The things that took her won't rest. The longer she's in their hands, the less likely it is we'll ever see her again." I rubbed at my eyes. "I need to rethink it."

Forthill nodded at me and rose. On the other side of the room, Charity was covering her exhausted son with a blanket. Even Alicia had surrendered to fatigue, and now only the adults were awake. "I'll leave you to it then. Have you eaten recently?"

"Sometime in the Mesozoic Era," I said.

"Sandwich?"

My stomach made a gurgling noise. "Only if you insist."

"I'll see to it," Forthill said. "Excuse me." He went over to Charity and took her arm, leading her out as he spoke quietly to her. Now that her children had been cared for, she looked like she might come apart at the seams. They left the room together, leaving me in the dimness with Mouse and a lot of sleeping kids.

I thought. I thought some more. I picked up all the facts I knew, turning them every which way, trying to figure out something, *anything*, that would let me put a stop to this insanity.

The phages. The answer was in the phages. Once I knew their identity, I could begin to work out who might be using them, and what I might do to learn more about them. There had to be a commonality to them, somewhere; something that linked them together, some fact that could provide me a context in which to judge their motivations and intentions.

But what the hell could they have in common, other than being monsters who fed on fear? They'd shown up randomly in a bathroom, a kitchen, a parking lot, a conference room. Their victims had been disparate, seemingly random. They had all appeared as figures from horror movies, but that fact seemed fairly unremarkable, relatively speaking. Try as I might, I could find nothing to join them together, to let me recognize them.

Frustrated, I rose and went over to Daniel's cot. I called up my Sight. It took me longer than normal. I braced myself and regarded the boy.

I'd been right. He'd taken a psychic flogging. The phage had been worrying at his mind, his spirit, even as it had threatened his flesh. I could see the wounds as long, bleeding tears in his flesh. Poor little guy. It would haunt him. I hoped he would be able to get a little rest before the nightmares woke him up.

I stared at him for a good while, making sure his suffering was burned indelibly into my head. I wanted to remember for the rest of my life what the consequences of my screw-ups might be.

I heard a sound to the side and glanced up without thinking, turning my Sight upon the source of the sound—a restlessly stirring Nelson.

If little Daniel had been the recipient of a savage beating, Nelson's spirit had been in the hands of Hell itself. His entire upper body was disfigured under my Sight, covered in hideous, festering boils and raw, bleeding burns. The damage was worst around his head, and faded gradually as it descended his torso.

And each of his temples bore tiny, neat holes, sharp and cauterized, as if by a laser scalpel.

Just like Rosie.

Chains of logic cascaded through my brain. My head swam. I shoved the Sight away from me, and my ass fell straight down to the floor.

I knew.

I knew why my spell had sent the phages after the Carpenters.

I knew why Molly had been taken. I could make a good guess at where.

I knew what the phages all had in common.

I knew who had sent them. The realization terrified me with a fear so cold and sharp that it literally paralyzed me. I could barely clap my hand over my mouth to keep from making whimpering sounds.

It took me a while to force myself to calm down. By the time I did, Forthill had returned bearing sandwiches. He settled down on a cot, clearly exhausted, and went to sleep.

I ate my sandwiches. Then I went looking for Charity.

I found her in the chapel, sitting up high in the balcony. She stared down at the altar, and did not react when I came up the steps to her and settled down on the bench beside her. I sat with her in silence for a minute.

"Charity," I whispered. "I need to ask you something."

She sat in stony silence. Her chin moved a fraction of a degree up and down.

"How long?" I murmured.

"How long since what?" she asked.

I took a deep breath. "How long has it been since you've used your magic?"

Chapter

Thirty-two

I couldn't have gotten more of a reaction if I'd shot her.

Charity's face turned sheet white, the blood draining from it. She froze in place grasping the edge of the wooden pew in front of her with both hands. Her knuckles turned white, and the wood creaked. She gnashed her teeth and bowed her head.

I didn't push. I waited.

She opened her eyes again, and she wasn't hard to read. Her thoughts and emotions were clear on her face. Panic. Desperation. Self-loathing. Her eyes flicked from one possibility to another. She considered denying it. She considered lying to me. She considered simply walking away.

"Charity," I told her. "Tell me the truth."

Her breathing quickened. I saw her desperation growing.

I reached out with one hand and turned her face toward me. "Your daughter needs you. If we don't help her, she's going to die."

Charity flinched and pulled away from me. Her shoulders shook with a silent sob. She fought to control her breathing, her voice, and whispered, "A lifetime."

I felt some tension ease in me. Her reaction confirmed that I was on the right track.

"How did you know?" she asked.

"Just putting lots of little things together," I said. "Please, Charity. Tell me."

Her voice was rough, half strangled, as though the breath that carried her words had been tainted with something rotten. "I had some talent. It showed just before my sixteenth birthday. You know how awkward that kind of thing can be."

"Yeah," I said. "How'd your family take it?"

Her mouth twisted. "My parents were wealthy. Respectable. When they had time to notice me, they expected me to be normal. Respectable. They found it easier to believe that I was a drug addict. Emotionally unbalanced."

I winced. There were a lot of situations that could meet someone with a burgeoning magical talent. Charity's was one of the worst.

"They sent me away to schools," she said. "And to hospitals disguised as schools." She waved a hand. "I eventually left them. Just left them. I struck out on my own."

"And fell in with a bad crowd," I said quietly.

She gave me a bitter smile. "You've heard this story before."

"It isn't uncommon," I said quietly. "Who was it?"

"A . . . coven, of sorts, I suppose," she said. "More of a cult. There was a young man leading it. Gregor. He had power. He and the others, all young people, mixed in religion and mysticism and philosophy and . . . well. You've probably seen such things before."

I nodded. I had. A charismatic leader, dedicated followers, a collection of strays and homeless runaways. It rarely developed into something positive.

"I wasn't strongly gifted," she said. "Not like you. But I learned about some of what happens out there.

About the White Council." The bitter smile returned. "Everyone was terrified of them. A Warden visited us once. He delivered a warning to Gregor. He'd been toying about with some kind of summoning spells, and the Wardens got wind of it. They interviewed each of us. Evaluated us. Told us the Laws of Magic, and told us never to break them if we wished to live."

I nodded and listened. She spoke more quickly now, the words coming out in a growing rush. They had been pent up a long time.

"Gregor resented it. He grew distant. He began practicing magic that walked the crumbling edges of the Council's Laws. He had us all doing it." Her eyes grew cold. "The others began disappearing. One by one. No one knew where they had gone. But I saw what was happening. I saw Gregor growing in power."

"He was trading them," I said.

She nodded once. "He saw my face, when I realized it. I was the next one to go. He came to take me away, and I fought him. Tried to kill him. Wanted to kill him. But he beat me. I remember only parts of it. Being chained to an iron post."

"The dragon," I said.

She nodded. Some of the bitterness faded from her smile. "And Michael came. And he destroyed the monster. And saved me." She looked up at me. Tears filled her eyes and streaked down her cheeks, but she did not blink. "I swore to myself that I would leave that behind me. The magic. The power. I had . . . urges." She swallowed. "To do things only . . . only a monster would do. When Siriothrax died, Gregor went mad. Utterly mad. But I wanted to turn my power against him anyway. I couldn't think of anything else."

"Hard to do," I said quietly. "You were a kid. No real training. Exposed to some nasty uses of power."

"Yes," she said. "Without Michael, I would never have been able to leave it behind me. He never knew. He still doesn't know. He remained near me, in my life. Making sure that I was all right. And . . . he was such a good soul. When he smiled at me, it was like all the light in the world was shining out at me. I wanted to be worthy of that smile.

"My husband saved my life, Mister Dresden, and not only from the dragon. He saved me from myself." She shook her head. "I never touched my power again after the night I met Michael. We married soon after. And in time, the power withered. And good riddance to it."

"So when Molly's talent began to manifest," I said quietly, "you tried to get her to abandon it as well."

"I was well aware of how dangerous it could be," she said. "How innocent it could seem." She shook her head. "I did not want her exposed to the things that had nearly destroyed my life."

"But she did it anyway," I guessed. "That's what really came between the two of you. That's why she ran away from home."

Charity's voice turned raw. "Yes. I couldn't get through to her how dangerous it was. What she might be sacrificing." She made no effort to stem or hide her tears. "And you were there. A hero who fought beside her father. Used his power to help people." She let out a tired laugh. "For the love of God, you saved my life. We named our child for you. Once she realized she had the talent, nothing could keep her from it."

Christ. No wonder Charity hadn't much liked me. Not only was I dragging her husband off to who knew where to fight who knew what, I was also setting an example to Molly of everything Charity wanted her to avoid.

"I didn't know," I told her.

She shook her head. Then she said, "I have been honest with you. No one else knows what you do now. Not Michael. Not my daughter. No one." She drew a Kleenex from her pocket and wiped at her eyes. "What has happened to my daughter?"

I exhaled. "What I've got right now is still mostly guesswork," I said. "But my gut tells me it all fits together."

"I understand," she said.

I nodded, and told Charity about the attacks at the convention, and about how Molly had gotten me involved. "I examined the victims of the first two attacks," I said quietly. "One of them, a girl named Rosie, showed evidence of a kind of psychic trauma. At the time, I attributed it to the phage's attack on her."

Charity frowned. "It wasn't?"

I shook my head. "I found an identical trauma on Nelson." I took a deep breath and said, "Molly is the link between them. They're both her friends. I think she was the one who hurt them. I think she used magic to invade their minds."

Charity stared at me, her expression sickened. "What? No . . ." She shook her head. "No, Molly wouldn't . . ." Her face grew even more pale. "Oh, God. She's broken one of the Council's Laws." She shook her head more violently. "No, no, no. She would not do such a thing."

I grimaced and said, "I think I know what she did. And why she did it."

"Tell me."

I took a deep breath. "Rosie is pregnant. And she showed physical evidence of drug addiction, but none of the psychological evidence of withdrawal. I think Molly took steps when she found out her friend was pregnant—to force her away from the drugs. I think she did it to protect the baby. And then I think she did the same thing to Nelson. But something went wrong. I think what she did to him broke something." I shook my head. "He got paranoid, erratic."

Charity stared down at the altar below, shaking her head. "Is it the Council then, that took her?"

"No," I said. "No. What she did to Rosie and Nelson left a kind of mark on her. A stain. I think she forced Rosie and Nelson to feel fear whenever they came near their drugs. Fear is a powerful motivator and it's easy to exploit. She wanted them to be afraid of the drugs. She had good intentions, but she wanted her friends to be frightened."

"I don't understand."

"Whoever called up these phages," I said, "needed a way to guide them from the Nevernever to the physical world. They needed a beacon, someone who would resonate with a sympathetic vibe. Someone who, like the phages, wanted to make people feel fear."

"And they used my Molly," Charity whispered. Then she stared at me for a moment. "You did it," she said quietly. "You tried to turn the phages back upon their summoner. You sent them after my daughter."

"I didn't know," I told her. "My God, Charity. I swear to you that I didn't know. People were dead, and I didn't want anyone else to be hurt."

The wooden pew creaked even more sharply in her grip.

"Who did this thing?" she said, and her voice was deadly quiet. "Who is responsible for the harm to my children? Who is the one who called the things that invaded my home?"

"I don't think anyone called them," I told her quietly. "I think they were sent."

She looked up at me, and her eyes narrowed. "Sent?"

I nodded. "I hadn't considered that possibility, until I realized what all of the attacks had in common. Mirrors."

"Mirrors?" Charity asked. "I don't understand."

"That was the common element," I said. "Mirrors. The bathroom. Rosie's makeup mirror in the conference room. Plenty of reflective steel surfaces in a commercial kitchen. And Madrigal's rental van's windshield was reflecting images very clearly."

She shook her head. "I still don't understand."

"There are plenty of things that can use mirrors as windows or doorways from the spirit world," I said. "But there's only one thing that feeds on fear and uses mirrors as pathways back and forth from the Nevernever. It's called a fetch."

"Fetch." Charity tilted her head, her eyes vague, as though searching through old memories. "I've heard of them. They're . . . aren't they creatures of Faerie?"

"Yeah," I said quietly. "Specifically, they're creatures of deepest, darkest Winter." I swallowed. "Even more specifically, they're Queen Mab's elite spies and assassins. Shapeshifters with a lot of power."

"Mab?" she whispered. "*The* Mab?"

I nodded slowly.

"And they've taken my daughter," she said. "Carried her away to Faerie."

I nodded again. "She'll be a rich resource for them. A magically talented young mortal. Compatible energy. Not enough experience to defend herself. They can feed on her and her magic for hours. Maybe days. That's why they didn't just kill her and have done."

Charity swallowed. "What can we do?"

"I'm not sure," I said. "It would be nice to have your husband along, though."

She bit her lip and sent what might have been a hateful look down at the altar. "He's out of reach. Messages have been left, but . . ."

"We're on our own," I said.

"We must do something," she said.

"Yeah," I agreed. "The problem is that we don't know *where* to do it."

"I thought you just said that they had taken her back to Faerie."

"Yeah," I said. "But just because I tell you Ayer's Rock is in Australia doesn't mean you're going to be able to find the damned thing. Australia's big. And Faerie makes it look like Rhode Island."

Charity clenched her jaw. "There must be something."

"I'm working on it," I said.

"What will . . ." She paused and cleared her throat. "How long does she have?"

"Hard to say," I told her. "Time can go by at different rates between here and there. A day here, but an hour there. Or vice versa."

She stared steadily at me.

I looked away and said, "Not long. It depends on how long she holds out. They'll get all the fear out of her that they can and then . . ." I shook my head. "A day. At most."

She shook her head. "No," she said quietly. "I will not let that happen. There must be a way to take her back."

"I can get to Faerie," I said. "But you've got to understand something. We're talking about opening a path into deep Winter. *If* I'm strong enough to open the way, and *if* I'm strong enough to hold it open while simultaneously running a rescue operation against at least one ancient fetch who ate my magic like candy earlier tonight, we're still talking about defying the will of Queen Mab. If she's there, there's not a damned thing I can do. I don't have enough power to challenge her in the heart of her domain. The whole damned White Council doesn't have enough power. On top of that, I'd have to know precisely where to cross over into Faerie, because I'd have only minutes to grab her and get out. And I have no idea where she is."

"What are you saying?" she asked quietly.

"That I can't do it," I told her. "It's suicide."

Charity's back stiffened. "So you're willing to leave her there?"

"No," I said. "But it means that I'm going to have to find help wherever I can get it. Maybe from people and things that you won't much like." I shook my head. "And it's possible I'll get myself killed before I can even make the attempt. And even if I get her out . . . there could be a price."

"I'll pay it," she said. Her voice was flat, strong, certain. "For Molly, I'll pay it."

I nodded. I didn't say the next thought out loud—that even if we did get the girl back, there might not be much left of her mind. And she'd broken one of the Laws of Magic. She could wind up on the floor of some lonely warehouse, a black bag over her head, until Morgan's sword took it off her shoulders. Or, maybe worse, she could already have been twisted by the power she'd used.

Even if I could find Molly and bring her home, it might already be too late to save her.

But I could burn that bridge when I came to it. First, I had to find her. The only way to do that was to learn where the fetches had carried her through to the Nevernever. Geography in the Nevernever isn't like geography in the normal world. The Nevernever touches our world only at certain points of sympathetic energy. The portion of the Nevernever that touched an empty and abandoned warehouse might not be anywhere near the area of the spirit world that touched the full and busy childcare center across the physical street from the warehouse. To make it worse, the connections between the mortal world and the Nevernever changed slowly over time, as the world changed.

There could be a thousand places in Chicago where the fetches might have dragged Molly back to their lair. I had to find the correct one. And I had to do it before dawn, before the rising sun scattered and dispersed the residual traces of her presence that would be my only trail.

I had about two hours, tops, to get my aching body back to my apartment to bathe and prepare for a spell that would have been dangerous had I been rested and entirely whole. Tired, hurting, pressured, and worried as I was, I would probably kill myself on Little Chicago's trial run.

But my only other option was walk away and leave the girl in the hands of creatures that made nightmares afraid of the dark.

"I'll need something of hers," I said, rising. "Hair or fingernail clippings would be best."

Charity said, "I have a lock of her hair in her baby book."

"Perfect," I said. "I'll pick it up from your place. Where's the book?"

She rose. "I'll show you."

I hesitated. "I don't know if that's wise."

"She's my daughter, Mister Dresden," Charity said. "I'm coming with you."

I was too tired to argue. So I nodded, and started down out of the balcony. My ankle twinged, and I wobbled and almost fell.

Charity caught me.

Chapter

Thirty-three

"This is Thomas," I told Charity, waving a hand at my brother, who had fallen into step beside me as I left the church. "He's more dangerous than he looks."

"I have a black belt," Thomas explained.

Charity arched an eyebrow, looked at Thomas for about a second, and said, "You're the White Court vampire who took my husband to that strip bar."

Thomas gave Charity a toothy smile and said, "Hey, it's nice to be remembered. And to work with someone who has a clue." He hooked a thumb at me and added, sotto voce, "For a change."

Charity's regard didn't change. It wasn't icy, nor friendly, nor touched by emotion. It was simply a remote, steady gaze, the kind one reserves for large dogs who pass nearby. Cautious observation, unexcited and deliberate. "I appreciate that you have fought beside my husband before. But I also want you to understand that what you are gives me reason to regard you with suspicion. Please do nothing to deepen that sentiment. I do not remain passive to threats."

Thomas pursed his lips. I half expected anger to touch his gaze, but it didn't. He simply nodded and said, "Understood, ma'am."

"Good," she said, and we reached her van. "You ride in the rearmost seat."

I started to protest, but Thomas put his hand on my shoulder and shook his head. "Her ride, her rules," he murmured to me in passing. "I can respect that. So can you."

So we all got in and headed for the Carpenters' house.

"How's Mouse?" Thomas asked.

"Leg's hurt," I said.

"Took one hell of a shot to do it," he noted.

"That's why I left him back there," I said. "Could be he's pushing his luck. Besides, he can help Forthill keep an eye on the kids."

"Uh-huh," Thomas said. "Am I the only one who is starting to think that maybe Mouse is something special?"

"Always thought that," I said.

"I wonder if he's an actual breed."

Charity glanced over her shoulder and said, "He looks something like a Caucasian."

"Impossible," I said. "He has rhythm and he can dance."

Charity shook her head and said, "It's a dog bred by the Soviet Union in the Caucasus Mountains for use in secured military installations. It's one of the only breeds that grows so large. But they tend to be a great deal more aggressive than your dog."

"Oh, he's aggressive enough for anybody, when he needs to be," I said.

Thomas engaged Charity in a polite conversation about dogs and breeds, and I leaned my head against the window and promptly fell asleep. I woke up briefly when the van stopped. Charity and Thomas spoke, and I dozed as they loaded some things into the van. I didn't wake up again until Thomas touched my shoulder and said, "We're at your apartment, Harry."

"Yeah," I mumbled. "Okay." I blinked a couple of times and hopped out of the van. "Thomas," I said. "Get in touch with Murphy for me, and tell her I need her at my place, now. And . . . here . . ." I fumbled in my duster's pockets and found a white napkin and a marker. I wrote another number. "Call this number. Tell them that I'm calling in my personal marker."

Thomas took the paper and arched a brow. "Can't you be any more specific?"

"I don't have to be," I said. "They'll know why I want them. This will just tell them that it's time for them to get together with me."

"Why me?" Thomas asked.

"Because I don't have time," I said. "So unless you want to play with dangerous magic divinations, call the damned number and stop making me waste energy explaining myself."

"*Heil*, Harry," Thomas said, his tone a bit sullen. But I knew he'd do it.

"Hair?" I asked Charity.

She passed me an unmarked white envelope, her expression a mask.

"Thank you." I took it and headed for my apartment, the two of them following after me. "I'll be working downstairs. The two of you should stay in the living room. Please be as quiet as you can and don't walk around too much."

"Why?" Charity asked.

I shook my head tiredly and waved a hand. "No, no questions right now. I'll need everything I've got to find where they took Molly, and I'm already rushing this thing. Let me concentrate. I'll explain it later." *If I survive it,* I thought.

I felt Charity's eyes on me, and I glanced back at her. She gave her head a brief, stiff nod. I took down the wards and we went inside. Mister came over and rammed his shoulder against my legs, then wound his way around between Thomas's legs, accepting a few token pats from my half brother. Then he surprised me by giving Charity the same treatment.

I shook my head. Cats. No accounting for taste.

Charity looked around my apartment, frowning, and said, "It's very well kept up. I had expected more . . . debris."

"He cheats," Thomas said, and headed for the refrigerator.

I ignored them. There wasn't time for the full ritual cleansing and meditation, but my day had exposed me to all kinds of stains, external and otherwise, and I considered the shower to be the most indispensable portion of the preparation. So I went into my room, stripped, lit a candle, and got into the shower. Cool water sluiced over me. I scrubbed my skin until it was pink, and washed my hair until my scalp got sore.

The whole while I sought out a quiet place in my mind, somewhere sheltered from pain and guilt, from fear and anger. I pushed out every sensation but for the bathing, and without conscious effort my motions took on the steady rhythm of ritual, something commonplace transformed into an act of art and meditation, like a Japanese tea ceremony.

I longed for my bed. I longed for sleep. Warmth. Laughter. I pinned down those longings one at a time and crucified them, suspending them until such time as my world was a place that could afford such desires. One last emotion was too big for me, though. Try though I might, I could not keep fear from finding a way to slither into my thoughts. Little Chicago's maiden run was an enormous unknown quantity. If I'd done it all right, I would have myself one hell of a tool for keeping track of things in my town.

If I'd made even a tiny mistake, Molly was dead. Or worse than dead. And I'd get to find out what the light at the end of the long tunnel really was.

I couldn't escape the fear. It was built into the situation. So instead I tried to make my peace with it. Fear, properly handled, could be turned into something useful. So I made a small, neat place for its use in my head, a kind of psychic litter box, and hoped that the fear wouldn't start jumping around at the worst possible moment.

I got out of the shower, dried, and slipped into my white robe again. I kept my thoughts focused, picked up my backpack and the white envelope, and went down to the basement lab. I shut the door behind me. If Little Chicago went nova, preventative spells I'd laid to keep energies from escaping the lab should mitigate the damage significantly. It wasn't a perfect plan, by any means, but I'm only human.

Which was a disturbing thought as I stared at the model on the table. Even a tiny mistake. Only human.

I set the envelope at the edge of the table, my backpack on a shelf, and went around the basement lighting candles with a match. A spell would have been faster and neater, but I wanted to save every drop of power for managing the divination. So I made lighting each candle a ritual of its own, focusing on my movements, on precision, on nothing but the immediate interplay of heat and cold, light and darkness, fire and shadow.

I lit the last candle and turned to the model city.

The buildings shone silver in the candlelight, and the air quivered with the power I'd built into the model. Some tiny voice of common sense in my head told me that this was a horribly bad idea. It told me that I was making decisions because I was in pain and exhausted, and that it would be far wiser to get some sleep and attempt the spell when I stood a reasonable chance of pulling it off.

I crucified that little voice, too. There was no room for doubts. Then I turned to the table, and to the elongated circle of silver I'd built into its surface.

Lasciel appeared between me and the table, in her usual white tunic, her red hair pulled back into a tight braid. She held up both hands and said, quietly, "I cannot permit you to do this."

"You," I said in a quiet, distant voice, "are almost as annoying as a sudden phone call."

"This is pointless," she said. "My host, I beg you to reconsider."

"I don't have time for you," I said. "I have a job to do."

"A job?" she asked. "Evading your responsibilities, you mean?"

I tilted my head slightly. In my current mental state, the emotions I felt seemed infinitely far away and all but inconsequential. "How so?"

"Look at yourself," she replied, her voice that low, quiet, reasonable tone one uses around madmen and ugly drunks. "Listen to yourself. You're tired. You're injured. You're racked by guilt. You're frightened. You will destroy yourself."

"And you with me?" I asked her.

"Correct," she said. "I do not fear the end of my existence, my host, but I would not be extinguished by one too self-deluded to understand what he was about."

"I'm not deluded," I said.

"But you are. You know that this effort shall probably

kill you. And once it has done so, you will be free from any onus of what happened to the girl. After all, you heroically died in the effort to find her and retrieve her. You won't have to attend her funeral. You won't have to explain yourself to Michael. You won't have to tell her parents that their daughter is dead because of your incompetence."

I did not reply. The emotions grew a little closer.

"This isn't anything more than an elaborate form of suicide, chosen during a moment of weakness," Lasciel said. "I do not wish to see you destroy yourself, my host."

I stared at her.

I thought about it.

She might be right.

It didn't matter.

"Move," I murmured. "Before I move you." Then I paused and said, "Wait a minute. What am I thinking? It isn't as though you can stop me." Then I simply stepped *through* Lasciel's image to the table, and reached for the white envelope.

The white envelope began to spin in place on the table, and abruptly became dozens of envelopes, each identical, each whirling like a pinwheel.

"But I can," Lasciel said quietly. I looked up to find her standing on the opposite side of the table from me. "I witnessed the birth of time itself. I watched the mortal coil spring forth from perfect darkness. I watched the stars form, watched this world coalesce, watched as life was breathed into it and as your kind rose to rule it." She put both hands on the table and leaned toward me, her blue eyes cold and hard. "Thus far, I have behaved as a guest ought. But do not mistake propriety for weakness, mortal. I beg you not to oblige me to take further action."

I narrowed my eyes and reached for my Sight.

Before I could use it, my left hand exploded into flame.

Pain, pain, PAIN. Fire, scorching, parboiling my hand as I tried to hold it back with my shield bracelet. The memory of my injury in that vampire-haunted basement came rushing back to me in THX, and my nerve endings were listening.

I fought down a scream, breathing, my teeth snapping together so suddenly and sharply that a fleck of one of my molars chipped away.

It was an illusion, I told myself. *A memory. It's a ghost, nothing more. It cannot harm you if you do not allow it to do so.* I pushed hard against that memory, turning the focus of my will against it.

I felt the illusion-memory wobble, and then the pain was gone, the fire out. My body pumped endorphins into my bloodstream a heartbeat later, and I drifted on them as my focus started to collapse. I leaned hard against the table, my left hand held close to my chest in pure reflex, my right supporting my weight. I turned my attention to the envelopes and forced my will against them until the illusions grew translucent. I picked up the real envelope.

Lasciel regarded me steadily, her beautiful face unyielding, determined.

"Sooner or later I'll push through anything you throw," I panted. "You know that."

"Yes," she said. "But you will not be able to focus on the divination until you are quit of me. I may force you to exhaust yourself resisting me, in which case you will not attempt the divination. Even if I only delay you until dawn, there will be no need for you to attempt it." She lifted her chin. "Whatever happens, the divination will not be successful."

I let out a low chuckle, which made Lasciel frown at me. "You missed it," I said.

"Missed what?"

"The loophole. I can kill myself trying it while you rock the boat. And after all, this entire exercise is nothing more than a suicide attempt in any case. Why not go through with it?"

Her jaw clenched. "You would murder yourself rather than yield to reason?"

"More manslaughter than murder, I'd say."

"You're mad," the fallen angel said.

"Get me some Alka-Seltzer and I'll foam at the mouth, too." This time I hit Lasciel with the hard look. "There's a child out there who needs me. I'd rather die than let her down. I'm doing the spell, period. So fuck off."

She shook her head in frustration and looked away, frowning. "You are quite likely to die."

"Broken record much?" I asked. I got out the lock of baby-fine hair, set my knife down on the table, and lit the ceremonial candles there. The fallen angel was correct, dammit. The fear stirred dangerously inside me, and my fingers shook hard enough to break the first kitchen match instead of kindling it to life.

"If you must do this," Lasciel said, "at least attempt to survive it. Let me help you."

"You can help me by shutting the hell up and going away," I told her. "Hellfire isn't going to be any use to me here."

"Perhaps not," Lasciel said. "But there is another way."

There was a shimmer of light in the corner of my eye, and I turned to see a slowly pulsing silver glow upon the floor in the middle of my summoning circle. Two feet beneath it lay the Blackened Denarius where the rest of Lasciel was imprisoned.

"Take up the coin," she urged me. "I can at least protect you from a backlash. I beg you not to throw your life away."

I bit my lip.

I didn't want to die, dammit. And the thought of failing to save Molly was almost worse than death. The holder of one of the thirty ancient silver coins had access to tremendous power. With that kind of boost, I could probably pull the spell off, and even if it went south I could survive it under Lasciel's protection. Somehow, I knew that if I chose to do it I could get the coin out from under the concrete in only a moment, too.

I stared at the silver glow for a moment.

Then I rolled my eyes and said, "Are you still here?"

Lasciel's face smoothed into an emotionless mask, but there was a subtle, ugly tone of threat in her voice. "You are much easier to talk to when you are asleep, my host."

And she was gone.

Fear rattled around inside me. I tried to calm it, but I couldn't regain my earlier detachment—not until I thought of young Daniel, mangled beneath my wizard Sight, wounded defending his family from something I had sent after them.

I thought of Molly's brothers and sisters. I thought of her mother, her father. I thought of the laughter, the sheer, joyous, rowdy *life* of Michael's family.

Then I pinked my fingertip with my ritual knife, touched the lock of baby hair to it, and laid it down within Little Chicago. I used a second drop of blood and an effort of will to touch the circle on the tabletop, closing it up and beginning the spell. I closed my eyes, focusing, murmuring a stream of faux Latin as I reached out to the model and brought it to life.

My senses blurred, and suddenly I was standing on

the tabletop, at the model of my own boardinghouse. I thought the silver-colored model had grown to life size at first, then realized that the inverse was more accurate. I had shrunk to scale with Little Chicago, my awareness now within the spell rather than in my own body, which stood over the table like Godzilla, murmuring the words of the spell.

I closed my eyes and thought of Molly, my blood touched upon her lock of hair, and to my utter surprise I shot off down the street with no more effort than it took to pedal a bicycle. The streets beneath me and the buildings around me glowed with white energy, the whole of the place humming like high-power tension lines.

Stars and stones, Little Chicago worked. It worked *well*. A surge of jubilation went through me, and my speed increased in proportion. I flashed through the streets, seeing faint images of people, like ghosts, the unsteady reflections of those now moving through the real Chicago around me. But then the spell wavered, and I found myself moving in a circle like a baffled hound trying to pick up a scent trail.

It didn't work.

I made an effort and stood back in my own body, staring down at Little Chicago, badly fatigued.

Exhausted, I reached for my backpack, sat down, and fumbled Bob into my lap.

His eyes lit up at once and he said, "Don't get me wrong, big guy, I like you. But not that way."

"Shut up," I growled at him. "Just tried to use Little Chicago to find Molly's trail. It fizzled."

Bob blinked. "It worked? The model actually worked? It didn't explode?"

"Obviously," I said. "It worked fine. But I used a simple tracking spell, and it couldn't pick up her trail. So what's wrong with the damned thing?"

"Put me on the table," Bob said.

I reached up and did so. He was quiet for a minute before he said, "It's fine, Harry. I mean, it's working just fine."

"Like hell," I growled. "I've done that tracking spell hundreds of times. It must be the model."

"I'm telling you, it's perfect," Bob said. "I'm looking at the darn thing. If it wasn't your spell, and it wasn't the model . . . Hey, what did you use to focus the tracking spell?"

"Lock of her hair."

"That's baby hair, Harry."

"So?"

Bob let out a disgusted sound. "So it won't work. Harry, babies are like one big enormous blank slate. Molly has changed quite a bit since that lock was taken. She doesn't have much to do with the person it got snipped from. Naturally the spell couldn't track her."

"Dammit!" I snarled. I hadn't thought of that, but it made sense. I hadn't ever used a lock of baby hair in the spell before, except once, to find a baby. "Dammit, dammit, dammit."

A tiny mistake.

I was only human.

And I had failed Molly.

Chapter

Thirty-four

I turned away from the table and hauled myself laboriously up the ladder to my living room.

Charity sat on the edge of the couch with her head
bowed, her lips moving. As I emerged, she stood up and
faced me, tension quivering through her. Thomas, who
had a kettle on my little wood-burning stove, glanced
over his shoulder.

I shook my head at them.

Charity's face went white and she slowly sat down
again.

I went to the kitchen, found my bottle of aspirin, and
chewed up three of them, grimacing at the taste. Then I
drank a glass of water. "You make those calls?" I asked
Thomas.

"Yeah," he said. "In fact, Murphy should be here in a
minute."

I nodded at him and walked over to settle into one of
the easy chairs by the fireplace with my glass of water,
and told Charity, "I thought I could find her. I'm sorry.
I . . ." I shook my head and trailed off into silence.

"Thank you for trying, Mister Dresden," she said
quietly. She didn't look up.

"It was the baby hair," I said to Charity. "It didn't
work. Hair was too old. I couldn't . . ." I sighed. "Just
too tired to think straight, maybe," I said. "I'm sorry."

Charity looked up at me. I expected fear, anger, maybe a little bit of contempt in her features. But none of that was there. There was instead something that I'd seen in Michael when the situation was really, really bad. It was a kind of quiet calm, a surety totally at odds with the situation, and I could not fathom its source or substance.

"We will find her," she told me quietly. "We'll bring her home." Her voice held the solid confidence of someone stating a fact as simple and obvious as two plus two is four.

I didn't quite break out into a bitter laugh. I was too tired to do that. But I shook my head and stared at the empty fireplace.

"Mister Dresden," she said quietly. "I don't pretend to know as much about magic as you do. I'm quite certain you have a great deal of power."

"Just not enough," I said. "Not enough to do any good."

In the corner of my eye, I saw Charity actually smile. "It's difficult for you to realize that you are, at times, as helpless as the rest of us."

She was probably right, but I didn't say as much out loud. "I made a mistake, and Molly might be hurt because of it. I don't know how to live with that."

"You're only human," she said, and there was a trace of pensive reflection in her voice. "For all of your power."

"That answer isn't good enough," I said quietly. I glanced at her, to find her watching me, her dark eyes intent. "Not good enough for Molly."

"Have you done all that you can to help her?" Charity asked me.

I racked my brain for a useless moment and then said, "Yeah."

She spread her hands. "Then I can hardly ask you for more."

I blinked at her. "What?"

She smiled again. "Yes. It surprises me to hear myself say it, as well. I have not been tolerant of you. I have not been pleasant to you."

I waved a tired hand. "Yeah. But I get why not."

"I realize that now," she said. "You saw. But it took all of this to make me see it."

"See what?"

"That much of the anger I've directed at you was not rightfully yours. I was afraid. I let my fear become something that controlled me. That made me harm others. You." She bowed her head. "And I let it worsen matters with Molly. I feared for her safety so much that I went to war with her. I drove her toward what I most wished her to avoid. All because of my fear. I have been afraid, and I am ashamed."

"Everyone gets scared sometimes," I said.

"But I allowed it to rule me. I should have been stronger than that, Mister Dresden. Wiser than that. We all should be. God did not give us a spirit of fear, but of love, of power, and of self-control."

I absorbed that for a moment. Then I asked, "Are you apologizing to me?"

She arched an eyebrow and then said, her tone wry, "I am not yet that wise."

That actually did pull a quiet laugh from me.

"Mister Dresden," she said. "We've done all that we can do. Now we pray. We have faith."

"Faith?" I asked.

She regarded me with calm, confident eyes. "That a hand mightier than yours or mine will shield my daughter. That we will be shown a way. That He will not leave his faithful when they are in need."

"I'm not all that faithful," I said.

She smiled again, tired but unwavering. "I have enough for both of us." She met my eyes steadily and said, "There are other powers than your magic, or that of the dark spirits that oppose us. We are not alone in this fight, Mister Dresden. We need not be afraid."

I averted my eyes before a soulgaze could get going. And before she could see them tear up. Charity, regardless of how she'd treated me in the past, had been there when the chips were down. She'd cared for me when I'd been injured. She'd supported me when she didn't have to do so. As abrasive, accusatory, and harsh as she could be, I had never for an instant doubted her love for her husband, for her children, or the sincerity of her faith. I'd never liked her too much—but I had always respected her.

Now more than ever.

I just hoped she was right, when she said we weren't in this alone. I wasn't sure I really believed that, deep down. Don't get me wrong; I've got nothing against God, except for maybe wishing He was a little less ambiguous and had better taste in hired help. People like Michael and Charity and, to a lesser extent, Murphy, had made me take some kind of faith under consideration, now and again. But I wasn't the sort of guy who did well when it came to matters of belief. And I wasn't the sort of guy who I thought God would really want hanging around His house or His people.

Hell. There was a fallen angel in my brain. I counted myself lucky that I hadn't met Michael or one of the other Knights from the business end of one of the Swords.

I looked at the gift popcorn tin in the corner by the door, where my staff and rod were settled, along with my practice fighting staff, an un-carved double of my wizardly tool, my sword cane, an umbrella, and the wooden cane sheath of *Fidelacchius,* one of the three swords borne by Michael and his brothers in arms.

The sword's last wielder had told me that I was to keep it and pass it on to the next Knight. He said I would know who, and when. And then the sword sat there in my popcorn tin for years. When my house had been invaded by bad guys, they'd overlooked it. Thomas, who had lived with me for almost two years, had never touched it or commented on it. I wasn't sure that he'd ever noticed it, either. It just sat there, waiting.

I glanced at the sword, and then up at the roof. If God wanted to throw a little help our way, now would be a good time to get that foreordained knowledge of who to give the sword to, at least. Not that it would do us all that much good, I supposed. With or without *Fidelacchius,* we had a fair amount of power of the ass-kicking variety. What we needed was knowledge. Without knowledge, all the ass kicking in the world wouldn't help.

I watched the sword for a minute, just in case.

No light show. No sound effects. Not even a burst of vague intuition. I guess that wasn't the kind of help Heaven was dishing out at the moment.

I settled back in my chair. Charity had returned to her quiet prayers. I tried to think thoughts that wouldn't clash, and hoped that God wouldn't hold it against Molly that I was on her side.

I glanced back over my shoulder. Thomas had listened to the whole thing with an almost supernatural quality of noninvolvement. He was watching Charity with troubled eyes. He traded a glance with me that seemed to mirror most of what I was feeling. Then he brought everyone a cup of tea, and faded immediately back to the kitchen alcove again while Charity prayed.

Maybe ten minutes later, Murphy knocked at the door and then opened it. Besides Thomas, she was the only person I'd entrusted with an amulet that would let her through my wards without harm. She wore one of her usual work outfits: black jacket, white shirt, dark pants, comfortable shoes. Grey predawn light backlit her. She took a look around the place, frowning, before she shut the door. "What's happened?"

I brought her up to speed, finishing with my failure to locate the girl's trail.

"So you're trying to find Molly?" Murphy asked. "With a spell?"

"Yeah," I said.

"I thought that was pretty routine for you," Murphy said. "I mean, I can think of four or five times at least you've done that."

I shook my head. "That's tracking down where something *is*. I'm looking for where Molly's *been*. It's a different bag of snakes."

"Why?" Murphy asked. "Why not go straight to her?"

"Because the fetches have taken her back home with them," I said. "She's in the Nevernever. I can't zero in on her there. The best I can do is to try to find where they crossed over, follow them across, and use a regular tracking spell once I'm through."

"Oh." She frowned and walked over to me. "And for that you need her hair?"

"Yeah," I said. "Which we don't have. So we're stuck."

She chewed on her lip. "Couldn't you use something else?"

"Nail clippings," I said. "Or blood, if it was fresh enough."

"Uh-huh," Murphy said. She nodded at Charity. "What about her blood?"

"What?" I said.

"She's the girl's mother," Murphy said. "Blood of her blood. Wouldn't that work?"

"No," I said.

"Oh," Murphy said. "Why not?"

"Because . . ." I frowned. "Uh . . ." I looked up at Charity for a moment. Actually, there was a magical connection between parents and children. A strong one. My mother had worked a spell linked to Thomas and me that would confirm to us that we were brothers. The connection had been established, even though she had been the only common parent between us. The blood connection was the deepest known to magic. "It might work," I said quietly. I thought about it some more and breathed, "Stars and stones, not just work. Actually, for this spell, it might work *better*."

Charity said nothing, but her eyes glowed with that steady, unmovable strength. I thought to myself, *That's what faith looks like.*

I nodded my head to her in a bow of acknowledgment.

Then I turned to Murphy and gave her a jubilant kiss on the mouth.

Murphy blinked in total surprise.

"Yes!" I whooped, laughing. "Murphy, you rock! Go team Dresden!"

"Hey, I'm the one who rocks," she said. "Go team Murphy."

Thomas snorted. Even Charity had a small smile, though her eyes were closed and her head was bowed again, murmuring thanks, presumably to the Almighty.

Murphy had asked the exact question I'd needed to hear to tip me off to the answer. Help from above? I was not above taking help from on high, and given whose child was in danger it was entirely possible that divine intervention was precisely what had happened. I touched the brim of my mental hat and nodded my gratitude vaguely heavenward, and then turned to hurry back to the lab. "Charity, I presume you're willing to donate for the cause?"

"Of course," she said.

"Then we're in business. Get ready to move, people. This will only take me a minute."

I stopped and put a hand on Charity's shoulder. "And then we're going to get your daughter back."

"Yes," she murmured, looking up at me with fire in her eyes. "Yes, we are."

This time, the spell worked. I should have known where the fetches had found the swiftest passage from their realm to Chicago. It was one of those things that, in retrospect, was obvious.

Charity's minivan pulled into the little parking lot behind Clark Pell's rundown old movie theater. It was out of view of the street. The sun had risen on our way there, though heavy cloud cover and grumbling thunder promised unusually bad weather for so early in the day. That shouldn't have surprised me either. When the Queens of Faerie were moving around backstage, the weather quite often seemed to reflect their presence.

Murphy pulled her car in right behind the minivan and parked beside it.

"All right Murph, Thomas," I said, getting out of the van. "Faerie Fighting 101."

"I know, Harry," Thomas said.

"Yeah, but I'm going to go over it anyway, so listen up. We're heading into the Nevernever. We've got some wicked faeries to handle, which means we have to be prepared for illusions." I rummaged in my backpack and came out with a small jar. "This is an ointment that should let you see through most of their bullshit." I went to Thomas and slapped some on him, then did Murphy's eyes, and then did my own. The ointment was my own mixture, based on the one the Gatekeeper used. Mine smelled better, but stained the skin it touched with a heavy brown-black tone. I started to put the jar away. "After we—"

Charity calmly took the jar from my hands, opened it, and put ointment on her own eyes.

"What are you doing?" I asked her.

"I'm preparing to take back my daughter," she said.

"You aren't going with us," I told her.

"Yes, I am."

"No, you're not. Charity, this is seriously dangerous. We can't afford to babysit you."

Charity put the lid back on the jar and dropped it into my backpack. Then she opened the sliding door on the minivan and drew out a pair of heavy-duty plastic storage bins. She opened the first, and calmly peeled out of her pullover jersey.

I noted a couple of things. First, that Charity had won some kind of chromosomal lottery when it came to the body department. She wore a sports bra beneath the sweater, and she looked like she could have modeled it if she cared to do so. Molly had definitely gotten her looks from her mother.

The second thing I noticed was Charity's arms. She had broad shoulders, for a woman, but her arms were heavy with muscle and toned. Her forearms, especially, looked lean and hard, muscles easily seen shifting beneath tight skin. I traded a glance with Murphy, who looked impressed. I just watched Charity for a minute, frowning.

Charity took an arming jacket from the first tub. It wasn't some beat-up old relic, either. It was a neat, quilted garment, heavy black cotton over the quilting, which was backed by what looked a lot like Kevlar ballistic fabric. She pulled it on, belted it into place, and then withdrew an honest-to-God coat of mail from the tub. She slipped into it and fastened half a dozen clasps with the swift assurance of long practice. A heavy sword belt came next, securing the mail coat. Then she pulled on a tight-fitting cap made in the same manner as the jacket, tucking her braided hair up into it, and then slipped a ridged steel helmet onto her head.

She opened the second tub and drew out a straight sword with a cruciform hilt. The weapon was only slightly more slender and shorter than Michael's blessed blade, but after she inspected the blade for notches or rust, she flicked it around a few times as lightly as she would a rolled-up newspaper, then slid the weapon into the sheath on the sword belt. She tucked a pair of heavy chain gloves through the belt. Finally, she took a hammer from the big tub. It had a steel-bound handle about four feet long, and mounted a head almost as large as a sledgehammer's, backed by a wicked-looking spike.

She put the hammer over her shoulder, balancing its weight with one arm, and turned to me. She looked ferocious, so armed and armored, and the heavy black stain around her eyes didn't do anything to soften the image. Ferocious, hell. She looked competent—and dangerous.

Everyone just stared at her.

She arched a golden eyebrow. "I make all of my husband's armor," she said calmly, "as well as his spare weaponry. By hand."

"Uh," I said. No wonder she was buff. "You know how to fight, too?"

She looked at me as though I was a dim-witted child. "My husband didn't become a master swordsman by osmosis. He works hard at it. Who did you suppose he's practiced against for the last twenty years?" Her eyes smoldered again, a direct challenge to me. "These creatures have taken my Molly. And I *will not* remain here while she is in danger."

"Ma'am," Murphy said quietly. "Practice is very different from the real thing."

Charity nodded. "This won't be my first fight."

Murphy frowned for a moment, and then turned a troubled glance to me. I glanced at Thomas, who was facing away, a little apart from the rest of us, staying out of the decision-making process.

Charity stood there with that warhammer over one shoulder, her weight planted, her eyes determined.

"Hell's bells," I sighed. "Okay, John Henry, you're on the team." I waved a hand and went back to the briefing. "Faeries hate and fear the touch of iron, and that includes steel. It burns them and neutralizes their magic."

"There are extra weapons in the tub, as well as additional coats of mail," Charity offered. "Though they might not fit you terribly well, Lieutenant Murphy."

Charity had thought ahead. I was glad one of us had. "Mail coat is just the thing for discouraging nasty faerie beasties with claws."

Murphy looked skeptical. "I don't want to break up the Battle of Hastings dress theme, Harry, but I find guns generally more useful than swords. Are you serious about this?"

"You might not be able to rely on your guns," I told her. "Reality doesn't work the same way in the Nevernever, and it doesn't always warn you when it's changing the rules. It's common to find areas of Faerie where gunpowder is noncombustible."

"You're kidding," she said.

"Nope. Get some steel on you. There's not a thing the faeries can do about that. It's the biggest edge mortals have on them."

"The only edge," Charity corrected. She passed me a sleeveless mail shirt, probably the only one that would fit me. I dumped my leather duster, armored myself, and then put the duster back on over the mail. Murphy shook her head, then she and Thomas collected mail and weaponry of their own.

"Couple more things," I said. "Once we're inside, don't eat or drink anything. Don't accept any gifts, or any offers from a faerie interested in making a deal. You don't want to wind up owing favors to one of the Sidhe, believe you me." I frowned, thinking. Then I took a deep breath and said, "One thing more. Each of us must do everything possible to control our fear."

Murphy frowned at me. "What do you mean?"

"We can't afford to carry in too much fear with us. The fetches feed on it. It makes them stronger. If we go in there without keeping our fear under control, they'll sense a meal coming. We're all afraid, but we can't let it control our thoughts, actions, or decisions. Try to keep your breathing steady and remain as calm as you can."

Murphy nodded, frowning faintly.

"All right, then. Everyone hat up and sing out when you're good to go."

I watched as Murphy got her gear into place. Charity helped her secure the armor. Her mail was a short-sleeved shirt, maybe one of Charity's spare suits. She'd compensated for the oversize armor by belting it in tight, but the short sleeves fell to her elbows, and the hem reached most of the way to her knees. Murphy looked like a kid dressing up in an adult's clothes.

Her expression grew calm and distant as she worked, the way it did when she was focused on shooting, or in the middle of one of her five trillion and three formal katas. I closed my eyes and tentatively pushed my magical senses toward her. I could feel the energy in her, the life, pulsing and steady. There were tremors in it, here and there, but there was no screaming beacon of violent terror that would trumpet our approach to the bad guys.

Not that I thought there would be. What she lacked in height, she more than made up for in guts. On the other hand, Murphy had never been in the Nevernever, and even though Faerie was as normal a place as you can find there, it could get pretty weird. Despite training, discipline, and determination, novice deepwater divers can never be sure that they will remain free from the onset of the condition called "pressure sickness." The Nevernever was much the same. You can't tell how someone is going to react the first time they fall down the rabbit hole.

Thomas, being Thomas, made the mail into a fashion statement. He wore black clothing, black combat boots, and the arming jacket and mail somehow managed to go with the rest of his wardrobe. He had his saber on his belt on his left side, carried the shotgun in his right hand, and made the whole ensemble look like an upper-class version of *The Road Warrior*.

I checked on Thomas with my wizard's senses, too. His presence had never been fully human, but like the other members of the White Court, the vampiric aspects of him were not obvious to casual observation, not even to wizards. There was something feline about his aura, the same quality I would expect in a hungry leopard waiting patiently for the next meal to approach; enormous power held in perfect balance. There was a darker portion of him, too, the part I'd always associated with the demonic presence that made him a vampire, a black and bitter well of energy, equal parts lust, hunger, and self-loathing. Thomas was no fool—he was certainly afraid. But the fear couldn't be sensed under that still, black surface.

Charity, after she finished helping Murphy, stepped back from her and went to her knees in the parking lot. She folded her hands in her lap, bowed her head, and continued praying. Around her I felt a kind of ambient warmth, as though she knelt in her own personal sunbeam, the same kind of energy that had always characterized her husband's presence. Faith, I suppose. She was afraid, too, but it wasn't the primitive survival fear the fetches required. Her fear was for her daughter; for her safety, her future, her happiness. And as I watched her, I saw her lips form my name, then Thomas's, then Murphy's.

Charity was more afraid for us than herself.

Right there, I promised myself that I would get her back home with her daughter, back to her family and her husband, safe and sound and whole. I would not, by God, hesitate for a heartbeat to do whatever was necessary to make my friend's family whole again.

I checked myself out, taking inventory. Leather duster, ill-fitting mail shirt, staff, and blasting rod, check. Shield bracelet and amulet, check. My abused left hand ached a little, and what I could feel of it felt stiff—but I could move my fingers. My head hurt. My limbs felt a little bit shaky with fatigue. I had to hope that adrenaline would kick in and make that problem go away when it counted.

"Everyone good to go?" I asked.

Murphy nodded. Thomas drawled, "Yep."

Charity rose and said, "Ready."

"Let me sweep the outside of the building first," I said. "This is their doorway home. It's possible that they've got the place booby-trapped, or that they've set up wards. Once I clear it, we'll go in."

I trudged off to walk a slow circle around Pell's theater. I let my fingertips drag along the side of the building, closed my eyes most of the way, and extended my wizard's senses into the structure. It wasn't a quick process, but I tried not to dawdle, either. As I walked, I sensed a kind of trapped, suffocated energy bouncing around inside the building—leakage from the Nevernever probably, from when the fetches took Molly across. But several times I also felt tiny, malevolent surges of energy, too random and mobile to be spells or wards. Their presence was disturbingly similar to that of the fetch I'd destroyed in the hotel.

I came back to where I'd begun about ten minutes later.

"Anything?" Thomas asked.

"No wards. No mystic land mines," I told him. "But I think there's something in there."

"Like what?"

"Like fetches," I said. "Smaller than the big ones we're after, and probably set to guard the doorway between here and the Nevernever."

"They'll try to ambush us when we go in," Murphy said.

"Probably," I said. "But if we know about it, we can turn it against them. When they come, hit them fast and hard, even if it seems like overkill. We can't afford any injuries."

Murphy nodded.

"What are we waiting for?" Thomas asked.

"More help," I replied.

"Why?"

"Because I'm not strong enough to open a stable passage to deep Faerie," I said. "Even if I wasn't tired, and

I managed to get it open, I doubt it would stay that way for more than a few seconds."

"Which would be bad?" Murphy asked.

"Yeah."

"What would happen?" Charity asked quietly.

"We'd die," I said. "We'd be trapped in deep Faerie, near the strongholds of all kinds of trouble, with no way to escape but to try to find our way to the portions of Faerie that are near Earth. The locals would eat us and spit out the bones before we got anywhere close to escape."

Thomas rolled his eyes and said, "This isn't exactly helping me keep my mind off my fear, man."

"Shut up," I told him. "Or I'll move to my second initiative and start telling you knock-knock jokes."

"Harry," Murphy said, "if you knew you couldn't open the door long enough to let us get the girl, how did you plan to manage it?"

"I know someone who can help. Only she's totally unable to help me."

Murphy scowled at me, then said, "You're enjoying this. You just love to dance around questions and spring surprises when you know something the rest of us don't."

"It's like heroin for wizards," I confirmed.

An engine throbbed nearby, and tires made a susurrus on asphalt. A motorcycle prowled around the theater to its rear parking lot, bearing two helmeted riders. The rearmost rider swung down from the bike, a shapely woman in leather pants and a denim jacket. She reached up, took off her green helmet, and shook out her snow-white hair. It fell at once into a silken sheet without the aid of a brush or a comb. The Summer Lady, Lily, paused to give me a slight bow, and she smiled at me, her green eyes particularly luminous.

The bike's driver proved to be Fix. The Summer Knight wore close-fitting black pants and a billowing shirt of green silk. He bore a rapier with a sturdy guard on his hip, and the leather that wrapped its handle had worn smooth and shiny. Fix put both helmets on a rack on the motorcycle, nodded at us, and said, "Good morning."

I made introductions, though I went into few details beyond names and titles. When that was done, I told Lily, "Thank you for coming."

She shook her head. "I am yet in your debt. It was the least I could do. Though I feel I must warn you that I may not be able to give you the help that you require."

Meaning Titania's compulsion to prevent Lily from helping me was still in force. But I'd thought of a way to get around that.

"I know you can't help me," I said. "But I wish to tell you that the onus of your debt to me has been passed to another in good faith. I must redress a wrong I have done to the girl named Molly Carpenter. To do so, I offer her mother your debt to me as payment."

Fix barked out a satisfied laugh. "Hah!"

Lily's mouth spread into a delighted smile. "Well done, wizard," she murmured. Then she turned to Charity and asked, "Do you accept the wizard's offer of payment, Lady?"

Charity looked a little lost, and she glanced at me. I nodded my head at her.

"Y-yes," she said. "Yes."

"So mote it be," Lily said, bowing her head to Charity. "Then I owe you a debt, Lady. What may I do to repay it?"

Charity glanced at me again. I nodded and said, "Just tell her."

Charity turned back to the Summer Lady. "Help us

retrieve my daughter Molly," she said. "She is a prisoner of the fetches of the Winter Court."

"I will be more than happy to do all in my power to aid you," Lily said.

Charity closed her eyes. "Thank you."

"It will not be as much help as you might desire," Lily told her, her voice serious. "I dare not directly strike at the servants of Winter acting in lawful obligation to their Queen, except in self-defense. Were I to attack, the consequences could be grave, and retaliation immediate."

"Then what can you do?" Charity asked.

Lily opened her mouth to answer, but then said, "The wizard seems to have something in mind."

"Yep," I said. "I was just coming to that."

Lily smiled at me and bowed her head, gesturing for me to continue.

"This is where they took the girl across," I told Lily. "Must be why they attacked Pell first—to make sure the building was shut down and locked up, so that they would have an immediate passage back, if they needed it. I'm also fairly sure they left some guardians behind."

Lily frowned at me and walked over to the building. She touched it with her fingers, and her eyes closed. It took her less than a tenth of the time it had me, and she never moved from the spot. "Indeed," she said. "Three lesser fetches at least. They cannot sense us yet, but they will know when anyone enters, and attack."

"I'm counting on it," I said. "I'm going to go in first and let them see me."

Fix lifted his eyebrows. "At which point they tear you to bits? This is a craftier plan than I had anticipated."

I flashed him a grin. "Wouldn't want you to feel left out, Fix. I want Lily to hold a veil over everyone else. Once the fetches show up to rip off my face, Lily drops the veil, and the rest of you drop them."

"Yeah, that's a much better plan," Fix drawled, his fingertips tracing over the hilt of his sword. "And I *can* cut up vassals of Winter, so long as it is no inconvenience to you, of course, m'lady."

Lily shook her head. "Not at all, sir Knight. And I will be glad to veil you and your allies, Lady Charity."

Charity paused and said, "Wait a minute. Do I understand this situation correctly? You are not allowed to assist Harry, but because Harry has . . . what? Passed his debt to me?"

"Banks buy and sell mortgages all the time," I said.

Charity arched a brow. "And because he's given me your debt to him, you're doing whatever you can to help?"

Fix and Lily exchanged a helpless glance.

"They're also under a compulsion that prevents them from directly discussing it with anyone," I filled in. "But you've got the basics right, Charity."

Charity shook her head. "Aren't they going to be in trouble for this? Won't . . . who commands her?"

"Titania," I said.

Charity blinked at me, and I could tell she'd heard the name before. "The . . . the Faerie Queen?"

"One of them," I said. "Yeah."

She shook her head. "I don't . . . enough people are already in danger."

"Don't worry about us, ma'am," Fix assured her, and winked. "Titania has already laid down the law. We've obeyed it. Not our fault if what she decreed was not what she wanted."

"Translation," I said. "We got around her fair and square. She won't like it, but she'll accept it."

"Oh yeah," Thomas muttered under his breath. "This isn't coming back to bite anyone in the ass later."

"Ixnay," I growled at him, then turned and walked toward the theater's rear entrance. I took up my staff in a firm grip and put its tip against the chains holding the door shut. I took a moment to slow my breathing and focus my thoughts. This wasn't a gross-power exercise. I wouldn't have to put nearly as much oomph into shattering the chain if I kept it small, precise, focused. Blasting a door down was a relatively simple exercise for me. What I wanted here was to use a minimum of power to snap a single link in the chain.

I brought my thoughts to a pinpoint focus and muttered, *"Forzare."*

Power lashed through the length of the staff, and there was a hiss and a sharp crack nearly as loud as a gunshot. The chain jumped. I lowered my staff, to find one single link split into two pieces, each broken end glowing with heat. I nudged the heated links to the ground with the tip of my staff, faintly surprised and pleased with how little relative effort it had taken.

I reached out and tried the doorknob.

Locked.

"Hey, Murph," I said. "Look at that zeppelin."

I heard her sigh and turn around. I popped a couple of stiff metal tools out of my duster's pocket and started finagling the lock with them. My left hand wasn't much help, but it was at least able to hold the tool steady while my right did most of the work.

"Hey," Thomas said. "When did you get those?"

"Butters says it's good for my hand to do physical therapy involving the use of manual dexterity."

Thomas snorted. "So you started learning to pick locks? I thought you were playing guitar."

"This is simpler," I said. "And it doesn't make dogs start howling."

"I might have killed you if I'd heard 'House of the Rising Sun' one more time," Thomas agreed. "Where'd you get the picks?"

I glanced over my shoulder at Murphy and said, "Little bird."

"One of these days, Dresden," Murphy said, still stubbornly faced away.

I got the tumblers lined up and twisted with slow, steady pressure. The dead bolt slid to, and I pulled the door slightly ajar. I rose, put the tools away, and took up my staff again, ready for instant trouble. Nothing happened for a moment. I Listened at the door for half a minute, but heard not a sound.

"All right," I said. "Here we go. Everyone ready to—"

I glanced over my shoulder and found the parking lot entirely empty except for me.

"Wow," I said. "Good veil, Lily." Then I turned back around just as if my nerves weren't jangling like guitar strings and said, "Ding, ding. Round one."

Chapter

Thirty-five

I kicked the door open, staff held ready to fight, and shouted, "And I'm all outta bubble gum!"

The pale grey light of the overcast sunrise coming in over the lake showed me a service corridor, the kind with walls that have marks and writing all over them, floors with the paint chipped off all down the middle of the walkway, and lots of stuff stacked up here and there. At the far end of the hallway was a door, propped open with a rubber wedge. A worn sign on the door read EMPLOYEES ONLY. A curtained doorway about halfway down the hall opened onto what must have been the concessions counter in the little theater's lobby.

Silence reigned. Not a single light shone within.

"Guess you had to see that one," I said to the empty building. "John Carpenter. Rowdy Roddy Piper. Longest fight scene ever. You know?"

Silence.

"Missed that one, huh?" I asked the darkness.

I stood there, hoping the bad guys would make this one easy. If they charged me, I could duck aside and then let my concealed allies take them apart. Instead, as bad guys so often do, they failed to oblige me.

I started to feel a little silly just standing there. If I went ahead, the narrow passage would negate the participation of those now lurking in veiled ambush behind me. But had I really been alone, the hallway would have been as reasonable a fighting position as I could hope to gain—no way for the fetches to encircle me, no way to use their advantage of numbers. Had I really been alone, I would have needed to jump on an opportunity like that. There are stupid faeries, but fetches aren't among them. If I didn't behave like a lone wolf come to party, it would tip off the presence of my entourage.

So, like a crazed loner with more death wish than survival instinct, I boldly strode into the building, staff held ready, teeth bared in a fighting grin. The place was dim, and cooler than it should have been, even given the time of day. My breath turned to frost in front of my nose. The movie-theater scent of popcorn had sunk into the very foundations, and was now as much a part of the building as its walls and floor. My stomach rumbled. Like certain other portions of my anatomy, it had a tendency to become easily sidetracked, and to hell with little details like survival.

The rest of me was nervous. I had seen how fast one of those creatures could move. I could have ducked out of the way if they'd come charging from the far end of the hall at me, but not by much. Maybe two or three steps in, I reached a point where I judged that I wouldn't have time to retreat and let my allies ambush the attacker. For a few seconds, at least, I'd be on my own.

A few seconds are forever in a fight.

I shook out my shield bracelet, willed power into it, and walked with my left hand before me, both providing me some protection against a possible charge and casting low blue light that would let me see as I moved forward. "Do you know what part of a movie this is?" I said to myself as I moved. "This is the part where the old farmer with the torch and the shotgun just can't keep himself from walking forward into the dark cave, even though he damn well knows there's a monster in there." I moved up to the hanging curtain and slid it aside with my staff. Several quick glances out showed me a small and dingy concessions stand to go along with the small and dingy lobby.

Nothing tried to eat my face.

"Oh, come on," I said, louder. "I'm starting to feel a little insulted, here. If you guys keep this up, I'm going to take drastic, clichéd measures. Maybe walk backward through a doorway or something."

My instincts suddenly screamed, and I flung myself through the curtained doorway, getting clear of the hall, as something darted toward me from the hall's far end. I didn't want to catch any bullets or blasts of fire or hurled hammers from my backup.

There was a roar of sound from the hallway—something letting out a ululating howl, a heavy handgun, a roaring shotgun, and the buzzing snap of an arc of electricity. Blinding blue-white light blazed through the curtain as I dove through it—and showed me the fetch that had lurked in ambush on the other side.

It was crouched on top of the glass cabinet atop the concessions stand's popcorn machine, and had taken the form of a creature that could only loosely be called a "cat." It was twice Mister's size, and its moldy black fur stood out in tufts and spikes. Its shoulders were hunched, almost deformed with muscle, and its muzzle was broad and filled with teeth too heavy to belong to any feline short of a lion. Its eyes gleamed with a sickly, greenish luminescence, and it flashed through the air, claws extended, teeth bared, emitting a mind-splitting howl of rage.

I had no time or space to strike first, and it was a damned good thing I'd prepared my shield ahead of time. I brought it up and into a quarter dome between me and the fetch, blue power hissing.

I should have kept in mind how easily the Scarecrow had shed my magic the night before. The lesser fetch must have had some measure of the same talent, because it changed the tone of its howl in the middle of its leap, impacted my shield, and oozed through it as though the solid barrier was a thick sludge.

There was no space to dodge in and no room to swing my staff, so I dropped it as the fetch's face emerged from my shield and drove my fist into the end of its feline nose. I dropped the shield as I did. With the shield gone, the only force acting on the fetch was the impact of my punch, and the shapeshifter flew backward into the old cash register on the concessions counter. It was made of metal. Blue sparks erupted from the fetch as its flesh hit the iron, along with a yowl of protest, tendrils of smoke, and an acrid odor.

I heard footsteps in the corridor behind me, and then a trio of gunshots.

"Harry!" Murphy called.

"Here!" I shouted. I didn't have time to say anything else. The nightmare cat bounced up from the cash register, recovered its balance, and flung itself at me again, every bit as swiftly as the fetch I'd faced earlier. I ducked and tried to throw myself under the fetch, to get behind it, but my body wasn't operating as swiftly as my mind, and the fetch's claws raked at my eyes.

I threw up an arm, and the fetch slammed into it with a sudden, harsh impact that made my arm go numb from the elbow down. Claws and fangs flashed. The spellbound leather of my duster held, and the creature's claws didn't penetrate. Except for a shallow cut a random claw accidentally inflicted on my wrist, below the duster's sleeve, I escaped it unharmed. I hit the ground and rolled, throwing my arm out to one side in an effort to slam the fetch onto the floor and knock it loose. The creature was deceptively strong. It braced one rear leg against the counter, claws digging in, robbing the blow of any real force. It bounced off the floor with rubbery agility, pounced onto my chest, and went for my throat.

I got an arm between the fetch and my neck. It couldn't rip its way through the duster, but it was stronger than it had any right to be. I was lying mostly on my back and had no leverage. It wrenched at my arm, and I knew I only had a second or two before it overpowered me, threw my arm out of its way, and tore my throat out.

I reached down with my other hand and ripped my duster all the way off the front of my body. Cold iron seared the nightmare cat's paws in a hissing fury of sparks and smoke. The fetch let out another shrieking yowl and bounded almost straight up.

Gunshots rang out again as the fetch reached the apogee of its reflexive leap. It twitched and screamed, jerking sharply. As it came back down, it writhed wildly in midair, altering its trajectory, and landed on the floor beside me.

Murphy's combat boot lashed out in a stomping kick that sent the fetch sliding across the floor, and the instant it was clear of me she started shooting again. She put half a dozen shots into the creature, driving it over the floor, howling in pain but thrashing with frenzied strength. The gun went empty. Murphy slammed another clip into the weapon just as the fetch began gathering itself up off the floor. She kept pouring bullets into it as fast as she could accurately shoot, and stepped with deliberate care to one side as she did so.

Thomas came through the curtain with preternatural speed, his face bone white. He seized the stunned fetch by the throat and slammed it overhand into the cash register, again and again, until I heard its spine snap.

Then he threw it over the concessions stand into the lobby.

Light flashed. Something that looked like a butterfly sculpted from pure fire shot over my head like a tiny comet. I scrambled to my feet, to see the blazing butterfly hit the fetch square in the chest. The thing screamed again, front legs thrashing, rear legs entirely limp, as fire exploded over its flesh, burned a hole in its chest, and then abruptly consumed it whole.

I leaned on the counter and panted for a second, then looked around to see the curtain slide aside of its own accord as Lily stepped through it. At that moment, the Summer Lady did not look sweet or caring. Her lovely face held an implacable, restrained anger, and half a dozen of the fiery butterflies flittered around her. She stared at the dying fetch until the fire winked out, leaving nothing, not even residual ectoplasm, behind.

Murphy reloaded and came over to me, though her eyes were still scanning for danger. "You're bleeding. You all right?"

I checked. Blood from the injury on my wrist had trickled down over my palm and fingers. I pushed back my sleeve to get a look at the wound. The cut ran parallel to my forearm. It wasn't long, but was deeper than I'd thought. And it had missed opening up the veins in my wrist by maybe half an inch.

My belly went cold and I swallowed. "Simple cut," I told Murphy. "Not too bad."

"Let me see," Thomas said. He examined the injury and said, "Could have been worse. You'll need a stitch or three, Harry."

"No time," I told him. "Help me find something to wrap it up good and tight."

Thomas looked around the concessions area and suggested, "Silly straws?"

I heard an expressive sigh. Charity appeared at the curtained doorway, flipped open a leather case on her sword belt, and tossed Thomas a compact medical kit. He caught it, gave her a nod, and went to work on my hand. Charity stepped back into the hallway, her expression alert. Fix glanced in and then went by the curtained doorway, presumably to the other end of the hall.

"What happened?" I asked Murphy.

"One of those things charged down the hall to jump on your back," she said. "Looked like some kind of mutant baboon. We took it down."

"*Nature Red,*" Thomas mused. "Remember that movie? The one where the retrovirus gets loose in the zoo and starts mutating the animals? Baboon was from there. That cat thing, too."

"Huh," I said. "Yeah."

"I don't get it," Murphy said. "Why do they all look like movie monsters?"

"Fear," I said. "Those images have been a part of this culture for a while now. Over time, they've generated a lot of fear."

"Come on," Murphy said. "I saw *Nature Red*. It wasn't *that* scary."

"This is a case of quantity over quality," I said. "Even if it only makes you jump in your chair, there's a little fear. Multiply that by millions. The fetches take the form so that they can tap into a portion of that fear in order to create more of it."

Murphy frowned and shook her head. "Whatever."

A light appeared in the hallway leading back to the actual theater. In an eyeblink, Murphy and Thomas both had their guns pointed at it and my shield bracelet was dripping heatless blue sparks, ready to spring into place.

"It's all right," Lily said, her voice low.

Fix appeared in the doorway at the far end of the

lobby, sword in hand. Fire gleamed along the length of the blade as if it had been coated in kerosene and ignited. He looked around, frowning, and said, "It isn't back this way."

"What isn't?" I asked.

"The third," Lily said. "There will be a third fetch."

"Why?" I asked.

"Because they're fetches," Fix answered. "We should check the bathrooms."

"Not alone," I said. "Murph, Charity."

Murphy nodded and slipped around the counter to join Fix. Charity slipped through the curtain and to the lobby in her wake. The three of them moved in cautious silence and entered the restrooms. They returned a moment later. Fix shook his head.

"There," Thomas said, finishing off the bandage. "Too tight?"

I flexed the fingers of my right hand and stooped to recover my staff. "It's good." I squinted around the place. "One room left."

We all looked at the double doors leading to the actual theater. They were closed. Faint lights flickered, barely noticeable from within the radius of our own illumination.

"If it ain't broke, don't fix it," I said, walking around the counter and into the lobby. I headed for the doors and tried to project confidence. "Same plan."

I paused at the doors while everyone gathered behind me. I looked back to check that they were ready, which is why I was the only one who saw what happened.

The plastic trash can about six inches behind Charity suddenly exploded, the top flipping off, and paper cups and popcorn bags flew everywhere. Something humanoid and no larger than a toddler shot from the trash can. It had red hair and overalls, and it held a big old kitchen knife in one tiny hand. It hit Charity just above her tailbone, driving her into the ground, and lifted the knife.

My companions had been taken by surprise—just a second or two, but as far as Charity was concerned it might as well have been forever. There was no time for thought. Before I realized what I was doing, I took a pair of long steps, shifting my grip on my staff as I went, and swung it like a golf club at the fetch's head. It impacted with a meaty thunk.

Its head flew off, bounced off of a pillar, and rolled to a stop not far from the rest of the thing. I had only a second to regard the doll's features before it began dissolving into ectoplasm.

Thomas blinked at it and said, "That was Bucky the Murder Doll."

"Kind of a wimp," I said.

Thomas nodded. "Must have been the runt of the litter."

I traded a glance with Murphy. "Personally," I said, "I never understood how anyone could have found that thing frightening to begin with." Then I went to Charity's side and offered her a hand up. She grimaced and took it. "Are you all right?"

"Nothing broken," she replied. She winced and put her hand to her back. "I should have stretched out."

"Next time we'll know better," I said. "Lily? Is that it?"

The Summer Lady's eyes went distant for a moment and then she murmured, "Yes. There are no longer agents of Winter in this place. Come."

She stepped forward and the doors to the theater proper opened of their own accord. We followed. It was your typical movie theater. Not one of the new stadium-seating fancy theaters, but one of the old models with only a slight incline in the floor. Light played over the screen, though the projector was not running. Spectral colors shifted, faded, changed, and melded like the aurora borealis, and I was struck with the sudden intuition that the color and light were somehow being projected from the opposite side of the screen. The air grew even colder as we followed Lily down the aisle.

She stopped in front of the screen, staring blankly at it for a moment, then shuddered. "Dresden," she said quietly. "This crossing leads to Arctis Tor."

My stomach fluttered again. "Oh, crap."

I saw Thomas arch an eyebrow at me out of the corner of my eye.

"Crap?" Murphy asked. "Why? What is that place?"

I took a deep breath. "It's the heart of Winter. It's like . . ." I shook my head. "Think the Tower of London, the Fortress of Solitude, Fort Knox, and Alcatraz all rolled up into one giant ball of fun. It's Mab's capital. Her stronghold." I glanced at Lily. "If what I've read about it is correct, that is. I've never actually seen the place."

"Your sources were accurate enough, Harry," Lily said. Her manner remained remote, strained. "This is going to severely limit what help I can give you."

"Why?" I asked.

Lily stared intently at me for a second, then said, "My power will react violently to that of Mab. I can open the way to the Arctis Tor, but holding the way open for your return will occupy the whole of my strength. Furthermore, so long as I hold the way open I run the risk of letting creatures from deep Winter run free in Chicago. Which means that Fix must remain here to guard the passage against them. I cannot in good conscience send him with you."

I scowled at the shifting colors on the screen. "So once we go in, we're on our own."

"Yes."

Super. Without Lily and Fix's power to counter that of the Winter fae within Arctis Tor, our odds of success would undergo a steep reduction—and I had hoped we would be attacking an independent trio of faeries lairing in a cave or under a bridge or something. I hadn't figured on storming the Bastille.

I looked up and met Charity's eyes for a second.

I turned back to the dancing lights on the movie screen and told the others, "Things just got a lot worse. I'm still going. None of you have to come with me. I don't expect you to—"

Before I finished speaking, Charity, Murphy, and Thomas stepped up to stand beside me.

A bolt of warmth, fierce with joy and pride and gratitude, flashed through me like sudden lightning. I don't care about whose DNA has recombined with whose. When everything goes to hell, the people who stand by you without flinching—they are your family.

And they were my heroes.

I nodded at Lily. She closed her eyes, and the shimmering colors on the screen grew brighter, more vibrant. The air grew colder.

"All right," I said quietly. "Each of you get a hand on my shoulder." I resettled my grip on my wizard's staff and murmured, "Round two."

Chapter

Thirty-six

Every time I opened a way to the Nevernever, it always looked pretty much the same—an uneven vertical rip in the air that let in the sights and sounds and scents of the world on the other side. The longer I wanted the rift to stay open, the bigger I'd rip the hole. More experienced wizards had made a comment or two over the years to suggest that I still had a lot to learn on the subject.

When Lily opened the way to Arctis Tor, I understood why. Light and color shifted over the screen, their flow quickening, deepening. At first nothing else happened. The movie screen was simply a surface. Then the hairs on the back of my neck rose, and a cold wind wafted into my face, bringing with it the dry, sterile scent of winter in high, barren mountains and the high, lonely cry of some kind of wild beast like nothing in the real world.

Deep blue came to dominate the colors on the screen, and a moment later resolved itself into the shapes of mountains towering beneath the light of an impossibly enormous silver moon. They were bleak and hateful stone peaks, wreathed in mist and wrapped in ice and snow. The wind moaned and blew frozen crystals into our faces, then sank into a temporary lull.

The blowing snow cleared just enough to get me my first look at Arctis Tor.

Mab's stronghold was a fortress of black ice, an enormous, shadowy cube sitting high up the slope of the highest mountain in sight. A single, elegant spire rose above the rest of the structure. Flickers of green and amethyst energy played within the ice of the walls. I couldn't make a good guess at how big the thing was. The walls and battlements were lined with inverted icicles. They made me think of the fanged jaws of a hungry predator. A single gate, small in comparison to the rest of the fortress, stood open.

Hell's bells. How the hell was I supposed to get in there? It was almost a relief when the wind rose again, and blowing snow once more obscured the fortress from view.

It was only then that I realized that the way was open. Lily had brought it forth so smoothly that I hadn't been able to tell when image gave way to reality. By comparison, my own ability to open a way to the Nevernever was about as advanced as the paintings of a particularly gifted gorilla.

I glanced back at Lily. She gave me a small smile and then gestured with one hand. One of the fiery butterflies fluttering around her altered course and soared over to me. "This much I can do for you all," she murmured. "It will lead you through the storm, and ward away the cold until you can return here. Do not tarry, wizard. I do not know how long I will be able to hold the way open for your return."

I nodded. "Thank you, Lily."

This time her smile was warmer, more like that of the girl she had been before becoming the Summer Lady. "Good luck, Harry."

Fix took a deep breath and then hopped up onto the stage floor at the base of the movie screen. He turned to offer me a hand up. I took it, stared at the frozen wasteland for a second, and then stepped directly forward, into what had been the screen.

I found myself standing in knee-deep snow, and the howling winds forced my eyes almost shut. I should have been freezing, but whatever enchantment Lily's blazing butterfly used seemed effective. The air felt almost as warm as that of a ski slope seeing its last day of the season. Thomas, Murphy, and Charity stepped out of a shimmer in the air, and Fix followed them a second later.

"Hey, Fix," I said. I had to raise my voice to be heard over the wind. "I thought you weren't coming."

The Summer Knight shook his head. "I'm not. But it will be easier to stop anything going through from this side," he said. He regarded us and asked lightly, "You bring enough iron, you think?"

"We're about to find out."

"Christ. You're going to piss off Mab something fierce, bringing iron here."

"I was doing that anyway," I assured him.

He nodded, then glanced back at the rift and frowned. "Harry," he said. "There's something you should know before you go in."

I arched an eyebrow and listened.

"We just got word from our observers that there's a battle underway. The Reds found one of the major headquarters of the Venatori Umbrorum."

"Who?" Charity asked.

"Secret organization," I told her. "Like the Masons, but with machine guns."

"The Venatori sent out a call for help," Fix continued. "The Council answered it."

I chewed my lower lip. "Do you know where?"

"Oregon, couple hours from Seattle," he said.

"How bad is it?"

"So far it's too close to call. But it's not good. The Reds had their sorcerous types mucking around with a lot of the Council's pathways through the Nevernever. A lot of the Wardens got sidetracked from the battle completely."

"Dammit," I muttered. "Isn't there anything Summer can do to help?"

Fix grimaced and shook his head. "Not with the way Mab's forces are disposed. If we pull enough of our forces from Summer to help the Council, it will weaken us. Winter will attack." He stared at the looming fortress, glimpsed in half instants through the gusting snow, and shook his head. "The Council's mind-set is too defensive, Harry. If they keep sitting tight and reacting to the enemy, instead of making the Reds react to them, they'll lose this war."

I grunted. "Clausewitz would agree. But I don't think the Merlin knows from Clausewitz. And this is a long way from over. Don't count us out yet."

"Maybe," he said, but his voice wasn't confident. "I wish I could do more, but you'd better get going. I'll hold the door for you."

I offered him my hand and he shook it. "Be careful," I said.

"Good hunting," he replied.

I glanced at my three companions and called, "Ready?"

They were. We followed the burning butterfly through the snow. Without its protection from the elements, I doubt we would have made it, and I made it a point to remember to wear sufficient cold-weather gear in the event that I somehow survived this ongoing idiocy and was crazy enough to come back a second time. Even with the Summer magic to protect us, it was a pretty good hike over unfriendly terrain. I'd done worse in the past, with both Justin DuMorne and Ebenezar, and there are times when having long legs can be a real advantage on rough terrain. Charity seemed all right, too, but Thomas had never been much of an outdoorsman, and Murphy's height put her at a disadvantage that the unaccustomed weight of her armor and cutlery exacerbated.

I traded a glance with Charity. I started giving Thomas a hand on rough portions of our climb. Charity helped Murphy. At first I thought Murphy might take her arm off out of wounded pride, but she grimaced and visibly forced herself to accept the help.

The last two hundred yards or so were completely open, with no trees or undulation of terrain to shield our approach from the walls of the fortress. I lifted a hand to call a halt at the edge of the last hummock of stone that would shelter us from view. Lily's butterfly drifted in erratic circles around my head, snowflakes hissing to steam where they touched it.

I peered over the edge of a frozen boulder at Arctis Tor for a long time, then settled back down again.

"I don't see anyone," I said, trying to keep my voice down.

"Doesn't make any sense," Thomas said. He was panting and shivering a little, despite Lily's warding magic. "I thought this was supposed to be Mab's headquarters. This place looks deserted."

"It makes perfect sense," I said. "Winter's forces are all poised to hit Summer. You don't do that from the heart of your own territory. You gather at strong points near the enemy's border. If we're lucky, maybe there's just a skeleton garrison here."

Murphy peered around the edge of the stones and said, "The gate's open. I don't see any guards." She frowned. "There are . . . there's *something* on the open ground between here and there. See?"

I leaned next to her and peered. Vague, shadowy shapes stirred in the wind between us and the fortress, insubstantial as any shadow. "Oh," I said. "It's a glamour. Illusion, laid out around the place. Probably a hedge maze of some kind."

"And it fools people?" she asked uncertainly.

"It fools people who don't have groovy wizard ointment for their eyes," I said. Then I frowned and said, "Wait a minute. The gate isn't *open*. It's *gone*."

"What?" Charity asked. She leaned out and stared. "There is a broken lattice of ice on the ground around the gate. A portcullis?"

"Could be," I agreed. "And inside." I squinted. "I think I can see some heavier pieces. Like maybe someone ripped apart the portcullis and blew the gate in." I took a deep breath, feeling a hysterical little giggle lurking in my throat. "Something huffed and puffed and blew the house in. Mab's house."

The wind howled over the frozen mountains.

"Well," Thomas said. "That can't be good."

Charity bit her lip. "Molly."

"I thought you said this Mab was all mighty and stuff, Harry," Murphy said.

"She is," I said, frowning.

"Then who plays big bad wolf to her little pig?"

"I . . ." I shook my head and rubbed at my mouth. "I'm starting to think that maybe I'm getting a little bit out of my depth, here."

Thomas broke out into a rippling chuckle, a faint note of hysteria to it. He turned his back to the fortress and sat down, chortling.

I glowered at him and said, "It's not funny."

"It is from here," Thomas said. "I mean, God, you are dense sometimes. Are you just now noticing this, Harry?"

I glowered at him some more. "To answer your question, Murph, I don't know who did this, but the list of the people who could is fairly short. Maybe the Senior Council could if they had the Wardens along, but they're busy, and they'd have had to fight a campaign to get this far. Maybe the vampires could have done it, working together, but that doesn't track. I don't know. Maybe Mab pissed off a god or something."

"There is only one God," Charity said.

I waved a hand and said, "No capital 'G,' Charity, in deference to your beliefs. But there are beings who aren't the Almighty who have power way beyond anything running around the planet."

"Like who?" Murphy asked.

"Old Greek and Roman and Norse deities. Lots and lots of Amerind divinity, and African tribal beings. A few Australian aboriginal gods; others in Polynesia, southeast Asia. About a zillion Hindu gods. But they've all been dormant for centuries." I frowned at Arctis Tor. "And I can't think what Mab might have done to earn their enmity. She's avoided doing that for thousands of years."

Unless, of course, I thought to myself, *Maeve and Lily are right, and she really has gone bonkers.*

"Dresden," Charity said. "This is academic. We either go in or we leave. Now."

I chewed my lip and nodded. Then I dug in my pockets for the tiny vial of blood Charity had provided, and hunted through the rocks until I found a spot clear enough to chalk out a circle. I empowered it and wrought one of my usual tracking spells, keying it to a sensation of warmth against my senses. Cold as it was, I would hardly mind anything that might make me feel a little less freeze-dried.

I broke the circle and released the spell, and immediately felt a tingling warmth on my left cheekbone. I turned to face it, and found myself staring directly at Arctis Tor. I paced fifty or sixty yards to the side, and faced the warmth again, working out a rough triangulation.

"She's alive," I told Charity, "or the spell wouldn't have worked. She's in there. Let's go."

"Wait," Charity said. She gave me a look filled with discomfort and then said, "May I say a brief prayer for us first?"

"Can't hurt," I said. "I'll take all the help I can get."

She bowed her head and said, "Lord of hosts, please stand with us against this darkness." The quiet, bedrock-deep energy of true faith brushed against me. Charity crossed herself. "Amen."

Murphy echoed the gesture and the amen. Thomas and I tried to look theologically invisible. Then, without further speech, I swung out around the frozen stone cairn and broke into a quick, steady jog. The others followed along.

I passed the first bones fifty yards from the walls. They lay in a crushed, twisted jumble in the snow, frozen into something that looked like a macabre Escher print. The bones were vaguely human, but I couldn't be sure because they had been pulverized to dust in some places, warped like melted wax in others. It was the first grisly memorial of many. As I kept going forward, brittle, frozen bones crunched under my boots, lying closer and thicker, and twisted more horribly, as we drew closer to Arctis Tor. By the time we got to the gate, I was shin-deep in icy bones. They spread out on either side in an enormous wheel of horrible remains centered on the gate. Whoever they had been, thousands of their kind had perished here.

Charity's guess about the portcullis had been bang on. Pieces of it lay scattered about, mixed among the bones. Where the gate arched beneath the fortress walls, there were still more bones, waist-deep on me, and slabs of planed dark ice, the remains of the fortress gate, stuck out at odd angles. The walls of Arctis Tor had been pitted with what I could only assume had been an acid of some kind. There were larger gouges blown out of the walls here and there, but against their monolithic volume, they were little more than pockmarks.

I pushed ahead to the gate, plowing my way through bones. Once there, I caught a faint whiff of something familiar. I leaned closer to one of the craters blown out of the wall and sniffed.

"What is it?" Thomas asked me.

"Sulfur," I said quietly. "Brimstone."

"What does that mean?" he asked.

"No way to tell," I half lied. But my intuition was absolutely certain of what had happened here. Someone had thrown Hellfire against the walls of Arctis Tor. Which meant that the forces of the literal Hell, or their agents, were also playing a part in the ongoing events.

Way, way, *way* out of my depth.

I told myself that it didn't matter. There was a young woman inside that frozen boneyard who would die if I did not burgle her out of this nightmare. If I did not control my fear, there was an excellent chance that it would warn her captors of my approach. So I fought the fear that threatened to make me start throwing up, or something equally humiliating and potentially fatal.

I readied my shield, gripped my staff, ground my teeth together, and then continued pushing my way forward, through the bones and into the eerie dimness of the most ridiculously dangerous place I had ever been.

Chapter

Thirty-seven

The black ice walls of Arctis Tor were sixty feet thick, and walking through the gateway felt more like walking through a railroad tunnel.

Except for all the bones.

Every breath, every step, every rasp of bones rubbing against one another, multiplied into a thousand echoes that almost seemed to grow louder rather than fading away. The bones piled higher as I went, forcing me to walk atop them as best I could. The footing was treacherous. The deep green and violet, and occasionally red or green, pulses of luminance in the black ice walls did nothing to light the way. They only made the shadows shift and flow subtly, degrading my depth perception. I started feeling a little carsick.

If one of the fetches appeared at the far end of the tunnel and charged me, things would get nasty, and fast, especially given how ineffective my magic had been against them and how the bones had slowed my pace. That was more than a little spooky, and it was hard to keep myself from thrashing ahead more quickly out of pure fear. I kept a steady pace, held it in, and refused to allow it to control me.

I had been shielding my thoughts from Lasciel for a couple of years now. Damned if I was going to give a bunch of murderous faerie monsters the chance to paw through my emotions.

I checked behind me. Charity had trouble managing the awkward task of crawling over the bones while armored and holding that big old war hammer, but she stuck to it with grim focus and determination. Behind her, Murphy seemed to have far less trouble. Thomas prowled along at the rear, graceful as a panther in a tree.

I emerged from the gate into the courtyard. The inside of the fortress was bleak, cold, and beautiful in its simple symmetry. Rooms and chambers had either never been built or had been built into the walls and their entries hidden. Stairs led up to the battlements atop the walls. The courtyard was flat, smooth, dark ice, and at its center the single spire reared up from the ground, a round turret that rose to a crenellated parapet that overlooked the walls and the ground beneath.

The courtyard also held a sense of quiet stillness to it, as though it was not a place meant for living, moving, changing beings. The howl of the wind outside and overhead did not reach the ground. It was as silent as a librarian's tomb, and each footstep sounded clearly on the ice. Echoes bounced back and forth in the courtyard, somehow carrying a tone of disapproval and menace with them.

Bones spilled out in a wave from the gate, rapidly tapering off after a few yards. Beyond that were only scattered groupings of bones. Thomas drifted over to one such and poked at it with his drawn saber. The blade scraped on a skull too big to stuff into an oil drum, too heavy and thick to look entirely human.

"What the hell was this?" Thomas asked quietly.

"Troll, probably," I said. "Big one. Maybe fourteen, fifteen feet tall." I looked around. Half a dozen other

enormous skulls lay in the scattered collections of remains. Another six had fallen very close to each other, at
the base of the spire. "Give me a second. I want to know
what we're looking at before we move ahead."

Charity looked like she wanted to argue, but instead
she took up position a few yards off, watching one way.
Thomas and Murphy spread out, each keeping their eyes
on a different direction.

Mixed in with the fallen trolls' bones were broken
pieces of dark ice that might have been the jigsaw-puzzle
remains of armor and weapons. Each fragment bore the
remnants of ornate engraving employing gold, silver,
and tiny blue jewels. Faerie artistry, and expensive artistry at that. "Thirteen of them. The trolls were Mab's,"
I murmured. "I saw some of them outfitted like this a
couple of years back."

"How long have they been dead?" Murphy asked
quietly.

I grunted and hunkered down. I stretched my left
hand out over the bones and closed my eyes, focusing
my attention on sharpening my senses, mundane and
magical alike. Very faintly, I could scent the heavy, bestial
stink of a troll. I'd only seen a couple of the big ones
from up close, but you could smell the ugly bastards
from half a mile away. There was a rotten odor, more like
heavy mulch than old meat. And there was more sulfur
and brimstone.

Below that, I could feel tremors in the air over the
spot, the psychic residue of the troll's violent death.
There was a sense of excitement, rage, and then a dull,
seldom-felt terror and a rush of sharp, frozen images of
violent death, confusion, terror, and searing agony.

My hand flinched back from the phantom sensation
of its own accord, and for just a moment the memories
of my burning took on tangible form. I hissed through

my teeth and held my hand against my stomach, willing the too-real ghost of pain away.

"Harry?" Murphy asked.

What the hell? The impression the death had left was so sharp, so severe, that I had actually gotten bits of the troll's memories. That had never happened to me before. Of course, I had never tried to pick up vibes in the Never-never, either. It made more sense that the substance of the spirit world would leave a clearer spiritual impression.

"Harry?" Murphy said again, more sharply.

"I'm all right," I said through clenched teeth. The imprint had been more clear than anything I had ever felt in the real world. In Chicago, I would have thought it was only a few seconds old. Here . . .

"I can't tell how old they are," I said. "My gut says not very, but I can't be sure."

"It must have been weeks," Thomas said. "It takes that long for bones to get this clean."

"It's all relative," I said. "Time can pass at different rates in Faerie. These bones could have fallen a thousand years ago, by the local clock. Or twenty minutes ago."

Thomas muttered something under his breath and shook his head.

"What killed them, Harry?" Murphy asked.

"Fire. They were burned to death," I said quietly. "Down to the bone."

"Could you do that?" Thomas asked.

I shook my head. "I couldn't make it that hot. Not at the heart of Winter." Not even with Hellfire. The remains of perhaps a thousand creatures lay scattered about. I'd cut loose once in the past and roasted a bunch of vampires—and maybe some of their victims with them—but even that inferno hadn't been big enough to catch more than a tithe of the fallen defenders of Arctis Tor.

"Then who did it?" Charity asked quietly.

I didn't have an answer for her. I rose and nudged a smaller skull with my staff. "The littler ones were goblins," I said. "Foot soldiers." I rolled a troll-sized thighbone aside with my staff. An enormous sword, also of that same black ice, lay shattered beneath it. "These trolls were her personal guard." I gestured back at the gate. "Covering her retreat to the tower, maybe. Some of them got taken down along the way. The others made a stand at the tower's base. Died there."

I paced around, checking what the tracking spell had to say, and triangulated again. "Molly's in the tower," I murmured.

"How do we get in?" Murphy asked.

I stared at the blank wall of the spire. "Um," I said.

Charity glanced over my shoulder and nodded at the spire. "Look behind those trolls. If they were covering a retreat, they should be near the entrance to the tower."

"Maybe," I said. I walked over to the tower and frowned at the black ice. I ran my right hand over its surface, feeling for cracks or evidence of a hidden doorway, my senses tuned to discover any magic that might hide a door. I had the sudden impression that the black ice and the slowly pulsing colors inside were somehow alive, aware of me. And they did not like me at all. I got a sense of alien hatred, cold and patient. Otherwise, I got nothing for my trouble but half-frozen fingers.

"Nothing here," I said, and rapped my knuckles on the side of the tower, eliciting the dull thump of a very solid object. "Maybe the trolls just wanted to fight with their backs to something solid. I might have to go all the way around checking for—"

Without any warning at all the ice of the tower parted. An archway appeared, the ice that had hidden it flowing seamlessly into the rest of the tower. The interior of the tower was all shadows and slowly shifting lights that did little to provide any illumination. Inside was nothing but a spiral staircase, winding counterclockwise up through the spire.

I glanced from the archway to my chilled fingers and back. "Next time, I guess I'll just knock."

"Come on," Charity said. She shifted her grip on the war hammer, holding it at something like high port arms, handle parallel to her spine, heavy head ready to descend. "We have to hurry."

Thomas and Murphy turned to join us at the door.

An idle, puzzled sense of familiarity gave way to my instincts' furious warning. Fetches were the masters of the sucker punch. Like the Bucky-fetch who had jumped us just as we opened the doors to the theater, they knew how to position themselves to attack just as their enemies focused their attention on some kind of distraction.

The suddenly opened doorway was it.

Mounds of bones around the courtyard exploded into motion. Fetches hurtled at us over the ground. There weren't three of them, either—there were dozens.

The fetches, here in Faerie, did not look like movie monsters. Their true forms were only vaguely humanoid, wavering uncertainly, as black as midnight shadows but for ghostly white eyes. I could see other shapes around them, translucent and faint. Here, another one of those alien monster things. There some kind of wolflike biped. There an enormous man with the head of a warthog. But the salve I had spread over my eyes revealed those illusions for what they really were, and showed me the thing beneath the mask.

My magic had a risky batting average against these creatures, but there were things I could do besides hosing energy directly at the enemy. Hellfire came to my call, and my staff's runes exploded into light as brilliant as a magnesium flare. Their flame lit the benighted courtyard while somehow not damaging my clothing or flesh. My will and the Hellfire roared through me in a torrent as I whirled the staff in a circle over my head and screamed, *"Ventas cyclis!"*

The howling winds thundered down into the silent courtyard as if I had torn off an unseen roof. They gathered along my spinning staff, fluttering with lightning the same color as the blazing runes on the staff. I cried out and hurled the winds, not at the oncoming fetches, but at the thousands of bones lying between them and me.

The wind picked them up with a wailing shriek; a sudden cyclone of broken bones and shattered armor, spinning them into a whirling curtain. The lead fetches were too late to avoid plunging into the cloud, and the ossified tornado began to rip them apart, battering to pulp whatever was not sheared away by the edges and points of bone and broken shards of ice. Fetches following in their wake skidded to a halt, letting out a startlingly loud chorus of hisses, the sounds filled with rage.

Thomas cried out and I heard heavy footsteps. Another fetch, this one much larger, came around the curve of the spire's wall. The ghost image of the Reaper was all around him. A beat later, another charged us from the other direction, just as large, this one with the faint image of Hammerhand, an almost obscenely muscled figure in black, heavy mallets emerging from the ends of his sleeves.

"Into the tower!" I bellowed.

The Reaper reached Thomas, and its arm rose up, tipped with gleaming black talons in its true form, the illusion superimposing the image of the Reaper's trademark scythe over them. Thomas caught the Reaper's sweeping claws on his saber, but instead of the ringing of steel on steel, there was a flash of green-white light and the Reaper-fetch howled in agony as the steel of the blade struck its claws cleanly from its appendage.

Thomas crouched, hips and shoulders twisting in a sharp, one-two movement. The saber's blade cut and burned a flattened X shape into the fetch's abdomen. The fetch roared in agony, and liquid green-white fire burst from the wound. The creature swung its other arm, its speed taking even Thomas by surprise. He avoided most of the power of the blow, but what was left slammed him into the side of the tower.

I heard a gunshot behind me, then another, and then Murphy snarled, "Damn it!" I turned in time to see her bob to one side and then to the other as Hammerhand swung a mallet limb down at her. The blow crashed into the courtyard with a cracking impact as loud as a rifle shot. Murphy danced in closer to the fetch, inside the awkward reach of its club-hands. It thrust one down at her. At first I thought she was slapping it aside, but then she grabbed onto the fetch and continued the motion, adding her own weight and strength to the fetch's and redirecting the force of the blow so that the fetch's weapon-hand crushed its own foot. The fetch bellowed in pain and lost its balance. Murphy shoved in the same direction and the fetch fell. She leapt away from it, for the tower door, while I grabbed Thomas and hauled him inside.

From somewhere up the stairs, I heard a terrified scream.

Molly.

Charity let out a cry and threw herself up the stairs.

"No!" I shouted. "Charity, wait!"

The doorway darkened as a fetch tried to come through. Murphy, her back flat against the wall beside the door, drew the long fighting dagger she had taken from Charity's box of goodies. Just as its nose cleared the doorway, she whirled in a half circle and with all the power of her legs, hips, back, and shoulders drove the knife to its hilt in one of the thing's white eyes.

The fetch went mad with agony. It slammed itself blindly against the inside of the doorway, more liquid fire erupting from the wound, and lurched back and forth until Thomas stepped up to it, lifted a boot, and kicked the fetch with crushing strength, hurling the mortally wounded faerie back out onto the courtyard.

"Go!" he cried. Another fetch began to press in, and Thomas went to work with his sword. His blows struck more burning wounds into the fetch, and its blood sizzled like grease on a stove when it touched the cold iron of his blade. Thomas dodged a return blow and pressed his attack with a sneer, driving the thing back from the doorway.

"Go!" he yelled again. "I'll hold the door!"

A snakelike, whipping limb shot in along the floor, seized Thomas's ankle, and hauled his foot out from under him. I clutched at him and kept him from being drawn into the open. "Murph!"

Murphy slid up, pointed her pistol out the door, and squeezed off several shots. A fetch screamed in pain and Thomas's leg suddenly came free. I pulled him in and he lunged to his feet again.

"We'll hold the door," Murphy said, her voice sharp. "Get the girl!"

Molly screamed again.

Charity's booted feet thudded unseen from the stairs above me.

I spat out an oath and sprinted after her.

Chapter

Thirty-eight

The spiral staircase spun me in a steady, ascending circle. The low, ugly light within the walls swirled sickeningly, adding to my sense of motion sickness and disorientation. Below me, I could hear Thomas's sharp, mocking laughter as he fought, together with the occasional report of Murphy's gun. My aching body hated me for forcing it to run up the stairs—particularly my knees. Anyone my size is prone to that kind of thing.

But there was nothing to be done about it, so I ignored the pain and went on, Lily's fiery butterfly keeping pace with me and lighting my way.

I had longer legs, and I caught Charity as she neared the top of the staircase. Molly screamed again, pure terror and anguish and pain, and her voice was very near.

"I'm coming, baby!" Charity gasped, panting. She was in great shape, but no one's exercise program includes running up several hundred feet of spiral stairs in full mail and helmet carrying a big-ass hammer and a sword. Her legs had slowed, and she staggered a little when she reached the top stair and found herself in a short, level, low-ceilinged hall leading a few feet to another open archway. The cold light of winter night, moonlight on snow, shone in through the arch.

I managed to snag her arm and check her advance just as a heavy door slammed to cover the archway with tooth-rattling force. If I hadn't delayed her, it would have hit her like a speeding truck. She recovered her balance, and while she did we heard a heavy bolt slide shut on the door. Charity shoved a hand at the door, which remained fixed. She kicked a booted foot at it, and failed to so much as rattle it in its frame.

Molly screamed again, still close, though muffled by the closed door. Her cry was weaker, shorter.

"Molly!" Charity screamed.

I thrust the spread fingers of my left hand against the door, and was instantly aware of the energy flowing through it, binding it, giving it strength beyond reason to resist being opened. I looked for a weakness, a soft spot in the adamant magic supporting the door, but there was none. The ward on the door was, simply put, flawless. It spread through the door's substance as coldly and beautifully as crystals of ice forming on a window, the magic of Winter drawn up from the heart of the land. There was no way for me to unravel the subtle, complex faerie magic.

But then, it *was* faerie magic. I didn't have to be subtle to counter it.

"Charity," I snapped. "It's faerie make! The hammer!"

She shot me a glance of comprehension and nodded. "Clear the door."

I hurried back, leaving her room to swing.

"Please," Charity whispered as she planted her feet and drew back the weapon. "Please, Father. Please."

Charity closed her eyes and took a deep breath, focusing her concentration on delivering the most powerful blow she possibly could in the confines of the hallway. Then she swung the weapon back, golf-club style, cried out, and swung, stepping forward.

Maybe Charity was way more buff than I thought. Maybe that particular ward had a particular weakness to cold iron. Maybe it had nothing to do with magic, and Charity had somehow tapped into the strength available to all mothers when their young are endangered. Hell, maybe God was on her side.

Whatever happened, that siege door of adamant ice and malevolent, obdurate magic screamed and shattered at the blow from her hammer, shattered like delicate glass, shattered into pieces no larger than grains of sand. The whole tower rang with the power of the blow, the very black ice it was made of seeming to shriek and groan. The floor literally shook, and I had to crouch to keep from taking a tumble back down the stairs.

I heard Charity choke down a cry of pain. She had broken the door before us, but the spells running through it had backlashed against the hammer, and it too had shattered. A flying piece of fractured metal had cut across her hip and lodged in one of the rings of her mail. It glowed red-hot, and she frantically slapped it away even as it burned her. Other pieces of shrapnel from the hammer had struck the walls of the tower, burning their way into the black ice, sending a network of cracks of green-white light all through the tower around us like some sort of bizarre infection. Black ice melted away from the red-hot steel. The tower rumbled again like some vast, agonized beast.

Charity dropped the handle of the hammer. I could see that her right arm hung limp and useless, but it didn't stop her from making an awkward left-handed draw of the sword at her hip. I slipped up beside her, staff held ready in both hands, and we stepped out onto the parapet of the tower of Arctis Tor together.

The parapet was enormous, a hundred feet across, twice as wide as the spire beneath us. It was a garden of sorts; a garden of ice.

Ice covered the parapet, somehow formed into ghostly

trees and flowers. There were seats here and there in the garden, and they too were made of ice. A frozen fountain stood silent at the center of the parapet, a bare trickle of water sliding from the top of a statue so coated in layers and layers of ice that one could not readily identify its particulars. Replica rose vines and thorns spread all around the place, all ice, all cold and beautiful.

Upon the branch of a tree perched a cardinal, its bloodred feathers brilliant, though the bird itself was utterly still. I peered a bit closer, and saw that it was covered in a layer of transparent ice, frozen into a sculpture every bit as much as the rest of the place. Not far from it, a spider's web spread between some tree branches, the spider at its center also transformed into ice sculpture. A swift look around showed me more beings entombed in ice, and I realized that this place was not a garden.

It was a prison.

Next to the fountain sat a lovely young girl in a Byzantine gown, hand entwined with that of a young man in similar historic costume. Not far from them, three females of the Sidhe, Mab's kindred, the nobility of faerie kind, stood back-to-back, their shoulders touching in a triangle. The three looked so much alike that they might have been sisters, and they each held hands with the others, expressions of determination and fear frozen onto their faces.

The ice sculpture of a thick, dead-looking tree held a dead, naked man upon it, crucified on its branches as a grotesque work of art. Bonds of ice held him there, transparent enough to let me see the blackened flesh of his hands and feet, the gangrenous darkness spreading upward through the veins of his arms and legs. His hair was long, unwashed, and fell over his face as he hung limp within his bonds, his body coated with layers of crystalline frost.

Molly sat at the base of the same tree. Her artfully shredded clothes had been shredded in truth, and they hung from her as loose rags. Her cotton-candy hair hung in a limp mass, uncombed and tangled. She shuddered with cold, and her eyes stared at nothing. Her expression was twisted as if in effort, her mouth open. It took me a minute to realize that she had never stopped screaming. She'd damaged her throat, and no sound would emerge. But that didn't stop her from trying.

Charity shifted her weight to hurry forward, but I cautioned her, "Wait. We'll do her no good if we're dead."

She clenched her jaw, but heeded me, and we paused for a moment while I swept my gaze over the rest of the parapet. Some movement in the shadows behind the crucifixion tree drew my eye, and I reached back for the handle of my blasting rod, sticking out of my nylon backpack. I drew the magical tool and primed it with an effort of will. Red-white fire suddenly glowed at its tip. "There. Behind the tree," I said.

A deep voice let out a rasping chuckle.

Then, from the darkness I couldn't quite see into, the Scarecrow appeared.

This thing was no fetch, no changer of form and image and illusion. There was no shadowy mask over an amorphous form, no glamour altering its appearance, which my salve would have enabled me to see through. This thing was a whole, independent creature. Unless maybe it was a fetch so old and strong that it could transform itself into the Scarecrow in truth and not simply in seeming.

Red flame glittered in the carved-pumpkin head. Its limbs, all long, tough vines as thick as my wrists, were clothed in ragged tatters of black that looked more like a funeral robe than a farmer's castoffs. Its long arms trailed almost to the ground, and one of them was stretched over to Molly. At the end of the arm, the vines tapered into dozens of slender, flexible tendrils, and the Scarecrow had them wrapped around Molly's throat and sliding up into her hair.

We stood in silence, facing one another for a while. Wind moaned somewhere overhead, not far above the parapet. The sounds of hissing and screaming fetches drifted up as if from a great distance. Thomas and Murphy still held the door.

I took several steps to one side and gave the Scarecrow a little smile. "Hi," I said. "Who the hell are you?"

"One who has served the Queen of Air and Darkness since before your kind can remember," he replied. "One who has destroyed hundreds like you."

"You know what, Captain Kudzu?" I asked. "I'm not here to play guessing games with you. Give me the girl."

The bizarre creature's face twisted in what might been amusement. "Or what follows?"

I wasn't absolutely certain the thing was quoting Shakespeare, but that didn't mean I couldn't do it. "Bloody constraint," I told him. "For should you try to hide the girl from me, even in your heart, there shall I rake for her."

Maybe the Scarecrow wasn't a Shakespeare fan. Its eyes flared with angry scarlet light. "Little man. Move an inch closer and I will crush her soft little neck."

"Inadvisable," I said, and raised my blasting rod to level it at the Scarecrow. "Because she's the only thing keeping you alive right now."

"I fear you not, wizard," the Scarecrow said. The creature narrowed its eyes, focusing upon me intently—perhaps preparing the same defense that had shed my spells in our first encounter. "Bring your fire, if you think it may survive the heart of Winter. It will avail you against me this time no more than last."

"You think I'd show up for round two without being prepared to finish what I started?" I asked him. I sidled a couple of more steps to one side. "The Council is already on the way here," I said. "I'm here to make you an offer before things fall apart. Give me the girl and your word not to go near her again, and I let you live."

The Scarecrow let out a laugh of pure scorn. "I shall enjoy killing you, mortal."

I prowled a few steps more and planted my feet, then brandished my staff and rod. The Scarecrow crouched in response, eyes burning even brighter.

I had to be careful. If I spooked him too much, he'd kill Molly as a prelude to closing with me. "You know what your problem is?" I asked him.

He stared at me for a blank second of incomprehension. "What?"

I showed my teeth in a wolfish smile. "You underestimate people."

While I'd drawn the Scarecrow's attention and eye, Charity had slipped around behind it, silent as a puff of smoke. As I spoke, she lifted her sword and swept it down at the appendage holding her daughter. The steel blade hissed and flashed and seared its way through the limb holding Molly.

The Scarecrow reared its head back in a sudden howl of rage. Molly's body bucked in panic as the severed limbs contracted on her throat. I lifted my staff and snarled, *"Forzare!"* Unseen force lashed out, caught up Molly as gently as I could manage it, and flipped her tail over teakettle away from the creature. No sooner had I moved her than its stumpy arm swung down to smash into the ground where the girl had been sitting.

The Scarecrow turned to grab at Molly, but Charity stepped into its path, cold steel gleaming, her eyes harder and colder than the black ice of Arctis Tor. She faced the thing squarely and snarled, "You will never touch my daughter again."

The creature roared in fury and rushed Charity. I whipped up my blasting rod and snarled, *"Fuego!"* A lance of flame as thick as my wrist lashed out from the tip of the rod—and died two feet away from it, the burning energy of the magical strike swallowed by an unfathomable ocean of cold, cold power. I had hoped that I could get in a shot while the Scarecrow was distracted, but I had already decided on what to try next if I couldn't.

I stuck the blasting rod through my belt, whipped my staff up to point the tip at the ground beneath the Scarecrow's feet, and shouted, *"Forzare!"*

Invisible force lashed out and struck the black ice under the Scarecrow like a mortar round. It threw the creature ten feet into the air, spinning end over end. Deadly chips of black ice flew. As the spell's energy roared out of me, I staggered and almost lost my balance. My vision tunneled for a second or two out of pure exhaustion. I'd been pushing too hard, for too long, with no rest. The magic I'd been using had drained my reserves entirely. The human body has limits that cannot be circumvented, and I had reached mine.

Charity rushed forward before the Scarecrow could rise. Her sword hacked down at it in elemental brutality, and the Scarecrow's blood and woodlike flesh sizzled on her blade. But she didn't kill it.

The Scarecrow regained its feet and lashed an arm at Charity. She swung her sword to meet it. Cold iron bit into faerie flesh, drawing forth another explosion of brilliant, liquid flame. The creature screamed, a sound louder than any living thing I'd ever heard, and its backswing slammed into Charity's limp right arm. The impact tore a grunt of pain from her and flung her several feet through the air, but the Scarecrow paid for it. Coming into contact with Charity's mail burned it again, and its furious howls redoubled.

It lifted a foot to stomp down on the helplessly writhing Molly, to flatten her like an aluminum can.

It was the kind of thing that draws suicidal levels of chivalry from me. I ran for the Scarecrow, ditching my blasting rod on the way. I took my staff in both hands, slammed it down like a pole-vaulter, and launched myself into the air, both feet aimed at the Scarecrow's back. I hit the thing with considerable force, but I'd been too tired to manage it as precisely as I wished. The blow only staggered the creature, and I bounced off it and flopped onto the icy surface of the parapet.

I had bought time enough, though, for Charity to regain her feet and charge forward with her blade, diverting the Scarecrow's attention from her daughter.

Before I could regain my feet, the Scarecrow snapped a foot at me in a clumsy, unbalanced kick. It landed with only a fraction of the force it might have had. Even so, that was enough to send me sprawling ten feet away and maybe crack one of my ribs. Pain washed through me and I suddenly couldn't get my lungs to take in enough air.

The Scarecrow stretched out an arm toward Charity, and ropy-looking vines shot from the ends of his arms, flickered across the ten feet between them like lightning, and wrapped her sword arm's wrist. The tendrils tightened. The Scarecrow shook Charity violently. She screamed, and the sword tumbled from her fingers. More vines wrapped around her throat, and the creature simply hauled her up into the air. Its wounds were already closing, rebuilding themselves. It seized Molly in its other hand and lifted her as well, holding the pair of them face-to-face. There was a malicious eagerness in the creature's stance.

"See," it murmured to the fruitlessly struggling Charity. "Look at her. Watch your daughter die."

Charity's eyes widened with terror. Her face turned dark red. Molly, meanwhile, simply lay limp, her own face darkening as she was strangled.

"Not long now," the Scarecrow purred. "There is nothing you can do to help her, mortal woman. Nothing you can do to stop me."

It *was* a fetch, I was sure of it, a creature who had been given talent or power enough to exceed its former status, to become the embodiment of the icon of fear mortals called the Scarecrow, to draw power from that image—power enough to block out my strongest magic. That was why it tormented both Molly and her mother— to feed on their terror.

I stared at it dully, while my mind ran through the logic tree and my lungs kept trying to get in a deep breath. I searched through myself for energy enough to do something, anything, to help.

I didn't have it in me.

I lay there on my side, too exhausted to feel fear, too exhausted to feel hate, too exhausted to feel anger. It was all that I could do to keep from lowering my head and going to sleep, and without will or emotion to fuel my spells, I might as well have been one more frozen sculpture in Mab's prison garden.

Charity's heels began to kick frantically, uselessly. The Scarecrow went on purring, and I thought I could actually see the damned thing grow a couple of inches taller. Lily's incendiary butterfly fluttered around my head, obscuring my view for a second.

And I suddenly got it. A sluggish hope surged up in me.

The fetch drew its power from fear.

And I had none. I was just too tired for it.

That was why I had thrashed the fetch at the hotel so badly. Not two minutes before I faced it, I had gathered up my fear and hurled it out on that decoy spell. When I faced the thing in the darkened hallway, I'd been nothing but angry. Without my fear to play on, the fetch could not disrupt my magic, and I had batted him around like a softball.

Similarly, when I decapitated the Bucky-fetch, I had been feeling no fear. It all happened too fast. I'd reacted on pure reflex, before any pesky thoughts or emotions could weigh in on the matter. There'd been no time to be afraid, and I'd struck the fetch down.

I would never have realized the weakness in the fetches' defenses had I not pushed myself to my limits; the only thing I had to fear was fear itself. I suddenly *knew* I could take this chump out, if only I had enough power left for one more spell. I'd done it twice. Third time's the charm.

The butterfly danced wildly in the air in front of me.

I stared at it for a second, realization dawning, and then I burst out into weak laughter. "Lily, you manipulative, deceitful, wonderful girl."

I held open my left palm, and the butterfly alighted on it. Its light flashed brighter for a second, and then my will touched it lightly. It fell apart into glowing threads that settled down on my scarred palm and rushed into my spirit. Pure flame filled me, the joyous heat of full summer, and I exalted in the sudden, overflowing *life* of it. It met the tiny spark of hope still glowing within me and the two multiplied, power unfolding and expanding inside me.

I found myself on my feet, arms spread to my sides, face turned up toward the enormous silver moon. Sunlight seemed to spill from me, to wreathe me in dancing fires that blazed their defiance of Winter. Arctis Tor itself, the fortress of black ice, groaned in protest at the intensity of the light.

I looked down to find the creature staring at me in utter shock. Its tendril-fingers had gone loose, and Molly and Charity lay moving weakly at its feet.

"You cannot do that," the fetch said in a shocked tone. "You . . . It is not possible."

I flicked out a hand, whispered a word, and my blasting rod flew from the ground where I'd dropped it and into my hand, its carvings bursting into light as the blazing heat of a thousand Julys welled up, ready to fly free. "You like movie villains, do you?" I lifted the blasting rod while Summer fire flickered around my outstretched arm. I peeled my lips back from my teeth and purred, "Have you seen this one?"

The carvings along the rod flooded with a blaze of scarlet-and-golden light.

"How about a little fire, Scarecrow?"

Chapter

Thirty-nine

The Scarecrow let out an ear-splitting trilling chirp, like a summer locust on steroids, and it bounded to one side in an effort to keep the mounded ice of the fountain between us. I'd already seen how fast a fetch could move, and didn't bother with a snap shot. Instead, I let it distance itself from Molly and Charity, until it reached cover behind the fountain's ice and stopped moving.

Then I blew two-thirds of that dome away in a single blast of light, thunder, and fire.

The golden Summer flame hammered straight through the ice and into the Scarecrow. The old fetch was taken off guard, and the lance of fire incinerated what would have been a hip and thigh on a human being. It bellowed a metallic roar of pain and anger, bounced off one of the white marble statues of the three sisters, and was forced to seize hold of one of the statues' ankles to keep from bouncing over the edge of the parapet.

But the Scarecrow wasn't the only faerie who cried out. Without warning, a hurricane of sound slammed into me, painfully intense. Once more Arctis Tor shuddered, the black ice trembling and heaving while deep, almost subsonic groans echoed through the fortress. The other fetches' screams arose from below, a frenzied chorus of berserk rage.

The heaving ground and the sonic sledgehammer tossed me into a bank of ice-sculpted rose vines with thorns three times as long as their flowers. The ice was not brittle, and it didn't break as my weight hit it. I felt a sharp pain from my ankle, a thorn stabbing underneath the hem of my duster, but the spell-worked coat protected me from further harm. I was on my feet again in a second, readying another blast.

But in that second, the Scarecrow had reversed its course with eerie agility. It headed for Charity and Molly, running on all three of its limbs like a wounded spider, awkward but still swift. This time I couldn't afford to take my time about lining up the shot. I flicked a lash of fire between the Scarecrow and the Carpenter women, but it sidestepped and I only burned a few loose-end tendrils from its vine-body. The Scarecrow hurtled toward Molly. Charity lay perfectly still beside her, sprawled on the black ice.

But only until the Scarecrow came within reach of her sword. Then Charity rolled and popped up into a low, slashing lunge. Her sword seared its way through the Scarecrow's undamaged leg, slicing it off at an angle that began at midthigh and finished just above the knee. It frantically rolled again, struggling to get out of sword range. Charity pressed ruthlessly, too close to the damned fetch to let me blast it again. The Scarecrow hopped and skittered on its remaining limbs, heading for the edge of the parapet.

"Charity!" I shouted. "Down!"

Michael's wife dropped out of my line of fire in an instant.

The fetch shimmered, body contorting weirdly, and leapt. On the way, it changed. Membranous wings unfurled from its body and beat powerfully down, and within a heartbeat the rest of the fetch's body had conformed to the shape of one of the monstrous, hang-glider-sized bats I'd seen in Faerie once before. It hurtled away, wings thrashing to gain altitude, and the faerie moon shone down in lunatic glee.

I had a perfect shot.

Once more, I called upon the fire of Summer I'd taken in. I could feel its intensity beginning to ebb, but if the fetch managed to slip away I might never have such an opportunity again. Besides, that creature had tormented my friend's wife and daughter, nearly murdered them right in front of my eyes, and now it was going to answer for it.

So I unleashed the fire again, this time so brilliant that it lit dark mountainsides five or ten miles away, so hot that the blowing snow hissed into instant steam in the wake of the flame. When it struck the fetch, it detonated into a blinding conflagration, an explosion that roared so loudly that it shattered every icy replica of a rose vine upon the parapet.

What tumbled burning from the Faerie skies toward the merciless mountains below could not have been identified as anything in particular. It trailed sparks, soot, and ash, and when it slammed into a granite cliff side, it hit with such force that an icy rockslide was jarred loose from the mountain's slope, burying the fetch under incalculable tons of stone.

I shook my staff at the rockslide in a primal gesture of triumph and shouted, *"Who's next!?!"*

The courtyard below become completely silent for a second, and then I could see fetches, too dark to make out clearly, darting away from the base of the spire, retreating from the fight.

"Harry!" Charity said, her voice strained.

I hadn't realized it when Charity had gotten her head down, but she'd dropped into a baseball player's slide.

Thanks to all the fire I'd been pitching around, the black ice had become slick with a thin layer of meltwater, and her momentum was carrying her with slow, dreamy smoothness toward the parapet's edge.

I turned to run toward her, and then used an ounce of brainpower to deduce that I'd only be duplicating the behavior that got Charity into the mess to begin with. Instead I dropped to all fours, crawling forward with my staff extended. Her ankles were over the edge by the time I got close enough to reach her. She was able to get her fingers around the end of the wizard's staff, and I locked onto the other end, halting her slide. I then began to move backward, very slowly, very carefully. The black ice of the parapet hardened once more in a moment, as though it had never thawed, and I pulled Charity carefully away from an involuntary education in skydiving.

Once she was clear, we both turned to look at Molly. The girl lay quietly, still breathing. I rolled onto my back until I could get my breath again. Charity rose and went to her daughter. I didn't follow her. It wasn't the kind of moment she'd appreciate me sharing.

I watched, and kept an eye out for trouble. Charity knelt down beside the young woman and gathered her into her arms as she might have a smaller child. Charity held Molly against herself and rocked gently, her lips murmuring steadily as she did so. For a moment, I thought that the terror and trauma had driven Molly too far away to return. But then she shuddered, blinked her eyes open, and began to weep quietly, leaning against her mother.

I heard a groan behind me, and spun up into a crouch, blasting rod ready again.

The sculpture of the crucified man groaned again. Though he was still crucified and horribly rotted, my fire spells, as augmented by Lily's extraordinary power, had melted the bonds around his left wrist, and now his left arm flopped bonelessly in the steady, howling wind. I had never seen human flesh so badly mangled. His fingers, wrists, and forearms had long since succumbed to frostbite, the blood gone poisonous as it flowed through them, causing the flesh to swell grotesquely. Despite that, I could see that the skin of his entire arm was covered in layers of scars. Burn scars. Knife scars. Scars from flesh torn by blunt force and left to heal incorrectly.

I've taken a few hits myself. But that poor bastard's *arm* had suffered more than my whole body.

Almost against my will, I walked over to the tree. The man's hair hung like Spanish moss over his bowed face, some of it light brown, some of it dark grey, some of it gone brittle and white. I reached out and brushed the hair back from the man's face, lifting his head toward me a little. His beard was as long and disgusting as his hair. His face had been ravaged somehow, and I got the unsettling impression that his expressions had so contorted and stretched his face that they had inflicted their own kind of damage, though there were no scars as on his arm. His eyes were open, but completely white and unseeing.

I recognized him. "Lloyd Slate," I murmured. "The Winter Knight."

The last time I'd seen Slate had been after the battle on the hill of the Stone Table, a place that served as the OK Corral for the Faerie Courts when they decided to engage in diplomacy by means of murdering anyone on the other team. Slate had been a first-rank menace to society. A drug addict, a rapist, a man with no compunctions about indulging himself at the expense of others. By the end of the battle he had killed a young woman who might have become a friend.

He stirred and let out a small whimper. "Who is there?"

"Dresden," I replied.

Slate's mouth dropped open, and a maniacal little giggle bubbled under his reply. "You're here. Thank God, you're here. I've been here so long." He tilted his head to one side, exposing his carotid artery. "Free me. Do it, quickly."

"Free you?" I asked.

"From this," Slate sobbed, voice breaking. "From this nightmare. Kill me. Kill me. Kill me. Thank God, Dresden, kill me."

The seedier neighborhoods of my soul would have been happy to oblige him. But some dark, hard part of me wanted to see what else I could think of to make him suffer more. I just stared at him for a while, considering options. After perhaps ten minutes, he dropped unconscious again.

From somewhere to my right, a delicious voice, at once rough and silky, purred, "You do not understand his true torment."

I turned to face the frozen fountain. Well. The remains of it, anyway. Maybe a third of the ice mound remained, but it had partially uncovered the statue within—no statue at all, but a member of the Sidhe, a tall, inhumanly lovely woman, her appearance one of nigh perfection. Or it would have been so in other circumstances. Now, partially free from the encasing ice, her scarlet hair clung lumpily to her skull. Her eyes were deeply sunken and burned too bright, as though she had a fever. She stood calmly, one leg, her head, one shoulder, and one arm now emerging from the ice, which was otherwise her only garment. There was an eerie serenity to her, as though she felt no discomfort, physical or otherwise, at her imprisonment. She seemed to regard the entire matter with amused tolerance, as though such trivial conditions were hardly worthy of her attention. She was one of the oldest and most powerful Sidhe in the Winter Court—the Leanansidhe.

And she was also my godmother.

"Lea," I breathed quietly. "Hell's bells. What happened to you?"

"Mab," she said.

"Last Halloween," I murmured. "She said that you had been imprisoned. She's kept you here? In that?"

"Obviously." Something extremely unsettling glittered in her eyes. "You do not understand his true torment."

I glanced from her to the Winter Knight. "Uh. What?"

"Slate," she purred, and flicked her eyes in his direction. She was unable to move her head for the ice about it. "There is pain, of course. But anyone can inflict pain. Accidents inflict pain. Pain is the natural order of the universe, and so it is hardly a tool meet for the Queen of Air and Darkness. She tortures him with kindness."

I frowned at Slate for a moment, and then grimaced, imagining it. "She leaves him hung up like that. And then she comes and saves him from it."

My godmother smiled, a purring sound accompanying the expression. "She heals his wounds and takes his pain. She restores his sight, and the first thing his eyes see is the face of she who delivers him from agony. She cares for him with her own hands, warms him, feeds him, cleans away the filth. And then she takes him to her bower. Poor man. He knows that when he wakes, he will hang blind upon the tree again—and can do naught else but long for her return."

I shook my head. "You think he's going to fall for that?" I said. "Fall in love with her?"

Lea smiled. "Love," she murmured. "Perhaps, and

perhaps not. But need. Oh, yes. You underestimate the simple things, my godchild." Her eyes glittered. "Being given food and warmth. Being touched. Being cleaned and cared for—and desired. Over and over, spinning him through agony and ecstasy. The mortal mind breaks down. Not all at once. But slowly. The way water will wear down stone." Her madly glittering eyes focused on me, and her tone took on a note of warning. "It is a slow seduction. A conversion by the smallest steps."

The skin on my left palm itched intensely for a moment, in the living skin of the Lasciel sigil.

"Yes," Lea hissed. "Mab, you see, is patient. She has time. And when the last walls of his mind have fallen, and he looks forward with joy to his return to the tree, she will have destroyed him. And he will be discarded. He only lives so long as he resists." She closed her eyes for a moment and said, "This is wisdom you should retain, my child."

"Lea," I said. "What has happened to you? How long have you been a Sidhe-sicle?"

Some of the strength seemed to ebb from her, and she suddenly seemed exhausted. "I grew too arrogant with the power I held. I thought I could overcome what stalks us all. Foolish. Milady Queen Mab taught me the error of my ways."

"She's had you locked up in your own private iceberg for more than a year?" I shook my head. "Godmother, you look like you fell out of a crazy tree and hit every branch on the way down."

Her eyes opened again, glittering and unsettling as hell. And she laughed. It was a quiet, low sound—and it sounded nothing like the laugh of the deadly Sidhe sorceress I'd known since before I could drive.

"Crazy tree," she murmured, and her eyes closed again. "Yes."

I heard heavy, thumping steps on the staircase, and Thomas came sprinting onto the parapet, fae-bloodied sword still in hand. "Harry!"

"Here," I said, and waved an arm at him. He glanced at Charity and Molly, and hurried over to me.

A little lump of fear knotted itself in my guts. "Where's Murphy?"

"Relax," he said. "She's downstairs guarding the door. Is the girl all right?"

I pitched my voice low. "She's breathing, but I'm more worried about damage to her mind. She's crying at least. That's actually a good sign. What's up?"

"We need to go," Thomas said. "Now."

"Why?"

"Something's coming."

"Something usually is," I said. "What do you mean?"

He gritted his teeth and shook his head. "Since last year . . . since the Erlking . . . I've had . . . intuitions, maybe? Maybe just instincts. I can feel things in the air better now than before. I think the Wild Hunt is coming toward us. I think a *lot* of things are coming toward us."

No sooner had he said it than I heard, blended with the distant cry of the wind, a long, mournful, somehow hungry horn call.

I stepped up onto the edge of the fountain and peered out into the moonlit night. I couldn't make out anything very clearly, but for an instant, far in the distance, I saw the gleam of moonlight on one of the odd metals that faeries used to make their weapons and armor.

Another horn rang out, this one more a droning, enormous basso—only the second horn came from the opposite side from the first. Over the next few seconds, more horns joined in, and drums, and then a rising tide of monstrous shrieks and bellows, all around us now. In the mountains east of Arctis Tor, one of the snowcapped peaks was abruptly devoured by a rising black cloud that hid everything beneath it. A quick check around showed me several other peaks being blanketed in shadow. Horn calls and cries grew louder and continuously more numerous.

"Stars and stones," I breathed. I shot a glance at my godmother and said, "The power I used here. That is what caused this, isn't it?"

"Of course," Lea said.

"Holy crap!" Thomas blurted, jumping like a startled cat when what he must have thought was another statue moved and spoke.

"Thomas, this is my godmother, Lea," I said. "Lea, Th—"

"I know who he is," my godmother murmured. "I know what he is. I know whose he is." Her eyes moved back to me. "You summoned forth the power of Summer here in Arctis Tor, in the heart of all Winter. When you did so, those of Winter felt the agony of it. And now they come to slay you or drive you forth."

I swallowed. "Uh. How many of them?"

The mad gleam returned to her eyes. "Why, all of Winter, child. All of us."

Crap.

"Charity!" I called. "We're leaving!"

Charity nodded and rose, supporting Molly, though the girl was at least mobile. If she'd remained unaware and walled away from the world, it would have been a real pain to get her all the way back down the tower. Molly and her mom hit the stairs.

"Thomas," I said. "See if you can chop off some of this ice without hurting her."

Thomas licked his lips. "Is that a good idea? Isn't this the one who tried to turn you into a dog?"

"A hound," Lea murmured, glittering eyes flicking back and forth at random. "Quite different."

"She was a friend of Mom's," I told Thomas quietly.

"So was my dad," Thomas said. "And look how *that* turned out."

"Then give me the sword and I'll do it myself. I'm not leaving her."

Lea made a sudden choking sound.

I frowned at her. Her eyes bugged out and her face contorted with apparent pain. Her mouth moved, lush lips writhing, twisting. A bestial grunt jerked out of her throat every second or two. The fingers of her freed hand arched into a claw. Then she suddenly sagged, and when she turned her eyes back to me, they were my godmother's again; one part lust, one part cool, feline indifference, one part merciless predator.

"Child," she said. Her voice was weak. "You must *not* free me."

I stared at her, feeling confused. "Why?"

She gritted her teeth and said, "I cannot yet be trusted. It is not time. I would not be able to fulfill my promise to your mother, should you free me now. You must leave."

"Trusted?" I asked.

"No time," she said, voice strained again. "I cannot long keep it from taking hold of . . ." She shuddered and lowered her head. She lifted her face to me a few seconds later, and the madness had returned to her eyes. "Wait," she rasped. "I have reconsidered. Free me."

I traded a look with Thomas, and we both took a cautious step backward.

Lea's face twisted up with rage and she let out a howl that shook icicles from their positions. *"Release me!"*

"What the hell is going on here?" Thomas asked me.

"Uh," I told him. "I'll get back to you after we get out of Dodge."

Thomas nodded and we both hurried toward the stairs. I glanced back over my shoulder, once. The fountain was already building itself up again, freezing water to ice. A thin sheet of it already covered my godmother. I shuddered and looked away, directly at the delirious Lloyd Slate. My footsteps quickened even more.

And then, just as I was leaving, only for an instant, I thought I saw one more thing. The triangle of statues of Sidhe noblewomen caught a stray beam of moonlight, while thin clouds made it jump and shift. In that uncertain light, I saw one of the statues move. It turned its head toward me as I left, and the white marble of its eyes was suddenly suffused with emerald green the same color as Mab's eyes.

Not just the same color.

Mab's eyes.

The statue winked at me.

The sounds of the approaching fae grew even louder, reminding me that I had no time to investigate. So I shivered and hurried down the stairs beside Thomas, leaving the parapet and its prisoners and—perhaps—its mistress behind me. I had to focus on getting us back to Lily's rift in one piece, so I forced all such questions from my mind for the time being.

The four of us were slogging through snow up to my knees a few moments later, while I spent the last reserves of power I'd taken from Lily's butterfly to keep us from going into hypothermia.

I took the lead and ran for the rift as a nightmarish symphony of wails and horns and howls closed in all around us.

Chapter

Forty

Shielded by the good graces of Summer, we fled Arctis Tor. The winds outside howled louder, kicking up increasingly intense clouds of mist, snow, and ice. Beyond the wind, still vague but growing slowly more clear and immediate, I could hear the cries of things that thrived in the dark and the cold. I heard drums and horns, wild and savage and inspiring the kind of terror that has nothing to do with thought, and everything to do with instinct.

I heard the cry of the Erlking's personal horn, unmistakable for any other such instrument.

I traded a quick glance with Thomas, who grimaced at me. "Keep moving!" he called.

"Duh," I grunted.

Immediately behind me, Murphy panted, "What was that about?"

"Erlking," I told her. "Big-time bad guy. Wants to eat me."

"Why?" she asked.

"Well. I met him," I said.

"Ah," Murph said. Even with her labored breathing, the nonword managed to be dry. "Last October?"

"Yeah. He thinks I insulted him."

"You're never mouthy, Harry. Must have been someone who looks like you." She grimaced and clutched at her belt, her balance wavering. There was a long, open slice in the tough leather, where a claw or blade had nearly struck home. The belt gave way, and the oversized mail she wore flopped down, binding her legs, almost tripping her. "Dammit."

"Hold up," I called before Murphy could fall down, and we all staggered to a halt. Molly all but dropped into the snow.

"We can't stand around like this!" Thomas called.

"Charity, Murph, we've got to travel as light as we can. Ditch the armor." I ripped off my duster and wriggled like an eel to get out of my own mail. Then I tossed it at Thomas.

"Hey!" he said, and scowled.

"Don't leave it on the ground," I said. "Thomas, carry it."

"What?" he demanded. "Why?"

"You're strong enough that it won't slow you down," I said, and got my coat back on. "And we don't dare leave this much iron lying on the ground here."

"Why not?"

I saw Murphy get out of her gear, and turn to support Molly so Charity could, too. "Would you want visitors leaving radioactive waste around behind them when they left your place?"

"Oh," he said. "Good point. Because we wouldn't want to get them mad at us." He started rolling the mail into a bundle, which he tied into a rough lump with a belt, and slung it over his shoulder.

Howls and wails and horn cries grew louder, though now all to our flanks and the rear. Somehow, in the gale of snow and wind, we had slipped out of the noose the encircling forces had formed around us. If we kept moving, we stood a real chance of getting away clean.

"This entire field trip isn't what we were meant to think it was," I told him. "We've been used."

"What? How?"

"Later. Now carry the damn armor, and don't leave anything lying behind. Move." The little flutter of Summer fire left in me began to waver, and for a second the wind gained frozen teeth sharp enough to sink all the way into my vitals. "Move!"

I started slogging through the snow again, doing my best to break a path for those coming behind me. Time went by. Wind howled. The snow slashed at my face, and the Summer fire sank to low embers that would not last much longer. They fluttered and faded at almost the precise moment I sensed a rippling of magical energy nearby, and got a whiff of stale popcorn.

The rift shone in the air thirty yards up the slope.

Things, big shaggy things with white fur and long claws, emerged from the snows behind us, running as lightly over the snow and ice as if it had been a concrete sidewalk.

"Thomas!" I pointed at the oncoming threat. "Murph, Charity! You get the girl out of here. Move!"

Murphy looked back and her eyes widened. She immediately ducked under Molly's other arm and began to help Charity. Charity staggered for a step, then drew the sword from her belt and thrust it into the snow at my feet, before redoubling her efforts to get Molly over those last few yards.

I transferred my staff to my left hand and took the deadly iron in my right. The last bit of the power Lily loaned me played out, and I didn't have enough magic left in me to light a candle, much less throw around fire or even use my shield. This was going to be about steel and speed and skill, now, purely physical. Which meant that I probably would have gotten myself quickly killed if Charity hadn't thought fast and armed me with iron.

As things stood, my brother and I only needed to hold the oncoming yeti-looking things off until the ladies escaped. We didn't have to actually beat them.

"What are those things?" Thomas asked me.

"Some kind of ogre," I told him. "Hit them hard and fast. Scare them with iron as much as we can, as fast as we can. If we can get them to come at us cautiously, we might be able to pull off a fighting retreat back up the slope."

"Got it," Thomas said. And then, when the first of the snow ogres was maybe thirty feet away, my brother took two steps and bounded into the air. The top of his jump was about ten feet off the snow, and when he came down he held the saber in both hands. The iron weapon sliced cleanly through the ogre's breastbone and filleted the monster, splitting him open like a steaming baked potato. Its faerie blood took flame, purple and deep blue, and gouted in a blaze of streaming energy.

But Thomas wasn't done there. The next ogre threw a rock the size of a volleyball at him. Thomas whirled, dodged it, faked to one side, and then cut across the second ogre's thighs, sending it howling to the ground.

The third ogre hit him with a small tree trunk, baseball style, and turned my brother into a line drive that missed slamming into me by six inches. The ogres howled in fresh aggression and charged.

I'm not a terribly skilled swordsman. I mean, sure, more so than ninety-nine percent of the people on the planet, but among those who know *anything* about it, I don't rate well. To make matters worse, my experience was largely in fencing—fighting with a style that uses long, thin blades; a lot of thrusting, a lot of lunging. Charity's sword would have been at home on the set of

Conan the Barbarian, and I had only a basic understanding of using the heavier slashing weapon. I have two advantages as fencer. First, I'm quick, especially for a guy my size. As long as something isn't superhumanly fast, I don't get massively outclassed. Second, I have really long arms and legs, and my lunge could hit a target from a county away.

So I played to my strengths. I let out a howl of my own to match the ogres', and when the one with the club drew near and swept it up over his head in a windup, I lunged, low and quick, and drove about a foot of cold steel into its danglies. I twisted the blade and rolled out to one side as I withdrew it. The club came down on the snow where I'd been. Fire fountained from the ogre's pelvic region. The ogre screamed and ran around in a panicked agony, and the ogres coming behind it slowed their steps, their charge faltering, until the ogre keened and fell over into the snow, the fire of cold iron consuming it. They stared at their fallen comrade.

Hey. I don't care what kind of faerie or mortal or hideous creature you are. If you've got danglies and can lose them, that's the kind of sight that makes you reconsider the possible genitalia-related ramifications of your actions real damned quick.

I bared my teeth at them, and ogre blood sizzled on the steel of my borrowed sword. Never turning from them, I started walking back step by slow, cautious step, tight agony in a fiery band around my ribs reminding me of my injuries. I reached Thomas a second later, and he was just then sitting up. He'd crashed into a boulder, and there was a knot already forming just above one eye. He was still too disoriented to stand.

"Dammit, Thomas," I growled. My left hand wasn't strong enough to grab on to him and haul him up the hill. If I used my right, the sword would be in my weak hand, and I wouldn't be able to defend either one of us. "Get up."

The ogres began gathering momentum, coming for us again.

"Thomas!" I shouted, lifting my sword, staring at the ogres as my shadow abruptly flickered out over the ground between us.

Wait. My shadow did what?

I had part of a second to realize that a new source of light had cast the flickering shadows, and then a bead of intense fire, maybe the size of a Peanut M&M, flashed over my shoulder and splashed over the chest of the nearest ogre. Summer fire slammed the ogre to the ground before it could so much as scream, and began to rip its flesh from its bones.

"I've got him!" Fix called, and I saw him in my peripheral vision, sword in hand. He got a shoulder under Thomas's arm and lifted him with more strength than I would have credited the little guy with. The ogres' charge came to a complete halt. I shoved my staff through the belt tying up the bundle of mail Thomas had been carrying, lifted it awkwardly to my shoulder, and we fell back toward the rift, never turning our backs on the ogres. They hovered at the edge of visibility in the gusting snow, but did not menace us again.

"Watch your step," Fix warned me.

Then I felt a rippling sensation around me, and then I stepped into an equatorial sauna.

I found myself on the thin stretch of stage before the screen in Pell's dingy old theater. I stepped to one side, just as Fix came through with Thomas.

Lily stood on the floor, facing the rift. She looked weary and strained. As soon as Fix came through, she waved a hand as if batting aside an annoying fly. There was a rushing sound, and then the rift folded in on itself and vanished.

Silence fell on the dimly lit theater. Lily melted down onto her knees, one hand holding her up, white hair fallen around her head as she shivered, breathing hard. The ice and frozen snow that had been coating me, gathering in my hair and in the creases of my clothing, vanished, replaced by the usual residual ectoplasm.

"Mmmm," Thomas observed in a slightly slurred voice. "Slime."

Fix lowered him to the ground and went to Lily.

"Fix," I said. "Did you hear what was happening out there?"

"Kicked a beehive, it sounded like." He knelt beside Lily, providing her his support. "The castle's garrison came out to meet you?"

"No," I said. "That was every other Winterfae on the map, apparently."

"What?" he demanded.

"I, uh, kind of threw a bunch of Summer fire around Mab's playhouse, and blew up most of this frozen fountain thing."

Fix's mouth dropped open. "You *what*?"

"The Scarecrow was hiding behind the thing and so . . ." I put Charity's sword down and waved a hand. "Kablooey."

Fix stared at me as if I'd gone insane. *"You poured Summer fire into Winter's wellspring?"*

"I can't sleep well any night I haven't inflicted a little property damage," I said gravely. "Anyway, I did that, and all hell broke loose. My godmother told me that anybody who was anybody in Winter had gotten their vengeance on and was coming to kill me."

"My God," Fix breathed. "That would do it all right.

Where did you *get* Summer fire to . . ." His voice trailed off and he stared at Lily.

The Summer Lady looked up, her weary smile gorgeous. "I only provided a minor comfort and guide in order to repay my debt to the lady Charity," she murmured, a small smile on her lips. "I had no way to know that the wizard would steal that power for his own use." She drew in a deep breath and said, "Help me up. We must go."

Fix did so. "Go where?"

I said, "All of those Winter forces are now at the heart of their own realm. Which means that they *aren't* on the borders of Summer waiting to attack. Which means that Summer has forces that can be spared to assist the Council," I said quietly.

"But it only took them a few minutes to show up," Murphy pointed out. "Couldn't they just run back and be there a few minutes from now?"

"No, Murph," I said. "They planned for that. This whole raid was a setup from the get-go." I jerked my head at Lily. "Wasn't it."

"That is one way to describe it," Lily said quietly. "I would not, myself, interpret it that way. I had no part in bringing the fetches here—but their presence and their capture of Lady Charity's daughter presented us with an opportunity to temporarily neutralize the presence of Mab's forces upon our borders."

"We," I murmured. "Maeve is working with you. That was why she showed up at McAnally's so quickly."

"Even so," Lily said, bowing her head at me in a nod of what looked like respect.

Fix blinked at Lily. "You're working with *Maeve*?"

"She couldn't have altered the flow of time at the heart of Winter," I said quietly. "Only one of the Winter Queens could do that."

Fix blinked at Lily as if I hadn't spoken. "Maeve's working with *you*?"

Lily nodded. "Like us, she fears Mab's recent madness." She turned back to me. "I provided you with power enough to threaten the wellspring, in the hope that you would draw some portion of Winter back into its own demesnes. Once that was done, Maeve altered the passage of time relative to the mortal realms."

I arched an eyebrow. "How long have we been gone?"

"It is nearly sunrise of the day after you departed," she replied. "Though the passage of time was only altered in the last few moments of your escape. Maeve will not be able to hold it for long, but it will give us time enough to act."

"What if I hadn't realized it in time?" I asked her. "What if I hadn't used your fire?"

She smiled at me, a little sad. "You would be dead, I suppose."

I glared at her. "And my friends with me."

"Even so," she said. "Please understand. The compulsion my Queen has laid upon me permitted me few options. I could not make explanation of what I had in mind. Nor could I simply stand by and do nothing while the Council was in such desperate need."

"But *now* you can tell me all about it?"

"Now we are discussing history," she said. She inclined her head to me. Then to Charity. "I am glad, Lady, to see your daughter returned to you."

Charity looked up at her long enough to give her a swift smile and a nod of thanks. Then she went back to holding her daughter.

"Lily," I said.

She arched a brow, waiting.

She'd manipulated me, turned me into a weapon to

use against Mab. She hadn't exactly lied to me, but she had taken an awful gamble with my life. Worse, she'd done it with the lives of four of my friends. She had good intentions all the way down the line, I suppose. And she had faced limitations that my instincts told me I still did not fully appreciate or understand. But she hadn't dealt with me head-on, open and honest.

But then, she was a Faerie Queen in her own right. What in the world had ever given me the impression that she would play her cards faceup?

I sighed. "Thank you for your help," I said finally.

She smiled, though the sadness was still in it. "I have not been as much a friend to you and yours as you have been to me and mine, wizard. I am glad that I was able to lend you some help." She bowed to me, from the waist this time. "And now I must take my leave and set things in motion to help your people."

I returned the bow. "Thank you."

She bowed again to the company, and Fix echoed her. Then they walked swiftly from the theater.

I dropped onto my ass at the edge of the stage, my feet waving.

Murphy joined me. After a moment, she said, "What now?"

I rubbed at my eyes. "Holy ground, I think. I don't think we're going to have any immediate fallout from this, but there's no sense in taking chances now. We'll get back to Forthill, make sure everyone is all right. Food. Sleep."

Murphy let out a groan that was almost lustful. "I like this plan. I'm starving."

I sat there watching Molly and Charity, and felt a twinge of nerves inside me. I'd been sent to find black magic. Molly was it. She'd used her power to renovate someone's brain, and as benign as her intentions might have been, I knew that it hadn't left her unstained. I knew better than anybody how much danger Molly was still in. How dangerous she might now be.

I'd saved her from the bad faeries, sure, but now she faced another, infinitely more dangerous threat.

The White Council. The Wardens. The sword.

It was only a matter of time before someone else managed to trace the black magic back to its source. If I didn't bring her before the Council, someone else would, sooner or later. Even worse, if the mind-controlling magic she'd already used had begun to turn upon her, to warp her as well, she might be a genuine danger to herself and others. She could wind up as dangerous and crazy as the kid whose execution had served as a prelude to the past few days.

If I took her to the Council, I would probably be responsible for her death.

If I didn't, I'd be responsible for those she might harm.

I wished I wasn't so damned tired. I might have been able to come up with some options. I settled for banishing thoughts of tomorrow for the time being. I was whole, and alive, and sane, and so were the people who had stood beside me. We'd gotten the girl out in one piece. Her mom was holding her so ferociously that I wondered if I might not have been the catalyst for a reconciliation between the pair of them.

I might have healed the wounds of their family. And that was a damned fine thing to have done. I felt a genuine warmth and pride from it. I'd helped to bring mother and daughter back together. For tonight, that was enough.

Thomas sat down on my other side, wincing as he touched the lump on his head. "Harry," Thomas said. "Remind me why we keep hurling ourselves into this kind of insanity."

I traded a smile with Murphy and said nothing. We all three of us watched as Charity, on the floor in front of the first row of seats, clutched her daughter hard against her.

Molly leaned against her with a child's gratefulness, need, and love. She spoke very quietly, never opening her eyes. "Mama."

Charity said nothing, but she hugged her daughter even more tightly.

"Oh," Thomas said. "Right."

"Exactly," I said. "Right."

Chapter

Forty-one

Father Forthill received us in his typical fashion: with warmth, welcome, compassion, and food. At first, Thomas was going to remain outside Saint Mary's, but I clamped my hand onto the front of his mail and dragged him unceremoniously inside with me. He could have gotten loose, of course, so I knew he didn't really much mind. He growled and snapped at me halfheartedly, but nodded cautiously to Forthill when I introduced him. Then my brother stepped out into the hall and did his unobtrusive-wall-hanging act.

The Carpenter kids were sound asleep when we came in, but the noise made one of them stir, and little Harry opened his eyes, blinked sleepily, then let out a shriek of delight when he saw his mother. The sound wakened the other kids, and everyone assaulted Charity and Molly with happy shouts and hugs and kisses.

I watched the reunion from a chair across the room, and dozed sitting up until Forthill returned with food. There weren't chairs enough for everyone, and Charity wound up sitting on the floor with her back to the wall, chomping down sandwiches while her children all tried to remain within touching distance.

I stuffed my face shamelessly. The use of magic, the excitement, and that final uphill hike through the cold had left my stomach on the verge of implosion. "Survival food," I muttered. "Nothing like it."

Murphy, leaning against the wall beside me, nodded. "Damn right." She wiped at her mouth and looked at her watch. She tucked the last of her sandwich between her lips, and then started resetting the watch while she chewed.

"Gone almost exactly twenty-four hours. So we did some kind of time travel?" she asked.

"Oh, God no," I said. "That's on the list of Things One Does Not Do. It's one of the seven Laws of Magic."

"Maybe," she said. "But however it happened, a whole day just went poof. That's time travel."

"People are doing *that* kind of time travel all the time," I said. "We just pulled into the passing lane for a while."

She finished setting the watch and grimaced. "All the same."

I frowned at her. "You okay?"

She looked up at the children and their mother. "I'm going to have one hell of a time explaining where I've been for the past twenty-four hours. It isn't as though I can tell my boss that I went time traveling."

"Yeah, he'd never buy it. Tell him you invaded Faerieland to rescue a young woman from a monster-infested castle."

"Of course," she said. "Why didn't I think of that?"

I grunted. "Is it going to make trouble for you?"

She frowned for a moment and then said, "Intradepartmental discipline, probably. They couldn't get me for anything criminal, so no jail."

I blinked. "Jail?"

"I was in charge of things, remember?" Murphy reminded me. "I was pushing the line by laying that aside and coming to help you. Throw in that extra day and . . ." She shrugged.

"Hell's bells," I sighed. "I hadn't realized."

She shrugged a shoulder.

"How bad is it going to be?" I asked.

She frowned. "Depends on a lot of things. Mostly what Greene and Rick have to say, and how they say it. What other cops who were there have to say. A couple of those guys are major assholes. They'd be glad to make trouble for me."

"Like Rudolph," I said.

"Like Rudolph."

I put on my Bronx accent. "You want I should whack 'em for ya?"

She gave me a quick, ghostly smile. "Better let me sleep on that one."

I nodded. "But seriously. If there's anything I can do . . ."

"Just keep your head down for a while. You aren't exactly well loved all over the department. There are some people who resent that I keep hiring you, and that they can't tell me to stop because the cases you're on have about a ninety percent likelihood of resolution."

"My effectiveness is irrelevant? I thought cops had to have a degree or something, these days."

She snorted. "I love my job," she said. "But sometimes it feels like it has an unnecessarily high moron factor."

I nodded agreement. "What are they going to do?"

"This will be my first official fuckup," she said. "If I handle it correctly, I don't think they'll fire me."

"But?" I asked.

She pushed some hair back from her eyes. "They'll shove lots of fun counseling and psychological evaluation down my throat."

I tried to imagine Murphy on a therapist's couch.

My brain almost exploded out my ears.

"They'll try every trick they can to convince me to leave," she continued. "And when I don't, they'll demote me. I'll lose SI."

A lead weight landed on the bottom of my stomach. "Murph," I said.

She tried to smile but failed. She just looked sickly and strained. "It isn't anyone's fault, Harry. Just the nature of the beast. It had to be done, and I'd do it again. I can live with that."

Her tone was calm, relaxed, but she was too tired to make it sound genuine. Murphy's command might have been a tricky, frustrating, ugly one, but it was hers. She'd fought for her rank, worked her ass off to get it, and then she got shunted into SI. Only instead of accepting banishment to departmental Siberia, she'd worked even harder to throw it back into the faces of the people who had sent her there.

"It isn't fair," I growled.

"What is?" she asked.

"Bah. One of these days I'm going to go downtown and summon up a swarm of roaches or something. Just to watch the suits run out of the building, screaming."

This time, her smile was wired a little tight. "That won't help me."

"Are you kidding? We could sit outside and take pictures as they came running out and laugh ourselves sick."

"And that helps how?"

"Laughter is good for you," I said. "Nine out of ten stand-up comedians recommend laughter in the face of intense stupidity."

She let out a tired, quiet chuckle. "Let me sleep on that one, too." She pushed away from the wall, drawing her keys from her pocket. "I've got an appointment with the spin doctor," she said. "You want a ride home?"

I shook my head. "Few things I want to do first. Thanks, though."

She nodded and turned to go. Then she paused. "Harry," she said quietly.

"Hmm?"

"What I said in the elevator."

I swallowed. "Yeah?"

"I didn't mean it to come out so harsh. You're a good man. Someone I'm damned proud to call my friend. But I care too much about you to lie to you or lead you on."

"It's no one's fault," I said quietly. "You had to be honest with me. I can live with that."

One corner of her mouth quirked into a wry half grin. "What are friends for?"

I sensed a change in tone as she asked the question, a very faint interrogative.

I stood up and put my hand on her shoulder. "I'm your friend. That won't change, Karrin. Ever."

She nodded, blinking several times, and for a moment rested her hand on mine. Then she turned to leave. Just then, Thomas poked his head in from the hallway. "Harry, Karrin. You leaving?"

"I am," she said.

Thomas glanced at me. "Uh-huh. Think I can bum a ride?"

Her car keys rattled. "Sure," she said.

"Thanks." He nodded to me. "Thank you for another field trip, Harry. Kind of bland, though. Maybe next time we should bring some coffee or something, so we don't yawn ourselves to death."

"Beat it before I kick your whining ass," I said.

Thomas sneered at me in reply, and he and Murphy left.

I ate the rest of my sandwich, idly noting that I had reached one of those odd little mental moments where I felt too tired to go to sleep. Across the room, Charity and her children had all fallen asleep where she sat on the floor, the children all leaning upon their mother and each other like living pillows. Charity looked exhausted, naturally, and I could see care lines on her face that I'd never really noticed before.

She could be a pain in the ass, but she was one gutsy chick. Her kids were lucky to have a mother like her. A lot of moms would say that they would die for their children. Charity had placed herself squarely in harm's way to do exactly that.

I regarded the kids for a moment, mostly very young children's faces, relaxed in sleep. Children whose world had been founded in something as solid as Charity's love for them would be able to do almost anything. Between her and her husband, they could be raising an entire generation of men and women with the same kind of power, selflessness, and courage. I'm a pessimist of the human condition, as a rule, but contemplating the future and how the Carpenter kids could contribute to it was the kind of thought that gave me hope for us all, despite myself.

Of course, I suppose someone must once have looked down upon young Lucifer and considered what tremendous potential he contained.

As that unsettling thought went through my head, Molly shifted herself out from under her mother's arm, removed her leg very gently from beneath a little brother's ear, and extracted herself from the slumbering dogpile. She moved quietly for the exit until she glanced up, saw me watching her, and froze for half a step.

"You're awake," she whispered.

"Too tired to sleep," I said. "Where are you going?"

She rubbed her hands on her torn skirts and avoided my eyes. "I . . . what I put them through. I thought it would be better if I just . . ."

"Left?" I asked.

She shrugged a shoulder, and didn't lift her eyes. "It won't work. Me staying at home."

"Why not?" I asked.

She shook her head tiredly. "It just won't. Not anymore." She walked out past me.

I moved my right hand smoothly, gripping her hand at the wrist, skin-to-skin contact that conducted the quivering, tingling aura of power of a practitioner of the Art up through my arm. She'd avoided direct contact before, though I hadn't had a reason to think she would at the time.

She froze, staring at my face, as she felt the same presence of power in my own hand.

"You can't stay because of your magic. That's what you mean."

She swallowed. "How . . . how did you know?"

"I'm a wizard, kid. Give me some credit."

She folded her arms beneath her breasts, her shoulders hunched. "I should g-go . . ."

I stood up. "Yeah, you should. We need to talk."

She bit her lip and looked up at me. "What do you mean?"

"I mean you've got some tough choices to make, Molly. You've got the power. You're going to have to figure out whether you want to use it. Or whether you're going to let it use you." I gestured with a hand for her to accompany me and walked out, slowly. We weren't going anywhere. What was important was the walk. She kept pace with me, her body language as closed and defensive as you please.

"When did it start for you?" I asked her quietly.

She chewed her lip. She said nothing.

Maybe I had to give a little to get a little. "It's always like that for people like us. Something happens, almost like it's all by itself, the first time the magic bubbles over. It's usually something small and silly. My first time . . ." I smiled. "Oh, man. I haven't thought about that in a while." I mused for a moment, thinking. "It was maybe two weeks before Justin adopted me," I said. "I was in school, and small. All elbows and ears. Hadn't hit my growth spurt yet, and it was spring, and we were having this school Olympics. Field day, you know? And I was entered in the running long jump." I grinned. "Man, I wanted to win it. I'd lost every other event to a couple of guys who liked to give me a hard time. So I ran down the blacktop and jumped as hard as I could, yelling the whole time." I shook my head. "Must have looked silly. But when I shouted and jumped, some of the power rolled out of me and threw me about ten feet farther than I should have been able to jump. I landed badly, of course. Sprained my wrist. But I won this little blue ribbon. I still have it back at home."

Molly looked up at me with a little ghost of a smile. "I can't imagine you being smaller than average."

"Everyone's little sometime," I said.

"Were you shy, too?"

"Not as much as I should have been. I had this problem where I gave a lot of lip to older kids. And teachers. And pretty much everyone else who tried to intimidate me, whether or not it was for my own good."

She let out a little giggle. "That I can believe."

"You?" I asked gently.

She shook her head. "Mine is silly, too. I walked home from school one day about two years ago and it was raining, so I ran straight inside. It was errands day, and I thought Mom was gone."

"Ah," I said. "Let me guess. You were still wearing the Gothy McGoth outfit instead of what your mom saw you leave the house in."

Her cheeks flushed pink. "Yes. Only she wasn't running errands. Gran had borrowed the van and taken the little ones to get haircuts because Mom was sick. I was in the living room and I hadn't changed back. All I wanted was to sink into the floor so she wouldn't see me."

"What happened?"

Molly shrugged. "I closed my eyes. Mom came in. She sat down on the couch and turned on the TV, and never said a word. I opened my eyes and she was sitting there, three feet away, and hadn't even seen me. I walked out really quietly, and she never even glanced at me. I mean, at first I thought she'd gone crazy or into denial or something. But she really hadn't seen me. So I snuck back to my room, changed clothes, and she was none the wiser."

I lifted my eyebrows, impressed. "Wow. Really?"

"Yes." She peered up at me. "Why?"

"Your first time out you called up a veil on nothing but instinct. That's impressive, kid. You've got a gift."

She frowned. "Really?"

"Absolutely. I'm a full wizard of the White Council, and I can't do a reliable veil."

"You can't? Why not?"

I shrugged. "Why are some people wonderful singers, even without training, and other people can't carry a tune in a bucket? It's something I just don't have. That you do . . ." I shook my head. "It's impressive. It's a rare talent."

She frowned over that, her gaze turning inward for a moment. "Oh."

"Bet you got one hell of a headache afterward."

She nodded. "Yes, actually. Like an ice-cream headache, only two hours long. How did you know?"

"It's a fairly typical form of sensory feedback for improperly channeled energy," I said. "Everyone who does magic winds up with one sooner or later."

"I haven't read about anything like that."

"Is that what you did next? You figured out you could become the invisible girl, and went and studied books?"

She was quiet for a moment, and I thought she was about to close up again. But then she said, quietly, "Yes. I mean, I knew how hard my mom would be on me if I was . . . showing interest in that kind of thing. So I read books. The library, and a couple others that I got at Barnes and Noble."

"Barnes and Noble," I sighed, shaking my head. "You didn't head into any of the local occult shops?"

"Not then," she said. "But . . . I tried to meet people. You know? Like, Wiccans and psychics and stuff. That was how I met Nelson, at a martial arts school. I'd heard the teacher knew things. But I don't think he did. Some of Nelson's friends were into magic, too, or thought they were. I never saw any of them do anything."

I grunted. "What did all those people tell you about magic?"

"What *didn't* they tell me," she said. "Everyone thinks magic is something different."

"Heh," I said. "Yeah."

"And it wasn't like I could just go running around all the time. Not with school and the little ones to watch and my mom looking over my shoulder. So, you know. Mostly books. And I practiced, you know? Tried little things. Little, teeny glamours. Lighting candles. But a lot of the things I tried didn't work."

"Magic isn't easy," I said. "Not even for someone with a strong natural talent. Takes a lot of practice, like anything else." I walked quietly for a few steps and then said, "Tell me about the spell you used on Rosie and Nelson."

She paused, staring at nothing, the blood draining from her face. "I had to," she said.

"Go on."

Her pretty features were bleak. "Rosie had . . . she'd already had a miscarriage, because she kept getting high. And when she lost the baby, she went to the hard stuff. Heroin. I begged her to go into rehab, but she was just . . . too far gone, I guess. But I thought maybe I could help her. With magic. Like you help people."

Hooboy. I kept the dismay off my face and nodded for her to continue.

"And one day last week, Sandra Marling and I had a talk. And during it, she told me how they were discovering that the presence of a very strong source of fear could bypass all kinds of psychological barriers. Things like addiction. That the fear could drive home a lesson, reliably and quickly. I didn't have much time. I had to do it to save Rosie's child."

I grunted. "Why do Nelson, too?"

"He was . . . he was using too much. He and Rosie sort of reinforced each other. And I wasn't sure what might happen, so I tried the spell out before I used it on her, too."

"You tested it on Nelson?" I asked. "Then did the same one on Rosie?"

She nodded. "I had to scare them away from the drugs. I sent them both a nightmare."

"Stars and stones," I muttered. "A nightmare."

Molly's voice became defensive. "I had to do something. I couldn't just sit there."

"Do you have any idea how much you hurt them both?" I asked.

"Hurt them?" she said, apparently bewildered. "They were fine."

"They weren't fine," I said quietly. "But the same spell should have done more or less the same thing to both of them. It acted differently on Nelson than Rosie." And then I put two and two together again and said, "Ah. Now I get it."

She didn't look up at me.

"Nelson was the father," I said quietly.

She shrugged. A tear streaked down her cheek. "They probably didn't even know what they were doing when it happened. The pair of them were just . . ." She shook her head and fell silent.

"That explains why your spell damaged Nelson so much more severely."

"I don't understand. I never hurt him."

"I don't think you did it on purpose." I waved a hand, palm up. "Magic comes from a lot of places. But especially from your emotions. They influence almost anything you can do. You were angry at Nelson when you cast the spell. Contaminated the whole thing with your anger."

"I did not hurt them," she said stubbornly. "I saved their lives."

"I don't think you realize the ramifications," I said.

She spun to me and shrieked, *"I did not hurt them!"*

The air suddenly crackled with tension; vague, unfocused energy centered on the screaming girl. There was enough energy to manage something unfortunate, and it was clear that the kid wasn't in anything like control of her power. I shook my head and swung my left hand in a half circle, palm faced out, and simply drew in the magical energy her emotions had generated and grounded it into the earth before somebody got hurt.

A tingle of sensation washed up my arm, surprisingly

intense. Her talent was not a modest one. I started to snap a reprimand for her carelessness, but aborted it before the first word. In the first place, she was ignorant of what she'd done. Not innocent, but not wholly at fault, all the same. In the second place, she'd just been through a nightmarish ordeal at the hands of wicked faeries. She probably couldn't have controlled her emotions, even if she wanted to.

She stared at me in surprise as the energy she had raised vanished. The rage and pain in her stance and expression faded to uncertainty.

"I didn't hurt them," she said in a rather small voice. "I saved them."

"Molly, you need to know the facts. I know you're tired and scared. But that doesn't change a damned thing about what you did to them. You fucked around with their minds. You used magic to enslave them to your will, and the fact that you meant well by it doesn't matter at all. Somewhere inside of them both, they *know* what you've done to them, subconsciously. They'll try to fight it. Regain control of their own choices. And that struggle is going to tear their psyches to shreds."

More tears fell from her eyes. "B-but . . ."

I went on in a steady voice. "Rosie was better off. She might recover from it in a few years. But Nelson is probably insane already. He might not ever make it back. And doing it to them has screwed around with your own head. Not as bad as Rosie and Nelson, but you damaged yourself, too. It'll make it harder for you to control impulses and your magic. Which makes you a lot more likely to lose control and hurt someone else. It's a vicious cycle. I've seen it in action."

She shook her head several times. "No. No, no, no."

"Here's another truth," I said. "The White Council has seven Laws of Magic. Screwing around in other people's heads breaks one of them. When the Council finds out what you've done, they'll put you on trial and execute you. Trial, sentence, and execution won't take an hour."

She fell silent, staring at me, crying harder. "Trial?" she whispered.

"A couple of days ago I watched them execute a kid who had broken the same law."

Her shocked expression could not seem to recover. Her eyes roamed randomly, blurred with tears. "But . . . I didn't know."

"Doesn't matter," I said.

"I never meant to hurt anyone."

"Ditto."

She broke out into a half-hysterical sob and clutched at her stomach. "But . . . but that's not fair."

"What is?" I said quietly. "One more hard truth for you. I'm a Warden of the Council now, Molly. It's my job to take you to them."

She only stared. She looked racked with pain, helpless, alone. God help me, she looked like the little girl I'd first met at Michael's house years before. I had to remind myself that there was another, darker portion of the girl behind those blue eyes. The snarling rage, the denial, they both belonged to the parts of her mind that had been twisted as she twisted others.

I wished that I hadn't seen flashes of that other self in her, because I did not want to follow the chain of consequence that sprang from it. Molly had broken the Laws of Magic. She'd inflicted incalculable harm on others. Her damaged psyche could collapse on her, leaving her insane.

All of which meant that she was dangerous.

Ticking-bomb dangerous.

It did not matter to the Laws that she had meant well.

She had become exactly the kind of person that the Laws of Magic—and their sentence—were created to deal with.

But when the law fails to protect those it governs, it's up to someone else to pick up the slack—in this case, me. There was a chance that I could save her life. It wasn't an enormous chance, but it was probably the best shot she was going to get. Assuming, of course, that she was not already too far around the bend.

I only knew one sure way to find out.

I stopped in the darkened hall and turned to her. "Molly. Do you know what a soulgaze is?"

"It . . . I read in a book that it's when you look into someone's eyes. You see something about who they are."

"Close enough," I agreed. "You ever done it?"

She shook her head. "The book said it could be dangerous."

"Can be," I confirmed. "Though probably not for the reasons you'd think. When you see someone like that, Molly, there's no hiding the truth about who you are. You see it all, good and bad. No specifics, usually, but you get a damned good idea about what kind of person they are. And it's for keeps. Once you've seen it, it stays in your head, fresh, period. And when you look at them, they get the same look at you."

She nodded. "Why do you ask?"

"I'd like to gaze on you, if you're willing to permit it."

"Why?"

I smiled a little, though my reflection in a passing window looked mostly sad. "Because I want to help you."

She turned away, as if to start walking again, but only swayed in place, her torn skirts whispering. "I don't understand."

"I'm not going to hurt you, kid. But I need you to trust me for a little while."

She nodded, biting her lip. "Okay. What do I do?"

I stopped and turned to face her. She mirrored me. "This might feel a little weird. But it won't last as long as it seems."

"Okay," she said, that lost-child tone still in her voice.

I met her eyes.

For a second, I thought nothing had happened. And then I realized that the soulgaze was already up and running, and that it showed me Molly, standing and facing me as nothing more than she seemed to be. But I could see down the hall behind her, and the church's windows held half a dozen different reflections.

One was an emaciated version of Molly, as though she'd been starved or strung out on hard drugs, her eyes aglow with an unpleasant, fey light. One was her smiling and laughing, older and comfortably heavier, children surrounding her. A third faced me in a grey Warden's cloak, though a burn scar, almost a brand, marred the roundness of her left cheek. Still another reflection was Molly as she appeared now, though more secure, laughter dancing in her eyes. Another reflection showed her at a desk, working.

But the last . . .

The last reflection of Molly wasn't the girl. Oh, it *looked* like Molly, externally. But the eyes gave it away. They were flat as a reptile's, empty. She wore all black, including a black collar, and her hair had been dyed to match. Though she looked like Molly, like a human being, she was neither. She had become something else entirely, something very, very bad.

Possibilities. I was looking at possibilities. There was definitely a strong presence of darkness in the girl, but it had not yet gained dominion over her. In all the potential images, she was a person of power—different kinds of power, certainly, but she was strong in all of them. She was going to wind up with power of her own to use or misuse, depending on what choices she made.

What she needed was a guide. Someone to show her the ropes, to give her the tools she would need to deal with her newfound power, and all the baggage that came with it. Yes, that kernel of darkness still burned coldly within her, but I could hardly throw stones there. Yes, she had the potential to go astray on an epic scale.

Don't we all.

I thought of Charity and Michael, Molly's parents, her family. Her strength had been forged and founded in theirs. They both regarded the use of magic as something suspect at best, and if not inherently evil, then inherently dangerous. Their opposition to the power that Molly had manifested might turn the strength they'd given their daughter against her. If she believed or came to believe that her power was an evil, it could push her faster down the left-hand path.

I knew something of how much Michael and Charity cared for their daughter.

But they couldn't help her.

One thing was certain, though, and gave me a sense of reassurance. Molly had not yet indelibly stained herself. Her future had yet to be written.

It was worth fighting for.

The gaze ended, and the various images in the windows behind Molly vanished. The girl herself trembled like a frightened doe, staring up at me with her eyes wide and huge.

"My God," she whispered. "I never knew . . ."

"Easy," I told her. "Sit down until things stop spinning."

I helped her settle to the floor with her back to the wall, and I did the same beside her. I rubbed at a spot between my eyebrows that began to twinge.

"What did you see?" she whispered.

"That you're basically a decent person," I told her. "That you have a lot of potential. And that you're in danger."

"Danger?"

"Power's like money, kid. It isn't easy to handle well, and once you start getting it, you can't have enough. I think you're in danger because you've made a couple of bad choices. Used your power in ways that you shouldn't. Keep it up, and you'll wind up working for the dark side."

She drew her knees up to her chin and wrapped her arms around her legs. "Did . . . did you get what you needed?"

"Yeah," I said. "You have a couple of choices to make, Molly. Starting with whether or not you want to turn yourself in to the Council."

She rocked back and forth, a nervous motion. "Why would I?"

"Because they're going to find you, sooner or later. If that happens, if they think you're trying to avoid them, they'll probably kill you out of hand. But if you're willing to cooperate and face up to what you've done, and if someone intercedes on your behalf, the Council might withhold a death sentence."

"Aren't you just going to turn me in anyway?"

"No," I said. "It's about choices, Molly. This one is yours. I'll respect what you want to do."

She frowned. "Would you get in trouble with them for that?"

I shrugged. "Not sure. They might kill me for being in collusion with an evil wizard."

Her eyebrows lifted. "Really?"

"They aren't exactly overflowing with tolerance and forgiveness and agape love," I told her. "They've almost pulled the trigger on me a couple of times. They're dangerous people."

She shivered. "You'd . . . you'd risk that for me?"

"Yep."

She frowned, chewing that over. "And if I turn myself in?"

"Then we'll explain what happened. I'll intercede for you. If the Council accepts that, then I'll be held responsible for your training and your use of magic."

She blinked. "You mean . . . I'd be your apprentice?"

"Pretty much," I said. "But you have to understand something. It would mean that you agree to accept my leadership. If I tell you to do something, you do it. No questions, no delays. What I can teach you is no damn game. It's the power of life and death, and there's no room for anyone who doesn't work hard to control it. If you go to the Council with me, you're accepting those terms. Got it?"

She shivered and nodded.

"Next, you have to decide what you want to do with your power."

"What are my choices?" she asked.

I shrugged. "You've got the juice to make the White Council, eventually, if that's what you want. Or you can find something worth supporting with your talents. I've heard of a couple of wizards who have made stupid amounts of money with their skills. Or hell, maybe after you learn to control yourself, you just set them aside. Let them fade." *Like your mom did.*

"I could never do that last one," she said.

I snorted. "Think about it, kid. You join up with the

wizards now and you wind up in the middle of the war. The bad guys won't care that you're young and untrained."

She chewed on her lip. "I should talk with my parents. Shouldn't I?"

I exhaled slowly. "If you want to, you should. But you've got to realize that this is going to be your choice. You can't let anyone else make it for you."

She was quiet for a long time. Then she asked, in a very small voice, "Do you really think I could . . . could like, join the dark side?"

"Yeah," I said quietly. "There are plenty of things out there who would be happy to help you along. Which is why I want to give you a hand—so that I can steer you away from that type until you know enough to handle them on your own."

"But . . ." Her face scrunched up. "I don't *want* to be a bad guy."

"No one *wants* it," I said. "Most of the bad guys in the real world don't know that they *are* bad guys. You don't get a flashing warning sign that you're about to damn yourself. It sneaks up on you when you aren't looking."

"But the Council . . . they'll see that, right? That I don't want to be like that?"

"I can't guarantee you that they'll believe that. And even if they do, they might decide to execute you anyway."

She sat very still. I listened to her breathe. "If I go to the Council . . . can my parents come with me?"

"No."

She swallowed. "Will you?"

"Yes."

She met my eyes again, this time without fear of a soulgaze beginning. That ship had sailed. Tear-stained cheeks gleamed and curved into a little smile that could not hide the fear behind it.

I reached out and put my hand over hers. "I'll promise you this, Molly. I don't intend to let them hurt you. Period. The only way anyone will lay a finger on you is over my dead body." Which would not be difficult for the Council to arrange, but there was no sense in mentioning that to the girl. Her day had been scary enough. "I think going with me is your best chance to get out of this," I continued. "If you decide that it's what you want, we'll sit down with your parents. They won't be thrilled with the idea, but they can't make the call on this one. It's yours. It has to be, or it won't mean anything."

She nodded and closed her eyes for a moment. Poor kid. She looked so damned young. I was fairly sure I had never been that young.

Then she drew in a deep, shaking breath and said, "I want to go to the Council."

Chapter

Forty-two

I talked Molly into staying at the church with her family until everyone had gotten some rest and we could talk things out with her mother. Any sane man would have hopped a bus for Las Vegas or somewhere rather than wait around and tell Charity Carpenter he wanted to haul her first baby in front of a gang of powerful wizards for trial and possible execution.

I found an unused cot and flopped onto it. My shins hung off the end of the undersized thing, and I didn't care a bit. Nails clicked in unsteady rhythm on tile, and I felt Mouse's warm, silent presence limp carefully to the floor beside my cot. I reached out, ruffled his ears, and laid my hand on the thick ruff of fur across his shoulders. I was asleep before he settled himself down to sleep beside me.

I woke up later, in the same position I'd fallen asleep. I had a crick in my neck, and one hand dangled over the side of the bed. It had lost enough circulation to feel numb and floppy, and I had to squint over the side of the cot to see that it was still resting on Mouse's furry back. The room was unlit, but the door to the hallway was open, and afternoon-flavored sunlight lit the hall.

I wanted to go back to sleep, but I hauled myself to my feet and stumbled down the hall to the bathroom, Mouse limping along beside me without complaint. I availed myself of indoor plumbing, and found myself wishing that they had a shower. I made do with a bird-bath in the sink, and shambled back down to Forthill's guest room.

The cots were all but empty. Nelson slept in one of them, faint twitches randomly stirring his limbs. His closed eyes rolled back and forth, and he had broken into a light sweat. Nightmares, I supposed. Poor kid. I wished I could have helped, but realistically there wasn't anything I could do for him.

Molly slept in another cot; the motionless, black sleep of the truly exhausted. Charity sat in a chair beside the cot, her head tilted back against the wall. She snored a little. One of her hands rested on Molly's hair.

I regarded them both in silence for a while. I thought about writing the whole thing off, conjuring up a wistful image of digging a hole, getting in, and then pulling the hole in after me. Hey, it worked for Bugs Bunny.

"I should have taken a left turn at Albuquerque," I sighed to Mouse.

Mouse settled down on the floor again, and lay on his side, holding his injured leg clear of the floor.

"Yeah, you're right," I said. "I'm too stupid to be uninvolved. No sense in putting off the inevitable."

So I got up, went over to Molly, and gently shook her shoulder. Charity woke up when I did, blinking disorientation from her eyes. Molly took a little bit longer, but then she took a sharp breath and sat up in bed, mirroring her mother.

"Yes? Is everyone all right?" Charity asked.

"As far as I know," I told her. "Where are the other kids?"

"My mother took them home."

"Any word from Michael?"

She shook her head.

"We need to talk about something fairly important, please."

"And what is that?" she asked.

"Worth waking up for. Maybe you could get up, get some water on your face while I hunt down some coffee."

"We do need to talk, Mama," Molly said in a gentle tone.

She frowned at me for a moment, and I thought she was going to argue with me about it. Then she shook her head and said, "Very well."

I made it so. I raided the small staff kitchen and came away with not only coffee, but several bagels and some fresh fruit. I left a few bucks on the counter under a saltshaker, then went back to Molly and Charity.

We sat down to eat our breakfast in the shadowy room.

I laid it out for Charity just as I had for Molly.

"Black magic," Charity whispered, when I had finished. She glanced at Molly, a faint frown troubling her features. "I never thought it had gone that far."

"I know, Mama," Molly said quietly.

"Is what he says true?"

Molly nodded.

"Oh, baby," Charity sighed. She touched Molly's hair with one hand. "How could I not have seen this happening?"

"Don't beat yourself up over it," I told her. "At least not right now. It won't help anyone."

Anger touched her features and she said, "Neither will this nonsense with the White Council. Of course she will not go."

"I don't think you get it," I told Charity in a quiet voice. "She's going. She can go voluntarily, or she can go when the Wardens find her. But she's going."

"You plan to inform them of what has happened, then?" Charity asked, her tone gaining frost as it went.

"No," I said. "But that kind of magic leaves a mark. There are plenty of things in the Nevernever who can sense it—and, in fact, they had already tipped off the Council that there was black magic afoot here. Even if I never say anything else about it, it's only a matter of time until another Warden investigates."

"You don't know that for a fact."

"I kind of do," I said. "And this isn't just about accountability, either. The things she's done have already left their mark on her. If she doesn't get support and training, those changes are going to snowball."

"You don't *know* that," Charity insisted.

"I kind of do," I said, louder. "Hell's bells, Charity, I'm trying to protect her."

"By dragging her in front of a kangaroo court of egotistic, power-mongering tyrants? So that they can execute her? How is that *protecting* my child?"

"If she goes in voluntarily, with me, I think I can get her clemency until she has a chance to show them that she is sincere about working with them."

"You *think*?" Charity said. "No. That's not good enough."

I clenched my fists in frustration. "Charity, the only thing I *am* sure about is that if Molly doesn't come out, and if one of the other egotistical, power-mongering tyrants finds her, they're going to automatically declare her a warlock and execute her. To say nothing of what will happen to her if she's on her own. It's more than likely that she'll deserve it by then."

"That's *not* true," Charity snapped. "She is *not* going to become some sort of monster. She is *not* going to change."

"My God, Charity. I want to help her!"

"That isn't why you're doing it," she snarled, rising. "You're trying to get her to go with you to save your own skin. You're afraid that if they find her, they will brand you traitor for not bringing her in, and execute you along with her."

I found myself on my feet as well. Silence fell heavy and oppressive on the room.

"Mama," Molly said quietly, breaking it. "Please tell me what Harry has done in the past two days to make you think that he is selfish. Or cowardly. Was it when he turned to face the ogres so that we could escape? Was it when he traded away the obligations the Summer Lady owed him in order to attempt the rescue?"

Charity was shocked silent for a second. Then her face heated and she said, "Young lady, that isn't—"

Molly went on smoothly, her voice quiet, calm, displaying neither anger nor disrespect—nor weakness. "Or perhaps it was when you were unconscious and no one could have stopped him from simply taking me to turn over to the Council, and he instead stopped to give me a choice." She chewed on her lip for a second. "You told me everything he's done since I was taken. Now he's offering to die for me, Mama. What more could you ask of him?"

Charity's face reddened further, and I thought I saw something like shame on her features. She sat down again, bowed her head, and said nothing. The silence stretched. Her shoulders shook.

Molly slid down to kneel at her mother's feet and hugged her. Charity hugged back. The pair of them rocked slowly back and forth for a moment, and though the dim room made it hard to see, I was sure they were both crying.

"Perhaps you're right," Charity said after a moment. "I should not have accused you so, Mister Dresden."

She squared her shoulders and lifted her head. "But I will not allow her to go."

Molly looked up very slowly. She faced Charity, lifted her chin a little, and said, "I love you very much, Mama. But this isn't your choice. I'm the one responsible for what I did. I'll face the consequences of it."

Charity turned her face away from Molly, a kind of terrible grief and fear making her look, for the first time in my memory, old. "Molly," she whispered.

Father Forthill had arrived at some point during the conversation, though none of us had noticed him in the doorway. His gentle voice was steady. "Your daughter is in the right, Charity," he said. "She's an adult now, in many ways. She's taken actions that demand that she accept the responsibilities that accompany them."

"She is my child," Charity objected.

"She was," Forthill corrected her, "if only for a time. Children are a precious gift, but they belong to no one but themselves. They are only lent us a little while." The priest folded his arms over his chest and leaned against the doorway. "I think you should consider what has happened, Charity. Dresden is perhaps the only one who *could* have helped you and Molly. I think it no accident that he became involved in this situation." He gave me a whimsical little smile. "After all, He does work in mysterious ways."

I walked across the floor and lowered myself to one knee before Charity. "I don't know anything about that. But for whatever it is worth, I promise you," I said very quietly. "I will bring your daughter back from the Council safe and well. They'll have to kill me to stop me."

Charity looked up at me, and I saw a dozen emotions flicker over her features. Hope, fear, anger, sadness. Twice she opened her mouth to speak, but bit down on the words before she uttered them.

Finally, she whispered, "I have your word on it?"

"You do," I said.

She stared at me for a moment. Then she looked up and said, to Forthill, "I wish Michael was here."

Forthill asked her, "If he was, what do you think he would say?"

Her eyes moved back to me, and she said, frowning faintly, "To have faith. To trust the wizard. That he is a good man."

The priest nodded. "I think he would say that, too."

Charity glanced at me without meeting my eyes. "How long will it take?"

"I'll contact the Council today. Depends on who is available, but this kind of thing gets high priority. Tomorrow, the next day at the latest."

She bowed her head again, and nodded. She said to Forthill, "Is there nothing we can do?"

"Molly's made her decision," Forthill said quietly. "And everything I've learned about the effects of black magic upon those who use it agrees with what Dresden has told you. Your daughter is in very real danger, Charity."

"Can't the Church . . . ?"

Forthill gave her a faint smile and shook his head. "There aren't many of us still standing sentinel against the Shadows. Of those who do, none of us have any real skill with magic. We could assist her in turning aside from her gifts, but given her age it would in effect be nothing more than imprisonment." He nodded to Molly. "And, no offense, child, but with your temperament, without your full cooperation, it would only push you more quickly toward the darkness."

"No," Charity said. "She's got to set this aside."

Molly folded her arms tightly against her stomach, and shook her head, lips pressed together. "No."

Charity looked up and all but pleaded, "Molly. You don't understand what it could do to you."

The girl was quiet for a moment. Then she said, "Do you remember the parable of the talents?"

Charity's eyes blazed. "Don't you *dare* attempt to use the scripture to justify this."

I held up a hand for silence and said, "I haven't read this one."

Forthill said, "Three men were given money by their lord in the amount of fifteen, ten, and five silver talents. The man with fifteen invested the money, worked hard, and returned thirty talents to his lord. The man with ten did the same, and returned twenty talents. The lord was most pleased. But the third man was lazy. He buried his five talents in the ground, and when he returned them to the lord, expecting to be rewarded for keeping them safe, his lord was angry. He had not given the lazy man the money to be hidden away. He'd given it to the man so that he could use it and make his lands better, stronger, and more productive. The moral being that, to whom much is given, much is required."

"Oh," I said. "Stan Lee said it better. Or at least faster."

"I'm sorry?" Forthill said.

"Spider-Man. With great power comes great responsibility," I said.

Forthill pursed his lips and nodded. "That *is* faster, I suppose. Though I'm skeptical on how it could be worked into a sermon."

I frowned and glanced at Charity. She had her head bowed, and her hands clenched into fists over and over again. Another insight about her hit me, then.

Charity had been the one given five talents. She'd had the power, and she buried it in the ground.

"My teacher told me something once," I heard myself

say in a quiet voice. "That the hardest lesson in life is learning when to do nothing. To learn to let go."

Molly laid her head in Charity's lap and said, "You know bad things are out there. I have a chance to make a difference. I want to help."

Something inside the steely will of Michael's wife suddenly broke. She gathered Molly up into another hug and just held her there while she shivered. Then Charity whispered, "Of course you do. You're your father's child. How could you want anything else?"

Molly let out a choking little laugh and leaned closer. "Thank you."

"I will pray for you," Charity said quietly. She looked up at me and tried to smile. "And for you, Harry."

Chapter

Forty-three

Forthill led me to a small, cluttered office I was sure was his own. He pointed me at the phone and then shut the door, giving me privacy before I could ask him for it. I sat down on the edge of his desk, got the notebook I kept my contact information in from my duster pocket, and called up the Wardens.

I did a password and countersign routine with the young-sounding woman who answered the phone, after which she asked, in accented English, "What is the nature of your call?"

"A report," I said. "I've got a young woman here who's broken one of the Laws."

"You've captured a warlock?" the woman asked.

"She turned herself in, full cooperation. There are extenuating circumstances around it. I want her to have a hearing."

"A hearing . . ." the young woman said. I heard paper rustling. "Warden, I'm sorry, but I don't think we do hearings anymore."

"Sure we do," I said. "We just haven't had one for ten or twelve years. Pass word to command and tell them we'll use the same location, sundown tomorrow. I'm tasking Warden Ramirez with security."

"I don't know," the woman hedged. She sounded young and uncertain. Our recent losses to the Red Court had created openings for a lot of young wizards, and they had inherited a hellishly dangerous responsibility from the fallen. "I'm not sure if this is appropriate."

"This is how we're doing it," I told her. "All you have to do is get word to Morgan and Luccio. Tell them what I said. Understand?"

"Yes, sir," she said. She sounded almost grateful. "I'll pass word up the line."

"Thank you," I said, and hung up.

I took a deep breath. Word was on its way to the Wardens, and now I was committed.

There was a knock, and then Forthill opened the door. "Finished?"

"Yeah," I said. "Thanks."

"Of course. Is there anything else I might do?"

I shook my head. "You've done more than enough already."

He smiled a little. "Arguable," he said. "Though, may I ask you something?"

I nodded.

"The young man," he said. "Nelson. Is he truly pursued?"

I shook my head. "I don't think so. No reason for him to be. Molly worked a spell on him that forced him to feel fear of drug use."

He frowned. "And you think it brought on a sense of paranoia?"

"She didn't know how badly her own feelings for him would disrupt the spell. She didn't mean to do it, but she laid a world of hurt on the boy." I shook my head. "Paranoia. Nightmares. Phobias. And he's feeling the physical withdrawal from the drugs, to boot. He could be permanently damaged."

"Poor lad," Forthill said.

"I don't know how to begin helping him, Father," I

said. I paused for a moment, then said, "He's an orphan."

Forthill smiled and took off his spectacles. He polished them with a handkerchief. "You may not know where to begin to help. I do. Don't worry, Dresden. The boy won't be left alone."

"Thank you," I said.

"I don't do it for you," he said, "but for the boy. And from obedience to our Lord. But you're welcome."

I put the notebook away and stood up, but Forthill remained in the doorway, his expression direct.

"Tell me," Forthill said. He squinted at his glasses, making sure they were clean. "Do you believe that you'll be able to protect the girl?"

"I think so," I said quietly. I didn't have many friends on the Council. But the ones I did have were on the Senior Council—it's an executive body, especially in wartime. They'd support me. It wouldn't clear the kid completely, but at least she could be placed on a kind of zero-tolerance probation rather than executed.

Forthill watched me with patient, bright blue eyes. "You sound familiar with this situation."

I smiled a little. "Intimately."

"I begin to see," he said.

"Tell me," I said. "Do you really believe what you told Charity about me? That God arranged for me to be there for Molly?"

He regarded me as he replaced his spectacles, bright blue eyes steady. "I do. I know that you don't much hold with religion, Dresden. But I've come to know you over the years. I think you're a decent man. And that God knows His own."

"Meaning what?" I asked.

He smiled and shook his head. "Meaning, mostly, that I have faith that all things work together for the good of those who love the Lord. I meant what I said about you."

I snorted gently and shook my head. "Harry Dresden. I'm on a mission from God."

"Seems an awfully unlikely coincidence, does it not? That the one person Michael knows on the Council should be the one in the position to best help his daughter, just when he was called away?"

I shrugged. "Coincidences happen," I said. "And I don't think God's got me warming up in the bullpen to be one of His champions."

"Perhaps not," Forthill said. "But I think that you are being prepared, nonetheless."

"Prepared?" I asked. "For what? By whom?"

Forthill shook his head. "It's an old man's hunch, that's all. That the things you're facing now are there to prepare you for something greater. Something more."

"God," I said. "I *hope* not. I've got problems enough without working up to bigger ones."

He chuckled and nodded. "Perhaps you're right."

I frowned over a thought. "Padre. Tell me something. Why in the world would the Almighty send Michael off on a mission just when his family most needed him to protect them?"

Forthill arched an eyebrow. "My son," he said, "God knows all things at all times. By His very nature, His omniscience enables Him to know what has happened, is happening, and will happen. Though we might not be able to see His reasons, or to agree with them from our perspectives, they are yet there."

"So what you're saying is that the Almighty knows best, and we just have to trust Him."

Forthill blinked. "Well. Yes."

"Is there any reason that the Almighty couldn't do something blatantly obvious?"

Poor Forthill. He'd been preparing himself for years for a theological duel with the shadowy wizard Dresden, and when the moment came, I wasn't even giving him a real fight. "Well. No. What do you mean?"

"Like maybe the Almighty didn't send Michael away right when he was needed to protect his daughter. Maybe He sent Michael away because that's exactly what He wanted him to do." I let out a short laugh. "If I'm wrong, it would be one hell of a coincidence. . . ." I frowned for a moment, then said, "Do me a favor. Go get Molly for me. Council procedure says that I can't leave her alone. I've got to keep her with me until it's done."

He rose and nodded, agreeable if still slightly baffled. "Very well."

"And I need to know something, Father. Do you know where Michael is right now?"

Forthill shook his head.

"Could you get word to him?" I asked. "I mean, if you really had to?"

He tilted his head, frowning, and asked, "Why?"

"Because I've had an idea," I said. "Can you get in touch with him?"

Forthill smiled.

Chapter

Forty-four

My mechanic's skills bordered on the supernatural. He left word with me that the Beetle was ready to resume active duty, and that while it didn't look like much, the car would roll when I pushed the pedals—which was all I really needed it to do. So Molly and I rolled up to the lakeside warehouse where I'd met with the Council at the start of this mess.

When I shut down the engine, the Beetle rattled and shuddered hard enough to click my teeth together before it died. It continued wheezing and clicking for several seconds afterward.

Molly stared out ahead of her, her face pale. "Is this the place?"

The rundown old warehouse looked different in the orange evening light than it had at high noon. Shadows were longer and darker, and emphasized the flaws and dents in the building, giving the place a much more rundown, abandoned appearance than I had remembered. There were fewer cars there, as well, and it gave the place an even more abandoned atmosphere.

"That's the place," I said quietly. "You ready?"

She swallowed. "Sure," she said, but she looked frightened and very, very young. "What comes next?"

I got out of the car as an answer, and Molly followed suit. I squinted around, but no one was in sight until the air shimmered about twenty feet away and Ramirez stepped out of the veil that had hidden him.

Carlos Ramirez was the youngest wizard ever given the post of regional commander in the Wardens. He was average height, his skin glowing with bronze health, and he wore both the grey cloak of the Wardens and one of their—or rather, *our,* except that I don't have one—silver swords at his left hip. At his right he wore a heavy semi-automatic in a holster, and his military-style web belt also bore several hand grenades.

"Good veil," I said. "Way better than the other day."

"I wasn't here the other day," he assured me with bland confidence.

"Your work?" I asked.

"I make it look easy," he said without a trace of modesty. "It's a curse to be so damned talented when I'm already obscenely good-looking, but I try to soldier on as best I can."

I laughed and offered him my hand. He shook it. "Dresden," he said.

"Ramirez." I nodded to my right. "This is Molly Carpenter."

He glanced at the girl, looking her up and down. "Miss," he said, without a polite bow of his head. He glanced at me, indicated a direction with his hand, and said, "They're ready for you. But walk with me for a minute? I need to talk with you." He glanced at Molly. "Privately."

I arched a brow at him. "Molly, I'll be right back."

She bit her lip and nodded. "O-okay."

"Miss," Ramirez said with a somewhat apologetic smile. "I need you to remain exactly where you're standing now. All right?"

"Hell's bells," I muttered. "You think she's that dangerous?"

"I think it's security protocol," Ramirez said. "If you didn't want me doing it, you shouldn't have asked me."

I started to snarl an answer, but I choked it down and said, "Fine. Molly, just stand there for now. I won't go out of sight of you."

She nodded, and I turned with Ramirez. We walked several paces away over the gravel before he asked, "That the kid?"

Ramirez wasn't old enough to get good car insurance rates himself, much less to refer to someone as "kid," though he'd had to grow up awfully swiftly. He'd been an apprentice when the war with the Red Court erupted, and he'd done good service for the Council upon attaining status as a full wizard, fighting in several nasty engagements with the vampires. It was the kind of thing that made a man age in a hurry.

"That's her," I confirmed. "Did you get a chance to examine the victims?"

"Yeah." He frowned and watched me for a moment before he said, "She's someone you know."

I nodded.

He glanced back at her. "Crud."

I frowned at him. "Why?"

"I don't think today is going to go well for her," Ramirez said.

My stomach suddenly felt cold. "Why not?"

"Because of how the battle in Oregon played out," he said. "Once the forces from Summer attacked their rear, we gave the vamps one hell of a beating. Morgan got within about twenty feet of the Red King himself."

"Morgan killed him?"

"No. But it wasn't for a lack of trying. He cut down a Duke and a pair of Counts before the Red King got away."

"Damn," I said, impressed. "But what does that have to do with Molly?"

"We had the Reds by the balls," Ramirez said. "Sunrise was coming in the real world, and when they tried to retreat into the Nevernever the faeries were on them like a school of piranha. The Reds had to find a way to draw off some of our heavies and they found it. Luccio's boot camp."

I drew in a breath. "They attacked Luccio and the newbies?"

"Yeah. McCoy, Listens-to-Wind, and Martha Liberty led a force from the battle to relieve the camp."

"They did, huh? How'd it go?"

He took a deep breath and said, "They haven't reported in yet. And that means . . ."

"It means that my support in the Senior Council isn't here to help me."

Ramirez nodded.

"Who has their proxies?"

"We didn't hear from you until after they had left, so they didn't entrust their proxies to anyone."

I sighed. "So the Merlin holds them by default. And he doesn't much like me. He'd cast the votes to condemn her just to spite me."

"It gets better," he said. "Ancient Mai is still in Indonesia, and LaFortier is covering the Venatori while they relocate. The Merlin has their votes too—and I don't think the Gatekeeper is coming."

"So the only one whose opinion counts is the Merlin," I said.

"Pretty much." Then Ramirez frowned at me. "You don't look surprised."

"I'm not," I said. "If something can go wrong, it does. I've accepted that by now."

He tilted his head. "I've just told you the kid will probably be found guilty before she's been tried."

"Yeah," I said. I chewed on my lip. This would make things more difficult. I had been counting on at least a little help from Ebenezar and his cronies. They knew the Council procedures better than I did, and how to manipulate them. They also knew the Merlin, who, magical talents aside, was a damned slippery fish when it came to maneuvering through a Council meeting.

The Merlin had every reason to oppose me, and therefore Molly. Now, if he wielded the votes of the people I'd been counting on to support me, he could literally be Molly's judge, jury, and executioner.

Well. Judge and jury, anyway. Morgan would do the executing.

I ground my teeth. My plan could still work, theoretically, but there was very little I could do to alter the outcome from here on in. I glanced back at Molly. Here we were. I'd brought her to this turn. I'd see it through.

"Fine," I said. "I can deal with this."

Ramirez arched an eyebrow at me. "I thought you'd look more upset."

"Would it help anything if I started foaming at the mouth?"

"No," Ramirez said. "It might *explain* a few things, but it wouldn't help, per se."

"Water, bridge," I said. "Spilt milk. Accept things you cannot change."

"In other words, you have a plan," Ramirez said.

I shrugged and smiled tightly at him, and just then a low, throbbing engine approached the old warehouse.

Ramirez's hand went to the butt of his gun.

"Easy," I told him. "I invited them."

A motorcycle wound its way through the maze of alleys and potholes between warehouses, and then crunched to a stop in the gravel beside the Blue Beetle. Fix flipped the bike's kickstand down, and then he and Lily got off the motorcycle. Fix flipped me a little salute, and I nodded back to him.

Ramirez arched an eyebrow and said, "Is that who I think it is?"

"Summer Knight and Lady," I confirmed.

"Well, crap," he said, and scowled at me. "You going to turn this into some kind of fight?"

"Los," I chided him. "Would I do that?"

He gave me a steady look and then said, "You just *had* to ask me to handle security."

"What can I say, man? No one else was pretty and talented enough."

"No one is so talented that you couldn't make him look bad, Dresden," he muttered. Then he gave Lily and Fix a calculating look and said, "Well. This should be interesting, at any rate. Introduce me?"

"Yep."

I did. Then Ramirez led us through the veil protecting the warehouse from perception. Two Wardens at the door searched everyone for weapons. They even had one of the animate statues of a temple dog they used to detect hostile enchantments, veils, and concealed weaponry. The stone construct made me a little nervous—I had nearly been attacked by one over a false alarm once—but this time it passed me by without showing any interest. It lingered longest on Molly, once emitting a grindstone growl, but it subsided after a moment and returned to its post beside the door.

I started to go inside, but Ramirez touched my arm. I stopped and frowned at him. He glanced at Molly and drew a black cloth from his belt.

"You've got to be kidding me," I said.

"It's protocol, Harry."

"It's sadistic and unnecessary."

He shook his head. "I'm not offering an option, here." He lowered his voice so that only I could hear him. "I don't like it either. But if you violate protocol now, *especially* in a case that involves mind-control magic, it will be all the excuse the Merlin needs to declare the proceedings potentially compromised. He'll be able to pass summary judgment on the girl, and put you and me both on precautionary probation."

I ground my teeth, but Ramirez was right. I remembered when I'd been brought before the Council for the first time. One thing, more than any other, stuck in my memory of that night—the scent of the black cloth hood they'd had over my head, over my face. It had smelled slightly of dust, slightly of mothballs, and no light whatsoever had come through to me. Some terrified corner of my brain had noted that so long as the hood was over my face, I wasn't really a person. I was only a creature, a statistic, and one that was a potential threat at that. It would be far easier to pass and mete out a death sentence when one did not have to look at the face of the damned.

I took the hood from Ramirez and turned to Molly. "Don't be afraid," I told her quietly. "I'm not going anywhere."

She stared back into my eyes, terrified and trying to look brave. She swallowed and nodded once, then closed her eyes.

I cast a resentful look at the warehouse. Then I slipped the hood over Molly's pink-and-blue hair and pulled it down over her pale face.

"Good enough?" I asked Ramirez.

It wasn't fair of me to blame him for it, but the note

of accusation in my voice came through far more strongly than I had intended. Ramirez glanced away, shame on his face, and nodded. Then he held open the warehouse door.

I took Molly's hand and led her inside.

Chapter

Forty-five

Blood might not stain a Warden's cloak, but it's all but impossible to get it out of an old, porous concrete floor. The Merlin, Morgan, and a dozen Wardens stood in the same places they had before, a loose circle that surrounded the dark brown stain that yet remained in the spot where the young warlock had been beheaded.

Morgan had a fresh cut on one of his ears and his left wrist was tightly wrapped in medical tape. Even so, he stood calmly and steadily, the sword of the White Council's justice resting with its tip on the floor, his hands folded over the weighted pommel. His expression, as he saw me, was impossible to read. I was used to flat contempt and hostility from the man. Hell, I was used to feeling the same thing about Morgan in reply.

But I'd seen him in action. I'd learned a little bit about what his life was like. I understood what moved him better than I had in the past, and I couldn't simply dislike him anymore. I respected the man. It didn't mean that I wouldn't pants him on national television if I got the opportunity, but I couldn't simply dismiss him outright anymore, either.

I nodded to the man who might be ordered to murder Molly in the next few minutes. It wasn't a friendly nod. It was more along the lines of the salute one gave to an opponent at a fencing match.

He returned it in exactly the same manner, and I somehow sensed that Morgan knew that I wasn't going to let the girl get hurt without a fight. The fingers of his right hand drummed slowly on the hilt of the sword. It wasn't meant as a threat: It was simply a statement. If I fought the White Council's justice, I would be fighting him.

We both knew how that kind of fight would end.

I would never survive it.

We also both knew that, if given the right reasons, I'd do it anyway.

Beside Morgan, the Merlin also watched me, speculation in his features. He knew that I didn't plan on slugging it out if the hearing didn't go Molly's way. In the past, the Merlin might simply have sneered at me, spat in my eye, and dared me to do my worst. Now, he was sure I was up to something else, and I could all but see the gears spinning in his head as I entered holding Molly's hand and guiding her blind steps, followed closely by Fix and Lily.

Morgan nodded to Ramirez, and he went to pull the doors closed and to close the circle around the building, a barrier that would prevent magical intrusion while the Wardens guarded the purely physical approaches. But just before Ramirez reached up to chain the doors closed, they opened to reveal the tall and ominous figure of the Gatekeeper. Dressed in his formal black robes, with a deep purple cowl that left his features shadowed but for the glitter of his dark eyes, the Gatekeeper stood in the doorway for a moment, and something gave me the impression that he was staring at the Merlin.

If so, the Merlin wasn't rattled. The old wizard inclined his head in a regal nod of greeting and respect to the Gatekeeper, and he gestured for the man to join him. Instead, the Gatekeeper walked to a point in the circle midway between the Merlin and myself, and stood quietly, leaning on an aged, slender staff.

The Merlin regarded this positioning for a moment, eyes narrowed, and then addressed the room, in Latin. "Wardens, close the circle. Warden Dresden, please step forward and introduce us to your guests."

I gave Molly's hand a squeeze of reassurance, then let go of her and stepped forward. "First thing," I said, looking around at the dozen or so Wardens present, plus a few other noncombatant Council members who had been in the area or who were on the Senior Council's staff. "Is there anyone here who doesn't understand English?"

The Merlin folded his arms, a slight smile curling his lips. "Council meetings are conducted in Latin."

The old bastard knew that my Latin wasn't so hot. I could understand it pretty well, but speaking it myself tended to result in words being transposed in increasingly odd ways until linguistic surreality ensued. If I tried to defend Molly in Latin, I'd sound like an idiot from the get-go, and the Merlin knew it. While he technically held all the power he needed to quash any defense, he was still accountable to the rest of the Council, so he had to do everything he could to justify his actions. He'd planned on undermining me with Latin from the moment he heard about the conclave.

But I can plan things too.

"Granted that Latin is our traditional lingual medium," I replied, giving the Merlin a big old smile. "But our guests, Lily, the Summer Lady, and Fix, the current Summer Knight, do not speak it. I would fain not show the slightest lack of consideration to such prestigious visitors and envoys of our allies in Summer."

Choke on that, jerk, I thought. *Let's see you snub the ally who just bailed the Council out of ass-deep alligators.*

The Merlin narrowed his eyes and chewed on his options for a moment before he shook his head, unable to find a way to counter the move. "Very well," he said in English, though his tone was grudging. "The Council welcomes the presence of the Summer Lady and Knight in this conclave, and extends its hospitality and protection while they remain within our demesnes."

Lily bowed her head in acknowledgment. "Thank you, honored Merlin."

He bowed his head to her in turn. "Not at all, Your Highness. It is hardly our custom to involve outsiders in confidential internal affairs." He pointedly shifted his gaze back to me. "But given the recent development between our peoples, it would be ungrateful indeed to evict you."

"It would, wouldn't it?" I agreed.

The Merlin's eyes went flat for a moment, but his expression shifted back to neutrality. "Warden Dresden. As a regional commander of the Wardens, you have the authority to summon a conclave in matters pertaining to your duties and your area of command. As soon as it is quite convenient, would you enlighten us as to the purpose of this conclave?"

"Two reasons," I said. "The first is to allow the Summer Lady to address the Senior Council." I turned my head and nodded at Lily, who stepped forward into the circle, while I faded back to stand beside Fix.

"Honored Merlin," she began, her tone serious and formal. "My Queen Titania has bidden me to pass her compliments to you and yours, and for two in particular whose courage has gained the admiration of the Summer Court."

I frowned. "What's this?" I whispered to Fix.

"Shhh," he said. "Pay attention. She'll get there."

"All I needed her to do was verify what we did."

"Be patient," Fix whispered. "She will."

Lily glanced over her shoulder at me and winked. I twitched. It looked exactly like the gesture from the statue that might have been Mab atop the spire at Arctis Tor.

Lily turned to Morgan and said, "Warden Morgan. Your courageous defense of the Venatori and their retainers, and your assault upon the Red King, were feats she has never seen bettered. My Queen extends her compliments and congratulations to you, Warden, and to the Council you serve. Furthermore, she will not let such acts of daring and dedication go unremarked or unrewarded, and so she has bidden me bestow upon you this token."

Lily held up a small, intricately detailed oak leaf of pure silver. She walked over to him and pinned the oak leaf to his grey cloak, just over his heart. "I name thee friend and esquire to the Summer Court, Warden Morgan. An you find yourself in peril near the realm of the Sidhe, once, and once only, you need but touch this device and call aloud upon Titania for aid."

Morgan got an odd look on his face, as though he had tried to make several expressions at once and gotten stuck halfway there. His mouth opened, shut, and then he settled for a deep bow at the waist and replied, "I thank thee, Your Highness."

"What the hell is that?" I whispered to Fix.

The little guy grinned. "The Order of the Silver Oak is nothing to sneeze at. Hush."

Lily smiled, laid a slender hand over the oak leaf in benediction, then walked back over to me. "Warden Dresden," she said. "Your own contribution to the battle is every bit as admirable. My Queen has bid me—"

"His contribution?" the Merlin said, interrupting her.

I blinked at Lily.

"Dresden was not present at the battle," the Merlin protested.

"Indeed not," Lily said, turning while she spoke to address every wizard there with some of her words. "In the late hours two nights ago, Warden Dresden planned and led a small force in a raid upon Arctis Tor itself."

A collective inhalation went through the room, and was followed by a nebulous buzz of murmurs and whispering. The Merlin's poker face was too good to tell me anything about his reaction, but Morgan's eyebrows went up.

"Warden Dresden and his team won through the defenders of the fortress and launched an assault of fire upon the icy wellspring at the heart of Arctis Tor. His actions disrupted the dispositions of the forces of Winter upon our borders, compelling them to retreat to the fortress to deal with the offenders. Once there, the flow of time through the region was slowed, creating an opportunity for our own forces to come to your aid."

"What is she talking about?" I whispered to Fix. "I didn't know I was going there until I got there, and the only fighting left to do was all the fetches."

"Mmmm," Fix murmured back. "And yet not one word she's said has been untrue."

I snorted.

"In short, honored Merlin," Lily continued, "and honorable members of the Council, had Dresden not attacked the lair of Mab herself, the mightiest fortress in Winter, had Dresden not stormed the gates of Arctis Tor, the battle would surely have been lost. Every soul who came safe home again from the battle owes his life to Harry Dresden and his courage."

Silence fell.

She looked slowly around the circle, and let the silence emphasize her previous words far more ably than any speech. "It is for this reason," she said after a moment, "that my Queen confers upon Warden Dresden status as friend and esquire of the Summer Court." She turned to me and pinned another silver leaf over my heart, then laid her hand over it. She looked up at me and smiled. "You, too, may once call upon us at need. Well done, Harry."

She stood on tiptoe and gave me a kiss on the cheek, and then turned to face the Merlin. "My Queen wishes you to know, honored Merlin, that, while glad to be able to go to the aid of the Council against the threat posed by the Red Court, Winter's forces have returned to their original positions, and once again the forces of Summer must remain vigilant of our borders. Until that situation changes, she cautions you that Summer will be able to offer its allies only limited assistance."

The Merlin was staring at me so hard that for a second I thought he hadn't heard Lily's warning. Then he blinked and shook himself a little. "Of course, Your Highness," he said. "Please convey to Her Majesty the gratitude of the White Council and assure her that even in these desperate times, her friendship will not be forgotten."

She bowed her head again. "I shall do so. And so are my duties discharged." She retreated back to her original position, beside Fix.

"Why," I muttered under my breath, "do I get the feeling that Titania handing me a medal can't possibly be as simple as it looks?"

"Because you can tell a hawk from a handsaw when the wind is southerly," Lily murmured in reply. "But it offers you some benefit today." She smiled at me.

"Surely you didn't actually expect a Summer Queen to do simply as you bid her and no more?"

I grumbled something under my breath, while the Merlin turned to confer quietly with Morgan. A general round of whispers rose up as the wizards took the opportunity to bandy rumors and theories around.

I found Molly's cold, trembling hand and squeezed it again.

"What happened?" the girl asked me.

"Lily talked me up like I was a hero," I said. "Everyone seems sort of shocked."

"Can I take this off yet?" Molly asked.

"Not yet," I told her.

"Harry," Ramirez said, stepping over to me. "She's not supposed to speak."

"Yeah, yeah," I muttered to him, and lowered my voice to speak to Molly. "Pipe down, kid. Try not to worry. So far, so good."

Which was true enough. I had managed not to look like an illiterate idiot, and Lily's impromptu medal ceremony had tacitly established my fighting credentials as something comparable to those of the Council's most capable soldier. It didn't mean that Molly was out of the woods, but it would give me a solid foundation for presenting her case. My credibility was everything, and I had done all that I could to establish my presence before the Council.

The Merlin had been in the game a while, and he knew exactly what I was up to. He didn't seem too happy about it. He beckoned the Council's secretary, a dried-up old spider of a man named Peabody, and put his head together with the old man in whispered conference.

"Order," the Merlin called after a moment, and the room settled down immediately. "Warden Dresden," the

Merlin said. "May we continue with your explanation for the necessity of this conclave?"

I stepped back into the circle, tugging Molly along with me until we were standing on the heavy bloodstain where the boy had been executed. There was a psychic remnant of the death there, a cold, quivering tension in the air, an echo of rage and fear and death. Molly shuddered as her feet came to rest atop the stained concrete. She must have felt it, too.

I had a sudden flash, a horrible image of the future, where Molly's body lay in spreading scarlet a few feet from a black cloth bag, so bright and detailed that it almost replaced the reality before me.

Molly shuddered again and whispered, so softly that no one but I could hear, "I'm afraid."

I squeezed her hand and answered the Merlin's question in the manner prescribed by protocol. "I have brought a prisoner before the Council, one who has broken the Fourth Law. I have brought her here to seek justice, Merlin."

The Merlin nodded at me, his expression serious and distant. "This woman with you is the prisoner?"

"This girl is," I replied, and put no emphasis on the correction. "She comes to face the Council openly, of her own will, and in open admission of her wrong."

"And this wrong?" the Merlin asked. "What has she done?"

I looked at Morgan. "She broke the Fourth Law of Magic when she imposed a fear of drug use upon two addicts in order to protect both them and their unborn child from the damage of their addictions."

Morgan stared back at me as I spoke. I thought I saw a faint frown in his eyes.

The Merlin remained silent for half a minute, then

slowly arched one brow. "She violated the free will of another human being."

"She did—but in ignorance, Merlin. She knew neither the Laws nor the side effects of her actions. Her intentions were only to preserve and protect three lives."

"Ignorance of the Law is never an excuse, Warden Dresden, as you well know, and has no bearing upon this judgment." The Merlin glanced at Peabody, then back to me. "I assume you have examined the victims?"

"I have, Merlin."

"And have you had their condition confirmed by another Warden?"

Ramirez stepped forward. "I have done so, Merlin. The psychic trauma was serious, but it is my belief that both will recover."

The Merlin eyed Ramirez. "Is that your opinion, Warden Ramirez? Based, no doubt, upon your extensive experience?"

Ramirez's eyes glittered with anger at the Merlin's tone. "It is the opinion of the duly appointed regional commander of the western United States," he replied. "I believe that the Merlin should remember that he personally appointed me. If it hasn't faded into a blur of senility."

"Warden," Morgan barked, and his tone was one of absolute authority. "You will apologize to the Merlin and moderate your tone. At once."

Ramirez's gaze smoldered, but he glanced at Fix and Lily, and then a little guiltily at Morgan. "Of course, Captain." He drew himself up and gave the Merlin a proper, polite bow. "I ask your forgiveness, Merlin. The last days have been difficult. For everyone."

The Merlin let it hang in the air for a minute. Then his rigid expression softened somewhat, and I saw a flash of bone-deep weariness in the old man's eyes. "Of course," he said in a quieter voice, and bowed his own head. "My choice of words was less polite than it could have been, Warden Ramirez. Please do not take it as a slight upon your performance."

Clever old snake. Establishing himself as oh-so-reasonable and understanding with the younger members of the Council. Or maybe he really was apologizing to Ramirez, who was the unofficial poster boy of the younger generation of wizards. Or, more likely, he was doing both. That was more the Merlin's style.

The Merlin returned his attention to me. "To continue. Warden Dresden, have you soulgazed the prisoner?"

"I have," I said.

"You are convinced of her guilt?"

I swallowed. "I am," I said. "But I am also convinced that her actions do not represent the malice that defines a true warlock."

"Thank you for your *opinion*, Warden Dresden." His voice turned drolly unapologetic. "Doubtless offered to us out of your own extensive experience."

"I beg your pardon, Merlin. But when it comes to the Council sitting in self-righteous, arrogant judgment over a young wizard who made an honest mistake, I believe I have more experience than anyone in this room."

The Merlin's head rocked back as if I had slapped him. I wasn't as subtle and proper as him when it came to insults, but if he was going to do it, I saw no reason not to return fire. I pressed on before he could speak, stepping forward and turning to address the room as I spoke.

"Wizards. Friends. Brothers and sisters in arms. You know why this is happening. You know how thinly stretched our resources have become. In the past three years, the Council has tried and condemned more war-locks than in the past twenty. Children who are raised in societies that do not believe in magic suddenly inherit powers they could hardly have imagined, and certainly cannot control. They have no support. No training. No one to warn them of the consequences or the dangers of their actions."

I reached out and jerked that fucking black hood from Molly's head, and the girl suddenly stood blinking at the light. Tears had streaked her makeup into dark stains running down her face. Her eyes were red with crying, her expression haunted and terrified. She shuddered and lowered her eyes, staring down at the blood-stained floor.

"This is Molly," I said to the room. "She's seventeen years old. Her best friend had already lost one unborn child because of the drugs she'd been addicted to. She knew it was going to happen again. So to protect that child's life, to protect her friends from their addiction, Molly made a choice. She used her power to intervene."

I faced Morgan. "She made a wrong choice. No one denies that. She admits to it herself. But look at her. She's no monster. She understands that what she did was wrong. She understands that she needs help. She submitted herself to this Council's judgment freely. She wants to learn to control her power, to handle it responsibly. She came here hoping to find help and guidance."

Morgan didn't look at me. He was staring at Molly. His fingers kept drumming on the hilt of his sword.

"I've soulgazed her. It's not too late to help her. I think we owe her the chance to redeem herself," I continued. I looked at the Gatekeeper. "For God's sake, wizards, if we are to survive this war, we need all the talent we can get. Molly's death would be a foolish waste."

I drew in a breath and turned to face the Merlin. "There's been enough blood spilled on this floor. I beg you to consider clemency. Levy the Doom of Damocles, if you must, but I beg you to spare her life. I will take personal responsibility for her training and accept the consequences of any actions taken under my mentorship."

Silence fell.

I waited for the Merlin to speak. Molly began trembling harder, and small whimpering sounds came from her throat.

The Merlin's eyes narrowed, and with that single revealing expression I suddenly knew that I'd made a terrible mistake. I'd outmaneuvered him. I'd startled him with my insult and delivered my speech effectively to the wizards present. I could see it on their faces; the uncertainty, the sympathy. More than one wizard had glanced at the bloodstains at my feet and shuddered as I spoke to them. More than one looked at Molly's face, and grimaced in sympathy for her fear.

I'd beaten the Merlin. He knew it.

And he hated it.

I had forgotten to take into account his pride, his ego, his self-image. He was the mightiest wizard on the planet, the leader of the White Council, and he was not accustomed to being insulted and manipulated—and especially not in front of outsiders. I, a mere puppy of a young wizard, had stung him, and his wounded pride sprayed arterial anger. He had it under control, but it was no less terrible or dangerous for that.

"Warden Dresden," he said in a deadly quiet tone. "Your compassion does you credit. But as you yourself pointed out, our resources are spread too thin already. The Council cannot afford to have a regional commander of the Wardens burdened with a hazardous rehabilitation of a warlock. The duties of the war and of containing the increasing occurrence of black magic must have your full attention."

Oh, God.

"The Laws of Magic are clear. The prisoner admits her guilt. I am not unmoved by the prisoner's plight, but we are involved in a war for our very survival."

Ohgodohgodohgod . . .

"I therefore take no pleasure in pronouncing the prisoner's fate. It is the judgment of the Senior Council that the prisoner is a warlock, guilty of breaking the Fourth Law." He lifted his chin and said, very calmly, "The sentence is death. To be carried out immediately."

Chapter

Forty-six

"**M**organ," the Merlin said quietly.

Morgan stared at Molly. Then at the Merlin. He drew in a sharp breath and took a grip on the sword, lifting it vertically before him.

I looked frantically around the room. Ramirez, like most of the rest of the wizards there, had a stunned look on his face. He looked back at me with a blank expression, and gave me a little twitch of his shoulders. Lily looked remote and troubled. Fix's expression was blank, but his jaws were clenched hard, muscles standing out and creating shadows on his face.

"Harry?" Molly whispered, shaking so hard she could hardly speak. "Harry?"

I turned back to the Merlin. His eyes were hard, his face as unyielding as stone. Morgan looked as if he might be about to throw up—but it didn't stop him from moving toward Molly with a steady, dreamlike slowness, sword in hand.

"Harry," Molly sobbed.

I promised Charity.

I took my staff in both hands and stepped forward, putting myself between Morgan and the girl. "Morgan," I said. "Stars and stones, man. Please don't do this. She's a *child*. We should be *helping* her."

My words slowed him, and he froze in place for a terrible heartbeat. Then he closed his eyes and swallowed, his face twisting with nausea. He opened his eyes again and whispered, "Stand aside, Dresden. Please."

I looked wildly around the room for someone, anyone to help, for some way to stop this madness. I felt a sudden pressure against my spine, and I looked over my shoulder.

My eyes fell on the Gatekeeper.

I whirled back to Morgan and lifted my hands. "Point of order!" I cried. "Point of order! The Senior Council has not yet made its decision."

Morgan paused, head tilting, and frowned at me. He lowered the sword and glanced back at the Merlin.

"The Senior Council has decided the issue," the Merlin snarled.

"No," I said. "The Senior Council must decide any capital crime in an open vote." I pointed my finger at the Gatekeeper. "He has not cast his vote."

The Merlin spoke through clenched teeth. "I hold six of seven votes. However the honored Gatekeeper decides, it will not change the outcome."

"True," I said. "But that doesn't change the fact that he gets a damned vote."

"Why are you doing this?" the Merlin demanded. "It is over. You only torment the prisoner with this unnecessary charade."

"He gets a vote," I repeated, and folded my arms on my chest.

The Merlin stared at me hard, and I could actually sense the pressure of his rage, like the end of a baseball bat poking steadily at my chest.

Morgan said, very, *very* quietly, "He's right, honored Merlin."

The Merlin narrowed his eyes. Then he turned his head to the Gatekeeper. "As you wish. We shall play this farce to its conclusion. Gatekeeper, how find you in this matter?"

And the Gatekeeper said . . . nothing.

He just stood there, face almost invisible beneath his cowl.

"Gatekeeper!" the Merlin called. "How find you?"

"I find the need for deliberation," the Gatekeeper responded. "I beg the Council's indulgence while I ponder this matter."

"Ridiculous," the Merlin said.

The Gatekeeper tilted his head. "Death is rather final, honored Merlin. I must consider carefully before I consign a soul, any soul, no matter how guilty, to that end."

"This is nonsense. It will make no difference how you vote."

"True," the Gatekeeper replied, very gently, the faintest shade of rebuke in his voice. "But that does not change my moral obligation to make this decision with care."

The Merlin took a deep breath and then said, forced calm in his voice, "I suppose a few moments for thought are not unreasonable."

"Thank you," the Gatekeeper said gravely.

Five minutes went by like five thousand years. Molly sagged against me, so frightened she could barely stand.

"Enough," the Merlin said, finally. "This travesty needs to end."

"On that point," the Gatekeeper said, "we agree." And then he stepped forward to the circle marked on the floor, and smudged it with his boot, breaking the circle. He flicked a gloved hand, and the lock on the chained door sprang open and fell away, followed closely by the chains.

"What is the meaning of this?" the Merlin demanded.

The Gatekeeper ignored him and pushed open the door. One of the Wardens on guard outside stood in front of it, one hand raised as if to knock. He blinked at the Gatekeeper, and then looked over his shoulder and said, "It's open, sir."

"Get clear of the door, fool," barked Ebenezar's voice. "Get them inside. Hurry, man! They're right behind us!"

Outside there was an eerie howl and a sudden detonation of thunder that shook the concrete floor. Young people in roomy brown robes began to hurry through the doorway, most of them around Molly's age or a bit younger. They were led by a young woman with short, curly hair and cheeks that had a dimple even when she wasn't smiling—Luccio, the commander of the Wardens, in the young body a necromancer had trapped her in. The kids must have been her trainees.

She was followed by more children and a tall, brawny woman with dark skin and short, iron grey hair, helping a lanky young man with a wounded leg. Martha Liberty helped the young man settle to the ground and barked out a command for a medical kit. An old man with braided hair and Native American features brought up the rear, shepherding the last few young wizards ahead of him. "Injun Joe" Listens-to-Wind made sure they were all inside, and then turned and shouted, "I'm closing the way now!"

There were several more howls, and a bell-like chime of steel. Something hit the wall of the warehouse hard enough to shake dust from the rafters. Then there was a rushing sound of wind that abruptly ended in heavy silence. Listens-to-Wind sagged and leaned against the doorway, panting. Then he rose and stood aside as Ebenezar McCoy came in.

My old mentor was wearing his usual overalls and T-shirt. His bald pate shone with sweat, and he looked tired, but he was smiling over the pugnacious set of his lower jaw. The air around him fairly crackled with intensity, a mantle of power that hung around him in a subtle haze. Ebenezar reached behind him to hold the door open.

Michael came in.

He wore his white cloak, his mail and breastplate, and he bore *Amoracchius* in his hands, stained with dark fluids. He glanced around the room, a smile firm on his face.

"Papa!" Molly shrieked, and threw herself at him.

Michael blinked and managed to get the sword out of the way before Molly hit him with a hug that nearly knocked him from his feet. He got an arm around her, smiling. "Ooof! Careful, girl, the old man needs his ribs right where they are."

"Who the hell is this?" Ramirez demanded, frowning at Michael. He looked like he didn't know whether to be upset or disturbed that an armed and armored stranger had just waltzed in and was now standing inside all of his security measures.

"He's a bloody hero is what he is," Ebenezar told him. "If he hadn't come along when he did, not a one of us would have gotten out of there alive." He offered Michael his hand. "I've only heard of you by reputation, Sir Knight. But I've got to say that I'm damned glad to meet you. Thank you."

Michael grinned and juggled his sword and his daughter so he'd have a hand free to shake Ebenezar's. "I'm only a servant," he said. "Any thanks are rightly owed to Him, not to me."

"Aye," Ebenezar said. "And thank God you came, Sir Knight."

"Secure the building," said the Merlin in a quiet voice. He walked forward to see what was happening, and stopped beside me. Michael nodded and moved out, tapping Ramirez and another Warden, and the three of them went to make sure the bad guys weren't still coming.

"Vote isn't over," I said in a very quiet voice. "Which means that the three of them will need to cast their votes as well."

"Obviously," the Merlin said in a neutral murmur.

"That's Michael. Knight of the Cross."

"Which Sword?" the Merlin asked idly.

"*Amoracchius,*" I said.

The Merlin lifted a brow and nodded, never looking at me.

"Looks like he just saved . . . about forty of our young people?"

"So it would seem," the Merlin said.

"Seems like the least we can do is save one of his."

The Merlin's eyes narrowed, and he did not speak.

"Look at it this way," I said quietly. "There's no downside to this for you. If you're wrong about Molly, the Council gets another wizard. Fairly talented one, too."

"And if I'm right?" he asked quietly.

"If you're right," I said, "you still get to kill the girl."

The Merlin glanced at me. "True," he said. "And you with her."

Forty-seven

After a second, much less lengthy round of questions and answers, the Senior Council voted, and Molly was officially declared my apprentice, to be granted clemency under the Doom of Damocles. "Doom of Damocles" was wizard-speak for probation. If Molly abused her magic or came anywhere near violating any of the Laws of Magic, she'd be executed at once—and I'd join her.

But I'd lived with that before. I could do it again.

It was full dark by the time the conclave ended and everyone filed out. As the wizard who had called the conclave, it was my job to make sure everyone departed safely and to take care of any last-minute details.

Between providing food and further medical supplies for the unexpected arrivals, and coordinating with Ramirez to make sure our comings and goings weren't being observed, I didn't get the chance to speak to anyone about personal matters. With Lily's help, we'd given the vampires a stiff kick in the balls, but the fight was far from over. The combat-hardened wizards and the talents of the Senior Council were needed elsewhere, and they departed with hardly a pause for food and drink.

Once it was done, I left the warehouse and sank down against the wall, just letting the cool summer evening wash over me.

I'd saved the girl from the bad guys. And more importantly, from the good guys. Which seemed the sort of thing that should pay my Warden's salary overtime, but for the moment I was simply glad it was over.

I'd gambled horribly in my attempt to play the collective will of the Council against the Merlin. I shouldn't have done it that way. The Merlin was a politician. If I'd been willing to eat a little crow, he probably would have come to some sort of compromise with me. A humiliating and disadvantageous compromise, from my perspective, but he might have worked something out.

Instead, I'd gained the moral support of the Council present there tonight, and I'd wielded it against him like a sword, chopping off his options and maneuvering him into bending to my will. I had exercised power over him in a way that no one had yet dared. I had struck a blow against his authority, declared myself an enemy of his administration. There was no way he could ignore that kind of challenge from a morally suspect young punk like me. He would have to bring me down. If I wanted to avoid that, I'd have to keep my eyes open, my wits sharp, and I'd have to continue to do whatever I could to secure myself against him.

In short: I'd become a politician.

But instead of moaning about it, I found myself laughing. Given all that had happened, matters could have been much, much worse. Molly was coming home safe. The murderous fetches had been dispatched. The vampires had been handed their first significant defeat since the cold war combusted.

After the events of the day, tomorrow surely held nothing for me to fear, and I trusted that it would take care of itself until I could rest, eat, and put an end to the last details of the business at hand.

Molly and Michael had waited with me: When Michael covered Luccio's retreat through the nearer regions of the Nevernever, he had gotten back to Chicago without paying for the gas, but his truck was still back in the middle of nowhere, Oregon. He'd need to have it shipped back, or else make a long drive with a partner. He needed a ride home, and I was it.

The Beetle's floorboards settled almost all the way to the ground by the time everyone was on board, and I drove carefully away from the warehouse. Molly chattered on about a confusing blur of things for maybe two minutes and then went abruptly silent.

Michael checked over his shoulder. "Asleep," he reported quietly.

"She's had a busy day," I said.

He sighed. "Tell me what happened?"

I told him everything. Except the parts with Lasciel in them. And I didn't mention Charity's neglected talent for magic. I thought for a second that I could hear a ghostly, amused laugh from somewhere nearby. Optimistically, I wrote it off to my fatigued imagination.

Michael shook his head. "How did you know that I would return as I did?"

"Oh, I didn't," I said. "I just figured that you must have been sent off to do *something* to help your kid, so I asked Forthill to get word to you that you needed to be back here pronto, and that if you were with any Council members they should come with you. You got the message?"

He nodded. "It found me at Luccio's camp in Colorado. We'd beaten off a vampire attack and were preparing to move. If I hadn't gotten the message, I wouldn't have followed them on their path through the Nevernever."

"What happened?"

"Demons," Michael said. "Quite a few of them, actually."

"What kind?"

"Oh. Fangs. Tentacles. You know, the usual."

I snorted. "No. I mean, were they Outsiders?"

"Ebenezar said something about Outsiders, yes, now that you mention it. Apparently his magic had difficulty dealing with them."

I shook my head. "I'm glad you were with them."

"Under the circumstances, so am I." He pursed his lips thoughtfully. "You assumed I had been sent to help the White Council so that they would show mercy to my daughter."

I shrugged. "It was either that or else I was the one meant to look out for her, which would mean that it was possible for me to do so. So I decided to lean on the Merlin."

Michael blinked and stared at me. "If I do not mistake your meaning, you just told me that you took a leap of faith."

"No. I took *your* leap of faith, by proxy." I shook my head. "Look, Michael. I try to stay out of God's way as much as I possibly can. I don't expect Him to send a rescue party for me if I'm in trouble."

"Harry, I know you aren't a churchgoing man, but God does help people who aren't perfect."

"Sure," I said, and I couldn't keep all the sneer out of my voice. "That's why the world is such a happy, orderly place."

Michael sighed. "Harry, God does protect us from harm—it's part of what I and my brothers in arms are tasked to do. But He's a great deal less involved in protecting us from the consequences of our choices."

"I know the theory," I said. "That God mostly only steps in when there's supernatural evil afoot, yeah?"

"That's an oversimplification, really, and—"

"Spare me," I said. "Hell, Michael, I had one of those

bastard Denarians here last year. Quintus Cassius. You remember him? While I was lying there watching him slice his way into my guts, I thought maybe it would be a good time for someone like you to show up. You know. One of those Denarian Knights. I thought to myself, hey, it would be a great time for one of the Knights of the Cross to show up, eh?" I shook my head. "It didn't work out that way."

"What is your point?" he asked quietly.

"Heaven ain't safeguarding me, Michael. But you're different than me. I figured God was going to look out for you and yours, out of professional courtesy if nothing else. And I've seen how He's arranged things for you in the past. So what I did wasn't about faith. It was just a matter of deducing probabilities."

He shook his head, not agreeing with me, but not pressing it, either. "Charity?"

"She's fine," I assured him. "Kids too. Should be back home by now."

"She and Molly?"

"Reconciled. Well. On polite speaking terms and hugging again, at least."

His eyebrows shot up, and then his mouth curved into a wide grin. "Glory to God, I wasn't sure it would ever happen."

I buffed my nails on my shirt. "Sometimes I amaze even myself."

Michael smiled at me, then looked over his shoulder again and frowned. "My Molly. Magic. Isn't that sort of thing passed through bloodlines?"

"Usually," I said. "But it doesn't have to be. Some people are just born with it. We don't really understand the how and why."

He shook his head. "But how could I not have realized what was happening to her?"

"I dunno. But if you find out, make sure to tell Charity. She asked me the same question."

"I suppose we're all blind to what is closest to us," he said.

"Human nature," I agreed.

"Is Molly in danger?" he asked me, his tone frank.

I frowned and thought about it. "Some. She's got real power. And she's abused it a little. She's going to be real tempted to use it again when she starts running into problems that look unsolvable. Not only that, but learning to harness the kind of strength she's got can be pretty tricky all by itself. But she's smart and she's got all kinds of guts. If her teacher keeps from making any stupid mistakes, I think she'll be all right."

"But if she isn't," Michael said. "If she abuses her power again . . ."

"Then clemency is revoked. They execute her."

"And you," Michael said softly.

I shrugged. "Isn't like I haven't lived with that over my head before. As far as the Council is concerned, I'm responsible for her now, until she either makes full wizard or sets her talents aside."

"Greater love hath no man," he said quietly. "Nothing I can say would be enough. She's my daughter, Harry. Thank you."

I felt my cheeks heat up. "Yeah, yeah. Look, don't make a big deal out of this. No one will enjoy that."

He let out a rumbling chuckle. "And this apprenticeship. What will it entail?"

"Lessons. Every day, at first, until I'm sure she's got herself under control. We'll have to practice some of it away from anything combustible. Trees, houses, pets, that kind of thing."

"How long will you need to work with her?"

"Until we're finished," I said, waving a vague hand.

"I don't know yet. I've never been on this side of an apprenticeship."

He nodded in acceptance. "Very well." We rode in silence for a moment. Then he said, "You remember the professional discussion I wanted to have?"

"Yeah," I said. "Shoot."

"*Fidelacchius,*" Michael said. "I was wondering if you found any candidates for a new wielder."

"Zippo," I said, frowning. "You think I should be looking?"

"Hard to say. But with only two of us in the field, Sanya and I are getting a little overworked."

I scratched my chin. "Shiro told me that I would know the wielder. There hasn't been anything like that. At least, not yet."

"I'm concerned that it may take more than simply patience," Michael sighed. "I've consulted our records. This is not the first time one of the White Council has been asked to be the custodian of one of the Swords."

I arched my eyebrows and looked at him. "Seriously?"

He nodded.

"Me and who?"

"Merlin."

I snorted. "You sure? Because the Merlin is kind of a jerk. Even you would think so, trust me."

"No, Harry," Michael said, his tone patient. "Not the Merlin of the Council. *Merlin.* The original."

I sat there with my jaw suavely flapping in the breeze for a minute. Then said, "Wow." I shook my head. "You think maybe I should find a big rock or something? Stick the sword in and leave it on the White House lawn?"

Michael crossed himself. "Heaven forbid. No. I just have an . . ." He scrunched up his nose. "An instinct."

"You mean like when you get sent out on a mission from God?"

"No. I mean a regular old human hunch. I think that perhaps you should investigate the history around how *Amoracchius* was passed on, back then."

Said sword now rested at a slant across Michael's chest, safely in its scabbard, point between the knight's boots.

"Wow. You mean . . . *that* sword right there. *Your* sword is . . ." I left it unsaid.

"Probably," he said, nodding. "Though the Church's records are fragmented, we've managed to establish that the other two Swords have been reworked from time to time, through the years. This one hasn't."

"That's interesting," I mused quietly. "That's interesting as he—uh, as heck."

Michael gave me a faint smile and nodded. "It's an intriguing mystery, isn't it?"

"You know what?" I said. "I can do mystery." I chewed my lip for a minute and said, "But I hope you're not in a hurry. You may have noticed that the Council is having a busy year. I'll have time sooner or later, but for now . . ." I shrugged.

"I know." He was quiet for a moment, and then said, "But knowing the sword's history could become important. Sooner is better than later."

Something odd in his tone made me look at him. "Why?"

His hand moved unconsciously to *Amoracchius*'s hilt. "I don't think I'll have the sword for much longer." His voice was very soft.

When the Knights of the Sword retired, they did it feetfirst from the inside of a box.

"Michael?" I asked. "Did the, uh, office send you a memo?" I carefully didn't say *Like they did with Shiro*.

"No. Instinct," he said, and smiled at me. "But I suppose I could be beginning my midlife crisis. But I'm not planning to change the way I live my life, and I certainly have no intention of an early retirement."

"Good," I said, though it came out more somber than I'd intended.

"Do you mind if I ask you something personal?" Michael said.

"I'm way too busy to answer rhetorical questions."

He grinned for a second and nodded. Then he pursed his lips and took his time about choosing his words. "Harry, you've avoided me for some time. And you seem . . . well, somewhat more dour than I've seen you before."

"I wasn't avoiding you, exactly," I said.

He regarded me with calm, steady eyes.

"All right," I said. "Yeah. But I've been avoiding most everybody. Don't take it personally."

"Is it something I've done? Or perhaps someone in my family?"

"Enough with the rhetoric. You know it isn't."

He nodded. "Then maybe it's something you've done. Maybe something you should talk about with a friend."

The fallen angel's sigil on my left palm throbbed. I started to say "no," but stopped myself. I drove for another block or two. I should tell him. I really should. Michael was my friend. He deserved my trust and respect. He deserved to know.

But I couldn't.

Then my mouth started moving, and I realized that what was bothering me the most had nothing to do with coins or fallen angels. "Last Halloween," I said quietly, "I killed two people."

He drew in a slow breath and nodded, listening.

"One of them was Cassius. Once he was beaten, I

had Mouse break his neck. Another was a necromancer called Corpsetaker. I shot her in the back of the head." I swallowed. "I murdered them. I've never killed, man . . . not like that. Cold." I drove a while more. "I have nightmares."

I heard him sigh. For a moment, his voice was bleak. Pained. "I've been in this business longer than you have. I know some of what you're feeling."

I didn't answer him.

"You feel like nothing is ever going to be right again," he said. "You remember it perfectly, and it won't leave you alone. You feel like you're walking around with a sharp rock in your shoe. You feel stained."

Stupid damned streetlights, getting all blurry like that. I blinked a lot and stayed quiet. My throat was too tight to speak, anyway.

"I know what it's like," he said. "There isn't any way to make it disappear. But it gets better with time and distance." He studied me for a moment. "If you had it to do again, would you?"

"Twice as hard," I said at once.

"Then what you did was a necessity, Harry. It might be painful. It might haunt you. But at the end of the day, so long as you did what you believed right, you'll be able to live with yourself."

"Yeah?" I asked, chewing on my lower lip.

"I promise," he said.

I darted a glance at him. "You don't . . . think less of me? Knowing that I'm a murderer?"

"It isn't my place to judge what you've done. I regret that those lives were lost. That their owners never found redemption. I worry for the pain you've inflicted on yourself in retrospect. But I don't for an instant think that you would choose to take a human life unless you absolutely had to."

"Seriously?"

"I trust you," Michael said, his voice calm. "I would never have left my family in your protection if I didn't. You're a decent man, Harry."

I exhaled slowly and my shoulders loosened. "Good." And then, before my brain could get in the way, I added, "I picked up one of the Blackened Denarii, Michael. Lasciel."

My heart skipped several beats as I made the admission.

I expected shock, horror, outrage, maybe with a side order of contempt.

But instead, Michael nodded. "I know."

I blinked at him. "You what?"

"I know," he repeated.

"You know. You *knew*?"

"Yes. I was taking the trash around the house when Nicodemus's car went by. I saw the whole thing. I saw you protecting my youngest."

I chewed on my lip. "And . . . I mean, you aren't going to slug me and drag me off to a private suite in the Asylum for Wayward Denarians?"

"Don't be ridiculous," Michael said. "Remember that the Knights of the Cross were not founded to destroy the Denarians. We were founded to save them from the Fallen. It is therefore my duty to help you in whatever way I can. I can help you discard the coin if that is what you wish to do. It's best if you choose to do it yourself."

"I don't need to discard it, actually," I said. "I haven't really taken the coin up. I buried it. Never used it."

Michael looked surprised. "No? That is good news, then. Though it means that the Fallen's shadow is still attempting to persuade you, I take it?"

This time the mental chuckle was a little more clear. I

thought *Oh, shut up* very hard and sent it in Lasciel's direction.

"Trying," I said.

"Keep in mind that Lasciel is a deceiver," he said quietly. "One with thousands of years of practice. It knows people. It knows how to tell you lies you want to believe are true. But it exists for a single purpose—to corrupt the will and beliefs of mankind. Don't ever forget that."

I shuddered. "Yeah."

"May I ask what it's told you?" He paused and narrowed his eyes. "No, wait. Let me guess. It's appeared to you as an attractive young woman. She offers you knowledge, yes? The benefit of her experience."

"Yeah." I paused and added, "And Hellfire. Makes my spells hit harder when I need them to. I try not to use it much."

Michael shook his head. "Lasciel isn't called the Temptress for nothing. She knows you. Knows what to offer you and how to offer it."

"Damn right she does." I paused a moment, then added, "It scares me sometimes."

"You've got to get rid of the coin," he said with gentle urgency.

"Love to," I said. "How?"

"Give up the coin of your own will. And set aside your power. If you do, Lasciel's shadow will dwindle with it and waste away."

"What do you mean, set aside my power?"

"Walk away from your magic," he said. "Forsake it. Forever."

"Fuck that."

He winced and looked away.

The rest of the trip to his home passed in silence. When we got there, I told Michael, "Molly's stuff is back at my place. I'd like to take her back there to get it. I need to have a talk with her, tonight, while everything is fresh. I'll have her back here in a couple of hours, tops."

Michael glanced at his sleeping daughter with a worried frown, but nodded. "Very well." He got out and shut the door, then leaned back in the window to speak to me. "May I ask you two things?"

"Shoot."

He glanced back at his house and said, "Have you ever considered the possibility that the Lord did not send me out on my most recent mission so that I could protect my daughter? That it was not His intention to use you to protect her?"

"What's your point?"

"Only that it is entirely possible, Harry Dresden, that this entire affair, beginning to end, is meant to protect *you*. That when I went to the aid of Luccio and her trainees, I did so not to free Molly, but to prevent you from coming to blows with the Council. That her position as your new apprentice had less to do with protecting her than it did protecting *you*?"

"Eh?" I said.

He glanced at his daughter. "Children have their own kind of power. When you're teaching them, protecting them, you are more than you thought you could be. More understanding, more patient, more capable, more wise. Perhaps this foster child of your power will do the same for you. Perhaps it's what she is meant to do."

"If the Lord was all that interested in helping out, how come He didn't send someone to help me against Cassius? One of old Nick's personal yes-men? Seems to be a solid rescue scenario."

Michael shrugged and opened his mouth.

"And don't give me any of that mysterious ways tripe."

He shut his mouth and smiled. "It's a confusing sort of thing," he said.

"What is?"

"Life. I'll see you in a couple of hours."

He offered me his hand. I shook it.

"I don't know of another way to end Lasciel's influence, but that doesn't mean there isn't one out there. If you should change your mind about the coin, Harry, if you want to get rid of it, I promise that I'll be there for you."

"Thank you," I said, and meant it.

His expression grew more sober. "And if you should fall to temptation. If you should embrace the Fallen or become ensnared by its will . . ." He touched the hilt of the great sword, and his face became bedrock granite, Old Testament determination that made Morgan's fanaticism look like a wisp of steam. "If you change. I will also be there."

Fear hit me in a cold wave.

Holy crap.

I swallowed, and my hands shook on the Beetle's steering wheel. There wasn't any attempt at menace in Michael's voice, or his face. He was simply stating a fact.

The mark on my palm burned, and for the first time I gave serious consideration to the notion that maybe I was overconfident of my ability to deal with Lasciel. What if Michael was right? What if I screwed something up and wound up like that poor bastard Rasmussen? A demonically supercharged serial killer?

"If that happens," I told him, and my voice was a dry whisper, "I want you to."

I could see in his eyes that he didn't like the thought any more than I did—but he was fundamentally incapable of being anything less than perfectly honest with me.

He was my friend, and he was worried. If he had to do harm to me, it would rip him apart.

Maybe the words had been his own subconscious way of begging me to get rid of the coin. He could never stand aside and do nothing while bad things happened, even if meant that he had to kill his friend.

I could respect that. I understood it, because I couldn't do it, either. I couldn't stand aside, abandon my magic, and cut myself loose of the responsibility to use it for good.

Not even if it killed me.

Life can be confusing. Good God, and how. Sometimes it seems like the older I get, the more confused I become. That seems ass-backwards. I thought I was supposed to be getting wiser. Instead, I just keep getting hit over the head with my relative insignificance in the greater scheme of the universe. Confusing, life.

But it beats the hell out of the alternative.

I went back to my place. I let the kid sleep until we got there, and then touched her shoulder with one hand. She jerked awake at once, blinking in weary confusion.

"Where are we?" she asked.

"My place," I said. "We need to talk."

She blinked her eyes several more times and then nodded. "Why?"

"Because you need to understand something. Come on."

We got out of the car. I led her down the steps to my door and said, "Come stand next to me." She did. I took her left hand and told her, "Spread your fingers and close your eyes." She did that too. I held her left palm up about two inches from the door. "Now, focus. See what you can feel."

Her face scrunched up. "Um," she said, shifting her

weight back and forth restlessly. "There's . . . pressure? Um, or maybe a buzzing. Like high-power lines."

"Close enough," I said, and released her wrist. "What you're sensing are some of the energies that I used to ward my apartment. If you try to come in without disabling them, you'll take a jolt of electricity that wouldn't leave much more of you than a smudge on the ground."

She blinked at me, then twitched and pulled her hand sharply away.

"I'll give you an amulet that will let you get through, until I'm sure you can disable them, go in, and start them up again. But for tonight, just don't try to open the door. In or out. Okay?"

"Okay," she said quietly.

We went in. My cleaning service had come through. Molly had left a bag with clothes and sundries spread over half of one of my apartment's couches. Now the bag was neatly closed, and suspiciously nonbulgy. I'm sure the cleaning service had folded and organized the bag so that everything fit in without strain.

Molly looked around, blinking. "How does your maid get in?"

"I don't know what you mean," I said, because you can't talk about faerie housekeepers or they go away. I pointed at the couch next to her bag and said, "Sit."

She did, though I could tell that my peremptory tone did not thrill her.

I sat down in a chair across from the couch. As I did, Mister drifted in from the bedroom and promptly wound himself around one of Molly's legs, purring a greeting.

"Okay, kid," I said. "We survived. I only had some very limited plans to cover this contingency."

She blinked at me. "What?"

"I didn't think I'd pull this off. I mean, raiding a faerie capital? Standing up to the Senior Council? All those movie monsters? Your mom? Hell, I'm shocked I survived at all, much less got you out of it."

"B-but . . ." She frowned. "You never seemed like . . . I mean, you just went through it all like you had everything under control. You seemed so sure what was going to happen."

"Rule number one of the wizarding business," I said. "Never let them see you sweat. People expect us to know things. It can be a big advantage. Don't screw it up by looking like you're as confused as everyone else. Bad for the image."

She smiled at me a little. "I see," she said. She reached down to stroke Mister and mused, "I must look horrible."

"Been a rough day," I said. "Look. We'll need to talk about where you're going to live. I take it that you had already decided to break things off with Nelson. I kind of picked up that vibe when we bailed him out."

She nodded.

"Well. Inappropriate to stay with him, then. To say nothing of the fact that he's going to need time to recover."

"I can't stay at home," she said quietly. "After all that's happened . . . and my mom will never understand about the magic. She thinks it's all bad, every bit of it. And if I'm there, it's just going to confuse and frighten all the little Jawas, Mom and me arguing all the time."

I grunted and said, "You'll have to stay somewhere. We'll work that out soonest."

"All right," she said.

"Next thing you need to know," I said. "As of now, you get no slack. You aren't allowed any mistakes. You don't get to say 'oops.' The first time you screw up and slip deeper into bad habits, it kills both of us. I'm going to be tough on you sometimes, Molly. I have to be. It's as much for my survival as yours. Got it?"

"Yes," she said.

I grunted, got up, and went to my tiny bedroom. I rooted around in my closet and found an old brown apprentice robe one of the shiny new Wardens had left at my place after a local meeting. I brought it out and handed it to Molly. "Keep this where you can get to it. You'll be with me at any Council meetings, and it is your formal attire." I frowned and rubbed at my head. "God, I need aspirin. And food. You hungry?"

Molly shook her head. "But I'm a mess. Do you mind if I clean up?"

I eyed her and sighed. Then I said, "No. Go ahead and get it out of the way." I stood up and went to the kitchen, muttering a minor spell and flicking several candles into light, including one near the girl. She took the robe and the candle, grabbed her bag, and vanished into my room.

I checked the icebox. The faeries usually brought some kind of food to stock the icebox and the pantry when they cleaned, but they could have mighty odd ideas about what constituted a healthy diet. One time I'd opened the pantry and found nothing but boxes and boxes and boxes of Froot Loops. I had a near-miss with diabetes, and Thomas, who never was quite sure where the food came from, declared that I had clearly been driven Froot Loopy.

Usually it wasn't that bad, though there was always a high incidence of frozen pizza, for which my housekeepers maintained the ice in my icebox with religious fervor. I often left most of a pizza lying around uneaten when I figured they'd be coming to visit, and thus continued my policy of shamelessly bribing my way into the Little Folk's good graces.

I was too tired to cook anything, and nothing was going to taste good anyway, so I slapped several hot dogs between two pieces of bread along with a couple of lettuce leaves and wolfed them down.

I got out some of my ice and dumped it in a pitcher, then filled the pitcher up. I got down a glass and filled it with ice water. Then I and my glass and my pitcher moseyed over to my fireplace. I set the pitcher on the mantel, idly flipped the neatly laid fire to life with my ignition spell, and then waited for the inevitable while sipping cold water and staring down at the fire. Mister kept me company from his spot on top of a bookcase.

It took her a little while to work up to it, but not as long as I had expected. My bedroom door opened and Molly appeared.

She had showered. Her candy-colored hair hung limp and clinging. She'd washed away the makeup entirely, but there were spots of pink high on her cheeks that I figured had little to do with cosmetics. The various piercings I could see caught the firelight in a deep, burned orange glow.

She was also barefoot. And wearing her brown robe.

I arched an eyebrow at her and waited.

She flushed more deeply and then walked over to me, quite slowly, until she stood not a foot away.

I gave her nothing to work with. No expression. No words. Just silence.

"You looked into me," she whispered quietly. "And I looked into you."

"That's how it works," I confirmed in a quiet, neutral voice.

She shivered. "I saw what kind of man you are. Kind. Gentle." She looked up and met my eyes. "Lonely.

And . . ." She flushed a shade pinker. "And hungry. No one has touched you in a very long time."

She lifted a hand and put it on my chest. Her fingers were very warm, and a rippling flush of purely biological reaction bypassed my silly brain and raced through me in a wave of pleasure—and need. I looked down at Molly's pale hand. Her palm glided over my chest, barely touching, a slow, focused circle. I felt faintly disgusted with myself for my reaction. Hell. I'd known this kid before she'd had to worry about feminine hygiene products.

I managed to thwart my hormones' lobby to start growling or drooling, but my voice had gotten a shade or two huskier. "Also true."

She looked up at me again, her eyes wide and deep and blue enough to drown in. "You saved my life," she said, and I heard her voice shaking. "You're going to teach me. I . . ." She licked her lips and moved her shoulders. The brown robe slipped down them to the floor.

The tattoo that began on her neck went all the way down to her pierced navel. She had several other studs and fine rings in places I had suspected (but never confirmed) they would be. She shivered and took swifter breaths. The firelight played merrily with her shifting contours.

I'd seen better. But mostly that had been from someone using her looks to get something out of me, and the difference had largely been one of presentation. Molly didn't have much experience in displaying herself for a man, or in playing the coquette. She should have stood differently, arched her back, shifted her hips, worn an expression of thickly sensual interest, daring me to come after her. She would have looked like the patron goddess of corrupted youth.

Instead, she stood there, uncertain and frightened

and too naive (or maybe honest) to be anything but totally sincere—and vulnerable. She was afraid, uncertain, the lost princess helpless in a dark wood.

It was worse than if she'd vamped onto me like a trained courtesan. What I saw in her was honest and hopeful, trusting and terrified. She was real, and fragile and precious. My emotions got together with my glands and they ganged up on me, screaming that she needed acceptance and that the kindest thing I could possibly do would be to give her a hug and tell her everything was going to be all right—and that if something followed, who would blame me?

I would. So I just watched her with a straight face.

"I want to learn from you," she said. "I want to do everything I can to help you. To thank you. I want you to teach me things."

"What things?" I asked in a quiet, measured tone.

She licked her lips. "Everything. Show me everything."

"Are you sure?" I asked her.

She nodded, her eyes huge, pupils dilated until only a bare ring of blue remained around them.

"Teach me," she whispered.

I touched her face with the fingers of my right hand. "Kneel down," I told her. "Close your eyes."

Trembling, she did, her breathing becoming faster, more excited.

But that stopped once I picked up the pitcher of ice water from the mantel and dumped it over her head.

She let out a squeal and fell over backward. It took her maybe ten seconds to recover from the shock of the cold, and by then she was gasping and shivering, her eyes wide with surprise and confusion—and with some kind of deep, heavy pain.

I faced her and squatted down onto my haunches to

meet her eyes. "Lesson one. This isn't going to happen, Molly," I said in exactly the same calm, gentle voice. "Get that through your head right now. It isn't *ever* going to happen."

Her lower lip trembled, and she bowed her head, shoulders shaking.

I gave myself a mental kick in the head and snagged a blanket from the couch. I went to her and wrapped it around her shoulders. "Get over by the fire and warm up."

It took her a moment to collect herself, but she did. She hunched her shoulders beneath the blanket, shivering and humiliated. "You knew," she said in a shaking voice. "That I would . . . do this."

"I was pretty sure," I agreed.

"Because of the soulgaze," she said.

"Nothing to do with that, really," I replied. "I figured there had to be a reason that you didn't come to me for help when you came into your powers. I figure you've been interested in me for a while. That you wouldn't want to come up to your favorite rock star and start fumbling around on a guitar so that the first thing he thinks about you is that you're incompetent."

She shivered and blushed even more. "No. It wasn't like that . . ."

Sure it was. But I'd hammered her hard enough for the time being. "If you say so," I answered. "Molly, you may fight with your mom like cats and dogs, but the two of you are more alike than you know."

"That's not true."

"It's trite but true that a lot of young women look for a man who reminds them of their dad. Your dad fights monsters. I fight monsters. Your dad rescued your mom from a dragon. I rescued you from Arctis Tor. Seeing the pattern here?"

She opened her mouth and then frowned at the fire—not an angry frown. A pensive one.

"Plus, you've just been scared real good. You don't have anyplace to stay. And I'm the guy who is trying to help you." I shook my head. "But even if there wasn't magic involved, it still wouldn't happen. I've done some things I'm not proud of. But I'm never going to take advantage of your trust.

"What we're going to have is not a relationship of equals. I teach. You learn. I tell you to do something, you damned well do it."

A touch of sullen teenager-ness gleamed in her eyes.

"Don't even think it," I said. "Molly, getting pierced and dyed and tattooed just because you want to break the rules is one thing. But what we're dealing with now isn't the same thing. A botched dye job affects you. You botch the use of magic and someone—maybe a lot of someones—gets hurt. So you do what I say, when I say it, and you do it because you don't want to kill someone. Or you can die. That was our deal, and you agreed to it."

She said nothing. Her anger had faded from her face, but that sullen trace of rebellion remained.

I narrowed my eyes, clenched my fist, and hissed a single word. The fireplace flared up in a sudden, fiery cyclone. Molly flinched back from it, one arm lifted to protect her eyes.

When she lowered it, I was hunkered down right in her face. "I'm not your parents, kid," I said. "And you don't have time to play teenage rebel anymore. This is the deal. You do what I say or you don't survive." I leaned closer and gave her the look I usually save for rampaging demons and those survey people at malls. "Molly. Is there any doubt in your mind—any doubt at *all*—that I can't damn well *make* you do it?"

She swallowed. The hard knot of defiance in her eyes suddenly shattered like a diamond struck at precisely the correct angle, and she shivered in the blanket. "No, sir," she said in a tiny voice.

I nodded at her. She sat there shivering and frightened, which had been the point of the exercise; to knock her off balance while she was still unsteady from recent events and drive home the notion of what she faced. It was absolutely necessary that she understand how things had to play out until she got her power under control. Anything less than willing cooperation would kill her.

But it was hard to remember that, staring down at her as she shivered and stared at the fire, its light turning tears to gold on her cheeks. Heartbreaking, really. She was still so damned young.

So I crouched down and gave her that hug. "It's all right to be scared, kid. But don't worry. Everything's going to be all right."

She leaned against me, shivering. I let her for a moment, and then got up and said, "Get dressed and get your things."

"Why?" she asked.

I arched an eyebrow at her. She flushed, took the robe, and hurried back into the bedroom. I had my coat on and was ready to go when she was. I led her out to the car and we took off.

"Can I ask you a question?"

"I hope so. It's going to take you a long time to learn if you can't."

She smiled a little. "Where are we going?"

"Your new digs," I said.

She frowned at me, but settled back in her seat. "Oh."

We pulled up to the Carpenter house, ablaze with lights despite the hour.

"Oh, *no*," Molly muttered. "Tell me you're kidding me."

"You're moving back in."

"But—"

I continued over her as if she hadn't spoken. "Not only that, but you're going to do everything in your power to be the most respectful, loving, respectful, considerate, and respectful daughter in the whole wide world. Especially where your mom is concerned."

She stared at me with her jaw hanging.

"Oh," I added. "And you're going back to high school until you're finished."

She stared at me for a long time, then blinked and said, "I died. And this is Hell."

I snorted. "If you can't control yourself well enough to finish a basic education and get along with a houseful of people who love you, then you sure as hell can't control yourself enough to use what I need to teach you."

"But . . . but . . ."

"Think of your homecoming as an extended lesson in respect and self-control," I said cheerfully. "I'll be checking up with your parents at least weekly. You'll do lessons with me every day until school is back in, and then I'll give you reading and homework for the—"

"Homework?" she half wailed.

"Don't interrupt. The homework will only be on weekdays. We'll do lessons on Friday and Saturday evenings."

"Friday and Satur . . ." She trailed off into a sigh and slumped. "Hell. I am in Hell."

"It gets better. I take it that you're sexually active?"

She stood there with her mouth hanging open.

"Come on, Molly, this is important. Do you boink?"

Her face turned pink and she hid her face in her hands. "I . . . I . . . well. I'm a virgin."

I arched an eyebrow at her.

She glanced up at me, blushed more, and added, "Technically."

"Technically," I said.

"Um. I've . . . explored. Most of the bases."

"I see," I said. "Well, Magellan, no baserunning or boldly going where no man has gone before for you— not until you get yourself grounded. Sex makes things complicated, and for you that could be bad."

"But . . ."

"And no, ah, solo exploration either."

She blinked at me and asked in a blank tone, "Why?"

"You'll go blind," I said, and walked up to her front porch.

"You're joking," she said, and then hurried to catch up. "That's a joke, right? Harry?"

I marched her up to her house without answering her. Molly wore a hopeless look on her face, as though she envied a condemned criminal, who could at least hope that the governor might call at the last minute. But when the doors opened and her family's delight washed over her in a roar like a breaking wave, she smiled from her eyes all the way down to her toes.

I made polite chat for a minute, until Mouse limped over to me, smiling and wagging his tail. There was something on his muzzle that I suspected to be honey mustard, or maybe buffalo sauce, doubtless slipped to him by a young accomplice. I clipped his lead on him and took my leave, heading back to my car.

Before I got there, Charity caught up with me. I arched an eyebrow at her and waited while she fidgeted and finally asked, "Did you tell them? About what I was?"

"Of course not," I said.

She slumped a little in relief. "Oh."

"You're welcome," I said.

She frowned at me and said, "If you hurt my little girl, I'll come down to that little closet you call an office and throw you out the window. Do you understand?"

"Death by defenestration, gotcha."

A few tiny cracks developed in her frown, and then she shook her head sharply, once, caught me in a hug that made my ribs ache, and went back into the house without another word.

Mouse sat there panting and grinning happily.

I went home and got some sleep.

I was working in my lab the next day, trying to make notes of all that had happened so that I wouldn't forget anything. Bob sat on the table next to me, helping me with the details.

"Oh," he said. "I found something wrong with Little Chicago's design."

I swallowed. "Oh. Wow. Bad?"

"Extremely. We missed a transition coupling in the power flow. The stored energy was all going to the same spot."

I frowned. "That's . . . like a surge of electricity going through a circuit breaker, right? Or a fuse box."

"Exactly like that," Bob said. "Except that *you* were the fuse. That much energy in one spot will blow your head off your shoulders."

"But it didn't," I said.

"But it didn't," Bob agreed.

"How is that possible?"

"It isn't," he said. "Someone fixed it."

"What? Are you sure?"

"It didn't fix itself," Bob said. "When I looked at it a few nights ago, the flawed section was in plain sight, even if I didn't recognize it at the time. When I looked again tonight, it was different. Someone changed it."

"In my lab? Under my house? Which is behind my wards? That's impossible."

"No it isn't," Bob said. "Just really, really, really, really, really, *really* difficult. And unlikely. He would have had to know that you had a lab down here. And he would have had to know how to get around your wards."

"Plus intimate knowledge of the design to tinker with it like that," I said. "To say nothing of the fact that he would have to know it existed at *all*, and no one does."

"Really, really unlikely," Bob agreed.

"Dammit."

"Hey, I thought you loved a good mystery, Harry."

I shook my head and started to tell him where to stick his mystery when someone knocked at the door.

Murphy stood on the other side and smiled at me. "Hey." She held up my shotgun. "Thomas wanted me to bring this by. Said to tell you he was getting his own toys from now on."

She offered it and I took it, frowning. "He didn't even clean it off."

She smiled. "I swear, Dresden. You can be such a pansy."

"It's because I'm a sensitive guy. You want to come in?"

She gave me another smile, but shook her head. "No time. Got to see the first shrink in half an hour."

"Ah," I said. "How are things playing out?"

"Oh, there's a long investigation and evaluation to be done," she said. "Officially, of course."

"Of course," I said.

"But unofficially . . ." She shrugged. "I'm losing SI. They're busting me down to detective sergeant."

I winced. "Who's getting the job?"

"Stallings, most likely. He's the next most experienced, better record than most of the department, and he's respected." She looked away. "I'm losing my seniority, too. All of it. So they're partnering me with their most experienced detective."

"Which is that?" I asked.

"Rawlins," she said, her mouth moving in a tight smile. "He did so good on this one they promoted him to SI."

"No good deed goes unpunished," I said.

"Ain't that the truth," Murphy sighed.

"That a bad thing? He seems like a decent guy."

"He is, he is," Murphy said, scrunching up her nose. "But he knew my father."

"Oh," I said. "And it's possible you have issues."

"Remotely," she said. "What about you? You okay?"

I met her eyes for a second and then looked away. "I, uh. I'll be okay."

She nodded, and then simply stepped forward and hugged me. My arms went around her without me telling them to do it. It wasn't a tense, meaning-laden hug. She was my friend. She was exhausted and worried and suffering, and she'd had what she valued most sullied and stained, but she was worried about me. Giving me a hug. Assuring me, by implication, that everything was going to be all right.

I gave as good as I got for a while. When we broke the embrace, it was at the same time, and it wasn't awkward. She smiled at me, just a little bittersweet, and glanced at her watch. "I have to get moving."

"Right," I said. "Thanks, Murph."

She left. A while later, my phone rang. I answered it.

"Everything work out?" Thomas asked. "With the girl?"

"Pretty much," I told him. "You all right?"

"Yeah," he said.

"Need anything?" Like maybe to talk about how he was feeding on people again and making money at the same time.

"Not especially," he told me. I was pretty sure he had heard the unasked question, because his tone of voice carried an unyielding coolness, telling me not to push. Thomas was my brother. I could wait.

"What's up with Murphy?" he asked me.

I told him about her job.

He was silent for an annoyed second and then said, "But what's up with Murphy?"

I glowered and slouched down onto my couch. "There isn't anything up with her. She isn't interested."

"How do you know?" he asked.

"She told me."

"She told you."

"She told me."

He sighed. "And you believed her."

"Well," I said. "Yes."

"I had a talk with her when she drove me home," he said.

"A talk?"

"A talk. I wanted to figure something out."

"Did you?" I asked.

"Yeah."

"What?"

"That you're both stiff-necked idiots," he said, his tone annoyed, and hung up on me.

I glowered at the phone for a minute, muttered a couple of choice words about my half brother, then got out my guitar and labored to make something resembling music for a while. Sometimes it was easier for me to think when playing, and the time drifted by. I played and mulled things over until someone else knocked. I set my guitar aside and went to the door.

Ebenezar stood on the other side, and he gave me a nod and a cautious smile when I opened the door. "Hot enough for you?" the old wizard asked.

"Almost," I said. "Come in."

He did, and I grabbed a couple of beers, offering him one. "What's up?"

"You tell me," he said.

So I told him all about the last few days, especially my dealings with Lily and Fix, Maeve, and Mab. Ebenezar listened to it all in silence.

"What a mess," he said when I finished.

"Tell me about it." I sipped at my beer. "You know what I think?"

He finished his beer and shook his head.

"I think we got played."

"By the Summer Lady?"

I shook my head. "I think Lily got suckered just as much as we did."

He frowned and rubbed at his head with one palm. "How so?"

"That's the part I can't figure," I said. "I think someone set Molly up to be a beacon for the fetches. And I'm damned sure that it was no accident that those fetches took Molly to Arctis Tor when it was so lightly defended. Someone *wanted* me there at Arctis Tor."

Ebenezar pursed his lips. "Who?"

"I think we got used by one of the Queens to one-up one of the others, somehow. But damned if I can figure out how."

"You think Mab really is insane?"

"I think it would be hard to tell the difference," I said in a sour voice. "Lily thinks so. But Lily wasn't exactly widely famed for her intellect before she became the

Summer Lady." I shook my head. "If Mab really is loopy, it's going to be bad."

The old man nodded.

"And since you can't swing a cat without hitting a cat's-paw lately, I think maybe someone was trying to use Mab for something. Like all the others who've gotten set up around here."

"Set up?"

I nodded. "Yeah. Starting with Victor Sells a few years ago. Then those FBI creeps with the wolf belts. I think that someone out there wants to get things done without getting his—"

"Or her," Ebenezar said.

"Or her own hands dirty," I continued. "Consider all these things running around with more power than they should have had or better connected than they should have been. The Shadowman, the hexenwulfen, the Nightmare, the last Summer Lady—and that's just for starters. The Red Court sure are a hell of a lot more dangerous than anyone thought they would be."

Ebenezar frowned, nodding.

"I think whoever is backstage moving things around tried to use Mab and got more than they bargained for. I think that's what the attack on Arctis Tor was about. Maybe they tried to put her down before she turned on them."

"Which she would," Ebenezar said.

"Of course she would. She's Mab. She'd keep any bargain she made, but she isn't the kind who takes orders real well."

"Go on, boy," Ebenezar said gently. "You've got facts. Where do they lead you?"

I lowered my own voice to a whisper. "A new power is moving around out there. Something big, smart, strong, and sneaky as hell. Something with a lot of strength and magical know-how." I licked my lips. "Put that together with the evidence of varied powers. Wolf belts handed out to those poor FBI bastards. Black magic being taught to small-timers like the Shadowman and the Nightmare. Vampires cross-training one another in sorcery. Hellfire used on Arctis Tor. And, of course, the White Council's highly placed traitor. All of that together doesn't point to just one person. It indicates an organization." I regarded the old man steadily. "And they've got wizards on the staff. Probably several of them."

Ebenezar grunted. "Damn."

"Damn?"

"I was hoping maybe I was starting to go senile. But I came to the same conclusion." He nodded. "Boy, don't breathe a word of this. Not to anyone. I got the feeling that this is information worth as much as your life." He shook his head. "Let me think about who else needs to know."

"Rashid," I said in a firm voice. "Tell the Gatekeeper."

Ebenezar frowned, though it looked more weary than anything else. "Likely he knows already. Knew already. Maybe even pointed you in a direction that would show you more. Assuming he wasn't simply using you to poke a hornet's nest and see what flew up."

Which was somewhat creepy to think about. If Ebenezar was right, I could count myself among the pawns in play, courtesy of the Gatekeeper.

"You don't want to tell him?" I asked.

"Rashid is a tough one to figure," Ebenezar said. "Three, four years ago, I wouldn't have thought twice. But with all that's happened . . . since Simon died . . ." He shrugged. "Better to be cautious. We can't put the genie back in the bottle once it's out."

"Or maybe that's the worst thing we could do," I said. "Maybe it's what these . . . Black Council assholes are counting on."

He looked up at me sharply. "Now why would you call them that?"

"Black Council?" I shrugged. "If the shoe fits. It's better than the Legion of Doom."

He regarded me for a moment more and then shrugged. "Times are changing, Hoss. That's for sure. But they always do. I know you're going to do what you think you need to do. But I'd like to ask that you be very cautious, Hoss. We still don't know what our enemies look like. That means we'll have to bring in our allies carefully."

"Meaning without troubling the White Council and the Wardens about it?" I asked, my tone dry.

He grunted in the affirmative. "Don't forget the other loose end."

I frowned and thought back over it. "Huh," I said. "You're right. Who was driving that car that ran into me?"

"Exactly," he said.

"More mysteries."

"Thought you were a professional investigator, Hoss," he teased. "For you, this should be fun."

"Yeah. Fun. Fun, fun, fun. I'm having fun already."

He smiled. "Mmmmph. It isn't good news that Winter isn't going to stand with us against the Reds, but it could have been worse. And we learned something valuable."

I grunted. "The traitor to the Council. Someone had to tell the Reds where Luccio's boot camp was hidden."

"Yes," he said, and leaned forward. "And outside of Luccio only four people knew."

I arched my brows at him. "Morgan?"

"That's one," he agreed. "Injun Joe, the Merlin, and Ancient Mai were the only others."

I whistled slowly. "Heavy hitters. But knock Morgan off your list. He didn't do it."

Ebenezar arched his brows. "No?"

I shook my head. "Guy is a dick," I said, "but he's on the level. We shouldn't tell him, but he's no traitor."

Ebenezar frowned for a moment and then nodded slowly. "Very well, then. I'll vouch for Injun Joe."

"So what comes next?" I asked him.

"Watching them," he said. "Waiting. Not letting on that we know. We won't get more than one chance to take them off guard. When we do move, we got to make it hurt."

I frowned at my now-empty bottle and nodded. "We wait. Lie in the weeds. Keep a low profile. Got it."

"Hoss," my old teacher said quietly. "What you did for that girl . . ."

"Yeah," I said, waving a hand. "Stupid. The Merlin is going to be royally pissed at me. He'll probably start insisting I go on shooting missions now, in hopes someone will take me out and remove a thorn in his side."

"True," Ebenezar said. "But what I meant to say was that what you did was damned brave. From what I hear, you were ready to take on everyone there if you had to."

"Wouldn't have lasted long."

"No. But then, that wasn't the point." He rose a little stiffly and said, "I'm proud of you, boy."

Something inside me melted.

"You know," I said. "You always told me you weren't at my trial. That the Council saddled you with me because you skipped out. I think that isn't true."

He grunted.

"It was all in Latin, which I didn't understand then. And I had that hood over my head, so I couldn't see anyone. But someone had to have defended me, the way I did Molly."

"Could be." He rolled one shoulder in a shrug. "I'm getting old, Hoss. I forget things."

"Ah," I said. "You know, I've missed a meal or three lately. And I know this little joint that's got the best spaghetti in town."

Ebenezar froze in place, like a man walking on ice who suddenly hears cracking sounds. "Oh?" he asked, tone careful.

"They've got this great bread that goes with it, too. And it's right by the campus, so cute waitresses."

"Sounds promising," Ebenezar said. "Makes me feel a mite hungry hearing about it."

"Absolutely," I said. "Let me get my shoes. If we hurry we can get there before the evening rush."

We looked at each other for a long moment, and my old teacher bowed his head to me. It conveyed a lot of things. Apology. Gratitude. Happiness. Forgiveness. Affection. Pride.

"You want me to drive us?" he asked.

I bowed my head in reply. "I'd like that, sir."

Author's Note

When I was seven years old, I got a bad case of strep throat and was out of school for a whole week. During that time, my sisters bought me my first fantasy and sci-fi novels: the boxed set of *Lord of the Rings* and the boxed set of the Han Solo adventure novels by Brian Daley. I devoured them all during that week.

From that point on, I was pretty much doomed to join SF&F fandom. From there, it was only one more step to decide I wanted to be a writer of my favorite fiction material, and here we are.

I blame my sisters.

My first love as a fan is swords-and-horses fantasy. After Tolkien I went after C. S. Lewis. After Lewis, it was Lloyd Alexander. After them came Fritz Leiber, Roger Zelazny, Robert Howard, John Norman, Poul Anderson, David Eddings, Weis and Hickman, Terry Brooks, Elizabeth Moon, Glen Cook, and before I knew it I was a dual citizen of the United States and Lankhmar, Narnia, Gor, Cimmeria, Krynn, Amber—you get the picture.

When I set out to become a writer, I spent years writing swords-and-horses fantasy novels—and seemed to have little innate talent for it. But I worked at my writing, branching out into other areas as experiments, including SF, mystery, and contemporary fantasy. That's how the Dresden Files initially came about—as a happy accident while trying to accomplish something else. Sort of like penicillin.

But I never forgot my first love, and to my immense delight and excitement, one day I got a call from my agent and found out that I was going to get to share my newest swords-and-horses fantasy novel with other fans.

The Codex Alera is a fantasy series set within the savage world of Carna, where spirits of the elements, known as furies, lurk in every facet of life, and where many intelligent races vie for security and survival. The realm of Alera is the monolithic civilization of humanity, and its unique ability to harness and command the furies is all that enables its survival in the face of the enormous, sometimes hostile elemental powers of Carna, and against savage creatures who would lay Alera in waste and ruin.

Yet even a realm as powerful as Alera is not immune to destruction from within, and the death of the heir apparent to the Crown has triggered a frenzy of ambitious political maneuvering and infighting amongst the High Lords, those who wield the most powerful furies known to man. Plots are afoot, traitors and spies abound, and a civil war seems inevitable—all while the enemies of the realm watch, ready to strike at the first sign of weakness.

Tavi is a young man living on the frontier of Aleran civilization—because let's face it, swords-and-horses fantasies start there. Born a freak, unable to utilize any powers of furycrafting whatsoever, Tavi has grown up relying upon his own wits, speed, and courage to survive. When an ambitious plot to discredit the Crown lays Tavi's home, the Calderon Valley, naked and defenseless before a horde of the barbarian Marat, the boy and his family find themselves directly in harm's way.

There are no titanic High Lords to protect them, no

Legions, no Knights with their might furies to take the field. Tavi and the free frontiersmen of the Calderon Valley must find some way to uncover the plot and to defend their homes against a merciless horde of Marat and their beasts.

It is a desperate hour, where the fate of all Alera hangs in the balance, where a handful of ordinary steadholders must find the courage and strength to defy an overwhelming foe, and where the courage and intelligence of one young man will save the Relam—or destroy it.

Thank you, readers and fellow fans, for all of your support and kindness. I hope that you enjoy reading the books of the Codex Alera as much as I enjoyed creating them for you.

—Jim

Furies of Calderon, Academ's Fury, Cursor's Fury, Captain's Fury, Princeps' Fury, and *First Lord's Fury* are available from Ace Books.

Read on for an exciting excerpt from
Jim Butcher's epic fantasy

FURIES OF CALDERON
Book One of the Codex Alera

Available now from Ace Books.

Prologue

The course of history is determined not by battles, by sieges, or usurpations, but by the actions of the individual. The strongest city, the largest army is, at its most basic level, a collection of individuals. Their decisions, their passions, their foolishness, and their dreams shape the years to come. If there is any lesson to be learned from history, it is that all too often the fate of armies, of cities, of entire realms, rests upon the actions of one person. In that dire moment of uncertainty, that person's decision, good or bad, right or wrong, big or small, can unwittingly change the world.

But history can be quite the slattern. One never knows who that person is, where he might be, or what decision he might make.

It is almost enough to make me believe in Destiny.

—FROM THE WRITINGS OF GAIUS PRIMUS,
FIRST LORD OF ALERA

"**P**lease, Tavi," wheedled the girl in the predawn darkness outside the steadholt's kitchen. "Just this one little favor?"

"I don't know," said the boy. "There's so much work today."

She leaned in closer to him, and the boy felt her slender body mold against his, soft and flower-scented and delightful. She pressed her mouth to his cheek in a slow kiss and whispered in his ear, "I'd be very grateful."

"Well," the boy said. "I'm not sure if, um."

She kissed his cheek again and whispered, "Please."

His heart pounded more quickly, and his knees felt weak. "All right. I'll do it."

Chapter

One

Amara rode atop the swaying back of the towering old gargant bull, going over the plan in her head. The morning sun shone down on her, taking the chill out of the misty air and warming the dark wool of her skirts. Behind her, the axles of the cart squeaked and groaned beneath their loads. The slave collar she wore had begun to chafe her skin, and she made an irritated mental note to wear one for a few days in order to grow used to it, before the next mission.

Assuming she survived this one, of course.

A tremor of nervous fear ran down her spine and made her shoulders tighten. Amara took a deep breath and blew it out again, closing her eyes for a moment and blocking out every thought except for the sensations around her: sunlight on her face, swaying of the pungent gargant's long strides, creaking of the cart's axles.

"Nervous?" asked the man walking beside the gargant. A goad dangled from his hand, but he hadn't lifted it in the entire trip. He managed the beast with the lead straps alone, though his head barely came to the old bull's brown-furred thigh. He wore the plain clothes of a peddler: brown leggings, sturdy sandals, with a padded jacket over his shirt, dark green on homespun. A long cape, tattered green without embroidery, had been cast over one shoulder as the sun rose higher.

"No," Amara lied. She opened her eyes again, staring ahead.

Fidelias chuckled. "Liar. It's not a brainless plan. It might work."

Amara shot her teacher a wary glance. "But you have a suggestion?"

"In your graduation exercise?" Fidelias asked. "Crows, no. I wouldn't dream of it, *academ*. It would cheapen your performance."

Amara licked her lips. "But you think that there's something I should know?"

Fidelias gave her a perfectly guileless look. "I did have a few questions."

"Questions," Amara said. "We're going to be there in a few moments."

"I can ask them when we arrive, if you prefer."

"If you weren't my *patriserus*, I would find you an impossible man," Amara sighed.

"That's sweet of you to say," Fidelias replied. "You've come a long way since your first term at the Academy. You were so shocked when you found out that the Cursors did more than deliver missives."

"You love telling that story even though you know I hate it."

"No," Fidelias said with a grin. "I love telling that story *because* I know you hate it."

She looked down at him archly. "This is why the Cursor Legate keeps sending you *away* on missions, I think."

"It's a part of my charm," Fidelias agreed. "Now, then. My first concern—"

"Question," Amara corrected.

"Question," he allowed, "is with our cover story."

"What question? Armies need iron. You're an ore smuggler, and I'm your slave. You heard there was a market out this way, and you came to see what money could be made."

"Ah," said Fidelias. "And what do I tell them when they ask where I got the ore? It isn't just found by the roadside, you know."

"You're a Cursor Callidus. You're creative. I'm sure you'll think of something."

Fidelias chuckled. "You've learned delegating skills, at least. So, we approach this renegade Legion with our precious ore." He nodded back toward the squeaking cart. "What's to stop them from simply taking it?"

"You're the harbinger of a smuggling network, representing several interests in the business. Your trip is being watched, and if the results are good, others might be willing to bring supplies as well."

"That's what I don't understand," Fidelias said, his expression innocent. "If this is indeed a renegade Legion, as rumors say, under the command of one of the High Lords, in preparation for overthrowing the Crown—aren't they going to object to *any* word about them getting out? Good, bad, or indifferent?"

"Yes," Amara said. She glanced down at him. "Which works in our favor. You see, if you *don't* return from this little jaunt, word is going to spread all around Alera about this encampment."

"Inevitable, since word would get out anyway. One can hardly keep an entire Legion secret for long."

"It's our best shot," Amara said. "Can you think of anything better?"

"We sneak in close, furycraft ourselves into the camp, obtain evidence, and then run like the crows were after us."

"Oh," Amara said. "I considered it. I decided it was too brainless and predictable."

"It has the advantage of simplicity," Fidelias pointed

out. "We recover the information, give solid evidence to the Crown, and let the First Lord launch a more comprehensive antisedition campaign."

"Yes, that's *simpler*. But once whoever is running this camp knows that they have been observed by the Cursors, they will *simply* disperse and move their operations elsewhere. The Crown will *simply* spend money and effort and lives to pin them down again—and even then, whoever is putting out the money to field their own army might *simply* get away."

Fidelias glanced up at her and let out a low whistle. "So you want to get in and out undetected, get word to the Crown and—then what?"

"Lead a few cohorts of Knights Aeris back down here and crush them where they lie," Amara said. "Take prisoners, have them testify against their backers, and wrap it all up right here."

"Ambitious," he commented. "Very ambitious. Very dangerous, too. If they catch on to us, they'll kill us. And it's reasonable to expect that they'll have Knights as well—and that they'll be on the lookout for a Cursor or two."

"That's why we don't get caught," Amara said. "We play the poor, greedy smuggler and his slave, haggle for all the money we can get from them, and leave."

"And keep the money." Fidelias frowned. "On general principle, I like any mission that involves a profit. But, Amara—there's a lot that could go wrong with this one."

"We are the First Lord's messengers, are we not? His eyes and ears?"

"Don't quote the Codex at me," Fidelias snapped, annoyed. "I was a Cursor before your mother and father had called their first furies. Don't think that because the First Lord has taken a shine to you that you know better than I do."

"You don't think it's worth the risk?"

"I think there's a lot you don't know," Fidelias said, and he looked very old for some reason. Uncertain. "Let me handle this, Amara. I'll go inside. You stay here, and I'll pick you up on the way out. There's no reason to risk both of us."

"No," she said. "In the first place, this is my mission to run. In the second, you will need your full attention to play your role. I'll be able to make observations—especially from up here." She slapped the gargant's broad back, and the bull snorted up a small whirlwind of trail dust in response. "I'll also be able to watch our backs. If I get the impression that they're onto us, we can get out of there."

Fidelias muttered, "I thought we'd just use this guise to pose as travelers. Get close and slip into the camp after dark."

"When no one else is coming in and when we're certain to arouse suspicion if we're seen?"

He blew out a breath. "All right," he said. "All right. We'll do it your way. But you're gambling yourself with the crows."

Amara's stomach fluttered again, and she pressed a hand to it, trying to will the fear away. It didn't leave. "No," she said. "I'm gambling both of us."

Though the gargant's plodding steps seemed slow, each covered many strides of a man. The great beast's thick-clawed feet ate the miles, though it stripped the bushes and trees of leaves along the way, adding to the layers of blubbery fat beneath its hide. If allowed, the hump-backed beast would wander into the richest forage and graze, but Fidelias handled it with a sure and calm hand, keeping the beast moving along the road, while he marched at the quickstep beside it.

A mile more, by Amara's estimation, and they had

come within picket distance of the insurgent Legion's camp. She tried to remind herself of her role—that of a bored slave, sleepy and tired from days of travel—but it was all she could do to keep the mounting tension from rising in her shoulders and back. What if the Legion turned out to be nothing more than rumor, and her intelligence gathering mission, so carefully outlined and planned, turned out to be a costly waste of time? Would the First Lord think less of her? Would the other Cursors? It would be a paltry introduction into the ranks, indeed, if she stepped forth from the Academy and straight into a monumental blunder.

Her anxiety grew, like bands of iron stretching across her shoulders and back, and her head started to pound from the tension and the glare of the sun. Had they made a wrong turn? The old trail they followed seemed too well-worn to be an abandoned lumber track, but she could be wrong. Wouldn't they be seeing the smoke of a Legion's fires? Wouldn't they hear something, by now, if they were as close as she suspected?

Amara was on the verge of leaning down to call to Fidelias, to ask his advice, when a man in a dark tunic and leggings and a gleaming breastplate and helmet melted into view beneath the shadows of a tree on the road no more than ten strides in front of them. He appeared without a warning of any kind, without a flicker of movement—furycrafting involved, then, and a fairly skilled woodworking at that. He was a giant of a man, nearly seven feet tall, and he bore a heavy blade at his side. He lifted one gloved hand and said, his tone bored, distant, "Halt."

Fidelias clucked to the gargant bull, slowing the beast to a stop after several steps. The wagon creaked and groaned, settling onto its wheels beneath the weight of the ore.

"Good morning to you, master," Fidelias called, his

voice oozing nervous, obsequious good cheer. The senior Cursor doffed his hat and clutched it in his slightly trembling hands. "And how are you doing on this fine autumn morn?"

"You're on the wrong trail," said the dark giant. His tone was dull, almost sleepy, but he laid a hand on the hilt of his weapon. "This land is not friendly to travelers. Turn around."

"Yes, master, of course we will, master," Fidelias simpered. "I am but a humble peddler, transporting his cargo in the vain hope of finding a ready market. I have no desire for trouble, good master, only for the chance to attempt to recoup my losses on this most excellent but lamentably ill-timed bounty of"—Fidelias rolled his eyes skyward and dragged one foot through the dust of the trail—"iron." He shot the giant a sly smile. "But, as you wish, good master. I'll be on my way."

The dark man stepped forward and said, "Hold, merchant."

Fidelias glanced back at him. "Master?" he asked. "Can I perhaps interest you in a purchase?"

The dark man shrugged. He stopped a few feet from Fidelias and asked, "How much ore?"

"Nearly a ton, good master. As you can see, my poor gargant is all but done in."

The man grunted, eyeing the beast, and swept his gaze up it, to Amara. "Who is this?"

"My slave, good master," Fidelias said. His voice took on a cringing, wheedling tone. "She's for sale, if you like the look of her, master. A hard worker, skilled at weaving and cooking—and more than capable of giving a man an unforgettable night's pleasure. At two lions, she's surely a bargain."

The man snorted. "Your hard worker rides while you walk, merchant. It would have been smarter for you to travel alone." He sniffed. "And she's as skinny as a boy. Take your beast and follow me."

"You wish to buy, master?"

The soldier gave him a look and said, "I didn't ask you, merchant. Follow me."

Fidelias stared at the soldier and then swallowed, an almost audible gulp. "Aye, aye, master. We'll be only a pace or three behind you. Come on, old boy." He picked up the gargant's lead straps in shaking fingers and stirred the great beast into motion again.

The soldier grunted and turned to start walking back down the road. He let out a sharp whistle, and a dozen men armed with bows appeared from the shadows and brush on the sides of the trail, just as he had a moment before.

"Keep the men here until I return," the man said. "Stop anyone from coming past."

"Yes, sir," one of the men said. Amara focused on that one. The men all wore the same outfits: black tunics and breeches with surcoats of dark green and dark brown. The speaker, in addition, wore a black sash around his waist—as the first soldier had. Amara checked around, but none of the other men wore a sash—only those two. She made a mental note of it. Knights? Possibly. One of them had to have been a strong woodcrafter, to have hidden so many men so thoroughly.

Crows, she thought. *What if this rebel Legion turns out to have a full contingent of Knights to go with it? With that many men, that many powerful furycrafters, they could be a threat to any city in Alera.*

And, as a corollary, it would mean that the Legion had powerful backing. Any furycrafter strong enough to be a Knight could command virtually what price he wished for his services. They could not be casually bought by any disgruntled merchant set to convince his Lord or

High Lord to lower taxes. Only the nobility could afford the cost of hiring a few Knights, let alone a contingent of them.

Amara shivered. If one of the High Lords was preparing to turn against the First Lord, then there were dark days ahead indeed.

She looked down at Fidelias, and he glanced up at her, his face troubled. She thought she could see the reflection of her own thoughts and fears there in his eyes. She wanted to talk to Fidelias, to ask him for his thoughts on the matter, but she couldn't break her role now. Amara ground her teeth and dug her fingers into the pad of the gargant's riding saddle and tried to calm herself again, while the soldier led them to the camp.

Amara kept her eyes open as the gargant's plodding steps brought them around a bend in the trail and over a small hill, into the valley beyond and behind it. There, the camp spread out before them.

Great furies, she thought. *It looks like a city.*

Her mind took down details as she stared. The camp had been constructed along standard Legion lines: a stake-wall and ditch fortification built in a huge square, surrounding the soldier's encampment and stores. Tents of white fabric had been erected within, row after row of them, too many for easy counting, laid out in neat, precise rows. Two gates, opposite one another, led into the camp. The tents and lean-tos of the camp's followers spread out around it in ragged disarray, like flies buzzing around a sleeping beast.

People were everywhere.

On a practice field beside the camp, entire cohorts of men were drilling in formation combat and maneuvers, ordered about by bawling centurions or men in black sashes mounted on horseback. Elsewhere, archers riddled distant targets with their arrows, while furymasters drilled other recruits in the application of their basic war-craftings. Women moved among the camp, as well—washing clothes at a stream that passed by, mending uniforms, tending fires, or simply enjoying the morning sunlight. Amara saw a couple of women wearing sashes of black, on horseback, riding toward the practice field. Dogs wandered about the camp and set up a tinny racket of barking upon scenting the gargant as it came over the hill. To one side of the camp, not far from the stream, men and women had established what looked like a small market, vendors hawking wares from makeshift stalls and spreading them upon blankets on the ground.

"You're here between breakfast and lunch," said the soldier. "Or I'd offer you some food."

"Perhaps we'll take lunch with you, master," Fidelias said.

"Perhaps." The soldier stopped and looked up at Amara, studying her with quiet, hard eyes. "Get her down. I'll send out a groom or two to care for your beast."

"No," insisted Fidelias. "I'll be keeping my goods with me."

The soldier grunted. "There're horses at the camp, and they'll go mad if they smell this thing. It stays here."

"Then I stay here," insisted Fidelias.

"No."

"The slave then," he said. "She can stay here with the beast and keep him quiet. He'd spook if strange hands cared for him."

The soldier squinted at him, hard and suspicious. "What are you up to, old man?"

"Up to? I'm protecting my interests, master, as any merchant would."

"You are in our camp. Your interests are no longer an issue, are they?" The soldier put no particular emphasis on his words, but he laid one hand on the hilt of his sword.

Fidelias drew himself up, voice shocked and outraged. "You wouldn't dare."

The soldier smiled. His smile was hard.

Fidelias licked his lips. Then shot a glance up at Amara. She thought she saw something in it, some kind of warning, but he only said, "Girl. Get down."

Amara slid down off of the back of the beast, using the leather straps to help lower herself down its flanks. Fidelias clucked to it and jerked down on its straps, and the gargant settled lazily to earth with a contented rumble that shook the ground nearby. It leaned its great head over, tore up a mouthful of grass, and began chewing on it, huge eyes half-closed.

"Follow me," the soldier said. "You too, slave. If either of you gets more than three strides away from me, I'll kill you both. Do you understand?"

"I understand," said Fidelias.

"I understand, master," echoed Amara, keeping her eyes lowered. They followed the soldier then and crossed the stream at a shallow ford. The water was cold and flowed quickly over Amara's ankles. She shivered, gooseflesh racing up and down her legs and arms, but kept pace with Fidelias and the soldier.

Her mentor dropped back beside her and murmured, very low, "Did you see how many tents?"

She jerked her head in a nod. "Close."

"Well kept and neat, too. This isn't a gang of malcontent Steadholders. Professional military."

Amara nodded and whispered, "Serious money behind them. Is it enough for the First Lord to bring it to the Council?"

"An accusation without anyone to accuse?" Fidelias grimaced and shook his head. "No. We have to have something that incriminates someone behind it. Doesn't have to be ironclad, but we need something tangible."

"Do you recognize our escort?"

Fidelias shot her a look. "Why? Do you?"

Amara shook her head. "I'm not sure. Something about him seems familiar."

The other nodded. "They call him the Sword."

Amara felt her eyes widen. "Aldrick ex Gladius? Are you sure?"

"I've seen him in the capital, in the past. I saw his duel with Araris Valerian."

Amara glanced up at the man ahead of them, careful to keep her voice down. "He's supposed to be the greatest swordsman alive."

"Yes," said Fidelias. "He is." Then he cuffed her along the head and said, loud enough for Aldrick to hear, "Keep your lazy mouth shut. I'll feed you when I please and not a second before. Not another word."

Ready to find
your next great read?

Let us help.

Visit prh.com/nextread

Penguin
Random
House